It was a routine case, a summer cold. . . .

A week, ten days at most, and Ashley Atkins would be back on the beach without a care in the world. A dozen waiting patients were exhibiting the same sniffling, flushed-face presentation. One of them began to cough again.

Carol saw the bluish cast of his lips.

My God, she realized, *he's cyanotic.*

His eyes rolled upward and he crashed heavily to the floor and lay motionless.

Then a woman standing wide-eyed amid the other stunned patients began to cough, loudly and painfully. If not for the fresh sea-horse tattoo, Carol would not have known it was Ashley Atkins.

What the hell is going on here? she asked herself.

FINAL EPIDEMIC

Earl Merkel

A SIGNET BOOK

SIGNET
Published by New American Library, a division of
Penguin Putnam Inc., 375 Hudson Street,
New York, New York 10014, U.S.A.
Penguin Books Ltd, 80 Strand,
London WC2R 0RL, England
Penguin Books Australia Ltd, Ringwood,
Victoria, Australia
Penguin Books Canada Ltd, 10 Alcorn Avenue,
Toronto, Ontario, Canada M4V 3B2
Penguin Books (N.Z.) Ltd, 182–190 Wairau Road,
Auckland 10, New Zealand

Penguin Books Ltd, Registered Offices:
Harmondsworth, Middlesex, England

First published by Signet, an imprint of New American Library,
a division of Penguin Putnam Inc.

First Printing, October 2002
10 9 8 7 6 5 4 3 2 1

REGISTERED TRADEMARK—MARCA REGISTRADA

Printed in the United States of America

PUBLISHER'S NOTE
This is a work of fiction. Names, characters, places, and incidents either are the
product of the author's imagination or are used fictitiously, and any resemblance to
actual persons, living or dead, business establishments, events, or locales is entirely
coincidental.

Again, for my family

WASHINGTON (WNS)—Citing a growing number of experts in international terrorism, a federal interagency commission will be established within the next six months to deal with what one prominent official termed "the virtual certainty" of an attack on the United States by terrorists using lethal viruses as biological weapons.

William MacKenzie Carson, the White House national security advisor, said the need to prepare for such an attack is "both real and urgent."

"In February 2000, more than 300 physicians, scientists, public officials and law enforcement agents gathered to discuss strategies for dealing with a potential biological attack," Carson said. "That was more than a year and a half before the World Trade Center fell, more than a year and a half before anthrax became a threat to anyone who received mail.

"Yet it is an undeniable conclusion—we remain ill-equipped to deal with such potentially cataclysmic assaults," Carson said.

Said the presidential advisor: "I can do no more to illustrate the danger than to quote Donald A. Henderson, the former director of the Johns Hopkins Center for Civilian Biodefense Studies, who warned this nation in 2000 that is was not a question of *if* an atttack will occur; it is only a matter of *when* it will happen here, among our citizens."

Carson noted that Henderson's statement, which received wide attention after the events of September 2001, concluded with both a warning and a probable timeline.

"In 2000, Henderson warned that the United States was likely to see an attack within the next five years," Carson said. "By that prediction, we are now alarmingly overdue."

—*Washington News Syndicate*
Release Date: January 18

"I know how not to get AIDS. I don't know how not to get the flu."

— Alfred W. Crosby,
historian and author of
*America's Forgotten Pandemic:
The Influenza of 1918*

Prologue

Another blast of frigid air swirled across the tundra, chilling flesh even through the layers of insulated garments they wore under their heavy arctic parkas. Occasionally, it was strong enough to rock anything merely human that stood in its path, particularly when weariness had brought on the mind-dulling blankness so common to cold-weather exertion. In this environment, a diet carefully planned to provide a daily minimum of nine thousand calories scarcely provided sufficient energy to fuel both the arduous work of excavation and the equally important task of maintaining a core temperature capable of sustaining life.

Anji Suzuki shivered involuntarily. He was born on Kyushu, one of the Home Islands far to the south. In the eleven days he had been here, on this godforsaken outcropping of frozen tundra and rock a few degrees above the Arctic Circle, he had never imagined anywhere so cold and desolate.

I will be glad to be gone from this terrible place, he thought, pressing his body weight hard against the pneumatic drill. He much preferred operating the ground-penetrating radar equipment. With the air drill, the vibrations shook him so harshly that his vision blurred each time the auger bit into the permafrost. After a few seconds, he released his grip on the trigger lever and leaned against the heavy tool.

On the barren tundra, near the mogul-like dome tents and stretched tarpaulins that served as housing and equipment shelters, almost two dozen parka-clad figures labored. A few worked with surveying transits, others strained against the weight of equipment-laden sledges; but most were engaged in the backbreaking work of driving hollow steel core-sampling rods into the ever-frozen earth along a geometric grid marked by yellow plastic cord. The heavy hammers rose and fell, but not even that tumult reached Anji's ears. The only sound not drowned by the banshee howl of the bone-numbing gale was his own labored breathing.

He was middle-aged, and the years he had spent in bio-genetic research laboratories were proper preparation for neither the manual labor nor the environment. Nor was the more recent confinement he had endured, even if it had been in a facility the medical staff had insisted on calling a "rest haven." There had been no rest there, not even during the sessions when he had been sedated.

In dreams, he could still recall the worst of it: the smooth, slick feel of unyielding nylon restraints; the cold electrodes taped to his temples; the taste of the rubber block they would force between his teeth; the acid sting of the sedative injection. Then the voltage would hit him, a vibrating fire that alternately paralyzed and convulsed his body. The sedative modulated the seizure, of course. Externally, it appeared little more than a ripple across his face. But inside, a terrifying electrical demon raged, slashing and ripping and throwing Anji against the walls of his very skull.

Anji's skin still prickled with the remembered horror, even if it had been the price of his Enlightenment.

"*Hai!*" a deep voice boomed, not far from his ears. As Anji turned, a heavy hand clapped him on the shoulder.

Fusaka Torji grinned at him, his stained and crooked teeth

a pedigree of childhood privation. Under the heavy quilting of his cold-weather gear, Fusaka's legs were short and bowed. But the man's upper body was barrel-chested and thick with muscle. Among the group of Aum faithful who had come to labor at this dismal site, he alone seemed tireless and unaffected by the climate.

Which made sense, Anji thought; the man was an Inuit, what the less enlightened still called an Eskimo — at least, his mother had been, and her genes had evidently dominated over those of his Yokahama-born father — and his earliest years had been spent on a cold and wind-swept island not wholly unlike the one where they now labored.

The two men leaned together so that the snorkel hoods of their parkas almost touched.

"Bring the drill," Fusaka shouted above the wind. He gestured to a figure behind him, which knelt beside a shallow excavation in the frozen ground. "One of the Initiates has found one, he believes."

Together, the two men wrestled the drill to the new location, its cold-stiffened pressure line dragging sullenly behind them. The young man on the ground stood up, his face a beatific smile.

"Here," he said, pointing his leather mitten to indicate the spot. "Quickly!"

This one is a True Believer, Anji thought, and smiled to himself. *As are we all now, those of us who remain. I, most of all.*

When the Sensei had chosen him for this assignment, Anji had bowed with the proper dignity — as had they all, Anji thought; even Fusaka, for once, had not committed some oafish breach of manners. But alone of the Select, Anji's mask of impassive devotion had almost slipped. His face had glowed when, with a touch on his forehead, the Sensei had selected him. Since the expedition had arrived here, he had been the most driven of the team, constantly urging them to arise earlier, to skip rest periods, to work harder. Some of his comrades had grumbled aloud, though most had contented themselves by staring at Anji behind an impassive mask that itself spoke volumes.

Like me, they are also Aum Truthseekers, Anji chided himself—he hoped sincerely. *That makes each of these men forever my brother, my cohorts in the Sensei's consciousness. But, oh—I have given much to ensure this hour will come to pass. I have sacrificed even the man I once was.*

Together, Anji and Fusaka positioned the drill where the younger man indicated. For several minutes they worked without speaking, the chatter of the tool and the wind rasping past their hooded heads competing in volume.

Suddenly, Fusaka grabbed Anji's arm and shouted something unintelligible. Anji cut the airflow to the drill and dropped to his knees, pawing with mittened hands at the loosened chunks of permafrost. Fusaka knelt close beside as the biogeneticist gradually exposed a mounded outline. Frozen hard to the ground was a rough-woven canvas form bound with hemp ropes.

"I told you," Fusaka said, poking Anji with an elbow. "This was where they placed the bodies. My mother's mother would tell her how they were sewn into sailcloth when there were no more sealskin robes." He looked around the flat tundra. "There will be several dozen more nearby. They were buried in a single trench. A meter or so below the surface, perhaps a little more."

Anji only grunted, watching closely as Fusaka pulled off his leather mittens and opened a pocket knife. Carefully, he worked the blade against the stiff cloth, cutting a semicircle that he peeled back with difficulty.

Underneath was the face of a young woman. Her features were the mix of Oriental and Indian that distinguishes the Komaji from other Inuit peoples. It was an unmarked visage, almost childlike, peaceful in repose in a way that belied the manner of her death.

Anji looked at her, filled with a reverence that came from

far more than a cultural respect for the dead. His awe was not
for the individual woman before him—how could it be? She
was insignificant, merely one of the tens of millions who had
died with her. No, Anji's awe was reserved for the instrument
of her death, which the biogeneticist fervently prayed still
lived on inside her, waiting to be awakened from a slumber
of almost a century. Waiting, he remembered the Sensei saying, for a man of Anji's unique skills to help it do so.

Now it begins, Anji thought, as the other members of the
party began to prepare this first corpse for the journey it
would take. He stood for a moment longer, his eyes locked
on the long-dead face swathed in its sailcloth cocoon. Unbidden, a phrase came to his mind.

I am Shiva, destroyer of worlds.

He shivered again, this time in a way that had nothing to
do with the cold.

Six months after the team's return from the expedition, Anji
Suzuki left for the United States. He worked hard to keep his
face stoic—as stoic as any of the other Japanese on the
plane. It was difficult, because his entire being was aflame
with the joy of having been selected—*by the Sensei himself!*
Anji remembered, in awe—for this final, divine mission.

Since the expedition to the frigid Arctic almost half a year
before, Anji had made this trip several times to meet with the
ganjini, the godless barbarian crazies that the Sensei had ordered him to find and cultivate in America. He had performed this duty well, finally selecting two of the *ganjini*
private armies—they called themselves militias, he reminded himself—one near the East Coast, one in the American West. He had supplied them with the unique weaponry
from the Aum arsenal and instructed them in its use.

In the coming days, he had been informed, it will be a useful diversion.

*It will be as if angry wraiths, swarming from every
crevice, seek to overwhelm them,* the Sensei had told Anji.

*Then shall come the final darkness, from which there will be
no escape.*

Anji savored the image with the zeal of a True Believer.

They had prepared, and waited. Among the Aum, some
still held hope that the unbelievers—the subhumans who
had mocked their Truths, the mindless beasts who had harried the Divine Aum Asahara mercilessly before finally removing him to their corrupt courtrooms—would somehow
find their own Enlightenment. They had steadfastly held to
that hope for several years—preparing for the worst, but be-
traying to the world nothing save a sense of their own harm-
lessness. So the Sensei had counseled them, with a wisdom
that had sustained them since the Divine One had been
seized.

All the while, the rituals of a sham justice painted their
leader as a murderous madman rather than a savior.

And then, only a few weeks before, their judges had condemned Aum Asahara—condemned the Divine One to what
they, in an unenlightened ignorance, considered the ultimate
punishment. And in so doing, unwittingly condemned themselves as well.

They will now learn, Anji pledged. *If the Truth of Aum is
to pass from existence, so too will the unworthy who rejected
it. And so too will we all.*

Hidden in the erstwhile biogeneticist's waistband was an
American passport that had once belonged to an Aum recruit;
the photo likeness was close enough to pass scrutiny, as it
had on the previous trips. Again, for safety Anji took the soft
route, flying first under his own name to Mexico City. There
he would change his plane and his identity for the flight to
Denver, while the original flight continued on to Miami.

His mission was not dissimilar to those of his countrymen
now filing aboard this aircraft: sent by their corporate mas-
ters to do battle with the outside world, to best it on its own
turf.

They wage a war of economics, Anji mused, *and carry as*

their weapons briefcases stuffed with contracts, business plans, proposals. So petty, so parochial in their limited aims.

His own war was much more direct; the weapon he carried was not in his briefcase, but inside his body—even now multiplying and girding for the final battle, the Great Apocalypse. He had, Anji knew, done his work well.

There were no symptoms to betray him, not yet; he had, in accordance with the incubation tables he had carefully calculated, waited until just before boarding to use the nasal inhaler. But soon, in a matter of days, he would become the first to take the path the Divine One had dictated for all the world to follow. By then, he would have cast the seed he carried so widely that none would be able to stay its destruction.

On the flight to Mexico, Anji flew tourist class, assigned to the aisle seat.

Despite the close quarters, it was an uneventful trip. Anji slept most of the way, as did his seatmate. To any who might notice, the pair was a study in contrasts: one a middle-aged Japanese with thick dark hair and the studious appearance of a man who had become accustomed to careful, intricate work; the other, an eight-year-old American girl. Her name was Emily Sawyer and she had been visiting her father, an Air Force E-6 stationed at a base in Japan. Emily shifted as she slept, for a while leaning against the snoring man in the seat beside her. Her blond hair moved slightly in the fitful breeze of his breathing.

Under the watchful eye of the flight attendant—a scrutiny that, in the end, was unequal to a danger far too minute to be seen—Emily was returning to her mother's home in Milton, a small town a few miles from Fort Walton Beach, Florida.

It was an easy landing at Denver International Airport, a smooth glide toward the geometric concrete ribbons and graceful white-tented canopies of the sprawling complex.

The connecting flight from Mexico City had been uneventful. Around the cabin, a Babel of English and Spanish rose in volume as the plane descended. Through the plastic window, blurred by the crosshatching of the inevitable fine scratches, Anji saw the purple-and-brown majesty of the Rockies jutting into a pale blue summer sky. In comparison, Denver itself—thirty-odd miles in the distance—appeared a jumble of children's blocks, carelessly strewn.

Denver's old Stapleton Airport is only a memory now, closed since the mountain metropolis greeted the new millennium with this five-billion-dollar, technology-laden facility. It is a much longer drive to the city now, and the traveler no longer gets a bird's-eye view of the city's streets and buildings that Stapleton's close-in location offered. But landing at Denver International Airport no longer requires visitors to the Mile-High City to endure sharp banking turns and steep descents on final approach, or the often-jolting touchdowns that were the inevitable result.

Neither are they required, as before, to look down upon the industrial expanse of the old airport's closest neighbor, the Rocky Mountain Arsenal; like Stapleton, the arsenal too is now closed, though spacesuited workmen still swarm over its otherwise idle grounds.

Here, the aggressive remediation program has not removed a stubborn plutonium contamination, the legacy of half a century of nuclear weapons assembly and storage. The radioactive mega-tonnage that passed through the Rocky Mountain Arsenal in its heyday could have exterminated humanity many times over.

Had Anji considered all this—had he not been distracted, first by the bilingual tumult of his fellow passengers, and later by the lengthy delay as he waited in line at the car rental counter—he might have been struck by the irony.

Finally, his suitbag over a shoulder, Anji struggled across the tarmac of the massive parking lot. He studied the numbers on the rental agreement he held, scrutinizing the rows of freshly washed autos through which he passed. He also wondered if his shortness of breath was the result of the thin mountain air or a first symptom of the lethal destiny he carried.

Thus distracted, the Japanese did not notice the figure that followed him, moving quietly without appearing to do so.

Anji stopped short, and dropped his suitbag to the pavement.

It was a Lexus, a pale gray mount for his final ride. As he fumbled with the keyring, Anji glanced over his shoulder in the direction from which he had come. There was no one to be seen.

He turned the key in the lock, and the trunk popped open. It was, he noted idly, surprisingly spacious.

"Excuse, please," a voice said from behind.

Anji spun, startled as much by the trace of a Slavic accent as by the interruption itself. For a split second, what might have been a smile of beatific delight flashed across his Asian features.

My Sensei! his mind cried out, knowing at the same instant it could not be.

And it was not.

He did not know the man who stood carefully outside Anji's attack radius with a genial smile on his cleanshaven face.

Anji's eyes dropped to an object the stranger held, waist-high. It was oddly shaped—an awkward black metal protuberance, vented on the sides and with what looked like a strip of masking tape affixed across the front of the tube. He had just recognized it as a weapon when the tape abruptly blew apart, leaving its edges frayed and tinged with black.

There was no sound, but Anji felt the shock of impact against his sternum. He staggered, catching himself for an instant; then his knees gave way and he felt himself tumble backward. He crashed onto metal, his head bouncing hard against what felt like thin carpet. There was still no pain, but when he willed his hand to touch his chest, it came away warm and dripping.

The world swam redly for a moment; when his eyes cleared again, he was looking up the pale blue sky framed by the inside of the open trunk lid. A face moved into his vision, peered down at him without apparent interest. Then it disappeared, and he felt his legs being lifted and folded into the trunk where he lay. They seemed very far away, no longer a part of his body.

Then the trunk lid slammed shut, plunging Anji into a semidarkness that, a few seconds later, became final and complete.

Day One:
July 21

Chapter 1

Fort Walton Beach, Florida
July 21

Breakfast today was an apple, a bright red Macintosh, and Dr. Carol Mayer bit into it with the aggrieved attitude of a hungry woman deprived of a decent meal. It made a satisfying crunching sound and tasted delicious and sweet. But it was still an apple, and as such, a woefully insufficient substitute for a real meal.

Her jaw working busily, Carol popped another chart from the ready-rack behind the reception counter and scanned it quickly. She frowned, pursing her lips.

Another upper-rez complaint? the young physician said to herself. *Third one I've fielded this morning.*

It was shaping up into a busy day, and the non-physician side of Carol sighed in disappointment. It was a beautiful day outside, and the waters of Choctawatchee Bay—*her* bay: the expanse of living waters that she had first seen on the incoming flight when she interviewed for the job here, the bay with which she had fallen into thrall from that instant onward—would be blue and inviting.

The emergency room at the Rossini-Evans Clinic was crowded—not unusual for a Tuesday during the summer season, when it seemed that every other tourist, traveler or random visitor to the Emerald Coast ran afoul of the perils of vacation. It might be sunburn, cherry red on newly arrived flesh unaccustomed to the searing rays of the Redneck Riviera. It might be jellyfish stings, or fishhook impalements. It might be cracked bones or abrasions on visiting skateboarders, whose chronic attitude of terminal teenage boredom was at least temporarily on hold.

But it's not often summer colds, Carol told herself. *At least, not this many.*

"Room Three," LaTonya Ferris said, interrupting the physician's musings. She was a large black woman in nurse's garb who ruled the clinic's immediate care operations with an iron hand. "But when you're finished there, honey, take a look at the boy in Five. He's wearing a cast that's past due the time to come off." She chuckled. "And the fragrance is something else, I want to tell you."

Carol Mayer checked to make sure no patients were watching. Then she stuck her tongue out at LaTonya. Both women laughed at the same time, and Carol was still grinning as she strode down the hallway to the examining room. She took a final bite of her apple, dropped it in the side pocket of her lab coat, and knocked once on the closed door.

Carol was all efficiency when she opened the door and stepped in.

Seated on the exam table was a woman who could not have been far out of her teens. She was wearing a multicolored tubetop and white shorts, and on her feet were bright red canvas Keds. Like so many of the girls who found their way to the sugar white beaches here, she had long blond hair and the body of a dancer. A sea-horse tattoo, acquired recently enough to still look raw on the margins of the ink lines, decorated the inside of her left thigh.

A young man in a faded Auburn T-shirt and cutoff Levi's sat on the table beside her, holding her hand and looking uncertain.

"How are we doing today"—Carol glanced at the name on the insurance form—"Ms. Atkins, is it?"

Ashley Atkins, whose sophomore year at Ole Miss had ended three weeks before she had informed her parents of the plan to summer on the beach, blew her nose in the handkerchief she held. Her eyes were red and puffy.

"Not so good. I truly feel like hell."

"She's been throwin' up all morning, Doctor," the young man interjected. His voice was worried. "I think she's running a fever, too."

"Let's take a look." Carol snapped on fresh latex gloves from a box on the countertop. She slipped a plastic sleeve over the sensor of an electronic thermometer and placed the tip in the younger woman's ear canal.

"Yep. You're elevated, a bit. I want to look at your throat, please."

There was inflammation. It was not major, and certainly fit the diagnostic profile Carol was building. Northwest Florida in July was an oven, which meant that air conditioners were working overtime in every motel room, beach house and condo. That kept the inside air dry, which dried out throat and nasal membranes; viruses tended to thrive in that kind of environment. Add to that the closed-circuit recirculated air in movie theaters, restaurants, rave halls and barrooms—*well,* Carol reasoned, *it's a wonder everybody isn't nursing the summer sniffles.*

She scribbled a note on the form. "About how long have you been feeling ill, Ms. Atkins?" she asked, without looking up.

"Day 'fore yesterday, she started sounding all clogged up," the young man said. "I don't think she got much sleep last night, either."

"It wasn't bad until this morning, Bobby," Ashley protested. "Doctor, you got something I can take to feel better?" She blew her nose again. "Penicillin or something? I tried Contac, but it didn't do any good."

Carol shook her head sympathetically.

"I'm afraid you've picked up a bad cold," she said. "Antibiotics don't work on a virus. I'm going to take some swabs and have a nurse draw a blood sample—don't worry, Ms. Atkins, you'll hardly feel it. We'll run some tests. There are a few medications that can help with the symptoms, and we'll write you up a prescription." She stood, peeled the latex gloves from her hands and tossed them into a wastebasket. "I'll be back in a minute."

Carol closed the door behind her. It was a routine case, a summer cold, and Ashley Atkins was an otherwise healthy young woman. Strictly speaking, Carol could prescribe two antivirals, amantadine and rimantadine, though it was probably too late in the cycle to do much good. In addition, the medical journals were all agog about neuraminidase inhibitors like zanamivir and oseltamivir, though the results were still less than predictable. There were also even newer formulations, most of them still in the pre-brand-name stage and tagged only by alphanumeric identifiers; sometimes they worked, usually they did not. Worse, the cost was horrendous; few HMOs or insurance companies would pay for what they termed such "experimental" treatment.

All you could really do was wait it out. A week, ten days at the most, and Ashley Atkins would be back on the beach without a care in the world. Carol fished the apple from her pocket and nibbled at it.

She was approaching the reception counter to order the tests when she heard a loud hacking from the waiting room. It rose above what suddenly seemed to her a cacophony of lesser coughs and a chorus of snuffling noses.

On a hunch, she walked around the counter and looked out at the waiting room. Of perhaps fifteen people there, she estimated a dozen were exhibiting the sniffling, flushed-face presentation she had already seen three times today.

As she watched, one of the waiting patients began to cough again. It was loud and phlegmy and extended, racking

the middle-aged man's beefy body. It was also evidently
painful, bending him forward from the waist as he sat. When
the man finally regained control, his eyes were watering profusely. He wiped at his mouth with a handful of paper tissues,
and Carol saw the bluish cast of his lips.

My God, she realized, *he's cyanotic.*

She was just starting forward when the man's eyes rolled
upward and he fell forward. He crashed heavily to the floor
and lay motionless. In an instant, Carol was crouched over
him, oblivious to the screaming and commotion in the room.
Her fingertips were still wet with the juice of the apple now
rolling into a far corner, and she pressed them firmly against
the man's carotid. She concentrated hard, only vaguely
aware of a figure that was now kneeling beside her. It was
one of the nurses, Jerry-something-or-other, who moon-
lighted at the clinic when not on duty at Eglin Air Force Base
hospital.

"There's no pulse," she told him, and began chest compressions as Jerry bent to clear the airway. They worked as a
team, with Jerry timing his mouth-to-mouth ventilation to
Carol's pace until LaTonya sprinted up with a bag and oxygen mask.

For the next few minutes, the waiting room was chaos.
Other physicians and nurses rushed in, some of them herding
the waiting-room occupants away from the tableau on the
floor. Patients, themselves alarmed by the clamor of the
frightened crowd, peered from behind half-opened doors of
the treatment rooms; several emerged to see better, adding to
the press of humanity in the room.

Carol noticed them only peripherally, all her attention focused on the medical crisis. The portable electroshock kit
was up and charging in seconds, but even repeated hits from
the paddles caused no change in the unit's monitors. She
heard somebody, a woman, asking loudly for an ambulance;
if Carol had not been so fiercely focused she might have
laughed.

Ambulance? This is a clinic, lady. He's already up to his butt in doctors.

She said nothing, except to call for syringes of adrenaline, bicarbonate, TPF—the full arsenal that modern medicine provides to restimulate cardiac activity.

But not even the most sophisticated treatments can reanimate dead tissue. After almost twenty minutes, Carol waved Jerry away from what was now only a bundle of slowly cooling meat. She looked at her wristwatch, trying to ignore the film of tears that blurred the digital numbers.

"Time of death," she said in a low voice, "nine-fifty-four A.M."

Around the room, there was a hushed silence from the medical staff and the patients alike.

But only for a moment.

Then a woman standing wide-eyed amid the other stunned patients began to cough, loudly and painfully. She was bent forward at the waist when Carol looked up, and had it not been for the fresh sea-horse tattoo she would not have known who it was. The paroxysm rocked Ashley Atkins's body, and she leaned heavily against the young man who held her arm.

There was an instant's hesitation before one of the clinic staff moved toward her. In that brief moment, the other patients already had begun to shrink back—all but one, whose own sudden racking cough ended in a projectile gush of bright crimson blood.

What the hell? Carol Mayer asked herself. *What the hell is going on here?*

She felt a shiver pass along her spine, and recognized it as fear.

Chapter 2

It was clearly not politically correct, but whenever Beck Casey landed in Atlanta there was a part of him that missed the Old South. He would look at the plastic kiosks advertising Japanese laptops, cellular phone services, the ever-changing and still-unmet promises of a dot-com technology, and wonder where the hell Scarlett O'Hara had gone.

At those moments, the historian in Beck would try to envision that world through the eyes of a Robert E. Lee or Jefferson Davis: vast feudal plantations doomed by the flaws and inequities that defined their agri-economic system but alive with the elegance that the system propped up. Beck saw the aristocratic young bloods, equally at home on horse and behind dueling pistol; and the proud Rebel beauties, as refined as they were fiery in their own varieties of passions. It was a romanticized imagery, and Beck knew it. But in recent years the picture had become increasingly difficult to summon, even though the capital of the New South took pains to remind all comers of its heritage. It had taken Beck several trips to understand what was wrong.

The problem, he had come to see, was in the sanitized version that was now being offered for public consumption.

Hartsfield Airport was now the nation's busiest; gone were the Confederate battle flags, the faux-lithograph postcards portraying red-clay fields of cotton, even the mural re-creating the Battle of Stone Mountain that had greeted travelers of an earlier year. All these had been replaced by ubiquitous photo-posters of Southern belles carefully posed in hoop-skirted coquettishness on the immaculate lawns of restored antebellum mansions. Today the Stars and Bars had been recast as a racist symbol; the plantations raised only tourist dollars; the coterie of modern Scarletts featured a more or less equal mix of races, skin hues and, presumably, creeds.

It was, he supposed, social progress of a sort—though Beck often wondered if blatant historical revisionism caused more problems than it cured. Better to embrace the past, or at least acknowledge its mistakes, than to remanufacture a homogenized history from random bits and scraps that survived the censor's scissors. All this was the Disney version of the Old South; and even as an unreconstructed Yankee, Beck felt the poorer for it.

He was jostled from his thoughts, bumped from the front by a woman in a rumpled business suit; then, almost simultaneously, from behind by a man in wilted shirtsleeves whose coat was draped over an arm. Both muttered their automatic pardons, their minds already otherwise occupied, before pushing past in opposite directions.

As always, the airport was chaotic. If you fly anywhere in the South, you change planes in Atlanta. The terminal was packed with throngs of the harried, the overwrought, the perplexed. Beck moved as quickly as possible through the gate area, pressed forward by his fellow arrivals still filing down the jetway behind him. Together they formed one of the countless tributaries that merged into a constant flow of humanity pouring through the airport terminal. Beck spotted an eddy, an empty space along the wall. He claimed it for his own, planting his bag at his feet.

"Dr. Casey!" The voice came from behind, and as Beck

turned he found himself face-to-face with a young woman almost as tall as himself. She was dressed in a light summer suit that was cut severely, almost like a uniform. Dark hair fell just short of her shoulders before curling slightly inward; it framed a face attractive in what Beck considered a serious-scholar sort of way. But her hands were delicate and lovely, not needing the adornment of jewelry and sensibly displaying none, and her eyes were a startling green.

"Dr. Casey?" This time the voice was interrogative. "Dr. Beck Casey?"

"Maybe," he said. "If I am, do we know each other?"

"Pardon me," she said, a hint of impatience in her tone. "I'm supposed to meet a Dr. Casey arriving from Chicago on Delta." She looked over her shoulder at the few Chicago passengers still milling about the gate area.

"Guilty as charged," Beck said, and grinned. "Let me guess: Larry Krewell sent you here, right?"

She nodded, and held out her hand. "I'm Andrea Wheelwright, Doctor. From CDC. Dr. Krewell had an unexpected schedule conflict, and I volunteered to meet your flight. You, uh . . . fit the description Dr. Krewell provided."

"And Larry's description said what, exactly?"

She colored slightly. "Well—tall. Dark hair." She smiled. "He described your age as—I'm quoting here—'either a well-preserved forty or a dissipated-looking thirty-five.' And he said you probably wouldn't be dressed like a doctor."

Beck looked down at an Iowa State T-shirt that had once been black, tucked into faded denim jeans. On his feet were salt-stained Top-Siders, no socks. On the carpeted floor beside them, an oversized gym bag that had seen better days bulged with Beck's traveling kit. Only the laptop Power-Book, slung over his shoulder in its spotless black ballistic nylon case, seemed out of place in an appearance that might, with extreme charity, be described as casual.

"Nailed it, didn't he?" Beck said, laughing.

The crowd jostled them again, and Andrea Wheelwright

scooped up the gym bag with an ease that belied its weight. "I have a car outside," she said, and—using the bag as a ram—led the way. She pushed through the throngs with enthusiasm, and forced a passage for herself and Beck on the crowded tram to the main terminal. There, she surged ahead to a long escalator that led upward to natural sunlight. He followed in the wake she left, deferring to what he recognized as an expert pathfinder.

Outside, an illegally parked Ford Mustang pressed against the curb under a sign that read TOWAWAY ZONE. It drew annoyed glances from the airport traffic police, but little more: a printed card propped inside the windshield said CDC/CENTERS FOR DISEASE CONTROL—OFFICIAL GOVERNMENT VEHICLE in large letters, above an impressive block of smaller type. The woman beeped the door locks and moved quickly to the driver's side. Tossing the bag in the seat behind her, she slid in and the engine roared to life. Before Beck could completely close the passenger door, she was pulling into the passing stream of vehicles.

"Pretty handy, I bet." Beck nodded at the card. He pulled the seat belt around himself and locked it with a click, just as his driver cut hard into a faster lane. He heard the sound of brakes squealing and involuntarily braced for an impact that did not materialize.

"Are we in a hurry?"

"Actually, Dr. Casey, " she began, "I just assumed—"

"Please, let's drop the 'doctor,' " Beck interrupted. "Why don't you call me Beck? Then I can call you Andrea."

"Andi, if you please. Only my mother uses the other name. Pardon me, but you're *not* a doctor?" She pulled from the airport ramp onto the expressway and accelerated in a manner that pressed Beck into the seat back.

"My doctorate is in history. And sociology."

"Ah, a professor."

"Yes and no. Having dual specialties seems to annoy both the sociology department and the history department at most

universities—at least, it sure pisses off their tenure commit-
tees."

"Really. I had no idea."

"I'm glad you saw that truck," Beck said, trying to sound
unconcerned. "So I've become a professional visiting academic. I've worked on four campuses in three years. Right now
I'm a guest lecturer at the University of Chicago—or will be
when the term starts next month." He glanced pointedly at
the speedometer. "If I live that long."

"Dr. Krewell seems to know you well. Have you worked
together?"

"I met Larry years ago, when I was living in D.C."

He noticed her eyes flicker toward him momentarily, and
he was careful to sound casual. "Georgetown, on a nice little
government grant. I was working on my master's then, and
was still afflicted with literary ambitions. So I was trying to
research a book."

"Really? What was the subject?"

Beck flinched as a minivan changed lanes in front of
them; Andi's Mustang swerved around it tightly and expertly.

"Looking back, it was a little pretentious. A history of the
impact of pandemic diseases on world history. You know—
the Black Death. Cholera. Smallpox. Plague books were considered sexy for a while back then. I thought I'd cash in on
the trend and maybe start building a reputation at the same
time. I interviewed a lot of people. Larry was sort of the
Army's up-and-coming resident expert."

"He would have been at USAMRIID—or was it still
called Fort Detrick, back then?"

Beck smiled, but said nothing. In the circles he had once
traveled, it was considered bad form to mention that someone had been posted to Detrick, despite the new reputation
the military installation had spared no effort to build for itself. At least USAMRIID—the acronym for the U.S. Army
Medical Research Institute of Infectious Diseases, where
today the work focused on vaccines and treatments—carried

fewer connotations of the biological weapons that was once Detrick's sole reason for existence.

"So, was your book a success?"

Beck made a show of scowling darkly, then grinned in unison with his driver.

"Took too long to write it," he said. "By the time I finished, public tastes had moved on. But at least I didn't have to give the grant money back."

And that's not exactly a lie, Beck thought.

In fact, ultimately the book had been published, though distribution had been limited to a small, select audience—all of whom received salaries from the United States government. It had also led to a job offer, then a career, in a profession he had once thought existed only in fiction. But he could think of no reason to proffer this information to Andi Wheelwright, or to anyone else who did not carry the requisite clearance.

After all, he thought with a flash of bitter regret, he had not offered it to Deborah—at least, not during the years when it might have made the difference to both of them. And by the time he might have been ready to do so, the information had already been devalued, torn from him by violent strangers whose calculated interrogations had been more intimate than anything he had shared with his wife. In the aftermath, Deborah had no longer seemed inclined to know.

He shook off the dark thoughts and turned to his driver.

"So, Andi—is it Dr. Wheelwright, or Ms. Wheelwright?"

She looked at Beck briefly, and—he thought—speculatively.

"I'm not a doctor," she said, easily, her eyes back on the traffic. "Most of my work involves public information."

"Aha—we're both in the same business," Beck said, and was puzzled at the look she shot him. "Writing and teaching, I mean. Do you always drive this fast?"

"Uh-huh." Another lane change snapped Beck's head sideways. "Beck, could we talk when we get to CDC? I'm sorry, but I kind of need to keep my mind on the road right now."

"No problem," Beck assured her, the cars outside a solid blur in his peripheral vision. Unconsciously, he drew his knees closer to his chest. "Absolutely. You go ahead and concentrate. Please."

The Centers for Disease Control are just what they sound like, a collection of six red-brick structures in Chamblee, just north of downtown Atlanta. Viewed from Clifton Road, which it faces, the complex is deceptive; built into one of the rolling Georgian hills, the bulk of the complex is actually underground. The overall appearance is not unlike the headquarters of a medium-sized corporation, though not a particularly prosperous one. This similarity continues into the various lobbies and reception areas, each comfortably appointed with an intentionally understated restraint. The effect is one of both scientific efficiency and a casual, almost folksy sense of welcome to the public.

The latter ends abruptly immediately inside the doors on the north side, where a lobby branches into an atrium. Those doors mark the outer boundary of Building Fifteen, officially designated the Viral and Rickettsial Diseases Lab. This is home for the CDC's Special Pathogens Branch, and the sunny visages with which staff greets most visitors elsewhere are conspicuous in their absence. Here, the uniformed guards take their jobs seriously indeed; the sidearms are clearly not for show. Here, a special system of fans maintains an air pressure that is slightly lower than the world outside; the negative air pressure ensures any exchange of microscopic life-forms will be in only one direction. It also causes a slight hiss that soon becomes unnoticed white noise.

Andi Wheelwright handed her laminated identification card to one of the guards, who passed it through what looked like an electronic credit card validator. He carefully studied the image that popped up on his computer monitor before returning the card.

"This is Dr. Beck Casey," Andi said, a hint of emphasis on the honorific. "He's on Dr. Krewell's access authorization. This morning's list."

The guard punched in a series of keystrokes.

"I'll need to see a photo ID, Dr. Beck."

"Sure," Beck said, and reached for his hip pocket and stiffened.

The wallet he always carried there was gone.

"Looks like we have a slight problem," Beck said.

"One of us does," said the guard. He glanced at Andi Wheelwright, who answered with a slight nod. Before Beck could speak, she was already heading down the hall.

"Can't admit you without an ID," the guard said. "But Ms. Wheelwright might be able to do something. It'll probably be a few minutes, though."

"I'll bet you have a little room where I can wait," he told the guard. "While all this gets straightened out."

"Uh-huh," the guard said, trying to keep a straight face. "I'll even keep you company."

Less than twenty minutes later, the guard escorted Beck past the lobby checkpoint. There was no ID check this time, and no sign of Andi Wheelwright. Instead, Beck walked in lockstep with the guard through a labyrinth of corridors. Occasionally, people passed them, traveling in the opposite direction. No one spoke.

Finally, they stopped outside one anonymous set of closed doors. The guard knocked once. He winked at Beck and gestured, palm up, at the door.

Inside, seated at a hardwood desk that butted against tall filing cabinets, was Larry Krewell. Spread out on the desk in front of Krewell was Beck's wallet and the contents thereof.

A man's history, or at least a significant part of it, is contained in the things he carries. Old business cards, receipts, the type and number of credit cards, a phone number scribbled on a napkin: each item adds another handful of pixels to the overall picture. Krewell had made an untidy pile: a commuter ticket, a prepaid phone card, an American Express and a MasterCard, five twenty-dollar bills and a similar number of singles. Apparently, Krewell had already read whatever stories they told and dismissed them as irrelevant.

All save the driver's license, which he was examining with a skeptical expression.

"Damn it, Beck—you trying to tell me you still weigh one-ninety?" Krewell raised his eyes, tracked up and down on his visitor. "Okay," he said grudgingly. "Maybe. You must have a *lot* of free time to spend in the gym, though." He tossed the license onto the pile of other official detritus. "By the way, my paranoid ol' buddy—whoever did up the other two licenses for you does good work. But where did he come up with the names? You just don't *look* like a Wayne or a Buford."

"Hello to you too, Larry," Beck said. "Don't lose the Metra ticket. It's a monthly pass, and I'll need it when I go back to Chicago." He pulled up the visitor's chair and crossed his legs. "Which will be on the next flight, unless you can explain why you had that pair of boosters lift my wallet."

Krewell grinned. "Bullshit. No way you made 'em." He thrust an impressive jaw at the monitor that occupied a corner of the desk. "I saw your face when you reached for your wallet, ol' buddy. About fell out of my chair laughing."

The door opened and Andi Wheelwright entered. In her hand was a sheaf of what looked like photos, which she laid in front of Krewell.

"You know, you should consider a cleaning service," she said to Beck, her impassive expression leavened by the hint of humor in her tone. "Your apartment is rather a mess, even for a bachelor."

Krewell glanced at the top photo—actually, a fine-

detailed laser printout, a vast improvement over the fax images it had replaced. It showed a small kitchen table that
evidently doubled as a desk; paper Starbucks cups and
opened take-out containers with Chinese characters badly
printed in red shared the tabletop with textbooks butterflied
open. Krewell flipped through the printouts rapidly, pausing
only at a picture of a bedside table in the middle of the stack.

A head shot of a smiling girl in her early teens filled the
right side of a hinged photo frame; the left side was conspic-
uously empty.

"How is Katie, by the way?" Krewell asked, still looking
at the photo. "She's what now—fifteen?"

"Fifteen, going on thirty," Beck said. "She spent two
weeks in Chicago with me last month—most of it, I think,
on the phone talking to her girlfriends back in Virginia.
Mainly about *boys,* from what I could overhear."

Krewell grinned. "Daughters are God's way of punishing
fathers for the sins of their youth. At least she's not driving
yet."

"Driver's ed starts in September," Beck replied. "Katie already has her learner's permit, courtesy of the Common-
wealth of Virginia."

"Wait till she asks for a car."

"Already asked and answered." Beck shook his head. "No
way, even if I *had* the money. So we compromised—I taught
her how to drive a stick shift. By the time she went back
home, my Beetle needed a new clutch."

"Back home." Krewell nodded, making it sound casual.
"How's everybody adjusting? To the divorce, I mean."

"Katie's fine."

"Good to hear. And Deborah? Is she fine, too?"

There was no answer. When Krewell looked up to repeat,
he saw Beck staring at him, unblinking. Krewell held Beck's
eye for a moment, then tossed the photos on the desk as if
they had no significance.

"Well, I hope you're getting a break on the rent," he told

Beck. "Looks like a bomb went off in your bedroom—and this was taken *before* our people searched the place."

Andi chuckled.

"You work in public information, you say?" Beck said to her, eyebrows raised in polite inquiry.

"Yes," Andi said. "Except my job is usually to *prevent* information from becoming public."

"Find anything interesting?" Beck asked. "In my wallet or my place?"

"Well, I for one find it interesting that your bank balance can be so low without knocking your credit rating all to hell," Krewell volunteered.

He smiled at the expression on Beck's face and shrugged in a way meant to convey good humor. "Oh, grow up. You know how the game is played. Of *course* we looked at your finances. Heck, ol' buddy, we turned your life inside out—did a pretty good job, given the time limitations."

"Behave, gentlemen," Andi said. "We didn't find anything incriminating or even mildly suspicious." She tried to look apologetic, and failed utterly. "Sorry. You never know until you check, and there wasn't time to go by the rule book."

"Andi is our security director here, Beck," said a grinning Krewell. "And since yesterday afternoon, it has been her people that you *didn't* see following you around. C'mon. Admit it, ol' buddy. It'll only hurt for a minute."

"I may be out of practice," Beck conceded. "A little." He twisted to address Andi. "Congratulations. Your guys are pretty good at the bump and lift. Dog and cat team at the airport gate. Right?"

Andi nodded. To Beck, she looked more than a little smug.

"Mario Andretti couldn't have beat your time getting out here, so I assume the dip handed off my wallet to you right there. What, ten feet from where I was standing? Nice touch."

"I like to get in a little fieldwork every now and then," Andi said. "Keeps *my* tradecraft from getting too rusty."

"Touché," Beck said. "Okay. What's this about, Larry? I gather all that sugar on the phone this morning was just bullshit to get me down here. All you had to do was ask me."

"You're wrong, my friend. I am indeed about to offer you a consulting contract. But not to research the history of the CDC, or whatever the hell I told you."

Beck frowned. "Why the cover story?"

"We have a for-real, double-barreled public health emergency," Krewell said, "and you've been drafted." He made a gesture with his thumb. "I have a roomful of silverbacks down the hall. Right now, they don't know how to do anything but bare their fangs and growl at one another. And throw dung, when they get the chance. They are one scared pack of old gorillas, I kid you not. But they're the ones who will have to go back to the President, damn soon, and give him our official recommendation."

"The President? Larry, what the hell is going on?"

"All that stuff you wrote for the Company on epidemics, pandemics, bioplagues, remember? The disruptions, the riots—hell, the whole ball of social breakdown they could create? I'll tell you—you painted one hell of a picture. Scared me, when the CIA sent over a copy."

Beck looked at his friend blankly. He realized that his heart had begun to beat faster, and that his face suddenly felt numb.

Krewell looked at his wristwatch.

"As of seventeen hours ago, ol' buddy, you officially became a prophet."

More than a dozen people were seated around the polished mahogany of the circular conference table, and as almost as many were in the theater-style chairs behind them. Each principal had been allowed only one aide; some, recognizing the sensitivity of the subject matter, had elected to come alone.

It was nearing lunchtime, and the meeting evidently had been going on for some hours. Plates and saucers, some bearing scraps of long-cold scrambled eggs and crusts of toasted muffins, still littered the table. The breakfast crockery had been pushed to the side to clear a space for legal pads or laptop computers, depending on each participant's note-taking preference. Only two or three people were squinting down, Beck noticed, trying to decipher the undersized screen of a Palm Pilot. Audio recorders might have been useful to these unfortunates; given the nature of the subject matter and its potential political sensitivity, these were strictly prohibited.

Despite an efficient air-conditioning system, the tang of burned coffee lingered in the air.

It mingled with a tantalizingly familiar odor that at first Beck could not place. Then it hit him: it was the smell of tobacco, and that fact alone confirmed to Beck that this was no ordinary meeting. Whoever was smoking had reached a stress level high enough to need a cigarette; needed one badly enough to ignore this most sacred of federal regulations.

And, Beck thought, *has the clout to get away with it.*

"Mr. Secretary, I would suggest that our most urgent need is to determine if we are indeed facing a threat. We should not forget the swine flu debacle that Jerry Ford initiated under much the same circumstances. More people died from the vaccine than even *caught* that flu."

The voice came from the far edge of the table, from the only person in the room who was still wearing a suit jacket. He was clearly not the smoker. Unlike the others, he appeared sleek and composed, and his eyes were bright as a ferret's. From television, Beck recognized him as the junior senator from Pennsylvania.

"Oh, for God's sake, Fred. That was 1976," another voice objected. "Mr. Secretary, rehashing what happened more than two decades ago is not a valid comparison. At least the Ford administration wasn't afraid to *act* when action was called for. I'd remind the gentleman that our science has come a long way since then—as has our ability to identify, and respond to, a critical danger to public health."

"Fine," the senator fired back. "*You* tell that to the President. Better still, tell the people of the United States they have to line up and get injected with some goddamn witches' brew—one that doesn't even exist yet."

Next to him, a woman in a tailored suit nodded in grim agreement; Beck recognized her as the surgeon general and assumed that a similarly serious-looking woman seated alongside was her aide.

Beck frowned, calculating the collective stature of the people at this table. Health and Human Services was Cabinet level, the surgeon general only a half-step below; add to that at least one senator, an assortment of expensive Brooks Brothers suits, and an impressive number of uniformed military, none of them below flag rank.

The heavy hitters were here in force, he realized.

A thin blue plume rose from one of the chairs, catching his attention. The occupant was facing away from the door where Beck, Krewell and Wheelwright had entered. Only the balding dome of the back of his head was visible, but Beck felt a sudden flash of recognition.

Carson, Beck thought. *Of course, it would have to be Carson.*

As if he heard Beck's thoughts, Billy Carson, national security advisor to the President, swiveled to look back at the entering trio. His face showed no sign of greeting, though his eyes locked on Beck's for what seemed like a long moment.

Then he turned away, leaning toward a stocky man in a short-sleeved white shirt who sat to his right. He murmured what might have been advice or instructions, then raised his voice to address the rest of the room.

"If I may. Please."

As always, Beck found the tone surprisingly mild, matching an appearance that would have better fit a stereotypical midlevel bureaucrat than the de facto head of the U.S. intelligence community. It was easy to underestimate Carson on the basis of how he looked and acted; in Beck's personal experience, a number of people had done just that, to their regret. In one notable instance, an undersecretary of defense had wondered aloud how "such a goddamn shoe-store clerk" could have risen so high in the intelligence community.

The remark had since become famous in the upper circles of government.

The undersecretary had seen neither the intellect nor the fierce pride that burned behind Carson's calculatedly mild demeanor. Only when the hapless official had found himself quietly outflanked and outmaneuvered had he looked closer, and by then it was too late to salvage his own career. The erstwhile undersecretary had left government, ironically to join a corporation that supplied footwear to the Army.

Beck had heard the story any number of times, even after he had left the job that kept him in regular contact with Carson. It had become a legend, and even the incumbent President was among those who regularly repeated the story. But rumor said he was the only one who did not smile when he told it.

Now Carson's quiet tone sliced through the debate like a bayonet.

"Thank you," he said. "Dr. Porter tells me he is prepared to address the nature of the situation we are facing. It might be valuable to hear him now."

Krewell touched Beck's arm. "Ray Porter heads CDC's Bio-Pathogen Forensics," he said in a low voice. "Knows his business. This guy, believe what he says about anything medical." They moved to the chairs behind Carson, where Wheelwright was already seated.

Porter fiddled with the keyboard, and an image lit up the room's large screen. It was a gray-and-white photo of what looked like fuzzy cotton balls, each corralled by a thick variegated circle. There were a number of them lumped together so tightly that some of the circles had flexed into the shape of hens' eggs.

"What you're looking at is an electron microscope's view of what we're calling H1N1-Florida," he said. "It's a virus culture sent to CDC by a pathologist in Niceville, Florida, down in the Panhandle. Patient was a thirty-six-year-old male, a limousine driver who had been hospitalized for a case of severe pneumonia. He died on the ninth of July. The sample was logged in here on July 11, and two days ago was assigned to a lab tech for A and I — analysis and identification."

"Thereby wasting almost two weeks," a woman sitting stiffly at the table did not quite mutter. The blue-black jacket draped over her chairback bore the gold shoulder boards of a Navy vice admiral and the bright silver caduceus of the medical corps.

Porter reddened, but his voice was unfazed.

"We get about a hundred and fifty culture samples here every working day," he said. "More on Mondays. You do the math, okay?" He pressed another key and a new image appeared along side the first.

"I'm not an expert," the ferret senator said, "but I don't see a difference."

"Genetically, there isn't one," Porter replied. "They're the same bug. Except this one came from in from a pathology lab in Mary Esther, Florida. An eight-year-old female presenting what the clinic's attending described as 'mild flulike symptoms.' That was last week — the sixteenth, I believe. We were sent the culture on July 18, the day the girl succumbed to severe respiratory failure."

Porter blew out hard. "Okay. We have a middle-aged male with pneumonia, which isn't all that uncommon even in the summer. This guy had all kinds of risk factors: he was a smoker, grossly overweight *and* in a sedentary job —"

He shrugged.

"Well. And sad as it is, sometimes when a kid catches the

flu, or even a common cold, there's a toxic-shock reaction. So the cultures came in. The first thing our people do is look over the paperwork that comes with 'em. Seemed routine. The clinical symptomology didn't raise any red flags, right? They had to wait in line for A and I."

"We all understand," the senator growled. "Your ass is covered. Get on with it."

Porter ignored the interruption.

"We ran the standard virological tests on the sample from the limo driver. It was an A-type, but we couldn't get a match on the strain. Wasn't Victoria, wasn't PR-34, wasn't WS. Then the lab tech ran an ELISA—that's shorthand for 'enzyme-linked immunosorbent assay'—and got some *very* confusing results. We seemed to have some kind of swine flu virus, non–type specific. *That* rang some bells—enough so the tech fast-tracked it to genetics for comparison.

"Yesterday, the computer came up with a hit—a form of Type A influenza, H1N1. Not an exact match; there are some very interesting antigenic shifts in the hemagglutinin protein that have us puzzled. But it was close enough for identification. More than close enough to make us start rescreening the paperwork backlog, looking for any cases with similar symptoms. That's how we found the other one, the girl."

He touched the keyboard again, and a map replaced the virus images. It was a detailed section of Northwest Florida, the stretch that ran along the Gulf Coast from the bulge of Applachicola to Mobile Bay in the west. Porter did something to the laptop that caused the display to zoom in, centering on the large patch of blue that was Choctawatchee Bay. Touching the northern shore was the town of Niceville; to the west, Mary Esther. Over both, a large red "1" was superimposed.

Between them, on the left side of the bay where the blue of the gulf touched a forest green shoreline, lay the city of Fort Walton Beach. There, on the display monitor, a large yellow "4-?" blinked relentlessly.

There was a stunned silence for a moment. Then the significance of what they were seeing dawned on those seated around the table, and several voices started to speak simultaneously.

Porter's next words rolled over the commotion like a tank.

"Approximately two hours ago, CDC fielded a call from a general practitioner in Fort Walton, which is on the coast about ninety miles west of Tallahassee. The physician—a Dr. Mayer—was reporting the death this morning of a fifty-three-year-old male who collapsed in the clinic where she works. Dr. Mayer indicated that the dead man presented with symptoms consistent with those of three other patients she had already examined this morning."

Porter paused for a moment.

"And here's worse news, people. Dr. Mayer says her waiting room was full of people with upper-respiratory complaints—an unusually high number, she believes."

The surgeon general spoke up.

"Can we confirm it's our virus?"

Porter shrugged. "I've got a team in the air now"—he glanced at the wall clock—"and they should be landing in a few minutes. We'll get swabs of the dead man and the three other patients, and run a field antibody test. My prediction is it's H1N1. If that's the case, I have no doubt that we will find others. It's only a matter of time."

From the chair beside Beck, Krewell's voice was hard, uncompromising.

"Time," he said, loud enough for the room to hear, "may be what we have the least of."

All eyes swiveled to Krewell. There was a silence for a moment, an appraisal of sorts. Then the senator spoke.

"Dr. Krewell, with all due respect, we're aware of your position. I'm certain the Special Pathogens Branch is sincere in its concern. But three or four cases of the flu—most of them not even confirmed—don't make for an emergency."

"This isn't just 'the flu,' Senator," Krewell said. "Not this variant of H1N1."

"Pardon me." Beck spoke up, feeling like a man come late to the party. "I don't know anything about this . . . H1-what-ever."

"Sure you do," Krewell said. "Maybe not by that name."

"The form of H1N1 we're looking at doesn't exist in nature," Porter said. "At least, we believe it hasn't for more than eighty years. But when it was making the rounds, back in 1918, it was called the Spanish flu. And now it's back."

"Jesus Christ," Beck said softly. "My great-grandfather died from that."

"Really?" Porter said. He spoke in a voice intended to carry throughout the room. "So did forty million other people."

Chapter 3

Fort Walton Beach, Florida
July 21

It was gloriously hot on the beach, moderated only slightly by the steady breeze that blew in from the sea. Gulls swooped in, hovering to investigate a scrap of bread crust on the sugar white sand before banking away in search of fresher sustenance. A sandpiper, either hungrier or less choosy than his larger cousin, darted in comically on its stiff bird legs and snatched up the morsel in his beak. Outside the surf line, fifty yards from shore, the occasional mullet broke the sun-dappled surface in fancy or in flight.

Katherine Casey—Katie to her friends—stretched languorously in the bright sunlight. She lay on her back, eyes closed, one knee carefully bent in a way she hoped displayed her fifteen-year-old charms to her best advantage. This, despite the fact that there were no teenage boys within view and only a handful of older male specimens in evidence. And most of *them* must have been thirty, maybe thirty-five—if not absolutely ancient, she told herself, then at least teetering on antique.

Still, Katie thought, savoring the sensation of warm sun on mostly bared flesh, *it doesn't hurt to practice.*

"Sure beats hanging around Arlington, doesn't it?"

The voice came from Carly Holmes, who at seventeen constituted the adult supervision for the trio. Carly had the car, a Chinese red LeMans; she had the credit card, a Gold American Express belonging to a mother both absent and indulgent; and she had the supreme self-confidence that came of past consequences habitually avoided. In this, she was the most experienced among her companions. It had been Carly's grand plan that brought them here, to the Florida Gulf Coast, in the first place.

"You said there'd be guys. Lots of guys."

The tone was not quite accusatory, not quite a question. It belonged to Jayne Lynn Soratelli, "J. L." to her close friends, "J. L.-bait" to the more literal-minded of her male classmates. Having just turned sixteen, J. L. was ready to prove her sophistication was at least the equal of her older friend's. Even without opening her eyes, Katie knew J. L. was propped up on her elbows, as if impatiently scanning the beach for likely prospects.

It was largely an act, and all three of the girls knew it. Of the trio, only Carly would be bold enough to initiate contact with the random passing male; she was also the only one of them who might take such an encounter to its logical conclusion.

Still, Carly had missed her only chance so far. When they pulled up outside the beachfront hotel late the night before, she had popped inside to see if there was a vacant room. Through the large glass lobby doors, Katie and J. L. had watched Carly lean over the counter, close to a skinny boy who was working the night desk. They saw Carly smile and pass her hand a little too casually through her blond mane. The clerk had nodded back at her, and the pair had talked for a moment before Carly had motioned her friends inside and unsheathed her Amex card. But the fates had intervened; it was close to three a.m., and even Carly was too bushed for more than the cursory flirtation. Worse, at close range the boy's appeal was somewhat muted by the rheumy cough of a bad summer cold.

Welcome to Florida, Katie thought to herself, remembering. This morning, when they had entered the lobby to walk to the beach, to her relief the desk was staffed by a large woman in a denim shirtdress.

"Oh, give it a chance," Carly was saying, listless in the morning heat, to J. L. "Most of the guys here don't even wake up before sundown."

"So why are we up at noon?" J. L.'s voice was now frankly challenging, as if she sensed an inconsistency that boded worse revelations. "Fourteen hours on the road! God, I'm still beat." Katie felt a sandy foot kick against her extended ankle. "Hey, Kates—you alive?"

"It's still better than hanging around at home," Katie said, eyes still closed. She hoped she sounded more enthusiastic than she felt.

"It's better than hanging around at your summer house, too," Carly said. "Sorry, Katie, but I *hate* that place."

"We used to have fun there," J. L. objected. "All of us."

"We were kids," Carly said, with less energy than Katie had become accustomed to when Carly was on the subject. "Now it's like going to kiddie summer camp. I have had my fill of hiking in the piney woods, thank you very much. I want to have some fun, and this is the place." There was a pause, and Katie could sense Carly working up her trademark wicked grin. "Come on. We're hot. We're three killer babes on vacation."

Still on her back, Katie raised her clenched fist in salute.

"Killer babes, on the beach," she said. "Get on board with it, J. L."

"Well," said J. L., "if I get caught, my folks will kill *me*."

"Look—nobody's going to get caught." Carly's voice was exasperated. "What're they going to do anyway? Call the cottage? There's no phone—right, Katie? So they'd have to call my cellular number, and then they'll get my voice mail and leave a message. You just block the number when you call back, that's all. I've done this before, dammit. It's *foolproof.*"

Katie knew better, just as she had known better in the first place than to sneak away on what Carly described as "a little road trip." The parents of all three girls had agreed—albeit reluctantly, in the case of Katie's and J. L.'s—to what was described to them as an extended weekend sleepover at the rural Virginia summer cabin Katie's mother had kept after the divorce. Had they been aware of the real plan, at least two of the young women involved would not have been allowed out of their respective rooms for the balance of the decade.

Hence Carly's precise timetable, under which they would be back home in Arlington, Virginia, after three days of non-stop sun-and-sand, extreme partying on the Redneck Riviera. With, presumably, no one the wiser.

Katie still felt guilty about the deception, though not as guilty as she had imagined she would. She had been nervous at first, particularly when Carly's LeMans had crossed the state line into North Carolina. But once her initial anxiety had cooled, she had analyzed her situation with all the logic of her years and experience.

I might as well enjoy myself now, Katie reasoned to herself philosophically. *Because when Mom finds out about this, I'll be grounded until I'm thirty.*

It was eerie, the way Deborah Stepanovich—she had dropped her married name, with an almost unseemly haste, after the divorce from Katie's father—could divine events that involved her only child. Perhaps it was her trained legal mind—Deborah was a lawyer on the partner track at a D.C. firm that specialized in representing the interests of obscenely large multinational corporations, and as such, accustomed to all manner of deception. Perhaps it was simply the finely honed instincts of every working mother.

Or maybe she's just a witch, with a "w," Katie told herself cattily, and bit off the thought as unworthy.

But whatever the skill, talent or supernatural power involved, there was no doubt in Katie's mind that her mother would, ultimately, discover the truth. It was a thought that surprised Katie with its mixture of apprehension and satisfaction, in roughly equal proportions.

The clashes were coming more and more frequently these days, and Katie admitted that it was usually her fault. She was tempted to attribute it to her parents' divorce, a still-raw wound that all three of the concerned parties pretended bled but a bare trickle; but instinctively Katie knew the conflict had far more elemental roots. Frequently, she found herself driven to challenge her mother even in matters where, secretly, they might have agreed.

It was as if someone else lived inside her, a malevolent being that automatically bristled at any suggestion, comment, observation or—especially—directive that came from Deborah. Invariably, Katie would respond, flint against her mother's steel. Then the sparks would fly, ignite the tinder of two women living in close proximity and raise a firestorm that indiscriminately blistered both of them.

The anger was automatic, virtually out of control, and in a very special way it frightened Katie—mainly because she could see the power she had to hurt her mother. But she could not stop, either. It was as if she were fiercely determined to prove that her mother had no answers, or at least not the right ones; at the same time, she was petrified at the prospect that this might be true.

It would have been useful to talk about what she was experiencing, Katie told herself; but to whom? Her mother was out, definitely; even on the days when an uneasy peace prevailed, the subject matter involved was decidedly too incendiary. It was, Katie believed, virtually guaranteed to bring about a less-than-fruitful exchange of ideas. There were, of course, the guidance counselors at school—a prospect Katie immediately rejected; only dweebs and losers went to them with their concerns, which were invariably passed along to the relevant parental unit anyway.

I wish I could have talked to Dad about it, Katie thought. In early June, she had spent two weeks with him in Chicago, where he was getting ready to work for a semester or so. *But he made it pretty clear that it was never quite the right time to bring up anything about Mom—exactly like she does, when I'm with her.*

Katie stopped short, surprised at the intensity of the sudden animosity she felt.

At both *of them, dammit,* she realized.

Katie understood that she was the fulcrum of a natural alliance that could pit one parent against the other; she could shift her allegiance between the two adult antagonists as her own necessities dictated. That fact, she reasoned, gave her a large measure of power—and should have given her, at least, a small measure of satisfaction.

Instead, it merely made her feel even more alone.

"Hel-l-lo—Earth to Casey. Anybody at home in there?"

Katie opened her eyes, squinting against the glare of the day.

"Carly's bailing on us," J. L. told her.

"I said, I'm going to call it a morning." Carly was standing, and despite the warmth of the day had pulled the large beach towel close around her shoulders. "I think maybe I've had too much sun. I'm going to go back to the room and sack out."

"What—you make a date with the front desk guy?" J. L. chided. Carly tried to smile, and for the first time Katie saw how tired her friend looked.

"Want us to come along?" Katie asked.

"No," Carly said. "You guys figure out where the parties are going to be tonight. I'm just pooped. Plus, I'm all achy from sitting in the car too long."

"Well," said Katie, "feel better."

"I just need to rest up." Carly added, "We've got a big night ahead. I guarantee it."

Chapter 4

Columbia Falls, Montana
July 21

The damnedest thing about the goddamn crazy Jap—the term Orin Trippett invariably used when referring to the emissary with whom he had met—the damnedest thing about him was that he had been so . . . so . . .

Well, "helpful" is the only word that comes right to mind, Trippett told himself. *Acts like he's Santy Claus and it's Christmas Eve. If Christmas came in July, that is.*

He had been suspicious initially, and he had not been alone. Orin had taken it to the leadership council, and just about everybody in the Mountain Warriors' Posse had been convinced that it was a government sting—a plot by the FBI or ATF or even those bastards from Internal Revenue, all aimed at undermining yet another citizens' militia.

And it would be just like Cousin Dickie to step into that kind of shit, Trippett thought sourly. *He's never been the sharpest pencil in the box.*

Early on, there had even been talk of bundling the lone Japanese into one of the panel trucks and taking him high enough into the mountains that no one would ever find the body. It had happened before, when the Posse had decided there was even a remote threat to the group.

But in the end, what the Japanese had been offering was simply too enticing to pass up. For the Mountain Warriors, it was the answer to their prayers. Nerve gas—sarin, the real thing. And another tantalizing prospect that the visitor would only hint at, but which—if true—would give Trippett's militia a capability beyond his very dreams.

They knew about CBW, of course—at least, the ones among the Posse who had been military or who used their home computers for more than hunting up porn sites on the Internet. To Orin Trippett, the idea of the Mountain Warriors posing a credible chemical and biological threat was enough to make him salivate.

But it was only when he had verified some of the Jap's claims that he began to consider the possibility was real.

That had come a month earlier, in late May, when Orin finally had decided to meet with his cousin in person. Dickie Trippett was an officer of the Empire State Legionnaires, a militia group in upstate New York. Despite his intellectual shortcomings, he was a man Orin trusted as much as he trusted anyone: they had done time together on a state weapons charge before Orin moved west in search of what remained of the real America. Now Orin had reestablished contact, and the two of them had met midway in an Iowa City motel.

"*Way* cool, man," Dickie had told him, a grin stretching across his face. "I couldn't believe it, y'know? This damn Jap—talks like some kind of egghead or something, doncha think?—anyways, he brings us this shit and, like, shows us exactly what to fuckin' do with it. I mean, we took those spray cans and laid the stuff anywhere there was lots of birds. Out in the woods, 'specially anywhere you got crows and jays—hell, one guy even drove into the Big Apple and sprayed it at the zoo. In the damn *bird house,* can ya dig it?" He laughed at the memory.

"You sure it was the real stuff?" Orin had asked.

"West Nile," Dickie had said, nodding. "It's a virus. Birds

get it, pass it to mosquitoes. They go bite people and presto! Encephalitis. Don't you read the papers, man? We got the stuff in, like, a year ago April. By the end of summer, people was comin' down with it all over the place. It's damn near everywhere in the country now." He had smiled thinly. "I'll give you two words: bug repellent. Don't leave home without it."

Orin frowned. "You think they had something to do with this other thing? You know, the foot-in-mouth shit over in England."

"I got my suspicions," Dickie said smugly.

Orin had been unconvinced.

"So how come you guys didn't, you know, take credit for it or something?"

Dickie had shrugged, in a manner decidedly nonchalant.

"Jap guy said it was just a test," he had replied. "So we could see how shit like that might work for us." He had leaned closer to his cousin, and his voice dropped. "But now we're gonna *really* make some noise, man. That's why I sent him along to you. Guy's got us something serious to work with."

"Like what?"

"He didn't tell you yet? Couple of new toys," Dickie had said, grinning. "One of 'em—well, you ever hear of sarin, man?"

Orin had shrugged noncommittally. Family was family, but in militia matters it was usually smart to listen more than you talked. That went double when it came to chemical weapons.

"Nerve gas, something like that?"

"Got that right. He's bringin' in a shitload of it." Dickie had leaned closer. "And he talks about having some kind of germ-warfare bug he can get us. Anthrax, maybe—fucker is playing it real cool, you know? But definitely military grade, can ya dig it?"

Orin had shook his head skeptically.

"Look," he had told his cousin, "how do you know this guy ain't federal?"

Dickie had looked up at him, and there was a serious expression on his face.

" 'Cause he brought a little sample with him, man," he had told Orin. "Had a spray can about the size of a can of Right Guard, okay?"

"Yeah, so what?"

"So we went out and found us one of those street bums—a homeless guy, you dig? Showed him a bottle of rye and he followed us back up an alley. And then my little Jap buddy sprayed that shit—*p-s-s-s-s-t*. Blast of nerve gas, right in his face."

"Jesus."

"It was intense, man. Fuckin' bum died *hard,* I'll tell you that. Glad I was standing upwind."

Orin had been silent for a long minute.

"Look, what do these Japs *want*? See, that's what I don't get."

Dickie had shrugged.

"Hell do I know? Like, maybe it's the emperor's birthday or something. All I know is we get this shit, and all we gotta do is use a little of it when they say the word. Raise a little hell. Screw with the G, right?"

Then Dickie had gone serious again, Orin remembered, and his tone shifted. For the first time, Orin had thought, his cousin sounded more like a militia leader than a kid who had been offered a new toy.

"All I know is, I get it, I sure ain't giving it back. I got my own ideas for the stuff."

That had been more than a month ago. Orin Trippett had returned to Montana, and plans had been made.

Now, looking at the crate that had been delivered this morning—*by FedEx,* Orin thought, *and how's that for laughs?*—Orin remembered what his cousin had said.

He felt the same way.

Chapter 5

Nominally, the Surgeon General's Office was a subordinate part of Health and Human Services. So there was not really an ongoing war between the secretary of HHS and the Surgeon General; it just seemed that way, which was almost as bad.

They were both political appointments, Beck recalled— HHS a former California congressman who had been instrumental in the current president's initial campaign, the SG a women's rights activist who had lobbied hard but fruitlessly for a cabinet-level post before settling for a position that was largely symbolic. Neither official was a physician. But both had brought to the CDC meeting aides who were, and that added an element of professional competition into the already volatile mix. The key question was the same that had bedeviled them throughout the day: Did the current situation warrant declaring an emergency? If so, there was no shortage of plans that could be put into action; but if they blew this call, the downside risk was, to appointees and career bureaucrats alike, potentially cataclysmic.

There had been heated words, some shouting, and no resolution. Porter had left in disgust, shaking his head as he stood to return to his office.

"I'm heading down to the outbreak site," he said to Krewell in an angry aside. "You don't need me here to deal with *this* crap. Not when people are dying down there." The physician stalked out without a backward glance.

"Damn it, Larry," Beck muttered to Krewell, who sat at his side. "He's right. How long do we listen to politicians and bureaucrats? Somebody has to show some leadership, for God's sake."

Krewell looked at his watch.

"The President expects a recommendation by six," he told Beck. "That gives them no more than—whoops. Here it comes. Watch this, ol' buddy."

Billy Carson had stood, and the figure he cut in his shirt-sleeves was enough to draw the attention of the room.

"There really is no room for discussion," Carson said. He half turned to address HHS. "Mr. Secretary, there is no statutory question as to your department's responsibility in the circumstances we face. In matters of public health, you are the lead authority. Like the rest of us here today, the Surgeon General's Office is an advisory body only. We have, I believe, heard its advice. It is time to act, sir."

The SG's aide, an emaciated woman who had been a family-planning specialist in Philadelphia before assuming her present post, spoke angrily.

"Mr. Carson, I resent the way you're—" she began, and Carson's voice overrode her firmly.

"As Dr. Krewell pointed out, we are dealing with a matter of available time. History alone demands that we accept Dr. Porter's analysis. H1N1 is, potentially, a catastrophic threat to public health. Look at the sheer numbers involved. Over the course of twelve months in 1918, at least a half-million Americans died of influenza. One in four was incapacitated. This disease constitutes a threat to our entire population— more than two hundred fifty million Americans."

"History demands that we not overreact, either," the senator said, and the SG nodded. "Do we want to risk a general panic? And as long as we're talking about 'potential,' how about the potential for making a bad situation worse? If we rush to produce a so-called vaccine, we're asking for a repeat of the swine flu fiasco in 'seventy-six. More people were harmed by the injections than even got the flu: some were in comas for months, others paralyzed by the Guillan-Barré syndrome the vaccine initiated. The lawsuits went on for years."

"If we're going to talk about history, let's allow an expert to have a word," HHS interrupted. "Dr. Casey, I apologize. I have not read the complete report you prepared, but I have reviewed the executive summary. You've been waiting patiently, and I'd appreciate your insights, sir."

"There's not much to add to my original work, Mr. Secretary," Beck said. "The question is, do we have an emerging epidemic here? To a society, epidemics are the biological equivalent of nuclear war. In extreme cases, as the disease spreads through the population, social systems break down. Plagues cause a social meltdown. The network of services and supports that civilization depends on fail, in varying degrees."

"Based on what?" HHS asked.

"Ironically, based on the technological level the society has attained," Beck said. "Historically, the more complex the civilization, the worse the collapse."

"Specifics, Doctor," the senator said.

"Specifically, Senator, the values that bind humans together progressively dissolve during an epidemic," Beck said. "This was the case during Europe's Black Death in the Middle Ages; the same effect occurred in 1918, the last killer-flu pandemic.

"In the beginning, a plague engenders fear, most commonly a sort of xenophobia. People begin to view 'outsiders' as the enemy, as potential disease vectors. They pull away—

for example, by ignoring people who collapse on public streets. As the outbreak expands, they build walls to keep the disease outside—and I mean that literally, in many cases. If you read Poe, his 'Masque of the Red Death' could well have been written as journalism rather than fiction. Extremes of behavior begin to occur—everything. Riots. Drunken orgies, group suicides. Fanatical religious fervor, complete with doomsday messiahs.

"Inevitably, as the plague expands and family members sicken and die, the social contract breaks completely. Parents are too frightened to care for their children, spouses abandon their dying mates.

"By then, of course, essential public systems are decimated. Health care is overwhelmed, both through the sheer volume of cases as well as the fact that many physicians and nurses have themselves contracted the disease. Fire or police protection is virtually nonexistent. And with all due respect to the representatives of our armed forces here, the military is no better off than the rest of society. They're usually worse off, in fact; living in barracks or on a ship is tailor-made for widespread disease transmission."

The senator snorted. "The Black Death. Edgar Allan Poe. There's a big difference between medieval Europe and the modern world."

"Not so different," Beck said, "if you're dealing with a disease you can't cure, or even prevent." He looked around the room. "Anybody here know how to keep from getting the flu?"

"Which raises the question of a vaccine." The SG spoke up. "We've been making influenza vaccines for years. Mass immunization has been around since the polio years."

"Assuming that this particular strain of H1N1 lends itself to development of an effective vaccine," Carson said, "we're looking at an immunization program that is unprecedented." He nodded in the direction of Krewell. "CDC's Special

Pathogens Branch has the figures. Dr. Krewell, what is your assessment? Is such a program possible?"

Krewell remained seated.

"Of course it is possible," he said. "We have a great deal of experience in developing flu vaccines. We do it annually, once we've analyzed which flu strain we're facing for the year. But H1N1 is not merely an evolutionary mutation of a virus we're already familiar with; it's a different animal entirely, and so there will be some time lost in our learning curve there.

"The key word is 'time,' " Krewell emphasized. "If we have enough time, we can dissect H1N1, decode any genetic mutations, develop and test possible vaccines. If we have enough time, the pharmaceutical firms can gear up to produce the two hundred and fifty million doses we'll need in this country alone. Given some breathing room, it is possible to set up a mass immunization in every city, town and one-stoplight crossroads in the country."

"In your opinion, do we have this time?"

HHS looked worried, Beck thought. *As well he might.*

"In my assessment," Krewell said, "no, sir, we do not. We'd need at best six months, more likely eight."

In his peripheral vision, Beck saw the head of the Federal Emergency Management Agency nod grimly. Alone among the group, the newly appointed head of FEMA had hands-on experience, in his former post as New York City's chief preparedness official, in planning for widespread public health emergencies. That experience had earned him his present position: New York City was acknowledged as the place best prepared to deal with critical situations, due in large part to the man's efforts.

In the months before he had left for his current Washington posting, he had tackled the specter of biological terrorism in America's largest urban center. He had written plans, devised contingencies, bullied funding for police and health personnel training. And then he had supervised exercises and drills to test how effective all the activity had been.

The news reports, even as sanitized and as spun as they had been, had been more accurate than kind, Beck recalled. It had been woefully apparent how unprepared even all the official's efforts had left his city.

And that was one *city,* Beck thought, *not the whole damn country.*

"This one scares me, people," FEMA was saying to the group. "Look, even limiting our concerns to the continental United States, this influenza is already here. And that means it's spreading as we speak."

"I concur," HHS said. "Short-term, mass vaccination is not an option. Given that, what is our best immediate course of action?"

"The only course of action is to contain it, at least as much as possible," Carson said. "We fight a delaying action, while we develop an effective vaccine."

"The girl in Florida died a week ago." Krewell spoke up. "Summer is vacation time, and people are traveling. It's reasonable to assume her death has a direct connection to the Fort Walton cases. I have people trying to draw up a contagion chart right now. I can already tell you, this could turn into a nightmare."

"Explain," HHS ordered.

"The first death involved a limousine driver," Krewell said, "a profession that has extensive contact with people who travel. Who gave it to the driver? Okay, we have determined the girl recently returned from a trip to Japan; if she took a limo home, maybe we've identified our Patient Zero—the index case, or at least the first carrier we know about. Who else did she infect? Who did the driver give it to, and did any of them get on a plane and fly somewhere else? Nothing has shown up in the WHO Weekly Epidemiological Record, but, believe it—we have to assume that these are not isolated infections."

"My God." The voice belonged to an Asian woman, the assistant director of the National Institutes of Health. "The airports. This could be spreading itself around the world already." She spoke directly to HHS. "The first step is for the President to declare an emergency. We have to inform the public, let them know what they're facing and what to look for."

"I'm inclined to agree," HHS said. "Of course, we would continue to explore all additional avenues. If the President declares a national health emergency, we can—"

"Start a national panic," said a man Beck did not recognize. "Two cases! That's all we have confirmed. Let's at least wait until we get the input from the CDC team in Florida. And before we start a worldwide panic, we better confer with WHO and the National Institute for Medical Research in England."

"At last, a reasonable suggestion," the senator said. "We cannot react blindly, just because—"

A shrill electronic chirp cut through the tense atmosphere and silenced the politician. The source came from next to Beck, and for an instant all eyes looked accusingly at him.

Then Krewell fished the cell phone from his pocket and spoke into it. His face stiffened, and when he spoke again it was in low and urgent tones.

Finally he finished and looked at Carson.

"That was Dr. Porter," Krewell said, and Beck could see the ashen cast that had spread on his features. "He was on his way to the airport when a call was transferred to him. CDC has just been formally contacted by its counterpart in the Russian Federation. They've had eighteen people die in the past two days, six in Moscow alone. Some kind of flu, they think."

Chapter 6

The matter of how Beck found himself aboard the plane that carried Carson back to Washington was not quite clear, least of all to Beck himself. "Ordered" was too strong a word, but "asked" was too cordial to cover it, either. However it happened, it had been some time since Beck had experienced the almost sybaritic pleasure of top-level government travel.

Beck had not changed from the clothes he had worn to Atlanta. The Air Force sergeant who had escorted Beck to his seat had been unruffled, but Beck had caught her quick appraisal of his outfit.

"You from Iowa, Sergeant?" he asked, settling against the pearl gray leather seat back.

"No, sir. Alabama."

"Should have worn my 'Roll, Tide' shirt, then. I save it for formal occasions."

He was rewarded with a quick; surprised smile before the no-nonsense expression of the professional soldier won out again.

"Yes, sir. I wear one under my Class A uniform, myself."

At that moment, Carson and Larry Krewell entered the cabin. As the sergeant retreated forward, they took seats flanking Beck. Both men snapped their seat belts tight before Carson spoke.

"It's been a while, Beck. Dr. Krewell says you have signed on with us again."

"It looks that way," Beck said. "You'd think I'd know better by now, wouldn't you?"

"Actually, yes," Carson said. "When you left government service, you didn't have much good to say about us. Though perhaps I can't blame you, given the condition you were in." He examined his fellow traveler with a skeptical eye. "You certainly *look* fit, Beck."

"Thank you. I eat a lot of roughage."

"You no longer see the Company's psychiatrist, I mean."

"I've left the CIA behind me," Beck said. "Along with everything associated with it."

"You haven't missed it?" Carson made an impatient gesture at Beck's expression. "I don't mean the fieldwork, necessarily. It was foolish to play the cowboy so often; you had to know it was inevitable that the odds would catch up to you."

He leaned forward, ignoring how his companion pulled back at the movement. "But the analysis, Beck. The access to so much data, to the secrets that people kill for—*die* for. Taking it, piecing it into a coherent picture. In that, you were quite good indeed. Surely you miss it?"

"Not much. I miss believing that it was worth what was expected in return."

Carson again studied Beck wordlessly. Then he turned to Krewell. "We meet with the President immediately; there will be a helicopter waiting at Andrews when we land. Brief him, please."

The craft's turbines spun up with a vibration that penetrated even the ultraefficient noise insulation of the fuselage. Outside, Beck saw a man in Air Force coveralls, the flashlights in his hands moving as if he were conducting an orchestra. There was only a small lurch when the plane began to roll. It was a tribute to the skill of the pilot and an acknowledgment of the status of his passengers.

"Here's the thing, Beck," Krewell said. "There's no doubt now, with the Russian outbreak and the new Florida cases, that the President will declare a health emergency. Health and Human Services will be in charge, nominally; I've been detached from CDC to serve as liaison, coordinator, whatever. By tomorrow afternoon, we'll have involvement from every federal office with a doctor on staff, and that's only the domestic stuff."

"I know the plan, Larry; I helped draft it. What I don't know is what you want from me."

"You wrote the book on riots and disruptions, ol' buddy," Krewell said. "With this virus on the loose, there's a potential for plenty of both. Officially, you'll be advising the people involved with public safety and security."

Beck caught the emphasis, and immediately understood. When he spoke, his voice carried a trace of wariness that made Krewell's lips twitch.

"And what will I be doing," Beck asked, *"unofficially?"*

"Oh, hell," Krewell said. "You've been around the block a time or two, boy. I don't guess it's a surprise to hear things are worse than you know."

"The possibility of a killer-flu pandemic isn't bad enough, Larry?"

"We've known about the Russian outbreak for almost two days, Beck. That's when your name first came up, ol' buddy. That's when we started the ball rolling to bring you back inside. Good thing, given the speed this thing's spreading at."

Beck's eyes flickered for an instant at Carson, who sat impassively. Then Beck turned back to Krewell; when he spoke, his voice had a new edge to it, cold and hard.

"What the hell's going on, Larry? What do you want from me?"

Krewell looked at Carson.

"I think the ball is in your court, Billy."

Carson had lit a cigarette as soon as the aircraft had rotated off the runway. He drew on it, then he carefully balanced it on the rim of the saucer he was using ᴀ an ashtray. To Beck, it seemed Carson was performing a ritual, steeling himself. But when Carson finally spoke, his voice betrayed no emotion at all.

"You'll be looking for the source of all this," Carson said. "You will investigate and analyze any leads or information that will help us determine the origin of this virus. As a first step, you will be working on where the first cases appeared—the Russian outbreak."

Beck looked at the two men. His mouth was a hard, thin line, and his silence spoke volumes. When he finally spoke, his voice was firm and final.

"I'm not going back into Russia. Not now. Not ever."

"The Russians guarantee your safety," Carson said. "We've received assurances from the highest—"

"That's final. You're wasting your time."

"We appreciate what happened to you over there, Beck," Krewell said, careful to keep his voice neutral. "Six weeks is a helluva long time to hold out. I don't know if I could have lasted *half* that long. But that was the *Mafiya,* not the Russian government—"

"Go ahead, Larry." Beck said. "Educate me about the difference. I spent almost two months becoming an expert on the subject, remember? It was a very hands-on curriculum."

"And we got you out," Carson interrupted. "As soon as we had the opportunity."

"Find somebody else."

"I wish we could," Carson said. "But the Russians want *you.*"

Krewell interrupted. "Putin made the request directly to the President, Beck."

"Putin doesn't know me from Adam," Beck retorted.

"But Alexi Malenkov does," Krewell said. "Okay, maybe you've been out of circulation, Beck. But you have to have heard how fast the power structure changes over there. Malenkov's not a field operative anymore—hasn't been for more than a year. He's Putin's director of state security now, and he is heading up the Russian efforts to deal with this virus."

"Then he knows I'm out of the business."

"He's like every other Russian spook—he sees secret plots and conspiracies everywhere he looks. Malenkov says, first off, he doesn't believe you are retired, and second, he doesn't give a damn even if you are. He says you're a wunderkind, Beck—a hotshot analyst who can see through brick walls and jump buildings in a single bound."

Krewell grinned at the face that Beck pulled.

"Okay, but you must have pulled something *serious* on that ol' boy back when you were playing spy versus spy. He has Putin believing you're some kind of genius, and Putin has the President thinking the same way. They all want you working on this. Doesn't give you a lot of wiggle room, ol' buddy."

"Even if I agreed to go—and I'm not—you need a medical expert who can—"

"You wrote the plague analysis," Carson interrupted flatly. "You were one of the Company's resident experts on biological warfare. In Russia, it's a matter of trust: we're dealing with your old contacts—you know them, they know you. This is a matter of national survival, Beck. There is no time to waste. If somebody drops the ball because they weren't up to speed with the people and issues involved, millions will die."

The national security advisor looked Beck squarely in the eyes.

"I will not try to minimize what you went through," he said. "But hear us out. You owe us that, at least."

Carson drew a thick packet from the briefcase at his feet and tossed it on the table beside Beck. On the cover was the presidential seal, and stamped across the bottom were the words COROMANT/US ARMY ULTRA.

"You'll find the historical background in there," Carson said. "Essentially, what we are now calling H1N1-AK—the original Spanish flu of 1918—was recovered by an Army medical expedition in 1951. In Alaska, hence the suffix. The expedition mission was to obtain any samples of a particularly virulent influenza virus. The theory was that the virus might be recoverable from corpses preserved in the permafrost."

"Whatever my opinion of the Army," Beck said, "it doesn't dig up dead Eskimos just for exercise."

"There was a weapons-development component," Carson admitted reluctantly. "But, in the event, that was deemed secondary to the potential for developing new vaccines."

"Because CIA had just stumbled onto Stalin's germwarfare project," Krewell interjected. He did not waver under Carson's hard stare. "Let's not pretend humanitarian motives here, Billy. Nobody in the room is a virgin."

Carson took a final pull on his cigarette before mashing it in the makeshift ashtray.

"I suppose not. By coincidence, a civilian research project along much the same lines was also undertaken that year," he continued. "In that case, they found that the bodies had been buried too close to the surface. Over the decades, there had been enough thaw-and-freeze cycles to allow at least partial decomposition of the corpses. That was certainly enough to kill any viruses, and none were found." Carson waved a hand dismissively. "Their project was severely underfunded, and—if I may say—rather amateurish in approach. They simply did not look in the right places, and finally ran out of time and money. The Army had no such problems. It also knew to look farther north. The expedition targeted villages that had been on Army survey maps in 1906. They just had to identify those that had completely disappeared on maps drawn in 1925."

"The official story is that the Army mission was a failure," Krewell said. "The Army, of course, encouraged this point of view. But in point of fact, a live virus was captured by the expedition."

"Did we release this thing?" Beck demanded. "Was there some kind of accident, or—"

"No," Carson said. "Not by us. As Dr. Porter told the group, the samples from the most recent victims show some specific, unusual genetic markers. They do not match the viral coding of the Army's virus. That's a definite, Beck."

"But we have the genetic map, the genome sequences," Beck pressed. "You can use it to develop a vaccine."

"H1N1-Florida, the new one, is a not a natural mutation of the base viral codes," Krewell said to Beck. "It is not what we call a wild virus."

"Not wild?" Beck repeated, puzzled. "How does a virus like this incubate if it doesn't—"

"It is a chimera—a genetically engineered virus," Carson said. "Is that simple enough? H1N1-Florida was created in a laboratory, intentionally. Whoever designed it grafted other genes onto the base influenza virus—genes that are specifically intended to increase the virulence factors."

Beck was stunned. "It's a weapon."

"Legally, a weapon of mass destruction," Carson said. "Release of which constitutes an act of war. Well, it's been released, and it's been aimed at us."

"A bioweapon, particularly one as contagious as this one, cannot be 'aimed' with any degree of precision," Krewell corrected. "The number of people infected will grow exponentially, in an ever-widening circle. Even under the most draconian quarantine measures, it is a virtual certainty that the disease ultimately will spread to the aggressor's population. Unless those who deployed it have already developed a vaccine, it is a suicide weapon."

"That would be insane," Beck said.

"No," Krewell interjected. "Just incomprehensible. At

least, to *us*. At Detrick, we were under a strict standing order. No chem or bioweapon could be developed unless there was a vaccine or antidote. But other folks didn't play that way, ol' buddy. For example, the old Soviet program took the position that the best bioweapons were those with *no* cure. Hell, by the late 'eighties, they were basing new biological weapons on multi-antibiotic-resistant bacterial strains, just so existing treatments would be worthless."

"Which might explain why the Russians are asking for assistance," Carson said. "The fact that they have an outbreak does not automatically clear them of responsibility or guilt."

"Are you saying the Russians started this plague? Without developing a cure for it?"

"What the national security advisor is saying," said Krewell, "is that at this moment we do not have a workable vaccine. Whether we can use what we know about the original H1N1 to come up with one—" He shrugged. "Frankly, we don't know."

"Why the act? Why pretend this is a natural outbreak?"

"Because the President actually *read* your report—the whole thing, not just the executive summary," Carson snapped. "He was particularly impressed by one of your conclusions. You cited evidence indicating the more violent upheavals in the social fabric—the rioting and vigilante activities, for instance—are less likely to occur immediately in so-called natural disasters than when the cause is a deliberate enemy action."

"He's trying to buy time, Beck," Krewell said. "At minimum, the time it will take to get troops and medical support where they'll be needed. And to come up with some kind of viable treatment."

Beck shook his head. "He'll need days just to start mobilizing, let alone—"

"The call-up began two days ago, when CDC finally got an ID on the Florida virus," Krewell said. "By tomorrow—day after, at latest—we'll have units in the major urban centers. With a little luck, by the end of the week the President can declare martial law and have it mean more than just national panic."

"Not enough time, Larry," Beck said. "Not with a contagious, airborne agent."

"That's why we must find who is behind this, and do it quickly," Carson said. "The Russians have been aggressively investigating since their outbreak began. Go there and assist. Your job is to find out who has declared biological war on the rest of the world. Whoever is responsible may have a vaccine."

"What if they do not?" demanded Beck. "What if they are madmen?"

"Then," Krewell said calmly, "the computer projections tell us to expect millions of people to die. Very likely, hundreds of millions."

Chapter 7

The telephone rang, and eight hundred miles away one of a row of computer screens in Fort Meade, Maryland, flashed an advisory to the technician on duty. He swiveled to the proper monitor and studied the lines that scrolled across the display. His fingers tapped on the keyboard; satisfied the call was being digitally recorded on the hard disk, the technician settled back to listen in real time.

The answering machine had no recorded salutation, instead greeting callers with a loud beep after the requisite four rings.

"Is she there?"

The voice was unmistakably that of a woman, and was unequivocally furious. The tech grinned in sympathy; the computer had already identified the caller's telephone number and location, cross-referencing that information against the known profile and calling pattern of the recipient.

"Poor guy," the tech muttered. "First he gets himself on a Priority Alpha watch status. Now he's got his ex all over his case, too."

He leaned back in his chair and popped a stick of gum in his mouth, idly wondering if this was a drug case or something to do with the latest terrorist threat. No matter. Surveillance like this was child's play, provided you had the right toys.

Here at the National Security Agency's Maryland headquarters, they did, if most of them were kept in specially constructed rooms with electronically baffled walls.

A number of these super-secret systems exist, some known and some only rumored. One of the former—Echelon, a spy system of satellites and listening posts that can intercept millions of telephone, fax and e-mail messages—had long been a source of concern to European governments, who believed at least part of its electronic product was turned over to U.S. corporations for competitive advantage. Overall, Echelon and its lesser-known sister systems constituted a technology that allowed the NSA to pluck virtually every signal from every subdivision of the world's communications spectrum.

It did not do this, of course; the staggering volume of signals traffic generated by today's world would have made this an impossible task, even had the NSA wanted to do so. But if a NSA client—say, the FBI, the CIA, or even the President's national security advisor—knew what to ask for, the NSA could quickly narrow its focus to envelop the target in an all-encompassing electronic bull's-eye.

The system had proven adept in counterespionage and the incidental guns-for-cocaine operation, and in the current crisis was now proving its capabilities in domestic surveillance. It would have all been quite illegal, had it ever come to the attention of a federal judge.

The voice—now logged by the computer as that of Deborah Stepanovich, intercept number 351-29, cross-referenced to a dozen other strings of databank entries—had paused, presumably to see if anyone would pick up in the apartment. Now it resumed, with no loss of its initial heat.

"I am going to assume that this was not your idea, Beck—that you had nothing to do with this little deception. If the three of them are in Chicago with you, please know they did not have permission to leave this state. Katherine *lied* to me, Beck, and I am very angry. I want her to call me immediately."

The phone slammed down with a bang in Arlington, Virginia—ironically, only a few miles from the monitoring center where the technician cross-checked the standing orders for this particular "account." He then punched in the number of Andi Wheelwright's pager, followed by a series of letters and numbers that would be meaningless to anybody without the key.

Then, as he had done with the two previous calls that had gone to the apartment in Chicago, he tapped in the code that erased the message from Beck Casey's answering machine.

"Sorry 'bout that," he quietly apologized to the erstwhile recipient, "but orders is orders."

In Arlington, Virginia, Deborah Stepanovich slammed down the receiver with enough force to rattle the tasteful side table on which it sat. Her hand trembled, she was so angry.

I should have guessed, she seethed, for the first time since the divorce wishing that she still smoked. *A sleepover, for God's sake. Teenage girls don't have sleepovers anymore.*

The problem was, of course, that she had wanted to believe Katie.

Increasingly, their relationship had foundered in shoal waters over the past year or so—probably, she did not doubt, a combination of the aftereffects of her divorce from Beck and the natural antipathy between mothers and daughters of a certain age. Any kind of interaction between the two of them risked turning into a conflagration of mysterious origin, and the result had been that both of them avoided any but the most mundane discussions.

No big surprise there, she thought. *Kids learn from watching how their parents act, don't they?*

But when Katie had raised the subject of spending an extended weekend with J. L. and Carly at the cabin—foolishly Deborah had ignored all the warning signals that had begun blinking deep inside her head.

It had seemed so . . . so damned *touching,* at the time. Over the years, she and Katie and—well, Katie's father—had spent no small amount of time together in the rural Virginia setting. Deborah had told herself that Katie was craving the simple nostalgia of it, and convinced herself that this was a good sign.

And so the trio of girls had left, driving off in the scarlet LeMans that Carly's mother had bought the girl the year before, and which always seemed to Deborah to be its own sort of warning flag. Uneasy thoughts had nagged at her all morning, even distracting her during a meeting with an Egyptian industrialist who had run afoul of U.S. import regulations.

Finally, she had excused herself and gone to her private office. Then Deborah had punched in the number she had been given, the cell phone Carly swore would always be with her.

No luck, that time or during the three subsequent calls she had made to it. Each call elicited only a vaguely female, automated cyber-voice advising the caller that—here, Carly's own voice supplied her name—was unavailable but would accept a recorded message.

Exactly when she had *known*—known completely, without doubt or equivocation—not even Deborah could have said. There had been no growing suspicion, no litany of the other possible circumstances in which Katie might have chosen to become involved. Deborah had simply *known* for an incontrovertible fact that her daughter had not gone where she had said she was going, and that it was time for a mother to act.

She had immediately telephoned J. L.'s parents, whom she once considered close friends; since the divorce from Beck, she had watched all parties reassign the relationship to a far more casual level. They too were concerned—no, they had not had word from J. L., and yes, they too had left a message with the cyber-femme—but they had not Deborah's capacity for the gestalt leap to what was truly going on.

A call to Carly's mother was, as Deborah suspected, a complete waste of time; Joyce Holmes was not even in town, let alone working the telephone to get word of her absent daughter. Deborah had no doubt she could track the woman down, if it proved necessary; but for the moment, there were other options and priorities.

Deborah Stepanovich was not without resources, nor without resourcefulness when the situation required it.

First things first: a very businesslike call to the office of the Van Dale County sheriff, where she took pains to assure that official that she was not merely a suburban hausfrau fretting over a tardy child. In her legal practice, Deborah Stepanovich dealt with corporate leaders and the international power elite; she could, when she wanted to, command respect not unlike that accorded to the heads of minor governments.

Within the hour, the deputy dispatched to the cabin was back on the phone with Deborah: there was no sign the cabin was occupied or had been visited in the previous month.

That her next reaction had been to call her former husband was, to Deborah, somewhat unnerving; that she had actually gone ahead and done it, extremely disturbing; that her automatic first words to him—rather, to his answering machine—had been harsh and accusatory, almost a relief. She had gone through too much, made too many hard decisions, to get to where it proved she now was. And to where Katie still adamantly refused to go.

Deborah had no doubt that the three girls, with Katie as their ringleader, had plotted this . . . this *outrageous* expedition. And whether Beck was privy to the plan or not—*probably not,* Deborah decided; *not even Beck would be that irresponsible*—the fact is that once more they had somehow succeeded in making her the outsider.

She almost got away with it, too, Deborah told herself, and as it had so many times before, the anger rose anew.

Secrets. She had lived most of her adult life on the wrong side of that wall, trying to accept that there were things she should not know, that she and her daughter needed to turn a blind eye toward.

And so she had tried.

Ultimately, it had all come crashing down on her anyway, and the price had been far too high to ever pay again. And now her daughter—*her only child!*—had chosen to follow the same hateful path.

And that made it hurt all the—

Oh, hell, Deborah thought, feeling the hot sting of tears she had not known she still possessed. *Damn him, anyway.*

She froze, suddenly aware of the pronoun she had used.

In Washington, Andi Wheelwright replayed Deborah Stepanovich's call again and again.

One missing fifteen-year-old, she told herself. *Not a major priority, when the whole damn country's about to go up for grabs.*

Andi was still surprised at herself when she found herself punching in the numbers and giving the order.

"There's three of them," she said, hearing herself add the professional toughness to her voice. "I imagine at least one of them is using a credit card on the parental account. I want to know where they are and what they're doing."

She listened for a moment to the voice at the other end.

"Do it anyway. This is no time for a damn road trip. God knows what kind of trouble they can get themselves into."

Chapter 8

An instant before the staccato chatter of the assault rifle cut through the sounds of the night, FBI special agent April O'Connor realized that everything had gone terribly wrong. She saw it in the face of Orin Trippett, the shipping clerk—in the sudden way his eyes narrowed, his expression hardened.

The metamorphosis had been swift and unexpected. A moment before, Trippett had shown the kind of behavior most people did when law enforcement credentials are held before their faces: startled, then ingratiatingly submissive.

Trippett had been standing on the shipping docks when they arrived, his breath making wispy clouds in the high mountain night air. Hadley and Morrisee, the other pair on the FBI-ATF tactical team, had elected to wait in the relative shelter of the car. That left April and Jesús Robles, a burly, dark-eyed agent from ATF.

And that's just dandy with me, she thought. *For an ATF cowboy, Robles isn't all that bad.*

She had been working with Hadley and Morrisee for almost a week, tracking a shipment of M-16s stolen ten days earlier from a National Guard armory in Missoula, Montana. In that time, she had learned much.

She had, for example, learned that she did not want to work with Hadley and Morrisee ever again.

She was no stranger to crude jokes, and even in the "new" FBI, suggestive language was not uncommon. During her four years in the field, April had learned to deal with it; in most cases, she could establish a working relationship with even the most recalcitrant chauvinist. Robles, at least, had waited almost two days before propositioning April. Unlike the two FBI men, he had accepted her refusal with a good-natured grace and gotten on with the job.

When Robles held up the search warrant for his inspection, Trippett had waved it away with a thin, polite smile. After Robles had disappeared down one of the long passages between the storage racks, Trippett nodded in the direction of the warehouse office.

"Cold night out here," he said in a mild country twang. "Lowlander'd never guess it was July. Cuppa coffee, ma'am?"

In any other circumstance, she would have smiled. But not tonight, not while serving a search warrant and not while feeling, after the week she had spent, a million years old.

Ma'am? April thought, and had been inwardly amused at the honorific. *Is that cowboy charm, or do I look as old as I feel?*

She declined the offer.

They stood for a moment in awkward silence.

"Whacha'll looking for, anyway?" he asked.

"It's on the warrant," she said in her best official tone, then relented slightly. "It's just routine, Mr. Trippett. Agent Robles will be back in a moment."

Trippett shrugged, smiling as if to apologize for some slight. Another long moment passed between them.

"That y'all's car?" he said finally. "Reason I ask, see, it's blocking the loading dock. Maybe you could ask them two fellows to move it."

"Agent Robles will be back soon," April repeated.

"Well, truck there's wanting in," Trippett said, looking past her shoulder. April turned to look.

In that instant, as her eyes slid past his face, she saw his features change from prey to predator. She stepped backward, automatically, trying to put some distance between the two of them.

The instinctive reaction probably saved her life.

Trippett grabbed at her, missing as April twisted sideways and smashed the heel of her left hand hard against his cheekbone. She backed away farther, her hand dropping to her waist, clawing to reach the weapon underneath her light leather jacket. Then she had it, the butt of the automatic hard in her hand as it cleared the holster and leveled on target.

"You move, you *die*!" April screamed, and she could hear the rage and fear in her own voice. Trippett froze, the muzzle of the Glock two feet from his head. Slowly, his hands rose.

The shots came from outside, a burst of three. Another. Then, much louder, a heavier automatic weapon firing in a sustained burst.

From the street, fifteen yards away, a pickup truck squealed to a stop. Whoever was driving had immediately recognized the car parked at the curb as a government vehicle. Before the first of the attackers even jumped to the ground, at least one automatic weapon had opened up at full tilt. Palm-sized blotches of fresh metal, each centered on its own bullet hole, stitched crookedly the length of the sedan. Where a bullet hit glass, the window spiderwebbed into a creamy opacity.

Other weapons began to fire in staccato bursts. One of them sighted on the streetlight outside, which shattered and flared before going dark. April heard someone shout commands, followed by the clatter of armed men moving quickly.

Gunfire walked its way across the loading dock, geysering chips of concrete along its path. April threw herself flat. Bullets, the sound of angry hornets, passed inches over her head.

When she looked up, Orin Trippett was no longer in sight.

Through the cacophony of shots all around her, she could barely make out the sound of running footsteps deep in the warehouse. She raised her head, looking in the direction Trippett had fled, then at the car where she had left Hadley and Morrisee. A fresh fusillade pockmarked the concrete near where she lay, making the decision for her. April rolled hard to the lip of the ramp and slid down into its relative cover.

In a crouching run, April sprinted up the sloping concrete ramp. She reached the head of it just as one of the dark figures outside wrenched open the passenger door of the ruined car. Somehow, the dome light had survived the hail of bullets. It still worked, illuminating the carnage inside.

Ten feet away, FBI special agent Michael F. Hadley slumped crookedly against the steering wheel, staring with unseeing eyes at the red-spattered windshield. Special Agent Thomas A. Morrisee lay crosswise on the seat. His face was out of sight, snugged intimately into the lap of the dead man beside him. What had been the back of his head was now a shattered exit wound; already, a thin wisp of steam rose from the gore into the cold night air.

The man at the door poked at Hadley's body with the muzzle of the M-16 he held. It was Vietnam-era issue, the old A1 model with the Buck Rogers forestock, and April immediately realized it had to be from the National Guard inventory. She centered her sights on the man and opened her mouth to announce herself and order him to drop the weapon.

At that instant, another figure stepped around the car.

Had he shot from the hip, April would have had no chance. Instead, the second gunman had raised his weapon to aim. It was a costly mistake. April's first shot struck just below his Adam's apple, passing upward through his brain stem. The second shot of her double-tap lodged in his upper chest just left of midline, though it was doubtful he felt its impact.

By then it was also too late for the first shooter, whose weapon was partially blocked by the open door of the ruined car. He sealed his own doom when he spun toward April and tried to fire the M-16 one-handed. The twin blasts of her second double-tap were swallowed in the long chattering burst from the assault rifle as his finger locked in a death spasm on the trigger.

Then the rifle's magazine ran dry, and in the sudden silence April heard the scream of tires. An instant later, too quickly for her to have reacted, a late-model pickup truck flashed past the bloody tableau and sped into the night.

Rapidly, she checked both of the shooters.

These guys are down for good, she thought, neither boasting nor apologizing. *I need backup, fast.*

She leaned into the ruined car, feeling the blood and broken glass that littered the dashboard. No good: the radio in the dash was shredded. Robles had the handheld with him.

At that instant, she heard the shots from inside the warehouse.

April O'Connor turned, gripping the pistol with which she had just killed two men, and sprinted back up the loading ramp into the warehouse. In a moment, moving serpentine to use what little cover there was, she was deep inside the cavernous building. She slid against what felt like a wooden box and waited.

It was even darker here, and the cold sharper. A steady draft blew toward the rear of the warehouse. April felt the chill through her leather jacket, felt it seep through the Kevlar vest she wore underneath. Even so, she was perspiring from the exertion of her run; the sweat that trickled between her breasts felt slick and clammy. The sounds of her breathing rasped loud in her ears, punctuated by the timpani of her heartbeats.

April had lost her White Sox cap shortly after the first shots had been fired. A strand from the ponytail she wore during her duty shifts brushed against her cheek, and she took one hand from her weapon to push it behind her ear. Momentarily, she worried whether, there in the dark, her blond hair made her a better target.

From the darkness to her left came a sudden crash, the sound of something hard and heavy smashing on a concrete floor.

Every sense heightened to an unnatural pitch, April stared into the dark as if she could, by sheer force of will, force her eyes to penetrate the inky blackness. She shifted her position slightly, aiming at where the sound had come from. April braced her gun hand on the crate and waited.

She stayed that way for several long minutes, unmoving, feeling her muscles stiffen. There was no movement, no sound except what she fashioned in her own mind.

As she pressed her body even closer to the rough wood of the shipping crate, she heard, or thought she did, another sound to her rear. Then April sensed Trippett's presence behind her, imagined that she felt the muzzle of his pistol brush against the back of her head.

Her head snapped to look, and she saw the dark form. It was crouched, arms extended in a two-handed Weaver stance, not more than ten feet away.

April O'Connor spun around and fired two shots into the third man she would kill that night.

That was how a tactical response team from the Columbia Falls police found her, seven minutes later. April was kneeling on the hard concrete floor beside a torn and bloody figure, her pistol within reach on the unfinished surface. Despite being near exhaustion, she was still performing cardiac compressions on a body the team leader could tell, with a single glance, had been dead before CPR started.

Wide in a surprise that would last forever, the already clouding eyes of Jesús Robles stared transfixed on a horrible emptiness.

For an instant, April fought the hands that tried to pull her away from Robles's body. Then she accepted what she too had known all along, and allowed one of the TRT members to half-walk, half-push her toward the outside. They followed the cold strong draft that blew in from the front of the warehouse. As they moved, April felt something heavy in her hand; it was her pistol, and she realized that she must have snatched it up without conscious thought.

When April was gone, the team leader, a lieutenant, squatted behind the same wooden box that had shielded April. He was armed with a shotgun, which he trained into the darkness. Around him, he saw his tac team in similar positions.

"We still have a suspect in here, and he may be armed," the team leader said. "Where the hell are the damn floodlights? Get 'em fired up, fast."

When they were mounted on their tripods, he made a thumbs-up gesture. Immediately, the cavernous warehouse lit up with several million candlepower of white light.

Of Orin Trippett, the lieutenant saw no sign. But movement on the floor next to a small packing crate that had smashed on the floor caught his eye.

"Hell is that?" he muttered to his second, a sergeant. "Looks like a rat, doesn't it?"

"Yeah," the sergeant said. "What's the matter with it? Damn thing's having a fit or something. Shit. There's another one."

The team leader squinted at the convulsing rodents. They reminded him of something, and he frowned in concentration, trying to —

Then it hit him, and the hairs rose on the back of his neck.

"Red ball, red ball!" His voice was unnaturally shrill as he called the code to abort. "Everybody! Pull back to the cars outside. *Leave the fucking lights, dammit!* Everybody move, *now!*"

As he moved, counting the heads of his team as they retreated, the lieutenant thumbed the microphone clipped to his shoulder.

"Eleven-Bravo — be advised, I got a haz-mat alert," he said, and he wondered if his voice broadcast how shaken he felt. "This is not, repeat, *not* a drill. I think we're dealing with some kind of poison gas here."

Day Two:
July 22

Chapter 9

Beck shifted, uncomfortable in the nylon webbing, Nomex flight suit, G-pressure pants, life vest, parachute strapping, oxygen mask and flight helmet into which he had been inserted. He tried his best to keep his eyes down, fixed on the green hues of the instrument panel. He rarely succeeded for more than a few minutes at a time. Then Beck would look outside the acrylic-composite canopy, at the dizzying blackness where no visible point of reference existed, and feel the wave of vertigo wash over him yet again.

Right then, the world tilted sharply, a fact felt by his inner ear if by no other sensory organ, pressing him sideways against the five-point harness. He felt the air bladders inflate against his legs as the pressure suit automatically worked to squeeze his blood back to where it was needed.

The voice of Major Carl Frankel, USAF, crackled in his headphones.

"Uh, just a minor course correction there, Dr. Casey," he said, and Beck wondered if all jet jockeys were sent to a secret school where they learned to talk like Chuck Yeager. "Madrid's got a little more turbulence than usual, so we're being vectored to new refueling coordinates south of León."

They had been in the air for slightly more than four hours, and Beck was no longer certain he could feel his own feet. In Washington, he had traded what in retrospect had been Cleopatra's barge for travel accommodations that were far more Spartan, though incomparably faster.

At first, it had sounded interesting—exciting, even—to be flown across the nighttime Atlantic to greet the morning sun as it rose over Europe. Beck had logged an impressive number of flight miles in his time, more than a few of them in small aircraft. But he had never before flown in a F-15J Eagle, the latest two-seater version of the Air Force's first-line fighter. It was capable of speeds in excess of Mach 2. *Significantly* in excess, particularly when afterburners were engaged—a fact that Major Frankel seemed intent on proving to his passenger.

But what they gained in speed, they lost in fuel efficiency. They were coming up on what was the last of three scheduled in-flight refuelings.

During the first two, Frankel had nudged the fighter in what to Beck seemed an alarmingly close proximity to the KC-135 tanker, itself visible only as a looming shape slightly blacker than the surrounding night sky. The tanker trailed a stingerlike retractable boom that ended in a ridiculously undersized docking coupling; he knew this because of Frankel's running commentary, not because any part of the fueling appendage was visible without the night-vision goggles the pilot had donned.

The Eagle's refueling probe lifted from a hatchway behind the cockpit, which gave Beck a ringside seat to the intricacies of docking. It seemed to him a perilous sort of mating dance. Nor was he comforted by the thought of thousands of pounds of flammable jet fuel pulsing over his head into the Eagle's tanks.

Presumably, they had been over terra firma for some minutes. To Beck, that was mere rumor, optimistic conjecture that he suspected was the pilot's attempt to soothe his passenger's nerves. When Frankel had announced landfall, Beck looked outboard, expecting that even from fifty-two thousand feet the vast geometric gridlights of modern cities would be visible. No such luck; a strong low-pressure wave off the Atlantic, unusual at this time of year, had socked in the larger part of Spain. They were approaching French airspace, and according to the pilot no break in the thick cloud cover was expected soon. That, and the fact that the sliver of new moon provided virtually no ambient illumination, only added to Beck's disorientation and jet-lag gloom.

He reached down to the panel and gingerly thumbed the only button he knew how to use. The omnipresent crackle in his headphones flattened, and he spoke.

"What's our time to Russia, Major?"

There was a slight dead-air pause until he remembered to release the intercom switch.

"—so our ETA is about seventy-two minutes, give or take." Frankel's voice came in midsentence. He chuckled. "I don't imagine Moscow logs many F-15 landings, Dr. Casey. Hope they remember we're friendlies. You let me know if their SAM batteries light us up, will you? It'll give me a chance to go evasive."

Beck hoped he was kidding.

There was a burst of static over the radio, and a woman's voice came in loud enough to make Beck wince.

"Uh, Night Rider, this is Auto Club," she said, and Beck wondered if Yeager had a daughter—make that a granddaughter—in the service. "We have you on scope as range oh-three-seven, two-two-five relative. You wanna take your foot off the pedal, we'll get set for a fill-up. Uh, while we're at it, you want us to check your oil?"

"Hang on, Doctor," Frankel said, and once more the Eagle banked hard right. "Guess you know the drill by now. This won't take long. Next stop, Sheremetyevo International Airport."

Moscow, Beck thought.

His stomach lurched again, though this time not entirely
because of the aerial maneuver. The only heartening aspect
was a thin sliver in the darkness, still too weak to be called
daylight, that was etching its faint line on the far horizon.

Mockba, it looked to Beck, the Cyrillic script disorienting in
its dyslexic mix of forward and backward lettering. He remembered the sign on the main terminal, but much else had
changed since his last visit. When the Eagle had nosed down
into its prescribed landing pattern, his rear-seat vantage point
had given him a panoramic view of the metropolis. Here, it
was already late morning; sunlight reflecting from the streets
and buildings made the city glitter.

Muscovites enjoy reminding their visitors that, like
Rome, Moscow is built on seven hills. This is difficult to
prove. Only the most expert eye can detect more than one or
two of these, the topographical formations themselves having long ago surrendered to maniacally fanciful czarist architecture and the bleak geometric designs of socialist
progressivism. Throughout much of the 'eighties, when
every available ruble was being thrown into a desperate attempt to match Western arms expenditures, there had been
little left over for construction. There was even less after the
Soviet system skidded into virtual bankruptcy. Neither had
the boom times of the 'nineties found its way into construction of anything except *Mafiya*-owned dachas and walled
compounds. This had brought an exhausted monotony to the
Moscow cityscape that Beck had found somehow comforting.

No longer.

To the north, urban sprawl had settled in; towns and what
looked like private estates had sprung up in what had, the last
time Beck had been there, been open fields. The activity
showed no signs of slowing; in the distance, along the route
to St. Petersburg, he could see bright yellow earthmoving vehicles scraping the curves of new residential roadways.

Beck also was surprised at the number of shopping malls; some of them were as large as their American counterparts, though with far fewer cars parked in far smaller lots. They flew over near the city's center, above the open expanse that was still called Red Square, and Beck sighted the Golden Arches of McDonald's. Just east of the triangular walls and minaret spires of the Kremlin, the F-15 had swept over what from the air looked like a Pizza Hut.

And in the final approach, as the F-15's wheels thudded into lowered-and-locked position, Beck looked closer at the glut of billboards he had noted from high overhead. They were also new and prolific as mushrooms after a spring rain. They advertised a cornucopia of Korean electronics, American cigarettes and Western European consumer goods. Capitalism, in all its forms and variations, clearly had come to the former workers' paradise.

By now, they had received instructions. Frankel taxied the fighter away from the main Sheremetyevo II terminal, bouncing over occasionally cracked or weed-tufted concrete toward a hangar undistinguished save for its sheer size. It was unmistakably military, and the ground personnel who swarmed around the Eagle as it braked were efficient as army ants, carrying tire chocks and wheeling out a green cherry picker. The latter had been spray-painted either inexpertly or carelessly; faintly, just below the fresher tricolor ensign of the Russian Federation, Beck could still discern the single red star.

Frankel opened the canopy. Beck caught the usual airport scents of scorched rubber and burned kerosene, and more: a smoky, earthy, semiacrid tang that his memory immediately recognized as uniquely Russian. While the Air Force major supervised the fighter's shutdown, Beck submitted meekly as a blond man in military-style coveralls disentangled him from the straps and wires he had worn for hours.

Within moments, Beck found himself hustled inside the hangar. He had left the helmet in the Eagle, but his Power-

Book and canvas carryall bag dangled by their respective straps from either hand. His body was stiff from inactivity and his gait bowlegged from the awkward embrace of the tightly laced G-suit. He looked like the world's most miserable tourist; as he walked, he waddled like a wounded duck.

"Ah, Beck Casey! You have injured yourself, my friend?"

Alexi Malenkov, wearing a Russian Army uniform, stood in jackbooted splendor near the open rear door of a Zil sedan. His tone was solicitous, but too much so; his face was split wide with a grin.

"Hello, Alexi. No, just not as flexible as I used to be." Beck eyed the collar insignia on the crisp uniform. "A General, I see. Last time I saw you, weren't you a Lieutenant Commander? In the Russian *Navy*?"

Alexi looked down at his tunic, and shook his head mock sadly.

"True. And I much preferred the Navy's taste in fashion. But what is there to be done, my friend? In our business, I have found it valuable to stay flexible."

He made a gesture, and the blond Russian quickly helped Beck strip off the G-harness. Malenkov watched with polite interest as Beck unzipped the Nomex flight suit, peeling himself out of it like an arthritic snake shedding skin.

" 'Iowa State,' " Malenkov read aloud, and pursed his lips theatrically. "Perhaps I could lend you something a little more . . . *formal,* my friend?" He shrugged at Beck's expression. "No matter, eh? So. Your pilot will stay here; there are accommodations waiting. We have business to do. Come."

As Beck settled in to the rear of the auto, Malenkov spoke to the driver in Russian.

"Yehat 'k Kremlin," he said.

Beck automatically translated: *To the Kremlin.*

The trip from Sheremetyevo to the center of Moscow is no more than twenty miles, but it can take as long as two hours—unless, that is, one is a passenger in a state vehicle equipped with a siren. Cars swerved aside to let them pass, some with alacrity and others with a studied indifference to the show of official impatience.

The back seat of the Zil was spacious. Beck stretched his legs, feeling his muscles threaten mutiny as he did. Outside on the right, they were passing what appeared to be a forest of massive concrete obelisks: concrete antitank hedgehogs arranged as a monument to the counteroffensive that sent Hitler's supermen reeling more than a half century earlier.

"I have missed you, Beck," Malenkov said.

"Three years is a long time, Alexi. Director of state security; you've done well for yourself."

"Bah." Malenkov tried to look humble, and failed utterly. "I have become a bureaucrat—the type of person that as field operatives, we both loved to hate."

There was an extended silence that threatened to become awkward.

"Your last visit to my country—" Malenkov frowned and shook his head. "Well, it is of no matter now. Necessary evils, eh?"

He lit a cigarette, without which no Russian feels complete. It was a Russian brand, the kind with the long cardboard tube that serves as a holder. Malenkov inhaled deeply of the fragrant smoke, and blew it toward the roof with obvious satisfaction.

"I myself have always feared torture," Alexi continued conversationally. "I knew that I would be unable to resist. In the end, one always talks, yes?"

"Of course you talk," Beck said tightly. "You answer every damned question they ask. If you don't know, you make up the answers that you think they want to hear. And finally, when they run out of questions, you tell them everything else I . . . you can think of."

"Ah, Beck—you are upset. I apologize. I thought it would be perhaps therapeutic, to talk of these things. And I am frankly curious. Few men survive an abduction by the *Mafiya*."

Beck looked out the car window.

"Alexi, we've known each other a long time. I even enjoy your company. Sometimes, you're so affable that I tend to forget what I know about you."

"And that is?"

"That you were a KGB thug before you started shaving. You're old school, Alexi—we both are, so please don't tell me how uninformed you are about the *Mafiya*. Half of the people who wired me up like a science project were working in your *Direktorate* back in the early 'nineties. Now they're *Mafiya*."

"Yes," Alexi agreed. "A sad commentary, how many of these criminals are former KGB men."

"And so convenient. They have such excellent contacts throughout your armaments industries. Even in those parts of it that make biological weapons."

Malenkov shrugged expansively.

"It is difficult to restrain commerce, my friend. Many countries seek such items. It is unrealistic to think that the less idealistic of my countrymen would not attempt to fill this demand. That they did so as . . . *private* businessmen—well, neither is that particularly difficult to understand. The state could no longer afford their services, so they became entre-preneurs."

"It's always valuable for a government to stay close to its business community. To work in each other's interests, so to speak. Of course, the relationship was very fortunate for me."

"Beck, we *bought* you from them," Alexi said, as if he was explaining to a child. "You awakened in a Moscow hos-pital. Did you think the gentlemen of our *Mafiya* were so considerate?"

"I always wondered about that," Beck said. "It wasn't as if the CIA was working overtime on my behalf."

Alexi laughed, and to Beck it sounded like genuine amusement.

"No, except for the usual inquiries between diplomats, the CIA was surprisingly inactive. While there were those in my government who wished simply to let the filthy *govnos* leave your body in Gorky Park, your survival was the result of Russian humanitarianism."

"I'm honored."

"You should feel so. Though, I admit, we did purchase several hours of audio recordings made during your . . . interviews. There was some official curiosity as to your presence in my country, you see. After all, my friend—a year earlier, you did arrange the defection of Comrade Alibelikov."

"He defected on his own, Alexi."

"If you say so. Still, it was quite embarrassing—having the head of our bioweapon program suddenly surface in Langley, telling your CIA all of our little secrets. Some of my people blamed you. Some continue to do so, I fear."

He lit another cigarette from the still-burning ember of his first.

"Now, your family. Your daughter, how is she?—young Katherine. Little Katie—but no. She can be no longer little. She must be what now? Fourteen years?"

"Fifteen," Beck said. "She lives with her mother. In Virginia, across the river from D.C."

"Yes. Your divorce is known to us. So sad. I am divorced myself—two times, and I do not expect my current wife to be my last. It is the nature of our business, no?"

"I don't believe in divorce, Alexi."

"Nor did my first wife, my friend. But only one of the two parties is required to do so, yes?"

"Perhaps."

"Ah, I see." Alexi nodded. "When I heard that you had left the employ of the CIA—well, had I believed it to be so, I would have been much saddened. Do not smile; in truth, our profession is populated with so many unimaginative brutes. On both sides, do you not agree? They see only what is on the surface; so superficial, so boring. You were so . . . so *unpredictable,* my friend!"

He leaned forward confidentially. "You will enjoy this, Beck: I was once told, in all seriousness, that you were believed to be possessed of *psychic* abilities. This, in an official KGB assessment. Ah, you laugh. So did I. I told them, no— Beck Casey is no wizard. He is merely a genius, I said, adept in analyzing what to most would be meaningless trivia. And in jumping to the most startling conclusions—many of which happened to be frighteningly accurate. I told them that you were most likely an idiot savant—that it was doubtful you yourself understood the mechanics of what you did. Oh, yes. You were quite a puzzlement to us, Beck."

Alexi sat back, a doleful expression on his features.

"And now you are—what, teaching history to children? A man with your gifts, a man with such value to his government. I am to seriously believe this?"

"Please don't tell me that you people stopped keeping files," Beck said. "That would truly break my heart, Alexi, lying to me like that."

"Files," Malenkov said, and waved his hand dismissively. "We need no files to tell our stories. We know each other too well. I still do not believe you are 'retired,' but it is a path you should consider with much seriousness. No, my friend, do not look at me like that. To play this game of ours, one must be ruthless and single-minded. This, you were never. Competent, yes. But not without scruples, and that is your failing."

Beck smiled. "After all we've been through. I'm hurt, Alexi, deeply wounded."

The Russian laughed. "I do not complain about this defect of yours, Beck. Had you been ruthless, you would have killed me. Remember? As you did poor stupid Borelovich, four years ago."

"Yes," said Beck. "At the cemetery."

"Did you know that those cemeteries grew out of another plague?" Alexi Malenkov asked. "Yes. In 1771, almost sixty thousand Muscovites died of the Black Death. It was forbidden to bury the victims within the city limits, so the bodies were taken to fields forty kilometers from the Kremlin's walls. Thus were established Danilovskoye, Kalitnikovskoye and Vagankovskoye. Our three great cities of the dead."

He drew again on the cigarette, and exhaled a prodigious amount of tobacco smoke.

"Well. Now Moscow may surpass them all, if what I am told about this virus is accurate. Since last we spoke to your CDC, we have confirmed another thirty-six cases of this 'flu.' That makes seventy-seven cases in all, and the number of deaths is now up to twenty-two."

"We have two deaths, out of two confirmed cases."

"Pardon me, but it is now three deaths and six confirmations. So far. We received word while you were in the air."

"Bad time to be in Florida," Beck said, and paused. "Or Moscow. Alexi, did this thing start here? Is this virus one of yours?"

Malenkov shook his head.

"Our virologists say no," he said. "The genome sequencing is wrong. There, you see, I have no secrets from you. I have admitted that my country possesses such things. This is not a time for the usual games, you see."

Outside the window, the roadway was now lined with ugly apartment buildings that resembled badly molded children's blocks. Beck could see that they were making good time. Moscow sits within five concentric rings of roadways, like a bull's-eye with the Red Square at the center; this was the first ring, and very soon they would traverse to a four-lane they would follow to the Kremlin. As if reading his thoughts, the Zil turned right onto a ramp that curved to meet yet another roadway. At this rate, Beck knew they would be at their destination in less than fifteen minutes.

Malenkov crushed out the cigarette, then leaned toward Beck and patted his knee.

"It has been too long, my friend," Alexi Malenkov said. "And what a hell of a way to renew our acquaintance, is it not?"

"I am very happy that you are not hiding anything, Alexi. But I do have one concern."

Malenkov shook his head in mock disappointment. "And that is?"

"You've assured me that this virus isn't one of yours," Beck said. "But why aren't you asking me if it is one of ours?"

Chapter 10

The Zil swept into the Kremlin, avoiding the main Trinity Gate used by most visitors in preference for a more discreet entrance closer to the Presidium, which houses the Russian governmental offices. Slowing only slightly, the vehicle turned right, past the great bell towers and cathedrals and armory.

Immediately, Beck could sense the tension that gripped the vast fortress of the czars. Normally, on a fine summer's day like this, throngs of tourists would be milling about the various courtyards and parade grounds in T-shirts and shorts, buying photo postcards or admiring in various languages the eighteen minarets that stood graceful sentinel around the triangular walls.

Today, no tourists were to be seen.

Instead, there were armed men everywhere—not the ceremonial guards dressed in Cossack costumes for the benefit of the foreign tourists, but soldiers in full battle dress whose posture and attitude displayed the casual toughness of the professional warrior. Nor were any pikes, ornate sabers or even fancifully engraved matchlock rifles in evidence; each of these troopers, Beck noted, carried the far less elegant but much faster firing AK-47. In addition, from each web harness hung a ceremonial knife, a stiletto with an ornate haft.

And that spells elite unit, he thought, *probably paratroop or even Spetznaz.*

Alexi Malenkov saw Beck's eyes scan the courtyard and correctly guessed his thoughts.

"Yes, there are more soldiers here than is usual," Alexi said. "Officially, the large number of soldiers throughout the city has been attributed to ceremonial requirements. Today we have yet another anniversary of the Great Patriotic War; Putin even placed a wreath somewhere, I believe."

"You can't believe you can keep this a secret, Alexi."

"There has as yet been no official announcement of the situation, and our media is being uncommonly cooperative in—how did I phrase the directive? Ah, yes—'in not spreading rumors that might encourage civil disruption.' All has been very orderly, so far. But even so—yes, there has been talk in the streets. The kettle is boiling, and it is always best to be prepared."

They turned a corner and the car skidded to a stop on the cobbled pavement. Opening his door, the Russian motioned for Beck to follow.

The location was correct for the presidential residence. But instead of the expanse of yellow-white marble and faux-Romanov architecture, a vast olive green canopy of rubberized fabric was tented over the entrance. To Beck, it looked not unlike the massive shrouds used in the States for building fumigation.

Two no-nonsense guards, assault rifles at the ready, flanked a clear plastic flap that served as the only entry. If they noticed Alexi's badge of rank, they gave no indication of deference. One of them carefully checked Malenkov's ID against a computer-printed list, then keyed a radio handset.

As they waited, Beck noticed the sign affixed to a stanchion. CONSTRUCTION—KEEP AWAY, it said in five languages, with the Russian added seemingly as an afterthought—it was, he thought, at best a transparent attempt to explain away the extraordinary activity.

Finally, the radio crackled with words too low for Beck to hear, and the soldier gestured the two men inside. They ascended the stairs, walking against a slight draft that blew toward the outside.

Upstairs, they passed through a foyer where throngs of Russian Army personnel were engaged in chaotic labor.

"Consider yourself fortunate," Alexi muttered to Beck. "Had we not come directly from the airport, neither of us would have been admitted. Perhaps not even with a good scrubbing down from these people."

He sidestepped two sweating soldiers who were unrolling heavy black plastic sheeting to cover the floor; others were draping the same material over the walls or affixing it to the ceiling. Electrical cables and rubber hoses twined with each other before branching off to conduits and brass manifolds around the large expanse.

The devices and apparatus being wrestled into place looked vaguely familiar, though it took Beck a moment to recall where he had seen this before.

Then he remembered: Israel, during the Gulf War.

Here, in the middle of the Russian Kremlin, a mobile decontamination station was being erected.

Beck had expected another meeting, perhaps even a mirror image of the bureaucratic free-for-all in Atlanta with which the day —*no*, he corrected himself mentally, *that was already yesterday*— had started. He had not taken into account the Russian disdain for group decisions, which roughly translated into an affinity for authoritarian rule.

Only one man was in the ornate room.

His back was to the door, away from the large television and VCR that stood between two low sofas. He was staring out a window that looked out over the Kremlin's walls; in the summer sun, the cityscape of Moscow glittered like a jewel.

The bright backlighting made him a silhouette, and to Beck he seemed to stand extraordinarily still.

Then the figure turned, and Beck recognized the thin, almost skull-like face of Vladimir Putin, president of the Russian Federation.

"I know you, Dr. Casey," the Russian president said, as Beck's mind automatically translated the Russian. "You have visited my country before." Beck heard neither threat nor admonition in his tone, and wondered if it was intentional. Putin gestured at the sofas, and Beck and Alexi settled on either side of the video screen. The Russian president handed the latter a sheet of thick, crisp paper, which Alexi scanned quickly before folding it into a pocket of his uniform.

"Vy gava'reet ye pa-Rooski," Putin said, his inflection not as a question.

"Not as well as you speak English," Beck said.

Putin nodded.

"I have conferred with your president," he said in the unaccented English his files said he learned in a KGB training academy. "We agree that our two countries are both in mortal peril; we have both pledged unconditional cooperation in this matter. Our medical authorities are exchanging what little information there is. At present, our official position is that this is a medical emergency, not an . . . attack. That may provide us time to determine who has done this. You wish to see the face of this atrocity?"

Without waiting for a response, he moved to the videotape machine and pressed a button. The screen flickered to life. It showed a head-and-shoulders close-up of what could have been a fully spacesuited cosmonaut. Any facial features were obscured by the blue-white flare of overhead fluorescent tubes on the helmet's plastic faceplate.

As the camera pulled back slightly, Beck could see that the figure wore a gray coverall, shiny with its rubberized coating; black gloves covered his hands, and what looked like double wrappings of duct tape sealed the wrist against the protective suit. The corrugated hose of a self-contained breathing supply snaked over his shoulder.

"This was recorded earlier today," Putin said, his words curiously flat. "At our Engelhardt Institute of Molecular Biology. As you see, it is much like the most stringent containment facilities at your Fort Detrick or your CDC. I believe you call these 'Level Four' facilities, where the most hazardous organisms are contained."

On the videotape, the cosmonaut now was walking down a corridor toward a steel door that looked like the hatch of a submarine. The camera followed him through the second door of the airlock, the man momentarily passing out of the camera's view. For an instant, the picture shimmied into a blur.

When the focus again steadied, it was on a scene of sheer horror.

Around the room, arranged like a dormitory from hell, were row upon row of hospital cots; at least two dozen, Beck estimated. Under sheets now stained and matted, human forms writhed and struggled — some frantically, fighting for breath with the panic of the drowning; others fitfully, feeble in their dying efforts to drag oxygen past bruise-blue lips. In several of the beds, the patients were in the midst of fevered seizures, mad convulsions that tore the intravenous tubes from their bodies and rocked the cots wildly. Everywhere, the floor was vile with puddled bodily fluids, skid-smeared where the spacesuited attendants had passed.

Beck watched wordlessly as the camera walked down the line of cots, the picture jerking and unsteady with each step of the operator. Face after doomed face passed in close-up, features contorted with pain as uncontrollable coughing ripped the tissues of their lungs. A number of the victims dripped a thick, bloody phlegm from their noses and mouths. Too weak to even lift their hands, only their eyes still looked human in faces ravaged by the virus's assault.

"The first case was reported three days ago — in Tuvelov, a village just outside this city," Putin said in the same curiously detached voice. "The first death came one day later, the same day we discovered it had spread to Arkadi, a neighboring village, and then to Moscow itself. Since then, our physicians have had no success in discovering a viable treatment. There are more than seventy identified cases, and our medical experts estimate that those already infected but still without symptoms number twenty to thirty times that figure. The contagion expands geometrically; within ten days, all of Russia could be infected. At present, our projections indicate the virus will be lethal in slightly fewer than eighty percent of all it infects."

The Russian president stopped, his eyes locked on the video screen. There, a young boy perhaps nine years old twisted in agony; frantically his hands clawed at his own throat, leaving red lines against the bluish, oxygen-deprived flesh.

Mercifully, the camera moved on; and Putin shook himself, as if to force his words to continue.

"Our attempts to contain this disease have fared little better," Putin said. "Last night, I ordered troops to cordon off the western quadrant of the city, well outside the area where this influenza already is found. Because Tuvelov and Arkadi have reported cases of this disease, they also have been sealed. No one is being allowed out, or in. No one. The units were ordered to employ lethal force."

He turned to face Beck and Malenkov directly.

"Already, this has been necessary," he said. "Perhaps fifty have been shot, maybe more. I have ordered that the bodies remain where they fall, in full view of others who might attempt to cross these lines."

Beck looked at Putin, thinking of bullet-torn bodies lying in a Moscow street. Unbidden, his mind's eye superimposed another image, another place, over the carnage.

"We too have considered containment," Beck said. "In Florida."

"I have advised your President that containment is at best a temporary measure," Putin said. "I am told, for instance, that parts of Moscow's sewer system do not exist on our maps; these will serve as an avenue of escape for some. Others will finally fear the disease more than bullets; they will merely overwhelm the soldiers at a given place in the line—overrun them, as you say. Is this not true, Alexi Malenkov? Or does my senior security advisor now have new counsel for me?"

Alexi stared back at him—without expression, but also without the pro forma respect that usually accompanied such an exchange. There was a hard tension between the two men that was obvious even to the American.

Finally Putin shrugged—rather bloodlessly, Beck thought.

"Inevitably, someone will elude our cordon," Putin said. "If I allow that to happen, this death will spread beyond all hope of stopping. There is but one manner of perhaps preventing this, and it is at best a doubtful proposition."

He looked at his watch, and raised his eyes to focus on a far wall above Beck's head.

"I have ordered my military to sterilize the areas where this virus is known to exist," Putin said.

Beck felt the skin at the back of his skull tighten; beside him, Alexi sat in his own stunned silence.

"In less than an hour, approximately one hundred helicopters will fly over western Moscow and the villages of Arkadi and Tuvelov. Each aircraft is equipped with aerial spraying devices, with which they will release chemical agents. This will be repeated as many times as is necessary. We are fortunate; the winds are favorable, and outside the sterilization zone deaths caused by our nerve gases will be minimized. I have been advised that by tonight at the latest, no one in the affected areas will remain alive."

"How many, sir?" Beck asked.

"Perhaps two hundred thousand," Putin said. "History may say it was a small enough sacrifice to save one hundred and fifty million other Russians. If this virus does not somehow outsmart us."

"*Soo'kin sin,*" breathed Alexi.

For a moment, Putin seemed not to have noticed the vulgarity. "Do not pretend such surprise, General Malenkov. You pressed hard enough for—how did you put it? *'Decisive* action,' I believe you wanted."

Alexi stared at his president wordlessly, but with eyes that spoke volumes. The two Russians' stares dueled for a long moment, before Putin turned to Beck.

"I have been waiting to hear the sounds of the helicopters," Putin said, and his voice was remote, distant. "There is a possibility, of course, that my order will not be obeyed." He suddenly smiled, as if in comradeship with the American seated before him. "Or that they will decide to release their weapons here, over the Kremlin. I have been wondering which choice I would make, were I one of the pilots. In truth, I cannot make up my mind."

The smile faded as quickly as it had appeared.

"I have given Alexi Malenkov my signed authorization to provide you with any information or assistance you need. He will accompany you to Lubyanka. There is an interrogation under way there—a cultist, one of the fanatics the FSB has had under surveillance for some weeks. Since before this virus appeared. I am told he may prove valuable to us."

The three men stood. No one offered to shake hands.

Putin's voice followed Beck to the door and stopped him there. When Beck turned, he saw that the Russian president was again at the window, looking out at the city.

"Four days ago, there was no sign of this virus in my country. Now I must sacrifice many lives, with no certainty it will prove successful."

"Russians have died for Russia before," Beck said, and Putin replied without turning.

"Americans may soon follow our example, Dr. Casey," he said. "I spoke to your president, to make him aware of what I must do here, to Russians. He is weighing the advice of your own experts even as we speak. This very same option, I believe, had already been suggested to him."

Chapter 11

The car carrying Beck entered Lubyanskaya Plaza, past the empty spot once occupied by a massive statue of Felix Dzerzhinsky, the man tasked by Lenin to create history's most draconian secret police organization. Until August 22, 1991, Iron Felix had stood in stern bronze vigilance, overlooking the yellow-brick headquarters of the KGB.

Beck remembered the day. He had been in the midst of the crowd of Muscovites numbering in the thousands who surrounded the monument. They had cheered as cranes toppled both the statue and, they thought, the system of terror it had represented. Some of the crowd—as giddy with vodka as with the prospect of democratic rule—performed various indignities on the statue as it lay facedown on the ground.

Beck had looked up at the windows overlooking the scene, noting the senior KGB officers who had watched patiently from their office windows. Afterward, pragmatic in their understanding of Russian history, they had had the statue removed to a warehouse and cleaned.

Many believe it remains in storage, waiting. But Beck, like other professionals who had watched Russia's subsequent mutation, knew better; like the institution founded by

Iron Felix—in its most recent incarnation, now known as the Federal Security Bureau—the statue had been quietly reerected. Lenin's dark angel again stands proudly, now in a park far from the eyes of the Russian public. Similarly, his legacy to the Russian national character is once again busily engaged in its traditional pursuits.

It had been a short trip from the Kremlin. Alexi Malenkov had said nothing during the two-block drive; nor had Beck encouraged conversation. Instead, both men stared straight ahead, each pretending not to be listening for the sounds of helicopters in the distance. No one challenged Alexi as he led Beck past the guards and checkpoints inside.

Only in the small elevator that Alexi had activated with his own key did he begin to speak.

"Madness," Alexi said, his voice barely under control. "We are attacked, and the only response our 'leader' can devise is to massacre our own people."

"Putin has tough choices to make, Alexi. It's what a leader does."

"A leader," Alexi repeated. "Is that what he is? Perhaps. In Russia, you see, we have created a new ruling class. It is made up of capitalists, our so-called oligarchs. Billionaires, all of them—and advised by your own very capable American public relations firms. These are the people who rule in Russia today, my friend."

"Putin was elected, Alexi. As was Yeltsin before him."

"Yes, please lecture me on the beauties of democratic government," Alexi retorted, sarcasm dripping. "Yeltsin was unstable. Even in his occasional lucid moments, he scarcely had the wit to dress himself, let alone provide leadership. A faction of our billionaires' club tired of his antics; they wanted more stability than could be provided under a manic-depressive alcoholic. So they found Putin."

He snorted. "Our wealthy ruling class thought he was merely an ambitious, midlevel KGB *apparatchik*. Ambitious, he certainly was. I fear they underestimated the rest of his personality—rather badly, no? You have perhaps heard the definition of an honest Russian politician? He is a man who, when you buy him, *stays* bought."

"You didn't make that up," Beck said. "I've heard it in Chicago."

"You know of the very public arrests my president has ordered recently? One was a Russian media baron, I believe you would call him; the second, an industrialist who has perhaps been too open in his views."

"They got rich by robbing your country blind," Beck said. "Come on. They share the blame for what happened in Russia. Maybe Putin does too, but there's a lot of blame to be shared."

"Now they are finding that President Putin is much like other leaders my country has had: disinclined to share anything, especially power." Alexi fell silent for a few paces, his brow dark with words unsaid. "If there is much of anything to share after this virus has done its work."

Beck said nothing.

"I have always been suspicious of the obvious," Alexi said after a moment. "The rational person does not wish to die; this is obvious. Who, then, would unleash a disease that kills so efficiently, spreads so rapidly and defies all efforts to discover a cure? What kind of person would be so irrational? Perhaps it is my early education as a good Communist, but to me the answer is obvious."

Beck looked at him patiently.

"A fanatic," Alexi said. "More specifically, a *religious* fanatic, who seeks his reward in the afterlife."

"And that narrows it down, does it?"

"As it happens, my friend, we have a number of quite fanatical religious cults in Russia. But I know of only one that has a previous record of chemical and biological terrorist acts."

The American frowned. "The Asahara cult? Aum Shinrikyo?"

"Of course, you would know of these Aum, as they call themselves," Alexi said to Beck. "Have we not all studied their murderous farce? Please, let me play the professor here: in the not-so-distant past, they released a quantity of nerve gas in the subway of Tokyo. They believed by so doing, they would trigger a worldwide religious uprising. They did not, though they succeeded in killing perhaps a dozen of their countrymen. Do you know why it failed?"

"The sarin contained impurities," Beck said, watching his companion closely.

"Ah, that is what the Japanese authorities announced. But it is not accurate. We have tested samples from that attack—no, do not ask how we obtained it, please. The nerve gas was quite adequately formulated. No, it was the delivery system that was faulty. In the subways, Aum soldiers had simply concealed sealed plastic sacks containing the gas inside briefcases, purses—even paper bags. At a prearranged time, the weapon bearer punctured the plastic and fled the scene."

Alexi smiled, grimly. "Even as a kamikaze delivery system, it was spectacularly unsophisticated," he said. "People died, surely; but only a handful, nowhere near as many as had been hoped for. Still, had the gas been delivered from pressurized containers in a properly coordinated assault, the results would have been far different."

Alexi looked as if he had tasted something foul, and shook his head in disgust.

"Idiots. After this lethal farce, the Japanese police supposedly arrested those responsible. I say 'supposedly' because, after the Japanese government courteously agreed that the peaceful rank and file of the Aum was no longer a public danger, they allowed it to continue in existence. This, despite the fact that sizable quantities of rather dangerous toys were found in their possession. I speak, of course, of the sarin. And also of biological cultures that, upon analysis, were determined to be anthrax."

Alexi shrugged, and was not quite capable of keeping his anger from emphasizing the gesture.

"Certainly, in the case of the anthrax, it was not that growing the organism was exceptionally difficult—early in World War Two, the British succeeded by using five interconnected metal milk cans and a simple vacuum pump. No, what we found impressive was the sheer energy of these Aum. They appear quite determined, once they have set themselves on a task. Do you know that some years ago they sent—you will perhaps enjoy the irony—a 'humanitarian mission' to Zaire? Not by coincidence, it was during an outbreak of Ebola. They wished to obtain a sample of this particularly nasty virus, and failed only because they could not reach the site of the outbreak in time.

"And so. The cult is Japanese in origin, supposedly formed by a half-blind leader said to have had an exclusive relationship with the Almighty. Since his imprisonment after the botched gas attack, he is now considered by his remaining followers as a god himself. In reality this Asahara was a petty thief, an embezzler who stumbled onto the far greener pastures of religious mysticism. He attracted unstable elements among his people, who made a practice of turning their own property over to their leader. Some of this wealth he decided to use in my country."

The elevator stopped and they exited into a subterranean level lighted by modern fluorescent strips. To Beck, it looked much like the windowless clerical areas of a large insurance operation.

"We have become very good capitalists," Alexi said. "We sold these fanatics air time on our most powerful transmitters, so the rantings of their insane leader could infect more and more Russian minds. We turned into what Lenin called your countrymen: merchants who would sell the rope to their own hangman."

He stopped at a door that looked far too heavy for an office or storeroom.

"Perhaps twenty or thirty thousand of my countrymen were gullible enough to adopt this Aum foolishness. Allow me to introduce you to one of them."

He waved Beck into a large room lit by powerful lights on the upper walls and ceiling. The brightness was dazzling, and Beck's eyes squinted against it. It took a moment before he could make out the three figures near the far wall. Two of them were in uniform, and their eyes were masked by the dark glasses they wore.

"I present Il'lych Valeri Davidovich." Beck heard Alexi sniff at the stench of urine and feces that hung in the air. "Do not stand too close. I believe our guest has become somewhat incontinent."

The prisoner was Slavic in his features and complexion—or would have been, had his hair not been matted with dirt and blood and his face not mottled with bruises. His eyes were mere slits, though whether because of the bright lights or the effect of physical abuse Beck could not discern.

Then Beck noted the curious pattern of angry red blotches, always in pairs, wherever the man's skin was exposed.

"What the hell, Alexi?"

"As a Russian citizen, Mr. Davidovich has constitutional rights that we have honored," Alexi said with sarcasm. "That is why he is here, rather than at Lefortovo Prison. He is freely assisting us in our investigation."

"I know electrical burns when I see them," Beck said.

"There is no virus here, and no nerve gas to fall on him from above," Alexi retorted. "Most of the persuasion we have employed has involved drugs and the deprivation of sleep. He is fortunate."

"Ask him if he thinks so," Beck said.

Alexi shrugged carelessly, his eyes on the scene.

The man swayed on his feet, and the inquisitor who stood behind him jabbed his kidney with a balled fist, hard and expertly. When the prisoner staggered, the interrogator to his front seized him by the windpipe and held him up. The uniformed man leaned close to the prisoner's face and said something sibilant and hard. When he released his grip on the man's throat, the prisoner sank to his knees.

He muttered something in Russian that was too low for Beck to hear.

The response was a vicious kick to the small of his back that sent the man writhing to the floor.

"Come." Alexi gripped Beck's upper arm. They turned and left the room. As they again walked down the corridor, Beck found his own fists were balled.

"Damn you," he spat at Alexi. "Why did you show me that?"

"Because there is no time for anything else," the Russian said. "Because you must understand that what I tell you now is true. Seven months ago, the man in that room attempted to bribe a senior Army officer, who happened instead to be a patriot. Our guest has been under surveillance ever since. He offered first eight million U.S. dollars, then increased it to ten million. Do you wish to know what he considered worth this vast sum?"

Beck said nothing, feeling his pulse pound angrily in his temple.

"He wished to purchase from us a biological weapon," Alexi said. "A virus."

Beck stopped short.

"You told me it was not one of yours, Alexi."

"And it is not. He did not acquire what he sought, not from Russia and not from your country. As a result of the interrogation methods to which you object so passionately, we have ruled this out completely."

"Have you?" Beck heard the anger in his own voice. "Then what does he know about the virus? Who engineered it? Where was it acquired?"

"My friend," Alexi said, "at this moment it does not matter how they obtained this virus. Perhaps through our old friend Saddam. Or perhaps an organization that has ten million dollars to spend can afford its own biogeneticists, no?"

"It matters if someone has a vaccine."

"Had he known anything about a vaccine, he would have already told us. This, I assure you."

"What other evidence do you have," Beck asked, "aside from the statement of a man under torture?"

Alexi snorted impatiently.

"Do you think he is the only member of this murderous cult we have taken into custody? No, my friend—in Russia, a group that engages in chemical warfare does not escape our attention. Certainly not if there are thousands of them inside our borders."

"I know how the Federal Security Bureau works, Alexi. People tend to disappear into the system, and many of them never emerge. I'll ask again: Do you have any hard proof that Aum is behind all this?"

"Do not play the lawyer with me, my friend. It is not a role that suits you. We have a man who is a member of a cult that has previously tried to wage biological warfare. He attempts to buy a deadly viral weapon. A few months later, people in both our countries begin to die from a virus we know is an engineered weapon. I need nothing more."

"It may be a smoking gun, Alexi. But it's not conclusive."

"When we have finished our interrogation," Alexi said, "we will know all that he does. He will wish only that he had more to tell us."

Beck bit off the retort that came to his lips. The two men walked on in silence for several paces before Alexi spoke.

"Beck, six weeks ago the Japanese convicted this Asahara, this cult leader. He was sentenced to die—a quite reasonable decision for a Russian court, though something of a surprise to come from the Japanese. They are, I fear, far too pliant, far too often."

"The Armageddon syndrome," Beck said. "As a cult, they believe their own annihilation is at hand, and they've decided to take the rest of us with them. This is what you believe has begun?"

Alexi nodded, and his expression was deadly serious.

"Report back to your president," he said. "Tell him that these fanatics, these Aum, are our most obvious—call them suspects, if you must. I would use a much more definitive description. We have gathered some intelligence on this group independently, and will share it with you. They are apparently led now by various people they call teachers—in Japanese, *sensei*. Who these sensei are, we do not yet know. But your people are much closer to the Japanese government than are mine, is it not so?"

Alexi reached out and gripped Beck's arm in a grip that was almost painful. "Understand, please. We must obtain all information on this cult immediately."

"What we have, you will have."

Alexi smiled coldly. "We cannot afford games in this, Beck."

"What are you saying, Alexi?"

"Your people already know much about this Aum, my friend. Your people infiltrated them some time ago."

Beck looked skeptical.

"And just how would you know this?"

"The man in the room—the one whose well-being you are so concerned about. He is Aum, certainly. But he is also one of yours. He is CIA."

Chapter 12

The first line of the helicopters—thirty Mi-24 Hinds, each adapted with aerosol spraying apparatus that protruded sideways from the landing skids and accentuated their insectlike appearance—swept in low over the target perimeter. They were no more than seventy feet above the street level, and the people below were easily visible as individuals to the two-man crews.

The words crackled in the headphones of Pilot Officer Yuri Gretnik, who recognized the voice of his squadron commander.

"Ajax Leader. This will be our orientation pass. Maintain formation throughout. Ajax-Three, tighten up." Yuri winced at the rebuke. He eased the collective, tweaking his craft back into alignment.

Below, there were no more barricades in place. When, a few minutes before, the cordon of troops had pulled back to the far side of the broad boulevard, the crowd had surged forward and crumpled the red-and-white-painted fencing. Yuri could see that the only obstacle now holding back the mass of humanity was the line of soldiers three deep and seventy yards away.

The margin of the crowd was dark and irregular against the lighter pavement of the street; seen from above, the scene looked not unlike the ebb and flow of waves upon a beach. Here and there, the white puff of a tear gas canister blossomed near the front ranks, and the people in the area scattered like birds disturbed in a park. Then the cloud would waft away, and the hole it had made would again fill with people, like a boot mark in a muddy field.

Before his conscription, Yuri, twenty-two, had been a literature student at Ekaterinburg University.

You are a master of descriptive language today, Yuri Gretnik told himself. *Perhaps you can use pretty words to describe what we do now. "Murder" sounds so . . . crude.*

"Ajax Cadre, prepare to deploy."

The protective suits and masks they wore made everything more difficult. Though they had drilled in them many times before, it was never pleasant. They were hot, hard to move in, and limited one's vision like a horse's blinders.

In fact, the only thing less pleasant would have been to be without them, Yuri thought, darkly. *Like those below.* He shook the black thoughts from his mind and focused on his flying.

He could see through the plastic windscreen and read the instrument panel; but unless he turned his head awkwardly, the copilot who sat behind him was out of vision's field. Warrant Officer Josef Pelov, riding in the helicopter's midline above and behind the primary pilot, might as well have been in Petrograd as far as Yuri was concerned. No matter. All Pelov had to do was trigger the spraying apparatus at the command and monitor its largely automatic operation.

The flight had linked up with the other squadrons now, and when he turned his head Yuri could see the line of helicopters stretching in precise formation to his right and left. Altitude was thirty meters, airspeed only high enough to provide sufficient control of the aircraft.

"Ajax Cadre, deploy at my mark," the headphones crackled, and a yellow ready light flashed on the dash: Pelov had heard, and was prepared.

No more than a dozen meters separated him from the helicopters on either side, demanding his full attention. Yuri kept his eyes level, forced himself to think of nothing but his flying. For that reason, the pilot did not see the small, almost palm-sized video camera that Pelov now raised to his goggled eye.

It had been an extravagance, a costly toy. When Josef Pelov had shown it to his family and told them what it had cost, they had been uniform in condemning his wastrel ways.

All except his brother-in-law, a former *Pravda* journalist who now freelanced for the various American news organs that maintained Moscow bureaus. He alone had shown respect and even suggested a few ways that the camera might pay for itself. Since then, Pelov and his sister's husband had split the profits from the occasional snippet of video shot during select military operations.

But none had been like this one. The audacity of what he risked made Pelov's hand tremble.

At the same instant, the words came: "Deploy weapon . . . mark."

With the hand not holding the camera, he flipped up the safety shield and pressed the button it had covered. A red indicator light flashed on and glowed steadily, and a new vibration—so slight as to be almost unnoticed, had he not been listening for it—mingled with the rest of the helicopter's din.

Atomized droplets hissed from the tubular spraying gear of a hundred aircraft.

Pelov twisted in his seat, the video camera silently recording.

Distanced by the viewfinder, Pelov could see it all happen objectively, even dispassionately. The spray itself was only visible for the brief instant when it flashed from the row of aerosolizing nozzles. Then it became invisible, a lethal cloud of mist released into the warm summer air.

Pelov tracked downward, imaging the path of the deadly cloud as it trailed in the helicopters' slipstreams. He held the moving shot for several seconds, then pressed the mini-button that operated the zoom lens. As if he were dropping toward them, the crowd mushroomed in his eye.

They fell as wheat under the scythe of an invisible hand — not singly, but as a rolling wave that trailed the shadows of the helicopters.

He imagined they screamed in their agony. The convulsions turned each figure into something clearly no longer human: a madly twisting creature tormented by some invisible fire that had ignited their flesh. Pelov ratcheted back, and the dying humanity he saw through his lens became a wider shot: a single writhing mass that tore at itself, an immense rag doll in the jaws of a particularly frenzied, though unseen, beast.

Pelov stared in terrified fascination at the scene below until Yuri's voice blared in his ear.

"Acknowledge, please. We are ordered to prepare for another pass."

"*Da,* Pilot Officer," Pelov responded. With his gloved left hand, he pressed the switch that cut off the flow of the nerve gas and prepared to reset the arming system. The palm-sized video cam he slipped into the map pouch affixed to the aluminum bulkhead. He would risk it, he thought silently, risk recording at least one more pass over the streets of death below.

He was certain his brother-in-law — the one who freelanced for the Americans journalists — could help him find the highest bidder.

Chapter 13

The spacesuited figure stood in the doorway, a stocky, bear-like form whose helmet had R. PORTER stenciled above the bubble of his faceplate.

"Dr. Mayer, I need your help for a moment."

The voice was oddly muffled through the acrylic bubble. Without waiting for a reply, he was gone.

Carol Mayer looked up from the computer screen, a frown pulling lines on her face. Aside from the CDC team, which had its own priorities, she was the only physician still on site. When Porter had arrived from Atlanta, Carol had volunteered to stay at the Rossini-Evans Clinic, arguing to Porter that she would be needed for the occasional walk-in that somehow missed being directed to newly established primary triage locations. Spreading the infection, if indeed she carried it, was a moot point: in actuality, if still unofficially, anybody who entered the clinic was taken into custody for quarantine.

Carol had examined five or six people, the first few under the critical eye of the CDC official. Then, his judgment made, the CDC physician had turned to areas where his supervision was actually needed.

The clinic was too small to assign each physician his or

her own office; like the rest of the junior staff, Carol shared both the cubbyhole and the computer with two other doctors. Had this been a normal day, at least one of them would have been lurking over Carol's shoulder in an unsubtle reminder that others might have a need for word processing or Med-Net data searches.

Today was not a normal day, nor had been the day before.

Had she needed any reminder of that, the sight of Porter and his field team from CDC's Epidemic Intelligence Service would have proven sufficient. Since the first units had arrived, its number had swollen to more than a dozen; Porter himself had shown up only an hour or so after the first EIS technicians.

The Rossini-Evans Clinic was now being used as a head-quarters—more accurately, a command center. From it, the CDC specialists were coordinating an expanding network of screening and evaluation, providing overall direction to what now threatened to turn into a quarantine of statewide proportions.

They had swept into the clinic the previous afternoon like an army of invading aliens—*and looked that way too,* Carol groused to herself, *with their Tyvek coveralls and damn Star Wars helmets.* What with the slight hiss of the HEPA-filtered air and the voice-deadening effect of their thick plastic visors, they even sounded a bit like Darth Vader.

The analogy brought a tight twist to her lips. Carol had been surprised to realize just how deep her resentment went. Of course she understood the reason for the protective gear; of course she wished that she too was sheathed head to foot in a sterilized-air, germ-free minienvironment. And of course she resented the forced change in her status from physician to—what?

Not patient, she thought. *Maybe lab rat.*

All this Carol knew, at least intellectually.

She also knew that it was not her intellect that drove her

anger; it was her emotions—specifically, her fear. She had to work hard to conceal it.

So she watched Ray Porter. From the moment he arrived, the man had been everywhere, never appearing to move hastily or without purpose. Carol had watched him supervise the lab setup, lean over another CDC physician to observe the exam, choreograph the doings of a dozen complex tasks.

Most impressively, Carol had seen him nod patiently inside his helmet, coolly waiting for an animated Sam Evans to run out of steam. Carol's boss looked old enough to have been in med school with Pasteur. He had been a Navy combat surgeon with the Marines in Korea before establishing this clinic. He knew all the words, and permutations thereof, needed to express his outrage in stentorian tones. But Porter had simply waited him out, impervious to his heat, and proceeded with the task at hand. Carol, who had herself occasionally felt the sting of her boss's displeasure, was grudgingly impressed.

The CDC field team, Carol had to admit, didn't fool around. They were efficient past the point of rudeness and had simply commandeered the clinic when they arrived. They gathered up the entire clinic staff as well as the patients still in the waiting room. Then each subject was, politely but firmly, probed, swabbed, examined and categorized. Their various fluids were placed by double-gloved hands inside tightly sealed specimen vials. From there, they were carefully walked to the portable laboratory that had been set up in Evans's private office, using his well-appointed wet bar for running water.

The initial examinations had taken almost two hours, and waiting for the lab results about the same. To all of this, for the most part, the patients and staff had submitted meekly.

The trouble began afterward, late in the day, when they found out they would not be allowed to leave—at least, not for their homes.

Carol had noticed the vehicles' arrival some time before:

several large yellow vans with RYDER emblazoned on the side, the drivers also dressed in anticontamination gear. The vans idled at the curb, presumably to allow the air conditioning to mitigate the Florida heat, but also suitable for speedy departure.

Finally, Porter had explained the drill.

"My name is Dr. Porter, and I'm a physician with the Centers for Disease Control. I want to thank all of you for your cooperation," Porter had said, as if he were addressing a Rotary Club meeting. "I have some news that I'm afraid you will not enjoy."

Around the waiting room, people had turned to look at one another. Some of the faces were puzzled, confused; others looked combative.

"Until we know more about the nature of this illness, we cannot risk your health, or that of the public. Those of you without symptoms—this, I want to reassure you, includes most of you—will be temporarily taken to a place we've leased for you." Porter carefully had not called it an isolation center. "A Ramada Inn, located not quite on the beach. There is a pool, all the amenities. After a period of a few days, my hope is you could all go home."

There had been silence for a moment, then a murmur that rose in volume. Above the buzz came a male voice.

"The *hell* with that. What about my kids—and my job? I run a charter fishing boat, and this is when I earn out for the whole year!"

Porter had raised a hand placatingly.

"Sir, your family will be allowed to join you. As for your business, the government will reimburse you for any lost income you may incur. That goes for all of you here."

The physician had paused to let that sink in.

He then continued. "A few of you are experiencing elevated temperature, some level of inflammation or respiratory distress. We need to transport you to a mobile treatment facility so we can keep you under observation and, if necessary, provide medical treatment. One has been set up at Fort Walton High School, in the stadium there."

A heavyset woman, her face flushed, had raised her hand as if she were in a classroom.

"What do we have?" she had asked, her voice husky and congested. "Are we going to be all right?"

"You know we would not be here, wearing all this"— Porter had gestured down at his spacesuit—"if we felt that the situation was not potentially serious. We believe it is a form of the flu, but as for how contagious it is, or how severe an illness it might cause . . ."

He had paused, and his helmet had moved slightly as he shook his head inside it. "Right now, we just don't know."

The man who had spoken earlier, the charter-boat owner, looked aghast.

"You don't know?" His voice had been loud, infuriated. "You want to lock all of us up, along with our families—no, you listen to *me*! You wear those damn things so you don't have to breathe the same air, and you say you don't know how bad it is?"

He had looked around at the others.

"Stay if you want," he had said. "He's lying. I'm getting away from here."

He then pushed past to the doorway and stepped through. Neither Porter nor any member of his team had moved to stop him.

But outside the glass of the entry door, two previously unseen figures had converged on either side of the fisherman. They were dressed in olive exposure suits and wore military helmets over the gas masks that covered their faces. The civilian had snatched his arm from the gloved hand that gripped it and cocked his fist. Before he could swing, the soldier's twin had moved.

To the others watching from inside, it had appeared that the second soldier merely jabbed a closed hand into the fish-

erman's chest. But the effect was extraordinarily out of pro-
portion to the apparent action.

The fisherman's entire body had stiffened, and his head
had arched back so abruptly that the tendons in his neck were
stretched tight. He had stood frozen for a long moment, eyes
clamped shut and his lips in a rictus that showed his tightly
clenched teeth almost to the jawline.

Then the soldier had withdrawn the military-strength
hand stunner. Had not both men supported him, the fisherman would have collapsed to the ground.

Porter had said nothing, allowing those in the clinic to
focus their full attention as the soldiers half dragged the inert
figure to one of the waiting vans. Then, other soldiers who
had waited unseen moved into position along the walkway.
In addition to the full chemical-bio protective gear, each
wore a sidearm holstered within easy reach.

"I'm very sorry," Porter had said to the now-quiet group.
"There really is no other option. We appreciate your cooperation."

Summoned, Carol Mayer shut down the computer.

Not much to do on it anyway, she thought, irritated. Electricity had already flickered twice, forcing her to reboot each
time. Worse, without Internet access—in fact, she had discovered that all phone communications outside the immediate area code were down—there was little new information
available to research.

She moved easily, unencumbered by protective gear.
Pragmatically, there would have been little to be gained from
it anyway, Carol knew; there was little doubt that she had already been exposed, if not during her cardiac resuscitation
efforts the previous morning then by one or another of the
patients she had seen since. She had prepared a cocktail of
the antiviral meds available in the clinic and injected herself
with it; for good measure, she followed up with a bolus of
gamma globulin. It was unlikely, she knew, that either of the

injections would prove prophylactic. But it made her feel as if she was doing something, was not a passive victim waiting for the onset of the symptoms.

Still, Carol admitted, as she walked toward the front of the clinic, *it would have been nice if somebody had offered a gas mask.*

By now, despite his all-encompassing protective suit, she could recognize Ray Porter from all angles—including from the rear, which is how she came upon the CDC physician.

"You rang?" Carol said, her voice unnaturally cheery.

Porter turned, and Carol saw that the clinic had visitors.

Three young women—girls, actually, Carol noted—stood awkwardly, two of them pretending not to notice the otherworldly aspect of the figures that surrounded them. The third, slumped between the pair, did not have to pretend. She was in no condition to notice anything outside the feverish universe she now inhabited.

"Can you help my friend?" Katie Casey said to Carol, her voice tight, only partly with the strain of holding Carly upright. "She's awfully sick."

Chapter 14

The satellite phone connection went through immediately, and the White House switchboard had obviously been alerted to treat it as a priority. In less than a minute, the national security advisor came on the line.

If Beck had expected Billy Carson to express shock, or even surprise, he was grossly mistaken.

"It's the kettle trying to call the pot black," Carson said, his voice tinny from the scrambling software. "Malenkov knows that. Have we cultivated sources inside groups like Aum? Of course we have; so have the Russians."

"Alexi didn't say Davidovich was an informant," Beck said. "He called him CIA—'one of yours,' is what he told me."

"Don't read things into it that aren't there," Carson said. "Malenkov's a professional. He may have motives that have nothing to do with the present situation."

"Meaning what, exactly?"

Over the sat phone, Beck heard Carson sigh theatrically.

"Look, Beck—ask Malenkov about a private security

company called Aum Protect. It's an Aum front they set up in Russia, ostensibly to provide bodyguards and industrial counterespionage to executives and companies operating over there. As staff, Aum recruited as many so-called former KGB thugs as it could find. It gave Aum connections in the Russian intelligence community, and through it to the military."

"So?"

"So we've been recruiting among the same people for years," Carson said. "Malenkov knows that, and knows FSB is compromised at least to some extent. All right—so he pulls in a suspect and puts him through the wringer. A plausible scenario is that Malenkov discovers this Davidovich used to work down the hall from him at Number Two Lubyanskaya. Perhaps Davidovich was RIF'ed out of the spook business during one of the Russian financial crises and ended up taking whatever work he could get. With Aum— *maybe* with us, and that might be what Malenkov is trying to get you to confirm."

"We don't have time for this spy-versus-spy nonsense," Beck said. "The Russians are as frightened as we are about this virus. Good God—you know what Putin intends to do; I don't know, it may have already started by now. They *want* to cooperate; we *need* them to cooperate, and that means the Russians have to trust what I say. Is Davidovich CIA?"

He had to wait for the reply. When it came, it was in measured tones without a trace of concession.

"Yes," Carson said. "He's a contract agent. We recruited him a year ago—rather, he came to us. By trade, he's a journalist. The product he gave us was strictly routine—interviews with politicians, economic reports, production statistics."

"What about the Aum connection?"

"We had no idea he was associated with Aum in any way. If it's true, we need to know the specifics. I already have our people interviewing his case officer: either he dropped the ball when he missed Davidovich's Aum relationship, or Malenkov is misleading you. We're also backtracking the other details—including who was involved in approving Davidovich's recruitment. Tell Malenkov he'll have what we find later today."

"What are you going to do about Davidovich? You can't simply leave him in a torture chamber."

There was silence on the line for a moment. When he spoke, Carson's voice was patient—almost, but not quite, solicitous.

"Beck, I understand how you feel," he said. "God knows, you have good reasons for it. But if Davidovich is involved with the virus—well, it doesn't matter what else he is or is not. He's the enemy. We need every piece of information we can get, any way we can get it. Right now, that includes Malenkov's way."

"For God's sake, Carson," Beck argued, "a person will say damn well anything when he's being tortured. We're acting as if we *know* this Aum group released the virus. What if we're wrong?"

"We're working to confirm that now," Carson replied. "Hold on." There was a muffled conversation that Beck could not decipher, then Carson came back on the line. "The President already has reached out to the Japanese—he's spoken directly to their prime minister. I'm informed that we've been promised full cooperation. They will direct their security forces to raid the known Aum facilities immediately. The prime minister assured the President that his forces will exercise all due restraint, consistent with the situation. It appears that they have not forgotten the Aum nerve gas attack in their country."

Beck frowned. "What does that mean?"

"It means," Carson said, and the tone in his voice raised the hairs on Beck's neck, "that they'll try to take them alive. At least, the important ones."

Chapter 15

The White House
Washington, D.C.
July 22

TRANSCRIPT, POTUS ADDRESS TO NATION
Network feed/pool camera.
White House Press Office.
FOR IMMEDIATE RELEASE—NO EMBARGO ON
AM OR PM OUTLETS
* * * * * * * * * * * * * *

TO:ACCREDITED WHITE HOUSE
CORRESPONDENTS
FROM:NEWS OFFICE/DIRECTOR OF
COMMUNICATIONS

(The following is a transcript of remarks made by the
President of the United States and televised from the Oval
Office 10:30 AM EDT, 7/22.
NOTE: Media briefing is scheduled for 11:00 AM EDT in
the Press Room. POTUS will be present for questions.)

"Good morning, my fellow Americans.

"In the history of our country, we have often faced
challenges that have, in the final analysis, only made us
stronger as a nation. Today I come before you to speak of

another challenge that has arisen, and which as a nation we must now address.

"I have been informed by the Department of Health and Human Services that a number of persons in the state of Florida have become ill as a result of an influenza outbreak. This flu has been severe enough to have caused several of those afflicted to succumb to respiratory failure. I am further informed that some cases of this flu have been reported in the Russian Federation, and that its leaders too are treating the matter as a potentially serious situation.

"As all of us know, influenza is a contagious disease. It spreads between individuals through close contact. We've all picked up a case of the flu because we've exposed ourselves to someone else who had it.

"This influenza comes at a time of year when many of us are taking well-deserved vacations. That's unfortunate, because it makes it harder to keep from picking up this bug. At the same time, it makes it much easier for the virus to move around. In addition, the timing creates difficulties for our pharmaceutical companies. Flu season is usually in the fall and winter months, which allows drug manufacturers more time to prepare and make available the vaccines we've all become accustomed to having on hand.

"I won't mislead you—for all these reasons, this influenza is potentially quite a serious health threat. It is a strain we have not seen for a number of years, and that means that more people are susceptible to it. It is prudent to do whatever can be done to limit the spread of this influenza.

"For that reason, I have been advised to declare a public health emergency. This morning, I signed an executive order to that effect.

"This order puts into effect a number of steps. They include:

"First, throughout the country I am asking for a voluntary, temporary suspension of all large public gatherings. This includes sporting and entertainment events, public meetings and gatherings.

"Now, if you're a baseball fan—as I am—please do

not worry. We do not anticipate more than a few days'
suspension of games, and I intend to ask the commissioner
of baseball to extend the season. I'm certain he will agree,
and that all games will be played. But at least for a while it
is wise for people to remain close to the comfort of their
own homes.

"Second, I am asking for all Americans to temporarily
postpone any vacation plans that involve travel outside
their immediate home communities. We want to limit any
opportunities for this influenza to spread before we have
completely assessed the situation and determined a full
course of action. To this end, effective immediately, I have
ordered a suspension of operation by most public
carriers—airlines, rail and bus.

"In addition, gasoline supplies are being placed on a
temporary rationing system. The final details of this
program—which, I again stress, is temporary in nature—
are being hammered out now. They will be announced in
the next day or so, but until then I have ordered all private
gasoline sales be suspended, except in cases of
demonstrated emergencies.

"Third, I am placing under federal control all National
Guard and state militia units to assist as necessary
throughout this period.

"And finally, I am ordering the creation of what we
have designated the Florida Quarantine Region, an area
currently limited to northwest Florida adjacent to Alabama
and Georgia. This is where the influenza has been reported,
and it is here that we will focus much of our activity. My
intention is to ensure that health care and related services
are not hindered unnecessarily until we can finish our
assessments. Effective immediately, all travel into and out
of this area will be restricted.

"My fellow Americans, it would be unwise indeed to
minimize the serious nature of this situation. But at the
same time, I do not want to create undue concern. The
situation is being vigorously addressed by your
government.

"Within a few days, I am confident that we will know

much more. We may well find that we have overreacted. If so, as your president I will have no apology to make. If we err, I want to err on the side of caution.

"I will be briefing the media after I speak to you, where I will try to provide whatever additional information I can. I assure you, my fellow citizens, that I will do my best to see that your questions and concerns are fully addressed, as information becomes available.

"For now, thank you. May God bless our country."

— end transcript —

Jason Sorenson, White House correspondent for NBC, had, like the rest of the journalists waiting in the briefing room, read the transcript a dozen times in the quarter hour since it had been broadcast to the nation. Like his brethren, he had scribbled notes and questions—his, onto the canary yellow legal pad he preferred over the more compact notebooks carried by the majority of the White House press corps.

It was partly for show, but mostly for necessity—Sorenson was more than moderately nearsighted and had never been able to tolerate contact lenses. When the cameras were on, he invariably slipped his wire-frame glasses into a pocket. Only the dimensions of his notepad and the proportional size of his precise handwriting allowed him to see the questions he always prepared.

This morning's presidential address had taken the news corps by surprise. The formal request for air time had been made only an hour before the scheduled broadcast time, making all of them scramble. The usual press secretary backgrounder was conspicuous in its absence, and neither threats nor cajoling shook anything loose from their usual sources in the executive branch.

And now it's time for the cattle call, he thought sourly.

Unlike many of those who covered the White House, Sorenson detested the press conferences that were so much a staple of the beat. For one thing, he was far more driven than

was considered seemly in a TV journalist; competitive by nature, he gauged his success on the job by the number of times
he had scooped not only his electronic-media cohorts, but
trounced the more rough-and-tumble newshounds of the
print side. This approach required an aggressive tenacity that
had given NBC both headaches and plaudits during Sorenson's tenure at 1600 Pennsylvania; wisely, the president of
NBC News considered the former a fair price for the latter.

But today, it availed the journalist nothing. If anybody
knew more about this flu outbreak, they were not talking to
Sorenson. It had been embarrassing to admit, but they had
the lid clamped tight on this one. And now broadcasting a
live press with no time for the newspeople to properly prepare their questions: few of the news pundits would relish
looking as if they didn't already know the details, which virtually ensured a session that would be fast and relatively
tame. The White House press people were professionals—
manipulative, devious, truth-twisting bastards, Sorenson
thought, *most of 'em. But clearly professionals.*

He had just settled into his seat near the front of the
room—TV jocks, many of them minicelebrities in their own
right, got the prime seats and the best camera angles—when
his cellular phone vibrated. The built-in caller ID showed an
extension number at NBC News's Manhattan headquarters.
It could only be one person.

"Talk to me, Dara," Sorenson said, without preamble.

"Did they start yet? No, don't talk—just listen." It was
the voice of Dara Chadwick, a former on-camera talent until
she succumbed to the enticements of a network V.P.'s title.
Now she managed international news operations—*as much,*
Sorenson thought, *as anyone could supervise that bunch of
hard-news cowboys.*

"You won't believe what we have," Dara said, stuttering
slightly in her excitement. "Or how much we're paying for it.
We just took the satellite download from Moscow. We have

tape, Jase. The quality's for shit, but that just makes it more effective. God, Jase. It's *killer* television—"

"Take a deep breath," Sorenson said. "Then start over, slower."

"The President—he mentioned Russia has this flu? Well, he's got *that* right, Jase. And you won't believe what the cold-blooded bastards did about it this morning."

Sorenson listened to her description, scribbling fiercely all the time.

"How many?" He waited impatiently. "Then an estimate, damn it." Another pause, longer. "Holy shit," he breathed. "And we've got all this on tape?"

There was a sudden movement as, around him, the assembled journalists rose to their feet in a gesture of respect, if not to the incumbent, then to the traditions of the room. Automatically, Sorenson whipped off his glasses and rose with them.

On the raised dais, in front of an ornate backdrop that read THE WHITE HOUSE, the President of the United States walked with a purposeful stride to the lectern. He nodded to the senior journalist from the Associated Press, and the session began.

"Cue it up," Sorenson muttered to Dara, ignoring the frowns this breach of etiquette elicited from the reporters seated on his either side. "Just make sure it's ready. You'll know when. Be set to roll when he calls on me." He listened for a moment. "Good. Uh-huh. Stand by."

He raised his hand, waited impatiently as the President instead chose the CNN reporter, raised his hand again. Finally, after several cycles, the President nodded to him.

"Sir, I have a question about the severity of this outbreak, here and in Russia," Sorenson said. "Particularly as to the options open to both countries."

"Jason, I've already responded that we're still assessing the situation," the President said smoothly. "President Putin and I are in agreement that we act vigorously, but I can't yet comment on the specific steps we'll take in our two countries."

He started to call on another reporter, but Sorenson's voice rose.

"A follow-up, Mr. President," he said, still standing.

For once, let New York be on the ball, he prayed silently.

"Mr. President, at this very moment, viewers tuned to NBC are watching videotape shot this morning in Moscow. It shows Russian helicopters releasing what appears to be nerve gas on a crowd there. These people had been cordoned off earlier by armed troops—because, we are told, a deadly disease was raging in this section of the city."

There was a sound as if an entire roomful of people had suddenly inhaled. Then the assembled journalists began to murmur, a buzz rising around the briefing room. Only Sorenson was silent, his eyes locked on the man at the lectern.

"I—I don't know that I can—"

Sorenson's voice overrode the suddenly ashen President.

"Our analysts have reviewed the videotape, Mr. President. They project that on the tape, sir, at *minimum* tens of thousands of people are being subjected to a lethal gas. Tens of thousands dead or dying, on the streets of Moscow.

"And my question, Mr. President, is this: What made the Russians decide they had to murder their own people? More to the point, sir—exactly how bad is this influenza virus?"

Chapter 16

More than two hundred specially trained members of the Kôan Chôsachô, the agency of Japan's national law enforcement responsible for public security, surrounded the walled Aum compound in the postmidnight blackness. They moved, quietly but quickly, through the light undergrowth that was, aside from the dark night, their only cover.

Group Lieutenant Hideo Hayakawa felt on his forehead the cool tang of the air that flowed from the heights of Mount Fuji. It was the only part of his body not covered by Kevlar, ballistic nylon or the heavy black twill of his assault coveralls. Even his hands were covered by tight black gloves. Unconsciously, the index finger of his right hand tapped lightly against the trigger guard of a Heckler & Koch MP5 submachine pistol strapped across his chest. Two flash-bangs—small explosive bombs designed to disorient defenders with their intensity of noise and light—were clipped to his belt.

Through his earpiece, clear as if the man were standing beside him, Hideo heard his unit commander's voice.

"Thirty seconds."

Hideo lifted his hand from his weapon and tapped twice

against the side of his head; the earpiece doubled as an induction microphone, picking up the vibrations and sending a wordless response that acknowledged the command. His left hand held the detonator, and a hair-thin wire leading from it to the puttylike substance pressed against the hinges of the compound gate.

It was not the policeman's first visit to the Kamikuishiki compound. The previous had come several years before, two days after the fanatics inside had attacked the Tokyo subway system with poison gas. It had been a night raid then, too, and Hideo remembered the way the crickets had filled the air with their ceaseless, ancient melodies.

Then as now, the police units were accompanied by biochemical-warfare experts from the Japanese military. The sight of the soldiers, whose protective gear appeared to be far more cumbersome than the body armor Hideo and his team wore, was not reassuring to the policeman. If anything, it was an unnecessary reminder of what they might indeed face in the next few minutes.

In their briefing, the Kôan Chôsachô assault teams had been told of the urgency of the situation. The Americans, they were informed, had made their request to the highest level of the Japanese government. They required all information on the Aum without delay; even more desperately, they needed information that only Aum leaders could be expected to have—particularly the person, or possibly group of persons, who might be called sensei. And they needed the information immediately.

It was not necessary to provide details of whatever dilemma the Americans faced; as professionals, the Kôan Chôsachô needed none. But they were also policemen and trained in both investigation and assessing motive. Nor had Hideo and his compatriots forgotten the incident in the Tokyo subways. Without fanfare, the more curious among them immediately began to tap into the network of mentors, protégés and other contacts that exists in every law enforcement operation.

It was not long before the exact nature of the Americans' concerns was common knowledge among the Kôan teams. This time, it was said, the Aum fanatics had attacked both the Americans and the Russians—not with poison gas, but with some kind of untreatable, incurable plague germ.

Hideo shivered. He was a brave man and valued his honor highly. But he did not relish wading into a den of religious death-seekers, to face weapons for which there was neither defense nor cure. Better to stand at a safe distance—which, for the MP5, was anything up to thirty meters—and blast away all remnants of this black-minded cult. Sensei or not.

"Ten seconds."

The voice sounded inside his skull, as if his conscience were chiding him for his attack of cowardice. It steeled him. He glanced at the others on his team, dark shadows pressed against the lighter stone wall. All professionals, all prepared to follow him to whatever waited inside.

"Three, two, one—*detonate*!"

The C-4 exploded with a noise that was somehow both sharp and flat, silencing the crickets as if a switch had been thrown. The acrid smell of pyrotechnics and scorched metal filled the night air, and the planned chaos of the attack surged forward.

Two of his men formed the vanguard, kicking past the collapsed gate and rushing across the courtyard inside. Simultaneously, another assault group appeared from the far side of the expanse, pincering with Hideo's men on the main building. There, an ornate mahogany door proved no match for the solid-slug shotgun blast that shattered the lockset. In a choreography precise in its execution, the invaders moved through a series of unlighted and unoccupied rooms. They charged down a wide corridor toward a wall of modern glass doors that opened, Hideo remembered, to a large auditorium. He skidded to a stop behind an arching free-form sculpture of heavy polished wood. From there, his submachine gun commanded both of the corridors as well as the auditorium entrance.

"Kami-Six actual," Hideo whispered, confident that the induction transmitter was picking up every word. "Main building access achieved. No resistance encountered."

His team now flanked the auditorium entrance. Hideo's second, a sergeant who had also been present on the first raid here, made an interrogative gesture with his black-gloved hand. In it he held the gray canister of a flash-bang.

Hideo shook his head once. His weapon at the ready, he spun around the statue in a crouching run. In an instant he had joined his men, flattening himself against the flanking wall. The policeman listened closely; aside from the noise of the other Kôan attack teams across the courtyard, he heard nothing.

"Kami-Six actual," he whispered. "No hostiles encountered. Entering auditorium."

He signaled to his sergeant to follow, and eased open one of the glass doors.

The stench that rose to greet him was horrendous, and unmistakable.

Mingled with it was the still-lingering, smoky perfume of a hundred candles.

Hideo risked a quick look inside, holding his breath as he did so.

A few of the larger candles, once tall as a man but now reduced to guttering stubs, still burned. They cast a flickering light, illuminating the carnage that covered the floor like a thick, uneven carpet.

Chapter 17

"They were all dead?" Alexi Malenkov's voice was carefully neutral. If it was an attempt by the Russian to mask his own turmoil—to push it aside simply in order to allow himself to function—it was done with a competence that Beck envied.

Beck nodded, also carefully professional.

"Not the flu, thank God. The Japanese police believe it was poison, a mass suicide. There were three hundred and seventeen bodies. All had been dead two, perhaps three days when the raid occurred."

"This does not help us, my friend," Alexi said. "It tells us nothing."

"At the very least, it confirms your theory about where this virus originated," Beck said.

"To confirm what we already knew is but cold comfort, Beck."

"It tells us is that the Aum felt there was a pressing need to self-destruct," Beck argued.

Alexi shrugged, and Beck saw defeat in the gesture.

"You wish to use logic on those whose actions defy it," the Russian countered. "Allow me, also. They fear the death they have unleashed—so they kill themselves?" He laughed bitterly.

"Maybe they did it to escape capture," Beck countered. "Maybe they did it to protect their last secret."

"I believe you try to convince yourself that there is still some chance, some small possibility, that we can coerce an antidote from these murderous madmen. This will not happen. Accept it. There is no antidote, no vaccine, because none was ever developed. The Aum saw no need for one. This lunatic act of self-immolation proves it."

And he's probably right, thought Beck.

He berated himself for not having foreseen it: the long trial of Asahara, the death sentence with which it had recently culminated, the final *Götterdämmerung* of the faithful themselves—all fit the traditional pattern that doomsday cults tended to follow. Beck disagreed with Alexi, but only as a matter of semantics: for the Aum, mass destruction *was* logical, simple and direct. The outside world was poised to destroy its Divine Leader, which meant that it intended to destroy Aum. For the cult, there was no recourse other than a preemptive action, and to make that action an Armageddon for all.

Alexi's voice broke into Beck's thoughts.

"And so—where does this now leave us?"

"It leaves us with Davidovich," Beck said.

"Ah, yes—the CIA's man inside the Aum," Alexi said mockingly. "Or is it the other way around? No matter. Have you now rethought your prejudice against our methods of interrogation?" He stopped abruptly. "I am sorry, Beck. At times, I speak before I think."

Beck fixed him with a level gaze. When he spoke, it was in a conversational voice that betrayed no sign of emotion.

"CIA records indicate Davidovich, described as a Russian national, was an agent-in-place here in Russia. He was covered as a journalist, Carson says. He insists that the only product Davidovich delivered was basic, low-level political and economic intelligence. Is that accurate, Alexi?"

"That is perhaps what he delivered to CIA," Alexi said. "In part. But it was not the activity in which he was engaged, either as CIA or as an Aum."

"Then what, Alexi? What was his assignment?"

"For the cultists, he was engaged as a provocateur. His instructions were to find and offer assistance to the various extremists that exist in the *Rodina,* in Russia."

"He was talent scouting," Beck said, and Alexi nodded grimly.

"I will provide you with the transcript of his interrogation. It is interesting reading. Our friend was to find in Russia those who oppose the direction our society has taken. Such people can be useful to groups like Aum, which deal in terror. We are today a turbulent nation. There is no shortage of ideologues who would embrace violence."

"Yes. Some of them with their own private armies. Like our militia movement in the States."

"We too have paramilitary organizations in Russia, my friend. They are no less crazy than your militias—and, I fear, ours are far better armed. Some of them are clearly fascists, others seek a return to socialist values. A few even wish to restore the czar."

"And the CIA?"

Alexi shrugged. "Your good associate was ordered by the CIA to report on these elements. To get close to the leadership. If possible, to become part of the movement. This he did very well. With great enthusiasm, in fact."

"And they knew he was Aum."

"Probably not," Alexi said. "Just as the Aum probably did not know he was affiliated with the CIA. But, my friend, I find it somewhat improbable that your people were unaware of his, shall we say, *religious* persuasions. I have not found CIA case officers to be totally incompetent; they certainly research the background of agents they recruit."

The Russian shook his head. "No. My belief is that your people thought that by recruiting Davidovich, they expected that they also acquired a window into this interesting little cult."

"So Carson lied," Beck said evenly. "Davidovich was providing information on Russian opposition movements, perhaps even channeling CIA assistance to them. And he was providing information, real or not, on the Aum." He looked up at the Russian, and his tone was chiding. "Unless you're lying to me now. Are you, Alexi?"

"Perhaps a little," Alexi admitted. "Old habits are hard to break. One must balance discretion against the requirements of our profession. For instance, it would be indiscreet to tell you that our people have agents in place close to your own paramilitary extremists. But of course, we do."

Beck nodded, filing away the information and wondering why it had been offered.

"And all the while, Davidovich was acting as an emissary for the Aum. I imagine he was very generous to your extremists."

"Yes, indeed," Alexi said. "He extended to them an assistance that far surpassed their own capabilities. Our friend Davidovich offered to provide them with nerve gases, which excited them greatly. And he hinted to them of even more interesting toys with which they might play."

Beck looked up. "Not this virus?"

"It is one possibility. I fear the Aum were disinclined to share the specific nature of this other plaything, even with our friend Davidovich," Alexi said. "Davidovich claims he does not know. Perhaps he is truthful in this."

"And your people were following him all the while," Beck said. "Watching and waiting."

"We waited perhaps not long enough," Alexi replied. "We took Davidovich into custody six days ago. It was a stroke of very bad luck. A day later, there was a visitor at his apartment. When he found no one at Davidovich's apartment, he knocked on the door of the building superintendent and spoke to the man who answered." Alexi snorted. "A Japanese—very polite, as they so often are to one's face. Our so-called building superintendent said he spoke abominable Russian. Very difficult to understand. It might have been because the man appeared to suffer from a bad cold." Alexi had the dark look of a man who wished he had someone to hit, hard. "Had we the wit to arrest this visitor, we might have been spared much sorrow."

Beck felt his heart beat faster.

"Now, how do you think we obtained this extensively detailed information?" Alexi's voice was mockingly professorial. "You will approve, my friend. No physical coercion was involved. Do you wish to guess?"

He waited for the briefest of moments before continuing.

"The superintendent was not the real superintendent! He was FSB, one of my oh-so-expert surveillance specialists. He made his report on this visitor—fortunately, by telephone—the day before he began to display symptoms of influenza. He died the next day."

Alexi took a deep breath; he did not look at Beck.

"You have, of course, guessed the final piece of this puzzle: Davidovich lived in Tuvelov, where the infection began."

"I want to talk to Davidovich," Beck said.

"The conversation would be a trifle one-sided, I fear. Like his fellow believers, Comrade Davidovich is no longer in a condition to discuss anything."

"You killed him?" Beck was aghast. "My God, Alexi. He could have—"

"No, my friend, though I certainly would have done so with pleasure. He saved us the effort. Last night, he did the job himself."

Chapter 18

Helena, Montana
July 22

"Provisionally, I'm going to rule it a clean shooting," said
Frank Ellis. "Under normal conditions, you'd be placed on
administrative duties pending a formal hearing." The Helena
special agent in charge looked up at April O'Connor and
eyed his subordinate steadily. "These are not normal times. I
need you on the job."

April nodded. She did not need to say anything; disclo-
sure that the Florida outbreak was a terrorist attack had galvanized the Bureau. Every available agent was called in,
pulled away from any other assignments and targeted on this
terrible new threat.

April had been filled in at the emergency midmorning
briefing, piped by video feed to all FBI field offices in
the United States. Every available agent was called in for the
event. Attendance was mandatory, as was evident from the
large number of agents who crowded into the Helena office:
financial and white-collar crime specialists, RICO task force
teams, even a number of agents pulled from deep-cover assignments. April had been painfully aware of the low buzz of
comments that had circled the room when she took a chair.
She had seen the surreptitious glances they had sent her way

and ignored them. Instead, April had donned an ice queen demeanor, narrowing her focus tightly on the FBI director's image on the oversized monitor and the procession of speakers who followed him.

Along with the others in the room, she listened with a growing sense of horror. The litany of the mortality rate, the projected spread, the lack of a viable response—all struck each agent like a physical blow. The additional updates focused on the mushrooming turmoil that was spreading its own wildfire in virtually every major city. When the teleconference was over, April walked down the hallway in a state near shock—a state mirrored on the faces of her FBI colleagues.

Now she was seated in her SAC's office and granted absolution, at least the official kind, for the previous night's tragedy. It was a relief, as well as a surprise. She had been certain she would be dismissed—transferred, at the least—and was not yet fully convinced such an action would have been unjust. Certainly, Robles's death weighed on her mind; she knew she would relive every moment for a long time. But from a professional viewpoint, she had come to grips with the killing as an accident of war. She was certain she could tough out any psychological aftereffects—without outside assistance, if possible. With it, if the Bureau insisted, as she assumed it would.

Ellis quickly disabused her of that notion. All the usual rules were off.

"Do *you* think you need a psychologist?" Ellis's voice was that of a man who did not brook fools well, or easily. "Neither do I. When this is over, we'll see if we're both right. Until then—hell, no. I need you to stay on the job you've been doing. Find Trippett. Track down this paramilitary group he's part of."

April was startled, and it showed on her face.

"You have a problem with that, O'Connor?"

"No, sir. I just assumed every agent would be working on the virus outbreak."

"That's right. You are."

The SAC pushed a thin sheaf of computer printouts across the desk to April. "Washington says there's a Japanese connection in the Florida virus. We've got one here also. The nerve gas in the warehouse—the manifest had it down as 'garden supplies—pesticide.' Shipped in by Federal Express yesterday morning, an international delivery from Kamikuishiki, in Japan. The town is headquarters for a religious cult called Aum. They're the same bunch that released nerve gas in the Tokyo subways a couple of years back."

April scanned the top sheet, a frown lining her features. "This cult is sending nerve gas to terrorists in the United States?"

"Looks like it," Ellis said. "Here's the thing: FedEx and Customs ran a search on every shipment that came out of this Kamikuishiki place and into the United States over the past six months."

"Let me guess," April said. "There were more of them."

"Yeah," Ellis said. "In addition to the container delivered yesterday morning to Columbia Falls, there was another sent to an address in upstate New York. Same size, same weight as the package that went to your warehouse."

"God, Frank," said April. "There's more of this out in New York?"

"No." Ellis smiled coldly. "We got lucky. FedEx tried to deliver yesterday morning, but nobody was around to sign. So it came back to the terminal. It was sarin, the same kind of nerve gas we found here."

"New York pick up the addressee?"

The SAC shook his head. "Alias. Probably used the foyer scam."

April nodded. It was a tactic common to credit card crimes. The perp uses stolen card numbers to make a purchase by phone, gives the number of an apartment building, and pays extra for next-day delivery. By ten o'clock, he is waiting in the foyer when the delivery arrives—to all appearances just one more overeager consumer.

"Here's the bad news," Ellis said. "Those two were only the most recent deliveries. Ten days ago, both addresses took receipt of another shipment. Manifest said it was food products, canned soup."

"We have any ideas what was really in there?" April asked.

"All we know about is the boxes it came in," Ellis said. "They were bigger, April. And heavier."

He straightened in his chair, assuming an almost formal posture.

"Start looking for Orin Trippett," Ellis said. "This Mountain Warrior bunch he's involved with had M-16s from the National Guard break-in. Trippett himself gets sent nerve gas from some crazy religious cult—the same one that may have let loose germ warfare on us. The thought of what else he may be carrying around now scares the hell out of me."

April stood. "Who do I work with, Frank?"

"Start solo. I'm trying to find you some help," Ellis said. "I'm working with Andi Wheelwright—used to be Bureau, now she's something or other with National Security. Washington's got her coordinating the security side of all this. She wants to send out a guy, an expert on terrorist groups, biological warfare. A professor—but apparently he used to work with the intelligence people."

"He's a spook?" April asked.

"Odds are good." Ellis's face twisted unpleasantly. "He's on his way back from that god-awful mess in Russia. I guess he was helping them, too."

April matched his expression.

"If that was his idea of help," she said, "we don't need him."

Chapter 19

Larry Krewell slumped in the borrowed chair that sat behind the borrowed desk in an office normally reserved for the use of visiting dignitaries. Health and Human Services was a typical government bureaucracy, housed in a typical government building built and furnished to typical government specifications.

Translated, that meant it possessed an empty ambiance that was so blandly regimented, so sterile as to be disorienting to anyone unaccustomed to such surroundings. Krewell, at heart an unrepentant elitist, firmly believed that it contributed heavily to brain rot; he attributed the current state of American democracy to the absence of individuality every bureaucracy represented.

Today, he was certain that he was its most recent victim. He felt drained, helpless and worse: useless.

Krewell had considered relocating his office to Fort Detrick, or even returning to Atlanta; in both locations, teams of research specialists were frantically working to dissect and decode the carefully convoluted secrets someone had built into H1N1-Florida. In either location, he would have felt closer to the efforts being made than he did here, in his borrowed HHS office.

He turned to the computer and his fingers tapped out an access code.

Thanks to the miracle of modern electronics, he was able to track everything that was happening across the country, as well as the larger part of the world. In the former, there was a firestorm of bad news, tempered only by a weak glimmer of good.

The CDC teams in Florida reported the present death toll at one hundred and forty-six, with current confirmed cases now numbering almost two thousand persons. More than three times that many were confined under armed guard—these persons still asymptomatic, but determined to have been in close contact with the infected. Soon there would be too many to guard, and at that point Krewell knew that all hell would break loose.

On the computer, Krewell called up the outbreak graphic, surveying the numbers that flashed above the communities. About half of the total caseload was in or around Fort Walton, though the contagion had now spread to a half-dozen surrounding communities in Northwest Florida. Panama City, fifty miles to the east, now reported twenty-three deaths due to the virus. Worse, three additional flu cases had been found outside the state—two in Mobile, the other in southern Georgia. The borders of the now-misnamed Florida Quarantine Region had been moved back accordingly.

He selected another item from the screen's menu, and a list of the latest reports from the medical research staffs appeared.

At present, there was no progress on vaccine development, despite the herculean efforts under way.

And there was one new, chilling report: at Johns Hopkins, virologists studying H1N1-Florida had theorized that it had the potential to cross species—most likely to infect swine, but possibly also able to spread to avian species.

If accurate, it was a nightmare scenario: even if by some miracle they could contain the current outbreak in the south, the virus could become endemic in pigs and birds. One could, conceivably, slaughter every pig in North America. But what did you do about billions of birds, forming a constantly moving reservoir of contagion?

There's no shortage of bad news, Krewell thought, though to his mind it still failed to encompass the full scope of the developing catastrophe.

The good news was that, as yet, no cases of the killer influenza had been reported elsewhere in the country.

As yet, Krewell repeated silently. It was inevitable, only a matter of time. Flu respected no boundaries, natural or manmade. *But if we can slow it down, even for a few days—well, who the hell knows?*

With the singular exception of the Russian Federation, the situation was the same elsewhere in the world. Thus far, no flu cases had been found.

Uniformly, the governments involved were determined to keep it that way, by any means necessary.

Virtually all international travel had come to a halt that was as sudden as it was complete. Taking their cue from the American action, foreign governments severely restricted civilian travel inside their borders at the same time they slammed shut all the doors into their countries. As an island, England drew into itself and halted all incoming travelers, including their own citizens returning from abroad. Stung, the Irish quickly followed suit.

In most countries, police preemptively scoured their databases to identify any persons whose travels had taken them to Russia or the U.S. within the past two weeks. These persons were visited by medical personnel, usually accompanied by armed escorts. Entire families were quarantined or, in some instances, removed to isolation facilities.

In some cases, enforcement was even more draconian: in one of the Balkan states, Krewell read, unconfirmed reports said that guards had opened fire on a caravan of Roma that had attempted, as was their routine, to slip across the border. According to rumors that had reached the embassy, there had been no survivors among the gypsy band.

Russia was, officially and ominously, silent. Since NBC had aired the videotape of the massacre, virtually every news organ in the world had broadcast pirated copies; newspapers printed stop-action frames, blurry in a way that did nothing to mask the horror. The Russian response, both to the world and to its own population, had been—nothing.

Krewell knew that Putin had been in contact with the President before the massacre. Presumably, he was still— but Krewell had as yet heard nothing about whether the mass killing had accomplished its mission, even as a stopgap measure. Had Putin burned out the contagion, or were new cases even now spreading elsewhere in Moscow and the rest of the country? There was simply no information.

And that may well mean the Russians don't even know themselves.

Krewell shook his head.

The most surprising aspect of the entire situation was the fact that this virus was mimicking a natural outbreak. The flu had appeared in only two locations: Florida and Moscow. In a biological attack, which this surely was, one would expect outbreaks of the disease to occur almost simultaneously in multiple, probably widespread locations.

That was indeed puzzling, and Krewell frowned as he contemplated.

What are we missing? he wondered, not for the first time.

Word of the Aum mass suicide had been bitter news to all of them, but it had hit Larry Krewell particularly hard. Krewell had not realized how much he had counted on their ultimate rationality, on the hope that nobody would unleash a certain death without first securing a way to save themselves.

The realization there would be no answers from the Aum

had shaken him profoundly. He had been unable to keep it from his voice when Beck Casey, seeking instructions, had called from Moscow on the satellite phone.

"Come home," Krewell had told him. "Billy Carson wants you back here. You'll probably end up advising on the riots. They want to develop a strategy they can use while the cities burn. Right now, the only idea anybody has is to hand out matches while we wait for the epidemic to spread."

"What do you mean?"

The realization that he had said too much came to Krewell at the same time he realized he did not care that he had.

"The Russian solution, Beck. The President is being told that he has to sacrifice Florida—that it's the only way to buy time, to come up with a viable plan to save the rest of the country. With every new case that gets reported down there, more people in D.C. agree. And we're getting a *lot* of new cases now."

Krewell laughed bitterly. "Hell of a note, ol' buddy. All that's left is for you to come home and help us play Nero. Say, you know how to play the fiddle?"

There was a silence on the line for a long moment.

"Good luck, Larry."

"You too, Beck. You too."

The line went silent, dead.

Larry Krewell was not a religious man. But at that moment, he felt an urge to pray.

And did.

Chapter 20

The way Dickie Trippett saw it, back when he first considered biowar against the United States, the most difficult part of the mission was going to be purely technical—that is, an overly complicated task that involved calculating wind direction and velocity, the optimal height of the release, even the relative humidity of the air itself. And these were only a few of the factors that, his helpful Japanese teacher had cautioned, would influence the dispersion of the biological agent. Learn, Anji had counseled the American; only then would the bioweapon be delivered to him.

The condition for delivery had been an unhappy surprise for Dickie. His original plan had been to select a suitable place and time—say, upwind of Rockefeller Center a few minutes past noon—open the sealed containers and shake them empty. To discover that considerably more preparation was required for effective dispersal of this particular weapon . . . To Dickie, it was very disheartening.

It's like getting a damn electric guitar for Christmas, he thought, finding a simile in his own soured experience. *Yeah—that's when they tell you that you gotta take lessons.* In his own case, the unforeseen prerequisite had sharply curtailed his musical career: he had attended the guitar class two or three times, learning a few basic chords before boredom drove him away.

The pattern was not much different with the bioweapon, though Anji's dogged persistence made it seem longer. Dickie was not a details sort of guy.

In the eyes of the man from Japan, the American failed to appreciate the sheer elegance of the weapon itself—a form of anthrax, he had told Dickie, deadly to those who breathe the spores but incapable of human-to-human transmission. The perfect weapon for the oppressed, the Japanese had termed it—but only if it is used wisely. Patiently, he explained to Dickie that one does not merely scatter such a material artlessly. That might kill only thousands, whereas a more scientific approach could take a toll tenfold higher.

The more Anji pressed, the more Dickie resisted. Mathematics had never been his strong suit, and even with the aid of the calculator his visitor had thoughtfully provided, Dickie found it a tedious process indeed. But Anji had persevered. Only when he was satisfied that Dickie had mastered at least the rudiments of basic biowarfare had he relented, assuring his student that it was all child's play from there.

Child's play. Uh-huh.— Dickie threw up his hands in frustration.

Ever since that asshole in Washington had gone on TV, the hardest aspect of the mission suddenly had become simply *getting* to the target area. The executive order had literally closed down the majority of transportation options. For the Empire State Legionnaires, most of whom were located far enough upstate to place Canada closer to them than Manhattan, it posed a sudden, critical logistical problem.

Dickie felt the urge to hit someone, anyone.

He looked at the three metal containers in the nylon athletic bag on the seat beside him. The Japs were damn clever, Dickie had to admit it. The canisters even looked like soup cans, he thought, even to the red-and-gold label with "Campbell's" in ornate letters and the pull-tab, peel-back tops. Easy to carry, easy to use, in a handy soup-for-one size that belied their lethal potential.

Three fuckin' cans, he raged internally. *More than enough to fuckin' annihilate every kike, nigger, spic, rag-head*— Mentally, he sputtered to a halt, frustration blocking his otherwise impressive capacity for racial and religious invective. *And take down every faggot New York yuppie asshole along with 'em, too.*

Except the trains were stopped and the airports shut down, almost completely. The restriction on gasoline purchases—a deviously clever ploy, Dickie had to admit—created more than the obvious problem, too. You could always steal gas from somewhere, and usually a vehicle to go with it. But for Dickie's plan, the worst practical impact of the fuel restrictions was to grossly reduce traffic volume on the highways leading to and from the Big Apple.

The law was taking advantage of the situation in a big way: on the radio, Dickie had already heard that roadblocks were being manned by police, sometimes backed by troops. Ostensibly, it was to screen for potential flu carriers.

Dickie snorted out loud. *Flu,* Dickie told himself bitterly, *as if that wasn't some kind of damn government ploy, too.* He was not surprised; the government couldn't afford to let people know that the revolution had finally begun.

He had expected some kind of government disinformation when the attacks began. His Japanese mentor had warned him that, when the patriots struck, the federals would devise some lie as an excuse for despotic oppression against them. The militia leader had no doubt the government was using the opportunity to detain or search cars and occupants and confiscate whatever it might find.

So far, Dickie had been lucky, motoring along in his Ford pickup at just under the legal limit. Figuring the majority of the attention would be on interstate routes, he had stuck as much as possible to the secondary roads that wound south-

ward toward New York City. At first, in the rural upstate region, that had not been difficult. He had a good set of USGS
charts and a hand-held global positioning system receiver
that gave him a constant update on his location. His progress
was slow, but relatively steady.

Dickie skirted population centers like Syracuse, where he
expected the authorities to give a high level of scrutiny to
anything moving on the road. It was a good strategy. Dickie
had been stopped only once, by a county deputy who had
been manning a crossroads blockade west of Middletown.
With a suitably abashed smile, Dickie had shown the policeman his license and insurance cards; his other hand—the
one holding the nine-millimeter Taurus automatic—was out
of sight low against the door. It helped that the deputy stood
at arm's length, and declined to touch Dickie's ID. Without
comment, the deputy had accepted Dickie's cover story of
working an upstate construction job and rushing home to a
wife worried about the flu scare.

Dickie found himself enjoying the trip: the rolling coun-
tryside, dotted with farmhouses that looked abandoned, and
sometimes should have been; the almost-empty two-lane
highways that curved and climbed over the wooded Alleghenies; even the increasingly industrialized landscape that
began immediately after the foothills flattened. It had given
him a good feeling to see what he considered the "real"
America, and he found himself humming along to the tunes
on his radio.

That is, until he had neared the Jersey shore. Here, even
the sparse traffic had gradually slowed and thickened; before
Dickie fully realized it, he found himself inching along in an
improbable gridlock.

He flipped through the dial until he found an all-news
radio station. It was as bad as he feared: the Holland and Lincoln tunnels, the bridges and even the ferries—all were
closed. Decisively so, according to the newscast: at each, the
imposing bulk of a buttoned-up Abrams tank straddled the

traffic lanes. One particularly breathless reporter noted the sandbagged automatic weapons positioned to support the flanks; she waxed poetic about the insectlike visages of exposure-suited troopers and the perverse grace of the helicopter gunships that flitted like lethal dragonflies overhead.

New York was under martial law and effectively quarantined.

It could have been music to Dickie's ears—Babylon was crippled, bleeding—had it not underscored one unimpeachable truth: the doors had all been slammed closed and nailed shut, with Dickie and his anthrax on the outside.

He worked his way farther south, through Hoboken. On the other side of an expanse of cocoa-colored water, the New York skyline was a gray range of craggy man-made peaks. It would have been a spectacular vista, for one more appreciative.

Briefly, Dickie considered the feasibility of attacking New York City from his location across the bay. No. Even if the wind direction was right, he could never find a place high enough. Without a lofty starting point, particularly at this kind of distance, the majority of the spores—conceivably, Anji had warned, *all* of them—would merely settle onto the intervening water.

It would be, Dickie decided, a criminal waste of the weapon's potential.

He could, of course, find an acceptable place and pop the top right here in New Jersey. Anthrax was decidedly democratic and cared not a bit whether the lungs where it would spawn inhaled the aromatic Jersey air or the sour tang of a Big Apple alley.

But the more Dickie pondered it, the more the idea seemed to him unworthy—even shameful. Normally, he would have had no qualms about inflicting a plague on the Garden State, starting with the grittier industrial sections. It was a job somebody would have to get to anyway, sooner or later. Another idea was that he could keep driving south;

Philadelphia, or perhaps even Washington, might prove a more accessible target.

But now, with the New York skyline seemingly close enough to touch, anything less felt like a cop-out, the worst kind of compromise.

He stared at the wall of towering structures for several moments, a modern-day Moses barred from his promised land.

Finally, after what seemed an interminable period, Dickie pulled off the turnpike and found a place where he could stop and consider his situation. In the foreground, the brown water was marked by whitecaps from a freshening sea breeze. It rocked the small forest of masts that jutted like leafless saplings above the low buildings at the waterfront before him, raising a chorus of clanking halyards that to a less preoccupied ear might have sounded musical. To Dickie, trying to think through his dilemma, they just sounded irritating, just sounded like a bunch of fuckin'—

Boats. Of course.

It was a converted cabin cruiser reconfigured as a fisherman, complete with a tuna tower made of welded aluminum tubing. The name *Corazón* was hand lettered across the stern, in paint that once had been the color of fresh blood.

Eddie, *Corazón*'s owner and at twenty-two the elder of the two brothers aboard, squinted up at the man standing on the pier. It was tempting: with this stupid flu scare, nobody was going to be out charter fishing for a while. But he did not like the look of this one, either—the words he spoke were a little too glib, the smile a little too slick. He knew no newspaper people, but this person clearly did not fit Eddie's notions of one.

Besides, what kind of man asks to be taken to a place where things were being done—very serious things, indeed—to keep people out?

"I dunno, man," he said, a trace of San Juan accenting the words. "Coast Guard was pretty clear about it. They don't want nobody crossing over to the city, or coming out of it."

"C'mon. Five hundred bucks," Dickie said, an encouraging smile on his features. *Fuckin' spic's not going for it,* he realized.

He showed Eddie a cheap plastic camera he had dug from his glove compartment. "Look—how's this instead? You just take me over to where I can get a couple good pictures for the newspaper. Then we're back here. No harm, no foul. Whaddaya say?"

"Six hundred." It was the younger brother, Tomás. He was seventeen, lean and fit, and on his shoulder an ornate tattoo of a unicorn cantered sinuously as he coiled a length of line. "Six hundred, cash up front, you got yourself a boat ride."

Dickie pretended to consider the offer. It was more than he had in his wallet. But he did not intend the transaction to be any more than temporary in nature.

"Six hundred," he said. "Half now, half when we get back. Deal?"

He looked down at Eddie, who nodded. Tomás broke into a wide smile.

"Let's go out on the salt, *amigo.*"

They were less than a football field's length from the narrow shoreline of Battery Park, beneath the towering mass of concrete crags and glittering glass of the city's skyline. On shore, a crowd of perhaps a hundred had formed, a testimony to the ineffectiveness of the prohibition against public gatherings. It had watched *Corazón*'s approach; now it was a moving, gesturing mass. Some of its members shouted words that were lost in the stiff sea breeze and the crash of waves that flung themselves headlong against *Corazón*'s hull, atomizing into high-flying spray.

"I guess they don't want us here." Eddie grinned, his right hand expertly jogging the throttle to keep the craft in position against the surging currents. "Either that, or they want us to get *them* the hell out of New York, eh?"

They had left the Jersey shore, moving in ∟ wide circle that skirted Staten Island before curling north, their speed slowed to a crawl to minimize any wake that might be spotted by the helicopters that periodically flitted across the horizon.

To port was the Statue of Liberty, torch high in what was, given the circumstances, an ironic beckon. To starboard was Brooklyn; Dickie was certain he did not want to land there. Behind the cruiser was an expanse of open bay that merged into the Atlantic, its cooler air rushing unimpeded from the south toward the upward convection of the warmer land.

Now the bow of *Corazón* pointed directly at the jutting point of lower Manhattan. Here, the swirl of currents from the Hudson River tumbled headlong into the stiffening winds from the south. Without the wind shadow of the shore as a buffer, *Corazón* danced with the stiffening breeze in a reckless tango.

"Take it in closer," Dickie said. "I want to get a tighter shot."

The two brothers exchanged glances.

"Can't do it, man," Eddie said. "We ain't supposed to be here at all. Cops get our hull number, we could lose the boat."

"I'm paying to get close to the action, friend."

"You get your pictures from here, okay?"

"Closer," Dickie insisted. "Newspaper'll pay if anything happens."

"Bullshit." Tomás spoke up. His voice, skeptical before, was now plainly mocking. "Wha'chu up to, anyway? You ain't no newspaper—not with that piece'a shit camera." The younger sailor stood easily in the cockpit, shifting his balance effortlessly as the swells lifted and dropped the craft. It was an intentionally casual posture, but from a lanyard around his left wrist a stubby fish billy dangled, its sweet spot stained dark with dried fish blood.

Uh-oh, Dickie thought. *Little bro wants to show off his cojones.*

"Chill out, man," he told Tomás. "I write the fuckin' story, then I sell it to the paper. They pay more if I get pictures." Dickie's annoyance was rising steadily, but he made an effort to sound reasonable. "Look, I'll even put your name in it. You like that? Get fuckin' famous? All you gotta do is take me a little closer to shore."

He shot a quick look at Eddie. The older brother was still at the controls. But something in his attitude had changed too; a message had passed between the two brothers, and Dickie had no doubt that the content involved him.

Time to stop dickin' around with these two, he decided.

"Look—you want a bonus, right? Hey, no fuckin' problem. Whatddya say to a little something extra, right now?"

He smiled broadly, ingratiatingly, and reached under the shirt he wore untucked over his pants.

Tomás winked at his brother, and grinned.

Then Dickie's hand emerged, and the smile faded on the younger man's lips. He opened his mouth to speak just as Dickie fired, a single shot that took Tomás high in the forehead and pitched him hard over the side as if he had been thrown. There was a heavy splash that Dickie heard rather than saw as he turned toward the other brother.

Eddie had not moved, except for his head. He stared first at where Tomás had stood an instant before, then swiveled to the man who had killed him. On his face was an expression that to Dickie looked more indignant than shocked.

Before Eddie could say anything, Dickie spoke.

"You know," Dickie told him conversationally, "it don't look so hard. I think I'll drive the fuckin' boat now." He pulled the trigger once, then again.

It was not as easy as Eddie had made it look. Without a skillful hand on her controls, *Corazón* grew balky and willful.

As Dickie knelt beside Eddie's body to retrieve his three

hundred dollars, she swung about on her stern, then wallowed wildly as she came crosswise to the waves. It almost knocked Dickie to the deck. He clutched at the steering post while Eddie's corpse slid across the cockpit. It thudded against the gunwale, a red streak marking its path.

Dickie clawed himself upright. When he arose, he found the craft significantly closer to the shore than it had been only a few moments before. He was near enough to easily make out individuals, some of whom were moving in his direction. Dickie had no doubt that his shots had been easily heard by those on shore, and some had probably seen Tomás go overboard. It might be only a matter of minutes before one or another of them decided, martial law or not, to try for the good citizenship merit badge.

It was time to go and find another place to enter New York.

Gingerly, he advanced the two large chrome levers on the console. Immediately, the engines that had been bubbling in idle deepened their volume. *Corazón* settled at the stern, digging in and moving forward.

A wave, its strength multiplied by the increased speed, foamed into the boat's bow with a hard blow, staggering Dickie. He had the bare presence of mind to turn the wheel to the right, into the sea, only to have *Corazón* nose deeply into an oncoming breaker.

The craft shuddered, pitching forward and throwing Dickie painfully into the wheel. Simultaneously, a storage locker near the cockpit door flew open. Amid the fish gaffs, mops and boat hooks that crash-bounced to the fiberglass deck was the athletic bag he had stowed there, the one containing three containers of anthrax spores. It skidded across the cockpit sole, finally coming to rest against Eddie's inert form.

"Shit!" Dickie wrestled with the unfamiliar controls, realizing that the boat was almost into the surf line.

Less than twenty yards away was the crowd, some of the

more foolhardy among them even venturing out onto the jagged concrete blocks that took the shuddering force of the crashing waves. One person, his arm locked around a wooden piling that disappeared from sight with every breaker, was only a few yards away from touching the side of the insanely pitching boat.

The bag, and the anthrax, knocked and rolled against Eddie's lifeless body, out of Dickie's reach. Still at the boat's wheel, he cut it hard away from the beach and the bow shouldered hard against the now-white surf.

Too slowly. Now more of the crowd had clambered down the slope of the rip-rapped shoreline, some shouting what could have been warnings or threats. The latter, Dickie had no doubt: he was certain they intended to swarm on board, whether to seize the boat or to wreak some vigilante justice.

For an instant, he had an image of being pulled away from the wheel, beaten and kicked, thrown into the churning waters to drown.

Near panic, Dickie reached under his shirt, his fingers clawing at the butt of the heavy Taurus automatic, clearing it just as the boat hit a deep wave trough and bounced, hard and viciously. The black automatic slipped from his grip, skidding out of sight under the bench seat.

He bellowed in anger and fear; no longer tentative, his hand slapped hard at the throttle quadrant.

Immediately, the engines roared, belching black exhaust as *Corazón* muscled itself from under the punishing seas. The boat pounded ahead for several seconds before Dickie looked toward the stern. He was out of range, safe for the moment from both the jagged lee shore and the New Yorkers.

"You crazy fuckheads!" Dickie Trippett screamed at them, his rage and the residual fear making his voice break like that of an adolescent. "You—" He found himself unable to speak. He looked furiously around the cockpit sole, intending for a moment to recover his pistol and empty it at the mass of humanity.

At that moment another wave hit *Corazón*, rocking the boat madly and sending the half-opened athletic bag skidding within Dickie's reach.

If he momentarily thought of all Anji's patient instruction, he gave no outward sign.

The wind was blowing inland, toward the objects of his rage.

"Hey, all of you!" he shouted. "Breathe deep, you motherfuckers!"

Trippett peeled back the tin disk that sealed the metal can that held the light, dusty power he had been told to expect inside.

Instead, the can hissed loudly in his hand.

For the briefest part of an instant, he felt a cool moistness on his face that evaporated immediately in the wind. Startled, Dickie dropped the canister to the deck, where it sprayed its contents for a moment more.

"What the fuck—" He stared at the red-and-white container as it rolled with the pitching of the boat.

Unseen, the atomized particles rode the wind—ethereal as they spread upward and outward. Some certainly drifted harmlessly onto the ocean. But much of it would hang in the air for a long time, weightless, moving with the salty smells of the ocean through the crowd.

Even beyond.

In that moment, Dickie understood.

At that instant he heard the helicopter, overhead and closing fast.

Chapter 21

12,000 Feet over Chesapeake Bay
July 22

Beck Casey had long since lost track of how many time zones he had circumscribed in the past two days.

By now, the sense of exclusivity that came from having a forty-eight-million-dollar taxi at his disposal was long gone. In its place rode the mother of all jet-lag headaches, which not even the pure oxygen he was breathing could burn through. Despite the discomfort, he had slept most of the way back from Moscow deeply and profoundly, even missing two of the F-15's in-flight refuelings. There had been five on the return leg, reflecting the headwinds that are routine in east-to-west transatlantic flight.

Still, he snapped to consciousness when Frankel's voice crackled in his earphones.

"Sorry to wake you, Dr. Casey. We're ten minutes out of Andrews AFB, and it looks like we part company when we land."

"Don't take this the wrong way," Casey said, wondering when sensation might return to his feet, "but if I never fly again, it will be too soon."

Frankel chuckled, a deep baritone rumble over the intercom.

"Sorry to hear that, 'cause it looks like you won't be on the ground long. You're heading out to Montana, Doctor."

"Montana?" Beck repeated, wondering if he had heard Frankel correctly. "Why would I want to go to Montana?"

"I was hoping you could tell me, Dr. Casey," Frankel replied. "Got the word while you were back there sawing z's. Sorry. I'm just the messenger here."

Beck's inner ear felt the F-15 tip forward for the descent.

"Tray in the upright position, please. And on behalf of your flight crew, thank you for flying Eagle Air."

Andi Wheelwright was waiting when the fighter eased to a stop at the ready-line in front of the airfield hangar. She waited while the ground crew disentangled Beck, relieved him of the flight equipment and deposited him on the tarmac. When she approached, Beck was eyeing a nearby Learjet with CDC markings.

She grinned at the expression on his face. Before he could speak, she did.

"We have a lead in Montana, Beck," she said. "Local militia there received a shipment of sarin, sent from Japan. That's confirmed, and it's one more finger pointing at your Aum. FBI field office says there's evidence of another package that we suspect may contain something even worse."

Beck frowned. "What am I supposed to do in Montana?"

"You're an expert in biological terrorism, or used to be," Andi said. "Work with the local Bureau agents. If there's one band of crazies with this stuff, there may be others; we may be facing biological attacks in a multitude of locations around the country. Advise, observe, assist. Maybe it will help us anticipate what these bastards might do next."

"If they're playing with this virus," Beck said, "what they'll do next is die."

"These militia people may be looney-toons politically, but they're not usually suicidal," Andi said. "If there's any chance they were provided a vaccine, or some immune factor—"

She shrugged, trying to put optimism into the gesture.

"Again, why me?"

Andi made her voice exasperated. "Because Billy Carson said so, how's that? Maybe he thinks your finely honed mind—pardon me while I salute—might be of more use there than sitting in a D.C. bunker."

"I'm not an investigator," Beck insisted.

"Well, I am," Andi shot back. "And I'm ordered to sit behind a desk at Health and Human Services while the world goes up in flames. Count your blessings and shut up. You take off when the Learjet's been refueled."

While Andi left to check the flight crew status, Beck turned to more mundane tasks. As he sat in the spartan passengers' lounge, he pulled from his computer bag the satellite phone Billy Carson had ordered issued to him, what seemed like a long time before.

There were no messages on his apartment answering machine—not particularly unusual, though Katie usually called once or twice a week, just to talk. *Summertime,* Beck thought. *Or maybe a new boyfriend's keeping her time filled.*

He checked his watch; it was late, but with the new semester looming, the college office kept long hours. Beck direct-dialed the office he had been provided at the University of Chicago. Instead of the voice-mail recording he expected, a crisply efficient human answered.

"History department, Ms. Tercella. How may I help you?"

"This is Dr. Casey—*Beck* Casey? I'm a guest lecturer for the semester."

As always, he felt the usual vague embarrassment; visiting faculty were academia's transients, and dealing with the permanent staff at most universities was uncomfortable at best. Beck had become accustomed to always being the new kid on the block, the one that more established members of any given academic community eyed quizzically, neither knowing his name nor appearing particularly inclined to learn it.

There was a pause of perhaps ten seconds, during which time Beck envisioned the secretary scrolling through the computerized faculty list to confirm his existence.

"Yes. Dr. Casey. How may I help you?"

"I can't seem to connect to my voice mail," he said apologetically. "I don't expect any messages, but—"

"That's because you have not yet been activated, Dr. Casey. I see here that you have neglected to return the office registration forms you were provided."

"I've been out of town," he began, "but I promise—"

"One moment, Dr. Casey."

He waited on hold, listening to Ravel's *Bolero* build through its second orgasmic movement, until she returned to the line.

"Since your office voice mail has not been activated, we have had to take your messages here, Dr. Casey. By hand." Her voice was accusatory, chiding.

"I'm sorry."

"Yes. You have two messages, both of which were received yesterday afternoon. Both of them are from the same individual. A Ms. Stepanovich."

Beck felt his stomach drop. One message from Deborah might be anything; two in the space of a single afternoon signaled potential cataclysm.

"Dr. Casey?" The voice was impatient. "I said, do you have something to write with?"

"Yes. Please go ahead."

"Message one: 'Please call me immediately.' Time-stamped at 1:18 P.M." The voice was openly disapproving now. "Message two, 2:07 P.M. 'Tell him his daughter is missing, and he must call me immediately.' Do you need the number, Dr. Casey?"

He clicked off without responding, and looked up to see Andi Wheelwright looking at him curiously.

"It's my daughter," Beck said, his mind churning. "Her mother says she's missing."

He stopped, frowning at the expression that suddenly appeared on Andi's face.

"We should talk about her," Andi said. "About Katie, I mean."

He called Deborah's numbers, both home and office, while Andi stood at his shoulder, voicing quiet objections.

"No answer," Beck said, only partly to the woman beside him. "What's the flying time to get down there?"

"There is no commercial air traffic in or out of Florida," Andi reminded him, grateful that Beck was once more addressing comments to her directly. "And don't start thinking you could get into Fort Walton, anyway. Not without official sanction. I'm sorry, Beck. Montgomery is as close as they'll let anybody get."

He nodded. On the map he had examined, Montgomery, Alabama, was perhaps one hundred fifty miles north of the Gulf Coast; there was no direct interstate route to Fort Walton Beach, which in the current circumstances was probably fortunate for the Alabama capital. He had traced down the various primary routes and two-lane blacktops that spiderwebbed southward from Montgomery.

Andi read his mind.

"Use your head, Beck. They're not at the motel anymore, and there's been no activity on the credit cards we know the girls have. They may not even *be* in Florida anymore."

"If you think I'm going to play spy in Montana when my only child is—"

"We've put out an urgent request to all our CDC teams in the Quarantine Region. They have Katie's photo and the names of all three girls. You want to locate her, that's the only way to do it."

"Do you know where Deborah is?" He did not turn to look at her.

"We've confirmed she is still in the Arlington area, Beck. We've monitored several phone calls she's made today. There's no reason to believe she even knows Katie has been in Florida. And as long as Deborah stays in Virginia, she'll be as safe as anyone else."

"Thank you. I appreciate all your . . . *efforts.*"

"Damn it, Beck! I'm sorry we—I—kept you in the dark about your daughter. But you know as well as anybody what it's like in there right now. If I had told you, you'd have done just what you're thinking about doing now. And that won't do Katie, or anybody else, any good."

"Don't," Beck said with heat. "Don't pretend you care about my daughter, or anything else that wasn't in your case orders."

"I made a decision, Beck."

"What does that mean, Andi?"

She kept her eyes locked on the terminal window; outside, the CDC aircraft waited.

"You're a valuable asset. During this emergency, we need your skills, the things you know how to do. Don't be so eager to go wandering around in a contagion zone."

"My daughter is more important than—"

"Than working to stop this plague?" Andi's voice was hard. "Use your head, if you still can. Even if you find Katie in that madhouse down there, what happens next? *There's no cure for this disease, damn it!* What does that mean, Beck? Think!"

In her peripheral vision, she could see the impact her words had on her companion. But her next words were still anything but sympathetic.

"I want us to save Katie, and all the other Katies out there. I just think you might prefer not to die foolishly trying."

"I've done enough for my country, for too many years," Beck said, his voice tight. "Now it's time to think about—"

"Unless this virus is stopped damn soon, it will keep spreading," Andi interrupted. "Your daughter—and millions of other daughters; the whole country, Beck, maybe the whole damn *world*—in all likelihood will be dead. Within ten days, maybe less."

Beck stared at Andi for a long moment. Then, with a violence that startled her, Beck Casey spun away; his fist hammered against the wall, leaving a pockmark deep in the plasterboard. As she watched, Andi saw him slump as if all strength had drained from his limbs. He leaned his forehead against the wall, his eyes shut tight.

She resisted the impulse to speak, waiting.

"What do you expect me to do?" Beck said through gritted teeth.

"Go to Montana," Andi said, her words level and without emotion. "Get us whatever information there is, Beck. It's all you can do right now."

Chapter 22

The football stadium was a scene that would have rivaled the best of Dante, or perhaps the worst; certainly, it was as close to the lowest circle of hell as Carol had ever imagined.

Across the expanse of summer-burned grass, huge tents had been erected; their sidewalls were rolled high for ventilation, leaving the rows of cots open to view. All were occupied, save for those only recently vacated by one of the increasing number who no longer required it. These cots then quickly refilled, the process not unlike some perverse assembly line.

Had she the strength or the leisure, Carol Mayer would have been appalled. As it was, she merely filed it deep in her subconscious, displaying only the absent demeanor of those preoccupied with more pressing matters.

They were dying at a steady pace, almost like the workings of a clock. Carol wondered when she would become numbed to it all. She hoped it would be soon.

Carol wiped the perspiration from her forehead. The heat rose steadily throughout the day, but aside from the thundershower that rumbled through almost every afternoon during the summer months, the weather, at least, was cooperating. It was a small mercy, and one that was noticed only vaguely by the majority of those whom the virus had felled.

She was tired—*no, exhausted,* she corrected herself.

Aside from herself, there were only a relative handful of health-care personnel attending almost four hundred desperately ill patients. This, despite the presence inside the stadium of a dozen exposure-suited physicians from Ray Porter's CDC contingent. They moved about purposefully, but their activities were focused not on treatment; rather, they concentrated solely on the larger picture of analyzing the viral outbreak with an eye to containment strategies. Once Carol had even buttonholed Porter and demanded he order his team to help; Porter had listened, curtly refused and moved on.

What help Carol did have came from a surprising source: the two teenage girls who had carried their friend into the Rossini-Evans Clinic.

She looked around for the two volunteers and spotted them working in the semishade of the large canvas tent fly that shielded a block of filled cots.

Right now, Carol noted, the one called Katie was gamely holding the shoulders of a thickset black man. He was convulsing, vomiting violently into a stainless steel pannier being held by her friend, Jay-something.

The three teenage girls had been the last patients to come to the clinic; the one who had presented with acute symptoms had been, Carol knew immediately, beyond hope. But the other two had refused to leave her with the CDC team, fought off the suggestion they go anywhere but with their friend. Finally, all three had been ordered transported to the Fort Walton Beach High School football stadium.

Almost as an afterthought, Ray Porter had ordered Carol along.

It was just as well: throughout the morning, electrical power had become fitful and petulant. Then it had died completely, and did not return. As a medical facility, the clinic had been summarily shuttered.

It was a short trip to the stadium, scarcely half a mile. But to those who traveled it, the journey took them into a different, terrifying universe. There, several hundred of the most critically ill victims had been sent.

The sick girl—*Carly Holmes was her name,* Carol remembered suddenly, *just a seventeen-year-old girl who had the bad fortune to vacation in a plague zone*—was in agonal convulsions when she was carried to the van. When the spacesuited soldiers lifted the stretcher into fittings that locked it to slots in the floor, Carly's limbs began to flail; to the uninitiated, it appeared as if she were fending off an assault by unseen demons.

It took a determined effort on Carol's part—the soldiers had pulled back, though whether in shock from the violence of the young girl's seizure or in simple resignation, the physician could not tell—to secure the nylon restraints around Carly's arms and legs. It did little good; Carly's entire body was now convulsing madly, thrashing inside the straps. Her eyes were open wide, and her teeth gnashed and clacked as her jaw muscles went into spasm.

"What's happening?" J. L. had screamed. "What's happening to Carly?"

Before Carol could answer, Carly's body arched bowlike inside the embrace of her restraints. A sudden geyser of phlegm and bloody fluids burst from her mouth in an impossible volume. Carol fought, only partly successfully, to keep Carly's face turned during the paroxysm. The other teenagers looked on in something akin to horror.

Then J. L. began screaming in hysterics, adding to the chaos.

"Can you quiet her?" Carol snapped at Katie. Another thick stream of vomit gushed from the thrashing girl whose head she held steady, clamped beneath her arms and body weight.

Katie Casey reached out to J. L., who turned and clung tightly to the younger girl. She buried her face against Katie's shoulder, muffling the short screams that her fear and revulsion still wrenched from deep inside.

"What are you doing to my friend?" Katie asked, her voice unsteady.

"I'm trying to prevent her from aspirating the discharge," Carol said, most of her weight now pressing Carly's head against the stretcher's edge. She shifted Carly's position, trying to clear the airway. Then she raised her voice. "Driver! Get this thing rolling, damn it! I can't do anything for this girl without assistance!"

Carly's body again bucked madly, and Carol rode the violent convulsions like a rodeo cowboy. When the seizure finally subsided, Carly's face was bloated and blue. Her breath came in short, rapid wheezes—not enough, never enough even to partially fill her ravaged lungs.

"Can you help her?" Katie's voice was a whisper, barely audible over the sobbing of her companion. "Please."

Carol looked up at Katie. She said nothing, but shook her head once, a hard negative.

The van lurched into movement.

A few minutes into the trip, Carly Holmes had died, mercifully.

Her friends had been too stunned even to cry at first.

That would come later, Carol knew, as she covered the body, tucking the sheet under straps that fought the jouncing of the transport van. *If,* she thought, *there is a later.*

By then, of course, it was too late to alter the destination of the other two.

When she arrived at the stadium, Carol discovered she was one of the few doctors in what had become a vast charnel house of the dead and dying. As in most epidemics, physicians and nurses had been among the earliest exposed to the virus; they had died, most of them, only shortly after the patients who had infected them. Among them was LaTonya Ferris, who had so effectively managed operations at Carol's clinic. She had been delirious, fighting for air when Carol found her, by accident, among a row of other fevered victims.

It had been a brief reunion.

LaTonya had died, quickly and painfully, despite all of the frantic efforts Carol had thrown against the viral invader. Like the majority of the flu victims, LaTonya had drowned, a victim of her own fluids flooding into lungs torn and damaged by the virus's onslaught. Neither the oxygen Carol had intubated into LaTonya nor the Lasix with which she had injected her had any but the most temporary of effects; the progress of the disease simply had been too swift and devastating.

It had been the same with other patients over whom Carol had labored. Both O_2 and Lasix were now in short supply; so too was almost every other basic commodity.

It did not matter, really. There was no effective treatment. As it was, the shortage of nurses was more critical than that of their physician colleagues, since a kind hand wielding a clean handkerchief at least provided a temporary comfort to the stricken.

Carol heard news, in scraps and tiny morsels. Rumors, rather—in the chaos of the outbreak, there was no reliable way to discern fact from fiction.

She heard that the pestilence had spread as far north as Birmingham and as far to the west as New Orleans; nobody really knew for sure. She heard that at Eglin Air Force Base, which occupied an area the size of Rhode Island from Fort Walton almost to Pensacola, the virus had spread like wildfire; she remembered Jerry-the-Moonlighter at the clinic, working alongside her to breathe life back into the victim at the clinic. She even heard that the Russians had come up with some kind of cure, or at least a treatment that kept the disease from spreading; this could not be confirmed either, and Carol was too busy to allow herself the luxury of hope.

She worked throughout the day, losing track of time in the mind-dulling rounds amid the dying. At some point, a generator chugged to life and the bulbs strung between the tent poles cast their yellow light on the scene. When next she noticed, outside the yellow glow the night was dark and still.

In one of the faded gray tents along the perimeter of the treatment area, Carol had commandeered a corner for herself and her two charges. It was there that she retreated, collecting Katie and J. L. as she passed through the crowded triage area. By the time they arrived at their refuge, the fatigue was acute enough to leave Carol lightheaded, though she felt anything but ready to sleep.

Neither did the two teenage girls, though initially they seemed equally adverse to any kind of discussion. They jury-rigged one of the olive gray blankets over a rope, darkening the corner. It was too warm to sleep covered, though they stretched out on cots Carol hoped had not been recently used.

Still, Carol found sleep elusive.

So she prodded Katie and J. L. to talk, asking them questions until they began to respond. It was the only palliative she could offer two young women who had been thrust deeply into this pact with death.

J. L. was quiet, almost sullen, and spoke mainly in monosyllables. She stayed close to the other, Carol observed, the one named Katie. But she had done her share, even through the tears that had washed tracks down the grime on her cheeks. For her own part, Katie Casey was dealing with the shock of Carly's death by plunging into the far larger cauldron of suffering she found everywhere around her. She had cried too, if her reddened eyes were any evidence. But when, Carol could not say; each time she had glanced at Katie, the girl had seemed calm and competent—even resourceful. If the teenager was frightened by her situation, she gave no outward sign.

For a while they spoke about meaningless subjects, tacitly avoiding the world outside their small corner. Carol told them about her job at the clinic, about the incongruities of living in an area where most people come to play, about the largely absent social life of a single, overworked physician. She described her infatuation with Choctawatchee Bay in terms that might have embarrassed a human lover, mercifully missing the eye-rolling glance J. L. shot Katie. She mentioned that she had purchased her first vehicle only a few months before, and admitted it was a pickup truck, now parked back in the clinic lot.

"Stick-shift transmission," she volunteered. "That marks me as a real player, at least down here. Do either of you drive stick?"

"I can," Katie said. "My father taught me. But I just got my learner's permit. I'm not supposed to drive without an . . . *adult* supervising me." She sounded rueful, but to Carol's ears insufficiently so.

Carol grinned wickedly. *I still remember . . .* "But I'll bet you do it anyway. Am I right?"

There was a rustling, as if Katie might have shrugged. Silence settled between them.

"You're doing a good job out there," Carol said finally. "Both of you."

Again, there was no response, and Carol was about to abandon the effort when Katie spoke.

"All these people," Katie said to Carol quietly. "They're going to die, aren't they?"

The question took the physician by surprise, and she hesitated for only an instant. But it was answer enough, and all three of them knew it.

"Why don't we have it?" J. L.'s voice was hard, demanding. "We were around Carly when she was sick—I mean, if she caught it in Florida, we were with her the whole time. So why aren't Katie and I—"

Her voice caught, broke.

"I don't know," Carol said. "I don't know why I'm not displaying symptoms, either. Possibly the virus takes longer to manifest itself in some people. Or it could have something to do with the way our individual immune systems are working."

Katie frowned. "You mean, there's a chance we won't catch it?"

When she spoke, Carol was careful to keep her voice neutral. "That's not likely, I'm afraid. We don't know—*I* don't know anything about this virus, except that it's a very contagious variety of the flu. Most people are vulnerable to influenza."

"But it's possible?"

"Anything is possible."

"Not if we stay here," J. L. interjected. She looked around the football field and shook her head in a hard negative movement. "Not in here."

"The entire state is quarantined," Carol said. "There are police and soldiers on all the roads—certainly the main ones, I guess. There's no place for you to go. They can't allow the infection to spread."

"But we don't have it," J. L. repeated stubbornly.

"I'm sorry."

Again, silence. This time it lasted longer.

"Do you have anybody you can call?" Carol asked suddenly, realizing even as she spoke that the question was inane. During processing, she had discovered that all contact with the world outside was 'temporarily' out of service. It made sense, from the point of view of those trying to keep the genie in the bottle: had word of the conditions here migrated outside, widespread panic would have been inevitable.

"We kind of—well, sneaked down here," Carol heard Katie say. "The . . . three of us." She took a deep, shuddering breath. "Right now," Katie said, "nobody even knows where we are."

There was nothing Carol could think of to say. In a short time, she found herself drifting off, finding sleep at last.

She snored, rhythmically but lightly.

It was then that J. L. and Katie began to talk again, in voices pitched low and secretive.

Chapter 23

Fort Detrick is forty-eight miles away from the White House, as the crow flies. There was a time when any crow unwise enough to fly over the base ran a substantial chance of falling from the sky, the victim of birdshot from guns wielded by PFCs charged with keeping the skies clear of avian intruders.

This was not because of any particular malice toward crows, or birds in general. Rather, it was the fear that some random feathered interloper might become an inadvertent vector for one or another of the agents undergoing testing at the site.

The Crow Patrol is a legend of the distant past at Detrick now, ever since chemical and biological weapon development was officially ended by Richard Nixon in the late sixties. Today it is the home of USAMRIID, the Army's infectious disease research branch. As such, Fort Detrick has been officially rehabilitated. The research there now focuses on studying antidotes, vaccines and other treatments or preventatives involving CBW. Officially, its former black arts are no longer practiced there.

Officially, they are practiced nowhere in the U.S. military.

It was late, even for a military operation, but few at Detrick had left their research stations since word of the first case in Florida.

It was almost midnight when a figure in a Class IV exposure system—the staff called them "Mr. Bubble" suits, for the obvious reason—had torn her eyes from the blue glow of a computer screen at which she had been staring intently. She clicked the mouse with an awkwardly gloved hand, toggling between two not dissimilar displays that she studied with equal intensity.

"I'll be damned," breathed Barbara Jones, who in addition to carrying a Ph.D. in biogenetics from Johns Hopkins was a major in the United States Army. She was "Dr. Jones" to the rare outside visitor, "Major Jones" to the enlisted personnel, and "B. J." to her close colleagues. But never, never was she "Major Barbara."

She reached around the controls of the electron microscope and pressed an oversized switch. Immediately, a voice rasped from the intercom speaker.

"What's up, B. J.?"

It was the voice of the man who had, almost singlehandedly, overseen the biowarfare research at Fort Detrick, Maryland, for the past three decades. For the past two and a half of them, the program's very existence had been classified "Ultra D"—an infinity above the merely "top" secret.

"I've been playing around with a sample of Agent VIX," Barbara answered.

For a moment, her supervisor was dumbstruck.

"Good God. Why are you even handling that stuff?"

B. J. screwed her face into an expression that would have been better suited to a much younger female; she did not like her work questioned, even by someone she respected as much as she did this man.

"The genome is pretty close to the killer flu. So I kind of played a hunch."

B. J. was famous for her hunches, and wore the idiosyncrasy as a badge.

"And?"

"I think I found something," she said, and this time her mentor heard the edge in her voice. "I think maybe I found something important."

Chapter 24

Deborah Stepanovich stared at the television screen, appalled by the events of the past twenty-four hours, by the sequence of shocks that threatened now to spin completely out of control.

When she had left her law offices in the District yesterday evening, all had been well — at least, as well as they could be when one's teenage daughter had taken French leave to a still-indeterminate location.

But Deborah had awakened today to find the capital in complete chaos. Things were still reasonably quiet here, across the river; but Deborah had decided that she wanted Katie home, immediately.

Not for the first time this morning, she wondered why Beck had not returned any of her calls from the previous afternoon. Whatever his faults or failings, Deborah did not doubt Beck's love for his daughter. For a long moment, she eyed the telephone, debating whether to try him in Chicago one more time.

Instead, she reached for her bag and removed the Palm Pilot in which she kept her records, notes and the telephone numbers she seldom felt inclined to call.

*   *   *

Deborah Stepanovich squeezed the telephone handset hard enough to feel the plastic flex beneath her fingers. Had the other woman been present in the room, instead of at the other end of a long-distance connection, Deborah was sure that by now she would have throttled Carly Holmes's mother.

"Joyce," she said, careful to keep her voice level. "Just tell me."

She could hear Joyce Holmes's sigh of exasperation, and seethed silently while she waited for a response.

"Mah Gawd. Theah' just out havin' some fun, Debbie. Ah'm sure theah' just fine."

Joyce Holmes's Southern accent was a relatively recent acquisition, Deborah realized; not too many years ago, when Katie and Carly had played on the same soccer team, Joyce's pronunciation had been the more clipped tones that reflected her upbringing in a Cleveland suburb.

Around the time that Carly's father had moved in with a real estate agent from Silver Springs, Joyce's almost-severe suburban-mom persona had begun a marked evolution to that of flirtatious Southern belle. Now she sounded as if she had never ventured north of the Mason-Dixon line and that her worst fear was the dreaded return of Sherman's raiders.

There was more rustling, as if quantities of paper were being riffled near the distant mouthpiece.

"Heah it is. Carly's using mah American Express—they send the bill right to her father, thank Gawd. Still and all, Ah just don't know about givin' out the numbers to just *anybody,* Debbie."

Joyce paused, and in the loaded silence Deborah envisioned a cat lazily toying with a fieldmouse. This time, Deborah could hear the handset creak with the intensity of her own grip. She forced herself not to speak.

"Oh, well—seein' it's *you,* darlin'." Joyce Holmes read off the credit card numbers, and added, "Now, don't you go shoppin' with mah card numbers, heah?" The giggle made Deborah's skin crawl. "Course, I'm jokin' with you, Debbie. Say hi to the girls for me, 'kay?"

Deborah was still livid by the time she got through to American Express, negotiating through the electronic menu until she reached a live operator. She bullied her way to a supervisor, then another; over the next quarter hour, she had been bumped in slow sequence again and again to whoever was next highest in the Amex pecking order.

She had lost track of names and titles by the time she reached what she sensed was her last hope. The voice was female and sounded both competent and unbending.

"Ms. Stepanovich, surely you understand that we cannot—"

"Look," Deborah said, and was surprised to hear her own voice sound reasonable. "I don't want you to violate any laws. I don't want any personal or confidential information on this account. All I want to know is where the card was last used, and how long ago."

She took a deep breath and played her last card.

"You know about this flu out there: I am just trying to find my daughter. She's fifteen. Please help me."

There was a momentary hesitation, and with a sudden sinking in her stomach, Deborah knew her appeal had failed.

Then the voice spoke, in a tone crisp and professional. "Hold, please." A pause. "That card was last used—Island Resort Properties, apparently a motel . . . yes. Two days ago. In"—there was a sudden hesitation, as if the speaker had been taken aback—"in Fort Walton Beach, Florida."

"Florida," Deborah repeated, her throat suddenly tight and dry.

For a moment, the fear rose within her and she could not speak.

"Hello? Are you still on the line?"

Deborah shook herself. "Yes. Thank you very much."

"Please don't mention it," the voice said, then dropped to a conspiratorial level. "To *anybody,* if you catch my drift. My prayers are with you; I've got a teenager too."

Chapter 25

In retrospect, Larry Krewell realized, it had been foolish to expect that New York City would be any better prepared to deal with a biological attack than anywhere else in the country — indeed, in the rest of the world.

It was not, despite the millions that had been spent on training and drills and equipment. Not even the imposition of martial law made a difference. A trooper could shoot a rioter, perhaps; but no number of soldiers could impose its will on a lethal, untreatable microbe driven by an almost supernatural impulse to spread.

Less than an hour before, a Coast Guard helicopter had swept down upon a boat that had ignored repeated hailing calls to heave to for boarding. It had sped on heedlessly, until a Coast Guard marksman had fired a single three-round burst from his M-14 into the bridge, then stitched a longer burst along the deck that silenced the boat's engines. The helicopter circled overhead until the Zodiac arrived with a boarding party, each member of which wore the full exposure suit that had been, only that morning, ordered mandatory in such circumstances. Three hooded and goggled Coast Guardsmen

clambered aboard, one tripping awkwardly against the first
of two bodies they would find in the cruiser's cockpit.

As *Corazón* wallowed in the waves, a red-and-white can
skittered back and forth across the blood-slick decking. It
was ignored initially by the Coast Guardsmen, until one
picked it up in his gloved hand, half intending to pitch it
overboard. Inside his mask, he did a double take. Then he
dropped the canister as if it were white-hot, and he pawed at
the microphone clipped against his rubberized tunic.

The cargo found on board *Corazón* was ominous in its implications. Neither Krewell nor General S. V. "Swede"
Brandt, the Army brigadier who had set up command headquarters at One Police Plaza, held any doubt as to what the
opened canister had contained; few soup cans come from the
factory complete with a pressurized atomizing apparatus inside.

Though New York City was already under martial law,
civilian government remained in charge, albeit unofficially,
of everything not directly related to administering troops on
the city's streets. That included public health, and it took
Krewell less than two minutes to get his counterpart in the
New York City Department of Health patched into the emergency conference call. In turn, that municipal official had
insisted on adding one more participant to the discussion.

Now there was a momentary burst of crackling static, followed by a voice Krewell recognized from newscasts. Almost immediately, Krewell found himself metaphorically
nose-to-nose with the city's mayor, an intense and demanding personage who was obviously unaccustomed to the desperation he now found his city facing.

The news Krewell delivered left the mayor at first
stunned, then infuriated.

"So what the *hell* is supposed to happen now?" demanded
the mayor, an angry and disembodied voice that crackled
from Krewell's speaker phone. "You expect me to seal off
the southern tip of Manhattan? It's too late. How many of

those people do you think are still there? They went back to work, or took a cab to some other part of the city."

"With all due respect, Mr. Mayor." Swede Brandt's tones were firm, measured. "It is no longer your decision to make."

The speaker box went silent for a moment.

"Jesus, this is a nightmare."

Krewell forced himself to stay calm. No drills, no academic course of study could have prepared a normal human being for the situation they all faced. Larry felt sympathy for the New York mayor: the man was a former prosecutor, and a tough-minded one at that. He had used the same approach as mayor, and was credited with spurring a renaissance in the city's quality of life.

But nothing in his experience could have been adequate preparation for the single harsh reality of biological terrorism. The concept was, under most circumstances, unthinkable: triage, on a massive scale. Those who could be saved had to be identified and selected; the others written off, coldly and deliberately. After a bioweapon had been deployed at a target like New York City, the question was no longer how to *prevent* deaths—widespread mortality had already become inevitable. Instead, the question became who must be left to die, so that others may live.

In Russia, Krewell knew, Putin had understood that truth instinctively; he had acted ruthlessly, but with a cold-blooded pragmatism. Not so in New York; its officials were still thinking of how to save everybody, and that was impossible.

Krewell understood.

Most people don't think that way, he told himself. *Firemen run into buildings because they need to believe they can save everybody. Well, this time they can't. The fire is about to burn very brightly in New York City.*

"We will proceed on the assumption that the virus has now contaminated an initial core group in New York City." In contrast to the mayor's, Brandt's tone was unemotional.

He could have been reading from a printed card. "Pending orders from the Joint Chiefs, I will—"

"*Damn* it, General. Dr. Krewell, you don't even know what was in those cans."

Krewell hardened his voice. "You're right, Mr. Mayor," he said. "We won't have confirmation from the lab for another five hours, at best. By that time, the majority of the people who were standing downwind on that shoreline will have infected whoever they've been in contact with. And those people will be incubating their own virus load, passing it to others."

"*So what the hell do I do?*"

"Mr. Mayor, we are still developing a . . . *proactive* course of action," Krewell said, wondering how much of his implied optimism either Brandt or the city official actually believed. "But the immediate response has to be containment. Slow down any spread of contagion for as long as possible."

"The city is already quarantined," the mayor said. "Your people have *tanks* blocking the bridges and tunnels, for God's sake."

"I'd suggest you clear the streets," Krewell said. "The less contact people have with others, the less their chance for immediate infection with the virus."

The mayor's voice was harsh and scornful. "A curfew," he said. "We have rioting in all five boroughs, and you think you can impose a curfew. What—you expect that I can just get on a bullhorn and convince people to go home?"

"We can order the streets cleared, Dr. Krewell," Swede Brandt said, ignoring the mayor. "Get everybody inside. Make certain nothing moves on the streets—no cars, buses, trains. I have sufficient assets in troops and helicopter gunships to enforce this order—at least, throughout most of the area of operation. But I must be authorized to employ lethal force." Both men knew that was a presidential decision, but one that had already been tacitly made, if not yet officially communicated.

"I concur, General," Krewell said.

"You're threatening to gun people down?" The mayor's voice was accusatory. "On the streets of New York?"

Krewell bit off the obvious rejoinder. "Mr. Mayor, all I can do is give you my advice as an epidemiologist," Krewell said. "My belief is that your city now has been exposed to this virus. Until a treatment strategy has been developed, the only option is to slow the spread of the contagion. By whatever means necessary."

"Like the Russians did?" The mayor's voice was furious. "Is that what's next? This is still the United States of America. This is *New York City,* man!"

"Yes, Mr. Mayor," Krewell heard himself saying. "But right now, it's also under attack. You're standing on a battlefield, at ground zero."

"God help you if you're wrong."

"No, sir," Brandt's voice corrected the mayor. "God help us if he's right."

Day Three:
July 23

Chapter 26

Columbia Falls, Montana
July 23

They had streaked west for another two hours, passing high above the Continental Divide; had it been daylight, Beck knew, the awesome brown and white spine of the Rockies would have stretched past the horizon on either side. Instead, only the occasional twinkling of mountain hamlets marked where the ground began.

Beck forced himself to read the thick sheaf of briefing documents Andi had provided, burying himself in the details of the American fringe groups who had been tracked and monitored as potential domestic security threats. The specifics of the various Montana militia organizations alone comprised almost sixty single-spaced sheets.

For almost a decade, the trend line of violence had been rising on an ever-steeper slope, though much of it had occurred below the radar scope of the general public. Many Americans believed that the tragic events of September 11, 2001, had constituted the climax of terrorism on U.S. soil. It had not, as the litany of antigovernment conspiracies through which Beck was plowing showed vividly; it had been only the most dramatic, at least thus far. Since then, several hundred major bombing or other terror plots — generally unknown to the public at large—had been shortstopped by the intensive efforts of the FBI and other police agencies throughout the United States.

It had become a savage game of odds and numbers, Beck realized. Even in the most draconian police state, no government could stymie every terror plot; the difficulty was a magnitude harder in a democracy that protected the constitutional rights of even the most cold-blooded criminal.

Inevitably, the statistics dictated, terrorists would slip past the cordon of American law enforcement and win another one.

As they had now, Beck thought—and was surprised at the warning light that flashed deep inside his mind.

Almost against his will, he felt his mind shift into a pattern that had once been familiar—one segment of his intellect logically analyzing, calculating, assessing the matter at hand; in the background, another simultaneously churned like a computer multitasking, more ethereal and far more subject to flashes of deductive insight that always seemed outside his command.

After his own experiences as a prisoner, Beck had learned firsthand not to trust the fruit of any interrogation based on torture. But as a paranoid sometimes has real enemies, sometimes a torture victim tells the real truth in lieu of merely what he thinks the torturer wants to hear. The Aum had tried both chemical and biological terrorism in the past; they had joined in a ritual suicide, among cults typically an act of final defiance, contempt and oblivion.

There was still no real proof, no evidence that was anything but circumstantial; no court in any civilized country would convict on such a flimsy basis. But all signs pointed to the cult. If Alexi was right, the Aum had initiated a suicidal war against all humanity and enlisted American militia groups as their allies.

Direct, logical and straightforward, the logical part of Beck's mind argued. Yet . . .

How, then, had the Aum persuaded the militias to join them in certain death? The Aum might hold self-immolation both a virtue and a virtual sacrament; in Beck's experience, few American militia groups held suicide in the same awed esteem. Had the Aum held out a promise, a vehicle of salvation that in the midst of plague would spare those engaged in spreading it?

Was there a cure, a treatment, a vaccine? Did the militia Beck now hunted possess it?

Again, the images on the videotapes he had seen—both the death rained on crowds from helicopters and the rows of dying flu victims in a Russian contagion ward—elbowed to the front of his thoughts.

But in his mind's eye, each of the victims bore the face of his daughter.

And Beck flew on, west into the night. Had either of the pilots looked back, they would have seen a man seemingly absorbed in the study of the documents piled on the seat beside him. Beck looked calm, focused.

Inside, he raged at his own helplessness.

At last, Beck felt the Learjet turn in a wide arching curve to the north, vectoring into the airspace over Kalispell, Montana.

"Nothing else flying," the pilot's voice crackled in Beck's earphones. "Looks like we have the approach path all to ourselves, Doctor. We'll be on the ground in a few minutes."

With a stomach-dropping maneuver, the plane nosed over into the sweeping descent of its landing pattern.

April O'Connor stood on the darkened airport apron and watched them touch down, suitably unimpressed at the expensive transportation that was delivering her new—*what?* she asked herself. *Observer? Partner? Supervisor?*

April was unclear as to the role her visitor was intended to play, and the uncertainty did not ease her mind. She had worked with the CIA before, and like most FBI agents had found it an awkward pairing. With spooks, one was never sure what priorities had been set, what plans had been made, what agenda was being followed. Invariably, it made for casework that to a law enforcement professional felt extremely loose—at times even inept, and one was never quite sure if it was intentionally so.

In the past few hours, April had wasted no time. She had run Orin Trippett through every electronic database available—not just the National Crime Information Center computer banks, but through systems that NCIC and the Bureau normally could not access directly: NSA and DIA, to name but two of the super-secret information banks that lurked behind the intelligence community's black firewall. Barriers that were normally insurmountable had melted away like frost under the midmorning sun, a fact at which April marveled.

And all it takes, she told herself, *is a killer plague that threatens to destroy world civilization.*

In the end, with one notable exception, it had availed her nothing.

Most of the yield from the government's electronic cornucopia was little more than a compilation of Trippett's arrests and convictions, which April already had. The remainder was a collection of conjecture, myth and sheer rumors from the variety of informants that would make even a rookie cop scoff.

So much for modern criminology.

April had retreated to the tried-and-true: pulling out-of-date hard-copy files, sending e-mails and faxed inquiries to select local and county law enforcement agencies, working the telephone to tap into the network of colleagues and sources that every cop guards jealously—*all of which,* she thought sourly, *I could be doing right now, instead of waiting for this guy to show up.*

The single notable exception to the dearth of information had involved Dr. Beck Casey. While her boss Frank Ellis had been unable to provide additional detail on Casey, April had found a number of cryptic, sometimes intriguing nuggets among the NSA archives.

The Middle East, she thought, impressed despite herself, *both Iran and Iraq. North Korea? And Russia. Lots of Russia, right up until—*

Three years ago, according to the files, Casey had been tracking a Russian informant's story involving a lost shipment of precursors—chemicals that were used in the manufacture of one or another lethal brew—said to have been diverted to a rogue North African country. He had followed the trail as far as Ekaterinburg, to a city that even April knew was a virtual fiefdom of the Russian *Mafiya.*

And then Beck Casey had gone missing.

Six weeks later he turned up in a Moscow hospital, a torn and scarred skeleton from the effect of the physical abuse and the drugs that had left him virtually psychotic. He was turned over to American authorities and subsequently repatriated to the United States. There, the record stopped abruptly. The final entry was the dates of his admission and release from Walter Reed Army Hospital, near Washington.

They were, she saw, nearly eleven months apart.

"Nice shirt," April said, after the ritual of introduction was complete. "Did somebody walk off with your luggage over there, Dr. Casey?"

Beck forced a smile onto his face.

"You can drop me off," Beck said. "Somewhere with room service and a hot bath. I slept on the plane"—he grinned, a little too brightly—"but I'm feeling a bit gamey right now."

"Place in Columbia Falls I know," she said. "Should do you until morning."

They climbed into her car, a Bureau-issued Crown Victoria. For several minutes, they drove in silence. Then Beck spoke.

"Maybe you can tell me why I'm here, Agent O'Connor."

April cocked an eye at him. "You don't know?"

Beck shook his head.

"You're supposed to help me find a man named Orin Trippett," she said. "He's Montana militia — you know, camo clothes and an AK-47 under the floorboards. But he's tied in with the Japanese who started all this insanity. They gave him a load of nerve gas he didn't get a chance to use. But we think he may be carrying something else they sent him. Something very bad."

"I guess we know what that means," Beck said. "The Russians say that the Aum dangled the same promise in front of some Russian extremists."

April nodded grimly. "I saw the transcript from their prisoner."

"Now we have our own loonies to worry about." Beck was silent for a moment. "Look — I'm not a cop. I'll help any way I can, but you need a trained investigator, not a historian."

"Couldn't agree more. No offense."

"None taken."

They fell into silence again, and Beck found himself lulled by the passing miles. He dozed, chin drooped upon his chest.

He awoke twenty miles later, as the sedan eased to a stop under the canopy of an unpretentious motel. April watched without comment as Beck climbed out, hefting his computer and traveling gear. For a moment, he leaned in the passenger window, tentative in posture. Finally, he aimed a thumb over his shoulder at the lobby.

"Let me try to catch up with the geniuses in Washington. That will keep me out of your way for a while. If you get a lead on this Trippett guy, I'll be glad to watch your back." He smiled — to April, it seemed an apologetic gesture. "If you want, I'll even carry your handcuffs for you."

"Fair enough," said April evenly. "I saw the videotape

from Moscow. If I need any help like that, I know where to call."

Without waiting for a reply, she stepped on the gas. From the look on Beck Casey's face as she drove away, April had no doubt that he had understood exactly what she meant.

Chapter 27

Columbia Falls, Montana
July 23

It was almost two a.m. when April O'Connor punched in the telephone number of the motel where she had deposited Beck Casey.

It had been a toss-up. No FBI support was yet available locally, and this was not an assignment to handle solo. Worse, her supervisor also had his orders from on high; he had ordered April to make the pairing more than a marriage of convenience. She had little desire to be chained to a spook, and even less inclination to deal with the shadowy motivations Casey might bring to this case. There were lots of reasons not to want—

She forced back the sudden memory of Jesús Robles illuminated by the muzzle flash from her weapon; April also did not want the responsibility that wet-nursing Beck Casey would inevitably entail.

But in the end she had decided: she had her orders, any backup was better than none, and Casey had been her luck of the draw.

For more than five hours, she had been asking, cajoling, threatening and otherwise gathering information from the various offices and enforcement agencies with which Trippett had run afoul during his life. Armed with this background, she had checked Trippett's fairly impressive criminal record, selecting as most promising a number of arrests outside the Columbia Falls area.

After several dead ends, she hit pay dirt.

According to state records she obtained from a computer sited in the Montana capital of Helena, Trippett had been arrested for felonious assault in White Bison County, a largely mountainous region seventy miles southwest of Columbia Falls. He was listed as a resident of White Bison County, a fact that caused April to sit upright in her chair. Then she reached for the phone and somehow talked the White Bison court clerk out of bed and into the office.

There, the court records told April that the original felony had been negotiated down to a misdemeanor, and the fine had been suspended. Trippett obviously had a gift for slipping through the system.

But it was here that she also struck gold, in the form of the name of the arresting officer. She thanked the clerk, sent him home and kept digging, working the computer and her telephone deftly as she slogged through layer after layer of the bureaucratic machine. And by half-past one—after working her way through an ascending hierarchy of third-shift line sergeants, lieutenants, shift commanders and captains—April had finally gotten to Senior Deputy Carl McGuire of the White Bison County Sheriff's Department.

She spoke to him in the jargon that makes up the lingua franca of the law enforcement profession. She tinged it with the codes and key words that communicate both the urgency and the importance of such inquiries to police brethren who are too often inundated by their own caseloads. And when she hung up—after long minutes of waiting while McGuire consulted his own notes and memories as well as those of his colleagues—she looked at the descriptions and directions she had scribbled and blew out a long breath.

She passed along the relevant information to Frank Ellis

in Helena. Ellis relayed it to an assistant United States attorney who already waited, cellular phone at his ear and the proper paperwork in his hand, outside the home of a federal district judge. Less than fifteen minutes later, April had the confirmation that the warrant had been issued and was being faxed to her immediately.

Then April dialed one more number.

The phone rang at the other end, and she heard a familiar voice.

"Yo." There was a television in the background.

"O'Connor. You doing anything special right now?" she asked without preamble.

"Oh, *hell* yes," Beck Casey replied. "They have cable TV. I found one of those *Funniest Videotapes* shows. They had a guy playing catch with his kid in the yard—he turns his head to look at something, kid throws the ball. Hits him . . . well, in the crotch. Then they showed somebody else trying to climb a tree—I think his kite was stuck in it." April smiled at Beck's dubious tone. "Anyway, he's climbing up, slips, comes down on a tree branch. Guess where it catches him? Right in the crotch."

"I think I'm beginning to sense a theme," April said.

"Yep," Beck observed, "it's a scream. Right now, there's this fellow trying to impress his girlfriend by walking tightrope on top of a chain-link fence." There was a moment's pause. "Ouch, that must have hurt. So if I can tear myself away from all this must-see TV, what do you have in mind?"

"I've got a possible location for Trippett, and the paperwork is arriving on my desk even as we speak," she said. "I was pretty sure you wanted to go along."

"Good deduction," Beck said. "Am I going as an official observer?"

"Depending on whether we find him there," April said, "I suppose we'll figure out how official you are as we go along."

Chapter 28

White Bison County, Montana
July 23

"You're sure, this time?" Beck's voice was doubtful. "I don't know how much more my kidneys can take. Probably less than the suspension on your car."

In the driver's seat next to him, April O'Connor peered out the window, and then squinted as she reread the notes she had taken earlier. The notebook pages glared brightly in the beam of her pocket light, rendering useless what was left of her night vision. She inched forward, turning slightly so that the headlamps illuminated a gravel road that led away from the blacktop of this rural county two-lane.

"Hell, I don't know," April muttered, only partly to Beck. *Who would have figured that the street sign hadn't made it out here in the sticks yet?* she thought, with an irritation made worse by the fact that she suspected her companion was somehow laughing at her.

"The odometer says we've driven a mile and a quarter from the bridge," she said louder. "This *could* be the road."

"It's possible," Beck replied unhelpfully. "Of course, the last *two* could have been."

He looked down the bright tunnel the car's lights bored into the night, then back at April.

April shrugged and stepped lightly on the gas. The car dropped several inches as each set of wheels left the county roadway, and the crunching of tires on a graveled surface mingled with the engine sounds. She accelerated slightly, but the weathered surface of the road was like an old washboard. An unhealthy vibration tried to tear the steering wheel from her hands. April eased back on the gas until the alarming shaking subsided to a thudding bounce that was merely maddening.

"Watch the ditch," Beck advised unnecessarily.

For Beck, the ride had been a replay of the night flight to Moscow, a disorienting ride in the dark. He enjoyed the mountains—by day, that is; at night, and with a relative stranger behind the wheel, they struck him as a particularly perilous place in which to wander. For no particular reason, he was now certain the road was flanked by sheer precipices littered with the rusted hulks of cars that had already taken the plunge.

"You think anybody's been down this road recently?"

Intent on her driving, April shook her head. "Can't tell a damn thing," she said. "For all I know, this could be what they consider an expressway out here. Thousands of people maybe use it at rush hour. Or this might *be* rush hour out here." She leaned forward, surveying the road through the windshield. "Look like it's getting narrower to you?"

"You want me to drive?"

"With all due respect, Dr. Casey, blow it out your—"

Abruptly, the road rose and dipped, curving to the right as it sloped downward. A quarter mile beyond and below the range of their headlights, specks of reflected starlight rippled over a dark area perhaps the size of a football field. April quickly reached forward and snapped off the car's lights.

"This is the place," April said. "See—that's gotta be the old quarry the deputy described. Trippett's trailer should be off to the left of it. In some trees." Once again, she squinted into the night. "You see anything?"

Beck shook his head.

"Uh-uh," he answered. "But if he's there, I vote we leave the car here and go in quiet."

April nodded, and switched off the engine. Before she could prompt him to do so, Beck reached above the rearview mirror and snapped the switch of the dome light to OFF. It was the action of a man who had done this sort of thing before, and for a moment it gave April pause. Then she opened her door carefully, stepped outside and gently pressed it closed until the latch engaged with an almost inaudible click.

Outside, the noises of the night filled the chill mountain air. Cicadas and other nocturnal insects crooned their ceaseless choruses of sex and procreation, sometimes enticing a willing mate, sometimes merely attracting the notice of a hungry predator. High overhead, shadowy forms darted in erratic flight, as sonar-guided bats zeroed in on unsuspecting targets. Motionless in the trees lining the road, great horned owls focused their night eyes in the low grasses, alert for the tiniest movement of some doomed prey.

Their heads close together, April and Beck spoke in low voices that carried even less than whispers would have.

"No flashlights," April cautioned. She looked up at the sky. Far from the light pollution of any city, the sky was a heavy black velvet curtain gleaming with uncounted blue-white pinpoints. The moon was a thin Moorish crescent almost directly overhead, exceptionally decorative but decidedly nonfunctional as illumination. April decided that was lucky.

"We follow the road down to the quarry," she told Casey. "Stick to the left side of the road, and stay close enough that we know where each of us is. Once we get down there, we ought to be able to see Trippett's trailer. If anybody's there, we take him down, fast. If there's any surprises, I want them to come from us."

"Fine with me," Beck volunteered. "You want to flip a coin to see who goes in first?"

She shook her head. "I'm FBI," she said. "In case you've forgotten the story you told me, you are a historian working for the CDC. Let's pretend to believe that for now, shall we? I go in first, you stay behind me. You know the standard entry drill?"

He nodded—a little too quickly, April thought.

"I'll sweep the left arc with my flashlight; you take the right. If we're lucky, Trippett's in there sawing wood; all that happens is he gets what you might call a rude awakening. We take him down, toss the place, bring him in. But if we run into somebody else—or if somebody else is in there with him—stay out of the line of fire, right? This case has enough bodies hanging on it."

"Just don't shoot me," Beck said. He saw the look that crossed her face, and frowned, puzzled. "Sorry. It was a joke."

"Then get serious, fast," April said.

An image rose in her mind, and she pushed it down.

"Just a minute," April said. She stepped to the car's trunk and fumbled with the key in the dark. Then she eased up the hatch, removed an object as long as her arm, and closed the trunk silently. She came back to Beck, who looked at her with what she could barely make out as a frown.

"You think you'll need that?" he asked.

April O'Connor hefted the object she had removed from the trunk, holding it firmly in two hands across her chest. It was a Mossberg shotgun, the 12-gauge pump model commonly issued to police tactical units. It was fully loaded with five rounds of double-ought buckshot, each shell packed with nine 32-caliber lead balls. At close range, she knew, its blast could cut a human being almost in half.

"The last time I ran into this guy, his friends were carrying automatic weapons," she said grimly. "You didn't see what happened next. I did."

*   *   *

They covered the quarter mile to the edge of the quarry in less than ten minutes, moving through the grass alongside the road as quietly as if they had been in a church. Twice, April had stopped short as something substantial had scurried out of her path; once, she had even seen a flash of movement in the grass, and wondered what variety of venomous snake called this region home.

She had not looked back, but she knew Beck was behind her. She could hear his soft footfalls occasionally; once, when he stepped too close to the soft incline of the drainage ditch, she heard his sharp inhalation as he slipped and caught himself. She even imagined she could hear the regular timpani of his heartbeats, though she knew it was more likely she was listening to her own.

A few yards away, the water slapped at the banks of the quarry, loud in the night. April dropped to one knee. In a moment, Beck was next to her. She pointed into the night, and he strained to see.

It was there, a patch of darkness thicker than that which surrounded it. April could make out the lines of a trailer, the kind with flat aluminum sides and top, engineered more with economy than stylishness in mind. She discovered that she could see the object better by not looking at it directly. In her peripheral vision, it contrasted more clearly from the copse of cottonwoods that framed it at a short distance.

April felt Beck's hand touch her shoulder lightly. She looked at him and saw him point to his eyes, then toward the trailer and lift his palms in a doubtful shrug. She mimicked his gesture; April, too, could see no sign of human presence.

They could have been playing musical instruments, these two whose approach he had heard long before he saw their silhouettes against the lighter crushed stone of the roadway. Such a clatter they made, each step rasping through the grass in a boringly regular pace that stood out starkly against the natural sounds of the night. Twice he had heard the one in front halt, then resume the approach; the one in the rear, he had decided in a flash of wit, either had a physical defect involving his equilibrium or was simply unnaturally clumsy.

Whoever they were, they approached this place in a manner doubtless meant to be of stealth. But the pair was without adequate training and devoid of natural skill.

And now, he thought with a shrug, *they will die.*

For a moment, he toyed with the idea of feeling sorry for them; it would not alter the fate he would deal them, but he had been raised by a grandmother who took upon herself the teaching of a faith that was officially discouraged, if not banned. Despite his experiences since then, and particularly since reaching the age when military service was compulsory, he occasionally found himself pondering such half-forgotten concepts as mercy and compassion.

But only briefly, and certainly not in this matter.

No, he decided—though deep inside, he also understood the decision had been made all along—*they will die. One of them may even be the person we seek. If so, all the better. If not, I may keep one alive long enough to find out why they, too, have come here.*

The thought filled him with something he might have described as joy.

Okay, April O'Connor told herself, *let's keep this simple. One: I move to the trailer door; Dr. Casey will be two steps behind, on my right. Two: I kick the door and that cheap piece of tin will pop open like a beer can. And three—well, once we're in, we'll see if there is a three.*

A sudden foreboding chilled her, and she felt her hair prickle along her neck. She recognized it as fear, and the realization startled her.

April looked at the shotgun she held, then once again eyed the trailer doorway. *Shit,* she thought, *that's one narrow-looking door. And I'm going to barge in there carrying this goddamn clumsy blunderbuss?* She pictured trying to swing the shotgun around in what were bound to be close, confined quarters; she had an image of the barrel hanging up against a wall while somebody carefully sighted on her.

That was the clincher. April softly laid the shotgun on the grass and drew her Glock. She checked the action by feel, and fished a small, powerful Maglite from her side pocket. This too she examined by touch, running her fingers lightly along the metal tube until she found the rubber thumb switch in its base.

Still April hesitated, and realized suddenly that she was dragging out the moment intentionally. *What's the matter?* she chided herself silently. *Hell of a time to turn chicken, lady. . . .*

Beck watched her, waiting for her sign. She pointed one forefinger toward her chest, held it upright and then jabbed it in the direction of the trailer. As one, they rose and rushed at the trailer door.

Despite the advantages he held, the speed with which the two figures moved surprised him. Almost before he realized they had risen, they were halfway across the space between the road and the concrete block being utilized as a front step.

Mi'shova mat, he thought, falling into his native tongue at the surprise, *the one in front runs like a woman!*

He felt as if he had been given a very good, and very unexpected, present.

Perhaps it was the memory of the warehouse, or perhaps it was the rush of adrenaline that coursed through her body. It may have been the shout of "FBI!" she gave, loud as any explosive scream from a martial arts master as every available erg of energy is focused on the target. It may even have been the fact that the trailer was not new, or that April O'Connor had spent hours in the gym to develop lower body strength even more impressive than what was already granted to her gender.

For whatever reason, the kick April delivered to the trailer door did not cause it to pop open like a beer can. Instead, it tore the hinge strip completely out of the light frame of the doorway and sent the entire assembly skittering across the inside width of the trailer. It smashed against the far wall and toppled to the side with a crash of metal and glass.

More important, it left no obstacle to delay, even momentarily, the entry of April and Beck.

"FBI! Nobody move!" April shouted again, and thumbed on her pocket flashlight. At that instant, she saw the movement on her left. She spun, her pistol in a right-handed grip and the flashlight in her left locked under the gun hand's wrist. In the circle of light at the end of her extended arms, the sights filled with the chest of a man wide-eyed in surprise, seated less than a dozen feet away in a folding chair. As he jerked his own gun upward toward her face, she could see the cylinder in his revolver already rotating and knew she was about to die.

April pressed her own trigger.

The room lit up as if from a photographer's strobe, the two flashes so close they appeared as one. Simultaneously, the concussion from the shots, vicious and flat, pressured her eardrums painfully as the pistol recoiled against her hand. Without conscious effort, as April O'Connor had learned in long hours on the firing range, she absorbed the recoil's energy in her forearm, letting the force of the slide as it snapped back to battery help her again center the sights on her target.

There was no need. His shot had missed, gone off to who-knows-where in the objective precision of ballistics. Hers had not. The bullet had torn into the man's left shoulder, and the impact jerked his body to the side. At the same time, the pistol flew from his right hand, clattering on the stained carpeting. The first pulse of blood jetted crimson from the wound.

"*Freeze,* you son of a bitch!" April screamed, her voice

blazing with what felt like rage. "Do not move or I *will* shoot!"

Through the ringing in her ears, she heard Beck step up close behind her.

"I've got this guy," she said, her heart still racing. "Shine your light on the rest of—"

Something hard exploded into the side of her head, and the man behind her—the man who was not Beck Casey, the man who had waited motionless from the shadows outside as she and Casey approached—now watched her fall heavily to the floor.

Chapter 29

Real life is seldom like the movies. In the movies, a blow to the head of the hero results in what appears little different from a brief nap. A short time later, the hero awakes, shakes her head to clear the cobwebs, and proceeds to analyze the intricacies of motive and opportunity.

The reality of April O'Connor's situation was starkly different.

Despite the crushing force, she was never completely unconscious from the impact to her head. She could still hear, though the ringing was magnified far beyond what had been caused by her shot. She could even see her flashlight where it lay on the trailer floor a few feet from her head, though now there were two flashlights, one slightly overlapping the other, and both moving sickeningly in and out of focus. Against her cheek, she could feel the rough nap of the carpeting that covered the floor; she was even aware of the sour smell of mildew it gave off.

But she could not move, not a muscle; not even when two black shoes—boots, really, ankle high and with nylon zippers along the side—stepped close to her face. She had no strength in her body, not even to react when she felt a sharp poke against one of her buttocks. Then a face, its identical twin again superimposed by the double vision of the concussion she had suffered, filled her field of view. April felt a thumb on her eyelid, the one that was uppermost as she lay, and then a light brighter than the midday sun exploded in her face and was gone again.

His tests completed, the man who had come up behind April straightened. He felt an irritated disappointment, as if he had broken a favored toy.

I struck harder than I intended, he thought, *perhaps too hard.*

He had seen people die before from a single blow to the head, their bruised brain seeping blood inside until all function stopped; he had even killed once or twice this way himself.

But her pupils still respond to light, so we will see. And if she does not—well, I still have the other.

He knelt beside the motionless woman. With the efficiency of an expert, he collected her weapon, field gear and personal effects. With a careless flip of his wrist, he opened her badge carrier.

She is FBI, he thought, unimpressed. *Their training leaves much to be desired, I believe.*

A few feet away, the idiot he had brought with him to bring back this Trippett—*American hoodlums have too much muscle,* the dark man thought with scorn, *and not enough brains*—lay in his own blood, moaning and muttering in a low voice. His right hand was locked over the wound, and had stoppered the pulsating arterial bleeding into a slower trickle that seeped through his fingers. With irritation, the dark man remembered how his companion's single wild shot had hissed close past his ear. He stepped over April and bent over the man.

Even in the near-darkness, he could see the black stain that was spreading from under the man.

I have no time for fools, the dark man thought, mentally

addressing the moaning figure. *If by some miracle you do not die, that will teach you to sleep when you should be working.* He reached into the wounded man's jacket and removed a set of car keys. *Thank you. I will drive myself now.*

Again stepping over the motionless FBI agent, he moved through the hole where the door had been. Sprawled on the ground outside, one foot still on the concrete block step and the other folded under at the knee, Beck Casey lay where he had fallen.

Almost nonchalantly, the man grabbed Beck's shoulder and rolled him roughly onto his stomach. The flashlight reflected wetly from the blood matting the hair just above the nape of Beck's neck. The dark man repeated the test he had made on April, jabbing one forefinger hard against a cheek of Beck's posterior.

A person can feign unconsciousness in a number of ways. But long ago, in a dirty little room in Chechnya, he had learned from a battle-hardened sergeant that no truly conscious person—even one trying to gain a momentary respite from the interrogator's harshest methods—can refrain from involuntary tensing the gluteus muscle against such a jab.

As Beck did, though sluggishly. And when the Russian thumbed up an eyelid to test pupil response, Beck groaned and weakly pulled his head away.

Satisfied, the Russian squatted and searched Beck, methodically pulling each pocket inside out. He made a small pile of the contents, examining each in the flashlight's beam. There was surprisingly little, though what there was told the dark man the most important fact.

Ah, he said to himself, *am I to believe most Americans carry two—no, make that three—different sets of identity papers?* He studied the photos on each of the driver's licenses and compared them to Beck's features. *So. Without doubt, he is a government operative. I would guess CIA, and*—he fingered the two twenties and a single five-dollar bill in Beck's wallet—*certainly an underpaid one.* He smiled at his own joke and stuffed the money in his own pocket.

And now, my heavy-footed little friend, it seems that the idiot who drove me here is feeling unwell. Perhaps you could provide me with directions? Never mind—I have a good map. He dropped the wallet carelessly to the ground and picked up one of the other items April had carried. *Well—let us begin, eh? You have things to tell me before I go.*

Beck Casey was aware that he was being pulled by his arms over what felt, and tasted, like mud and weeds. His head ached agonizingly, limply lolling facedown and occasionally bouncing against the uneven ground. Once, when he mustered enough strength to lift his head a few irritated inches, he found himself looking at the slightly scuffed, pointed toes of what appeared to be black leather shoes. He noted, with a remote curiosity, that they had no laces.

His head fell forward again, and all he could see was the damp grass over which he was sliding, sliding, sliding, his hands held high in some powerful grip. His eyelids drooped, and Beck drifted away.

And then they stopped, and he felt himself being lifted like a large, inert sack, held on his own unsteady legs by pressure against his chest while something cold tightened around first one wrist, then the other. Beck's eyelids fluttered open, and he looked into eyes as empty as death.

He was not quite hanging from, not quite leaning against, a metal framework. Despite all the rust he could feel powdery against his bare arms, the frame was unmoving and solid. Beck tilted his head back, wincing from the sharp pain as his wound pressed against the slightly inclined I-beam support. Above him, handcuffs that could have been FBI issue were locked around his wrists, threaded over and around a short, horizontal length of angle iron. Whatever they used this for, Beck realized, it had been built to last.

His mind was beginning to clear slightly, and he realized

his legs had also been secured to the steel frame. The dark man who had dragged him here straightened and stepped back. Then the stranger reached around to the small of his back and pulled out an object that glinted even in the light of the thin moon.

"I'm a police officer," Beck said, pushing each word past a tongue that felt thick and only partially under his command.

"No," said his captor, in a voice that, despite the accent, sounded almost cheerful to Beck. "I do not believe you are."

He moved closer and bent in a casual manner. Beck felt a tugging at his waist and the coolness of the predawn air on suddenly bared flesh.

The dark man again stepped back and held the knife close to Beck's face so that it filled his vision. The blade, Beck could see, was honed razor sharp, scalloped with serrations almost to its needle-tipped point.

"You must tell me about yourself. And about other things as well."

April O'Connor felt a terrible urgency, though she could not remember why. It did not matter. She had vomited, and the acid of it still burned her throat; it did not matter, either. Almost nothing mattered, except for the voice inside her head, urging her to stand, to kneel, to crawl if she must—but to *go,* to get out of this dark and evil-smelling place now.

Her fingers scrabbled for a hold, and she pushed with first one leg, then the other. In front of her was only more darkness, punctuated with an occasional pained sound that she had thought was hers until now. Something made noises, moved fitfully over there; April did not want to go in that direction.

She rolled her head, feeling the starburst of more pain as she did, until she was facing her other side. A rectangular patch—actually, two of them, though April had begun to understand she was seeing double—was slightly less dark than its surrounding blackness. It was, the voice inside told her, a way out; the thought spurred her to increase her efforts.

By inches at first, she crawled. By the time she got to the doorway, an infinity later, she had mustered enough strength to push herself to her hands and knees. She almost decided to rest there awhile, head hanging and mouth open, until a surprisingly vivid picture came unbidden to her mind. It was of an olive-skinned man, his shirt torn open and two ragged rents weeping blood, lying open-eyed on a cold concrete floor. She saw hands that may have been her own frantically pushing hard against the unmoving chest.

It was, for some forgotten but very important reason, an image that shamed her and mocked her desire to rest. She pushed herself through the doorway.

There was a drop of perhaps two feet, and she was barely able to break her fall with her hands. A concrete block lying on its side scraped her palms, dripping another measure of pain into the already full bucket of her agony.

The sky was still alive with stars, though on the far horizon a thinning of the darkness implied rather than indicated where the sun would ultimately emerge. Still, it gave April an objective, a direction away from the blackness she was fleeing.

Her mind was gradually clearing, April realized, at least to a certain degree. She remembered in snatches of clarity, like seeing individual scenes from a movie. She recalled approaching the trailer in the night, kicking through the door. She could picture a man lifting a gun toward her, and the bright flash seen past her gunsights illuminating everything for a frozen moment. She remembered calling back to Dr. Casey to check—

Casey. She stopped short, suddenly frantic. Ignoring the renewed pain it caused, she swiveled her head in every direction, trying to probe the darkness surrounding her. The historian had been with her, and now he was not. That realization, more than any other factor, cut through the patches of fog that still clouded her mind. It fired April, fueled her to push herself upright on her knees and then, haltingly, to her feet. She stood, swaying, and strained her ears to hear around her.

There was something, a sound that did not fit with the other sounds of the night. It came from her right, somewhere past the slapping noise of water against rock. April lurched in that direction, unsteady on her feet.

She had gone only a few yards when she heard it again, much louder this time and with an undercurrent of agony that raised goose bumps on her arms. And, separate from it, a low droning voice that sounded almost conversational. Dimly, she thought she could see the outline of a man standing in front of what looked like a framework scaffold. A shape she could not see clearly twisted against the uprights, arms high, hanging.

She took another step, stumbled and then fell again to her hands. *Help him!* her mind screamed, and she scrabbled forward again crabwise in the grass.

Her hands touched metal, a pipe of some sort, and she seized it, intending to rush forward swinging with all her strength. And then she felt the grooved foregrip beneath the barrel, and the smooth wood of the shotgun's stock lying in the grass where she had left it. She snatched it up in both hands.

Still on her knees, April O'Connor racked the pump action, back and forward. Using the butt stock to support her, she pushed to her feet. From her throat burst a wordless scream of fury and challenge and perhaps terror defied. She staggered toward the figures to her front.

Except now there was only one, hung by the arms from a framework pylon at the edge of a flooded quarry. April stopped next to it, shotgun at her shoulder. She saw Beck Casey's eyes look at her wildly, and then blink in disbelieving recognition. The sound of something heavy, moving fast, crashed through the underbrush thirty feet away.

April fired into the sound, worked the action of her shotgun and fired again. The sounds of flight continued, fading with distance. Then she heard a car motor start up, out of shotgun range, and she fired once more. She was answered by the sounds of wheels spinning on a gravel road, speeding away.

She turned to the hanging figure. He was naked from the waist down, and a trail of blood flowed steadily to the ground down his right thigh.

Before she could speak, he did.

"Get me down from here," Beck said, his words clear through clenched teeth.

"He's in treatment now," Andi Wheelwright said, the strain in her voice evident despite the professional tone she affected. "They're stitching up the knife wound."

She paused, taking a deep breath.

"I guess we're lucky the guy was such a sick son of a bitch," Andi said. "It's a puncture wound—moderately deep, but not a long slash. Beck said he stuck the knife into his thigh and just left it there. He'd ask a question, and give the blade a twist. Patient guy. He expected to have a long time alone with our boy. I don't want to think what would have happened if O'Connor hadn't gotten there."

"How's she doing?" Larry Krewell asked. He had not intended to limit the question to the FBI agent's physical injuries, but he found that he was relieved when Andi chose to interpret it that way.

"She has a concussion, the doctors say," Andi replied. "The X ray didn't find any skull fracture, but they're doing an MRI right now. She'll be in the hospital for a while, but it doesn't look like anything permanent. Thank God." There was a pause. "The two of them dragged each other back to their car—a quarter mile over a gravel road. It took an hour, and Beck says then she argued over who'd make the radio call."

In her tone was grudging admiration.

"So what now, Andi?"

"The second man in the trailer—a local thug, the cops say; probably just beef hired for the occasion—bled to death before the ambulance arrived. That leaves Casey as the only one who even knows what Knife Man looks like. I'll check with the Bureau to see who they can assign to Casey. With her head injury, I'd guess that O'Connor's out of the game."

"I see."

"Look—suddenly, we're not the only ones who want Trippett, Larry. Who's the psychopath with the knife? He's the wild card in all this. He's looking for Trippett, who is out there somewhere carrying around a bottle full of virus. And I'm sitting here, wasting oxygen. We need to find that filth."

"And we need Casey, specifically, to look for it. Does that sum it up?"

"Casey will be in pain, but the doctors say he's ambulatory." Wheelwright frowned at Krewell's expression. "There is no time to shed tears, Larry. Casey has to do what he has to do."

Krewell nodded.

A slow flush colored Andi Wheelwright's face. "I've read his files, Larry. Of course I have—look, they brought him out to the Farm to lecture a class of trainees. He obviously doesn't remember it, but I was one of them. He was *good,* Larry. Even after what happened in Russia, he still is. He knows biological weaponry; he understands terrorists. We need his mind on this. *All* of his mind."

"It's a fine plan," Krewell said, watching her closely. "But what about his daughter? Are you going to tell him?"

"He can't help her," Andi Wheelwright said. "Nobody can."

Chapter 30

The President was in his shirtsleeves when Krewell and Carson were ushered into the Oval Office.

They were not alone. A constant flow of people moved through doors normally closed, carrying folders, individual sheets of paper, even what appeared to be rolled-up charts. At the far end of the room, a cadre of advisors were intent, their faces reflecting the flicker of computer screens and television monitors around which they worked.

The President waved the two newest visitors to the sofa that covered the right corner of a large, deep-blue carpet on which was centered the presidential seal; he sat, with obvious weariness, in the red leather wingback chair nearby.

The chief executive wasted no time.

"Okay," he said. "Let's hear it."

Carson spoke first. "Mr. President, are you familiar with the acronym VIX?"

"No. What is it?"

Carson nodded to Krewell, sitting stiffly beside him.

Krewell said, "Yes, sir. VIX stands for Viral Influenza/Experimental. It is a prototype bioweapon that was developed in the mid-sixties, only a few years before President Nixon officially shut down our CBW program. Agent VIX, as we call it, was—*is*—a viral weapon based on the same general viral strain that is today being used against us."

"The United States developed a weapon based on the Spanish flu?" The President's voice was incredulous and tinged at the edges with fury.

"Not as a lethal agent, Mr. President," Krewell said. "VIX was intentionally—well, dumbed down, so to speak. Genetically moderated."

"Exactly what is that supposed to mean?" the President demanded.

"As a weapon, VIX was designed solely as an incapacitating agent," Carson said. "It was not intended to kill."

"Exactly, Mr. President," Krewell said. "Our scientists used the 1918 virus, yes. But that was largely because, unlike other influenza strains, it did not lend itself easily to a vaccine. Also because the target population—combatant soldiers—generally had no acquired immunity to the strain. They were too young to have been around in 1918."

"Unbelievable," the President said, his lips tight. "Un-*fucking*-believable."

"Sir, VIX conformed to our standing bio-agent development orders in place at the time," Krewell protested. "It is not persistent: the virus was engineered so that ultraviolet radiation from sunlight destroys it within three to five hours. Most important, it a self-correcting agent. It acts to trigger an aggressive immune response in those exposed to it. With VIX, you're sick as hell for a day or so—but then the symptoms generally subside. By design, it's merely a very bad twenty-four-hour flu."

"Which the United States of America turned into a weapon," the President said bitterly. "And which we have apparently maintained, in violation of international treaties that we as a country proposed and signed!"

"As a weapon, VIX has some very attractive features,"

Carson said. "It has an extremely high contagion factor. Physiologically, it spreads through the human body with an impressive speed. The onset of symptoms is within a twenty-minute time frame—that's comparable to some of the slower-acting chemical warfare agents. The psychological impact adds to the effectiveness of VIX. You can imagine the demoralizing impact of seeing the disease spread almost before your eyes."

"Billy, the last thing I want to hear right now is how great any of this . . . *filth* is," the President said. "I simply cannot understand the reasoning behind this kind of insanity—particularly now, when it looks as if it may well destroy all of us."

He gestured at the far end of the room. "See those people down there? That's the United States government, helpless to stop this country from disintegrating. Since the news from Russia got out, all hell has broken loose. We have major riots in New York and Chicago, and martial law has been completely ineffective. Civilians are taking the law into their own hands, and we can't stop them. Barricades are up around Salt Lake City to keep 'plague carriers' out, manned by regular citizens carrying shotguns and rifles. They've fired on police who ordered them to disperse. Los Angeles is being patrolled by the National Guard. There are all kinds of rumors going around about the Florida outbreak, and it's got people acting insane. An hour ago, a crowd in Detroit surrounded a tractor trailer with Florida plates; they set it on fire and shot the driver when he tried to get out of the cab. It is getting worse by the minute. God help us if—*when*—flu cases start showing up in New York."

The President's voice had risen throughout the tirade, and now it fell abruptly. "We need a vaccine, dammit—a *cure*, not another weapon."

"That is the point," Carson said. "VIX and the new virus come from the same root. They're related—cousins, if you will. But not *kissing* cousins."

"I'm too tired for riddles, Billy."

"An hour ago, I received information that an Army researcher had found something that may be vital. She was comparing VIX with H1N1-Florida—the lethal one."

"And?"

"There may be a way to use VIX to fight it. It's theoretical, but possible. Dr. Krewell can explain the details better than I."

"Mr. President," Larry Krewell began, "the human immune system uses three lines of defense against viruses: macrophages, antibodies and killer T-cells. The first two go after the virus itself; they're like bodyguards, sir. But when the virus gets inside a human cell and takes it over, macrophages and antibodies are helpless. T-cells are not; they are ruthless and kill the infected cells. But if the virus spreads in the body too quickly, T-cells can cause a path of destruction while never catching up to the disease itself."

"That's what happens with H1N1-Florida," Carson added. "Most victims die of respiratory failure or secondary infections due to the massive tissue damage. But VIX has been engineered to accelerate the immune process. In essence, it shortstops the virus before it can cause extensive tissue and organ damage."

"What does this have to do with the Florida virus?"

Carson took a deep breath, and wished he could light a cigarette here. "In humans, Mr. President, VIX triggers a sharply *accelerated* immune response. Specifically, it combats the infective process with hyperproduction of macrophages and antibodies. Essentially, VIX stimulates the body to successfully fight its own infection—for the most part, *before* T-cells go into action and cause further damage."

Carson took a deep breath to add emphasis. "And that response, Mr. President, also appears to effectively act against the H1N1-Florida virus."

The President looked at Carson with unblinking eyes. When he spoke, there was a new inflection in his voice.

"Do I hear you right? You're saying this VIX *cures* people who have this new disease?"

Krewell answered first, shaking his head firmly. "Mr. President, we don't know that," he said. "There has been no clinical testing—and, sir, there is not time for anything that would give us a conclusive answer to that. People already infected with the killer virus may be beyond any help. But VIX may give you a chance to save those who are not yet infected."

"It does appear likely that the two strains cannot exist in the same body," Carson added. "Not simultaneously. VIX appears to overwhelm the flu—to crowd it out, as it were."

"Can we use it as—I don't know, as a kind of vaccine?"

"It may confer some degree of subsequent immunity," Krewell said cautiously. "Certainly, antibodies are generated, in prodigious volume, during an acute VIX infection. H1N1 is an engineered virus. It's been artificially enhanced and modified, but some of the VIX antibodies might act against it." He made a gesture that conveyed, for an instant, his own frustration. "At least, that's one theory. The research simply isn't there, Mr. President."

"It may not be a cure or a vaccine, but Agent VIX might work as a firebreak," Carson insisted. "Herd immunity isn't a theory." The national security director turned toward the President. "We think VIX gives a fighting chance. Perhaps our only chance."

"You have a recommendation." It was not a question.

Carson nodded. "You order an intentional, widespread release of VIX—as a first priority, in a broad, concentric ring moving into the Florida Quarantine Region. We would then do likewise around New York, in both cases using existing VIX stocks." He looked at the President with steady eyes and admitted to the violation of international law. "There are limited supplies available for this purpose—here and at Porton Down, in England. Enough to initiate the VIX infection, at least. If successful, it will then begin to spread on its own."

"Explain to me—*precisely*—how this will stop the epidemic."

"Sir, a virus cannot live outside a host—in the case of the killer virus, an unprotected human," Krewell reminded him. "Unless it finds new hosts to infect, it burns out and is gone. That's what vaccination does. It takes people out of the pool of vulnerable hosts, which breaks the chain of contagion. Even if you can't immunize everybody, it makes it much harder for the virus to get to the unprotected ones. That's the herd immunity Mr. Carson referred to."

"If we release Agent VIX," Carson said, "we believe it will, at the very least, slow down the wildfire we're facing in Florida. The way you contain a forest fire is with backfires, and that's what we can do with VIX."

"It's a race, Mr. President," Krewell added. "If we can get enough people infected with Agent VIX, in a broad enough band around the foci of contagion, we believe that we can set up a herd immunity scenario."

"If they are infected with VIX," the President said, "they can't get the influenza."

"In a nutshell, Mr. President, that's it."

The President thought for a moment. "Forest fires can jump over backfire zones. What if the virus jumps past our band?"

"Very quickly," Carson said, "there would be no such band, sir. Agent VIX is highly contagious, Mr. President. That was the major reason it was considered experimental. No vaccine or antidote was successfully developed to prevent it from spreading to our own troops, which made it impractical as an operational weapon. If we release it, we must assume it will spread very quickly throughout the United States. On its own."

"In essence, you're recommending we use VIX to infect the entire country?"

Krewell and Carson exchanged glances.

"Yes, Mr. President," Carson said. "If it is going to be

done, it has to be done quickly, before the killer virus spreads further. As Dr. Krewell said, we cannot know for certain that VIX will save people who are already infected. Plus, there's reason to believe the flu virus has the ability to jump species, into pigs and migratory waterfowl. If we don't act, they could form a reservoir of contagion from which we may never escape."

"How quickly can this be done?" the President asked. "*If* I concur."

"We're making the arrangements now," Krewell said. "Contingent on your authorization."

"My authorization," the President repeated. "Give me the downside. What haven't you told me?"

"First, VIX is so contagious that it could easily spread *outside* the U.S.," Carson said. "Frankly, I believe this is desirable. But even if we made the attempt to minimize this, the possibility is there. Technically, Mr. President, it would be illegal. In effect, we'd be using a biological weapon in violation of numerous treaties and international law."

"The flu is highly contagious too," the President said. "If it's between H1N1 and VIX, I think most governments would make the obvious choice."

"The choice isn't quite that simple, sir. VIX was designed as an incapacitating agent against military targets," Krewell said. "Mainly young, healthy people whose immune system could deal with the overload. Even so, in tactical situations where we would employ VIX, our projections indicate a fatality rate of about two percent."

The President looked at Carson with hard eyes. "You're saying that if we use this, we intentionally kill two percent of the American people?"

"More," Carson said, and his voice was unflinching. "Widespread use will carry VIX infection far beyond its originally intended targets. To the elderly and the very young, persons with compromised immune systems. Other population groups probably have risk factors we can't even envision yet. When you factor in these groups, the projected percentage increases."

"How much?"

"Statistically, between four and seven percent," Krewell said. "As a realistic working percentage, we're using five percent."

The President sat very still, and Krewell could almost see him working the math in his mind, over and over. Krewell had done the same himself, done the horrific sums, the cold-blooded division, the ruthless subtraction.

The result always came out the same. The population of the United States, rounded off, came to about two hundred eighty million persons; world population was six billion souls. Five percent of those totals came to—

"Three hundred million people," the President said. "If I order this, the chances are that I will kill three hundred million people—fourteen million of them Americans."

"If you do not," Carson said, "you doom the rest."

Krewell spoke up. "There is something more to consider," he said. "The symptoms of both diseases are virtually identical. For H1N1-Florida, we've seen some wide swings in the incubation period between infection and the onset of symptoms—for some people, it's days. Others seem to succumb in eight hours or less. There's a possibility the flu has already spread and is simply incubating in many people who have not yet shown symptoms."

"And?" The President seemed not to understand.

"Well, sir," Krewell said. "If we release VIX on a widespread basis, we're certain to see flulike cases spring up all over—certainly in the U.S. and very likely elsewhere if it does spread to other countries. Millions upon millions of people will become ill within a short time span. We'll incapacitate whoever is still working in emergency services and the health system—doctors and nurses will be as sick as anybody else. Same with law enforcement, the military. VIX will literally shut everything down, very quickly. But—" His voice trailed off.

"But what?"

"Well, Mr. President," Krewell said, "as I said, the symptoms and antibody signatures of both are identical. We won't know which virus is activating the disease, the VIX or the killer flu."

The President clearly did not understand the implications. After a moment, his national security advisor spoke up.

"What Dr. Krewell means, sir, is that we won't know with certainty if the plan is working," Carson said. "Not until it's too late to do anything else. Except die."

Chapter 31

His leg, where one of the shotgun pellets had torn out a chunk of flesh, stung under the dressing he had improvised. He had easily stopped what little bleeding there had been. But now, after two hours spent parked casually in the vast parking area of a modern-looking rest stop, the wound had stiffened somewhat.

It hurts, he thought, *but worse—it is embarrassing. Forced to run like a rabbit, by a woman whose brains were all but pouring out of her ears! Ah, Ilya—it is well your old comrades are not here to see this, and to laugh at your ineptitude.*

He had been caught up in the dance of interrogation, too preoccupied in planning the rhythms and the choreography of pain to pay attention to the noises she must have made as she approached the tableau. Only the sound of the shotgun's pump mechanism—*hear* that *once, and survive it, and you never forget again,* he told himself wryly—only that sound had penetrated the exclusive relationship he had begun to establish with the man. He counted himself lucky to have escaped through the low underbrush with only this scratch as a souvenir.

The car was back on the interstate now, cruising at a speed only slightly above the posted speed limit. It was an untroubled drive on a fine road—particularly, he thought, one built through these most impressive mountains. Ilya considered himself a fair person, and ungrudgingly admired the quality of the highways he had found in this country. With the possible exception of the Autobahn, which he had driven a few months earlier while on another assignment, he had never seen finer roads.

Ilya regretted the lack of time with the man. He had resisted strongly, though the Russian had anticipated this from a fellow professional. But the breaking point certainly would have come; both of them knew it, he was certain. It was this shared knowledge, this . . . *intimacy* that had accounted for his inattention to his surroundings.

Unfortunate. He nodded silently. *On so many levels.*

Still, he now knew—almost for certain—that the CIA was working hand-in-glove with the federal police. This, he knew, was unusual for Americans. With only a few exceptions, they typically performed as wolverines locked in the same cage. Cooperation was rare, mutual animosity usually fierce.

So this Trippett and his play-soldier militia must have great significance to them too, he thought. *Even more interesting, if they are looking for this man, it is because they themselves do not have him. He is still a viable threat, and my assignment is still unresolved.*

No matter. He would look, and he would find Trippett. And then he would ask him the questions his employer wished answered. Ilya had no doubt the man would gratefully provide the information that was required, at some point in their conversation.

In his experience, almost everybody did.

Chapter 32

State Hwy. 241
Mielcarz, North Carolina
July 23

For Deborah Stepanovich, her eyes burning and her hands shaking in near exhaustion, the four hundred-plus miles she had traveled in the past seven hours had been a trip through hell.

It had not lacked for demons—many of them, she understood, of her own imagining, though that made them no less frightening. Neither had it lacked for sulfurous flames, a particularly vivid, dark orange corona against the black summer sky over several of the cities she had skirted.

Since leaving Virginia, Deborah had scanned the radio frequencies. Most were static filled, or—to her mind, worse—dead air. The few radio stations that were still broadcasting told tales of martial law, of riots breaking out even in smaller cities. There was little about the flu that she considered "news"; but the broadcasters still on the air made up for that shortage with an excess of rumors and wild conjecture.

Deborah had consulted her road atlas frequently, avoiding the main roads and skirting any city of significant size. She had skimmed the eastern edge of the Alleghenies, and their imposing bulk seen through her passenger window felt comforting and serene.

She had felt herself in personal danger only once, when halfway across North Carolina a two-vehicle covey had suddenly appeared in her rearview mirror. The first, a rust-dappled pickup truck, had spun from a side road seconds after she had sped past. Behind the pickup, a Firebird had fishtailed onto the pavement in turn, their wheels spitting gravel and dust.

Her stomach had dropped as the vehicles mushroomed in her mirrors, and for the first time Deborah wished she possessed a gun, even a knife. She pressed harder on the accelerator, but when she looked up again the pickup was so close she could read the letters on its grille: F RD, it read, the missing letter like a gap-toothed leer.

And then the truck swerved to the side and roared past with a broken-muffler flatulence that she felt even through her closed windows. Before her mind could register this fact, the other car shot past; from the Firebird, a girl who could not have been older than twelve waved excitedly from the passenger seat.

Deborah Stepanovich blew out the breath she had not realized she was holding, and willed herself to stop trembling. There was a moment of elation that flooded through her; then she felt the old anger rise—not surprisingly, at Beck.

Her temper flared. *Damn him!*

For an instant, she thought about what could have happened, what she had expected was about to occur; vivid images, some of them pornographic in their violence, flashed across her mental cinema.

He should have been here to help. But he never was, not when I needed—

She stopped short.

"Is this what it felt like, Beck?" she said aloud. "Is this what is was like out there in your world? Every day, every minute?"

She had seldom thought about that side of it.

But Katie is in danger and I—

Again she stopped herself.

I've spent my adult life without his help.

"And I did pretty fucking well on my own," Deborah said, again aloud, and was surprised at how much she savored the profanity. Despite herself, she smiled. "All on my . . . *fucking* own."

She drove on, not knowing there was a smile on her face.

Deborah saw only a few other cars before dusk fell, and none of them took any notice of her.

Outside Gaffney, South Carolina, Deborah filled her fuel tank at a BP station. There, she found that an executive order prohibiting fuel sales simply translated into a per-gallon black market price that roughly approximated that of single-malt Scotch.

The terms were non-negotiable: cash in hand. Deborah did not flinch as she handed the attendant two hundred-dollar bills, which he folded into his pocket with a nervous grin. But she supervised, tight-lipped and intent, as he filled the tank. She spoke sharply at the end, and glared until he topped off the last few ounces. She even pretended not to hear what he muttered as he replaced the hose in the pump.

Then she drove off, her stomach fluttering and her heart pounding madly.

Deborah swung far to the east of Atlanta, figuring to avoid whatever structures might be in place there, whether by law enforcement or those who defy it.

But even the most reasoned plans go awry in the face of reality; none of the alternate routes she traced on her map took her toward her destination. She pressed on for a while on roads that ran, more or less, due south; twice she found herself lost, even with her map open on the passenger seat beside her.

Finally, just before the nighttime darkness grew complete,

Deborah looked up through her windshield and mentally sighed. Above her idling Mercedes, the sign at the crossroads intersection pointed west. A blue-and-white shield gleamed in her high beams.

Interstate 85 it is, I guess, she told herself. *Here goes nothing.*

Ninety minutes later, she was one of the handful of vehicles speeding along the concrete ribbon of the interstate. To the north, a faint flickering glow marked where the skyline of Atlanta should have been; apparently, electrical power had failed, at least in the central business district. Her detour had added a hundred miles, and brought her only a dozen or so miles south of the metropolis.

But Deborah was past Atlanta now, and closer to where she knew, in her heart, Katie waited for her arrival. She sped up, slightly, at the thought.

She glanced at the sign as it flashed past.

MONTGOMERY, ALABAMA, it read, 192 MILES.

Chapter 33

If he pulled back the black-out drape slightly, Ray Porter could look out over the football field a scant fifty yards away. Occasionally he saw movement, dim figures moving ghost-like amid the canvas village. Most then disappeared into the darkness of the field, bearing what he assumed were stretchers.

Briefly, Porter wondered whether what they carried was alive or dead. He could not tell. The lights that the engineers had strung between the tents hung like a pale yellow necklace carelessly tossed, its weak glow waxing and waning with the fitful surges of the generators.

Here, in the elementary school gymnasium they had converted into a testing facility, illumination was anything but scarce.

No, Porter thought, and behind the acrylic faceshield of the physician's breathing apparatus his lips twisted wryly. *That's not quite accurate.*

It was light that was plentiful—an otherworldly blue-white light that filled every corner of the gymnasium with a cold glare. As for illumination—*well,* he thought, *we'll see how much of that we have here soon. Very soon.* Porter let the curtain drop, snapping the dark UV shield back over his helmet's faceplate before he turned back to the room.

"Dr. Porter? We're ready to start."

The voice was pitched low, but even so the physician could hear the near-exhaustion in the tone. It was not, Porter knew, a good sign. The whole team had been working non-stop, first on outbreak evaluation and then—after CDC had been advised that Fort Detrick was sending a very special package for Porter's people to live-test—on preparing a jury-rigged containment system. They were all tired.

And tired people make mistakes.

Which we damn well can't afford, Porter reminded himself wordlessly. *Certainly not with this damnable stuff.*

Porter had been briefed on the virulence of VIX and on the potential it carried for both good and ill. Of course he knew "Major Barbara" Jones—biological research and epidemiology are part of the same elite circle; everybody called her that, albeit behind her back—and during the conference call they had patched between Washington, USAMRIID, CDC-Atlanta and here, the Army researcher had been unable to keep the excitement from her voice.

"The lab work is sound, Ray," Jones had insisted. "VIX will *definitely* stimulate the immune system in any subject, even one already infected with your H1N1-Florida virus. You should see hyperproduction of antibodies within an hour of VIX exposure—and because the base virus was the parent organism for both VIX and your killer flu, the antibodies should be effective on both."

Ray Porter had grunted, a noncommittal response he hoped sounded professional. But when he spoke, he had carefully avoided the word "cure."

"As a theory, I concur," Porter said. "As a treatment therapy, Barb—well, I have concerns. VIX may work or it may not. But if it escapes and makes it into the general population . . ." He paused, leaving the words unsaid. "A live-subject test in the kind of field conditions we face here is very, very risky."

"Riskier than what? Than flying an infected subject out of the contagion zone to test up here?"

"That's simply not going to happen, Doctors."

It was a new voice, one that Ray Porter had known belonged to the only person with the power to make this decision final. The voice spoke firmly, in the manner of one accustomed to commanding others.

"Dr. Porter, you will devise a suitable containment there, in Fort Walton Beach—one that will prevent VIX from posing an immediate threat outside. No, please don't interrupt, Doctor. You will receive a sufficient supply of VIX to test its effectiveness on persons already infected with the killer flu; you will use as many subjects as needed to obtain results that will be representative of the U.S. population as a whole."

The voice had softened, and for a moment Ray Porter felt a twinge of profound sympathy for its owner.

"People will die as a direct result of your tests, Dr. Porter. For that, I accept complete responsibility." Then the tone hardened again. "You have your orders. Make the arrangements, and proceed."

"Yes, Mr. President," Porter had said, but the connection had already been broken.

Now, only a few hours afterward, Ray Porter turned from the shrouded window to survey the school gymnasium his team had labored to turn into a microcosm of Level 4 containment. The ultraviolet lights had been commandeered from tanning salons they had found in the Yellow Pages, rewired and configured in a ring around the gym's center court.

The lights surrounded a bubble of clear vinyl that in its original incarnation had been designed as a low-cost greenhouse; it had come from a garden supply store a few blocks south, as had the hand-pump sprayers now being used on its exterior surfaces. Empty gallon jugs of household bleach littered the far reaches of the parqueted floor. Other elements—ductwork, blowers, and more—had also been incorporated, Rube Goldberg–like.

It was an ingenious design, readily duplicated in field conditions anywhere. Or so the team hoped.

Inside the bubble, a half-dozen camp beds held the forms—some thrashing, some moving only feebly—of what were now the most important people on earth. Like worker bees attending a comatose queen, members of Porter's team moved among them, testing and measuring.

And waiting.

"Dr. Porter."

Ray tore his attention from the tableau and turned to the spacesuited figure who now stood at his elbow.

"There's a woman outside—a Dr. Mayer—who insists on talking with you immediately. She says it's urgent."

"What do you mean, gone?" Ray Porter's voice was frankly skeptical, even a little suspicious.

Carol took a deep breath, wishing she felt less like a traitor.

"I mean gone," she repeated. "Missing. Nowhere to be found. Out of here."

Porter snorted, the sound odd from behind the Plexiglas faceshield. "Not likely, Dr. Mayer. Not from here."

"Look," Carol said. "They're two teenage girls. They were showing no symptoms; they are not incapacitated in any way."

She waved her arm, a broad gesture that covered the entire grounds of the stadium. Outside the illumination that dappled the canvas treatment tents, an unyielding blackness reigned. Only a thin slice of the stadium's perimeter fencing could be seen.

"Those are chain-link fences. There's not even much of a moon tonight. Where are the guards? The only ones I've seen here are stationed around your incoming operations. The people here are too sick to *want* to escape."

Carol forced herself to remain calm.

"Correct me if I am wrong, Dr. Porter. My guess is that you did not choose a high school football field with the intention of preventing someone from going over the wall—certainly not two kids who think they're healthy and feel like leaving."

Porter looked hard at Carol. "You're certain they're not still here, somewhere?"

"I'm certain I can't find them," Carol retorted, "and I looked. If I were you, I'd start looking too. And you should ask someone to look in the parking lot of the clinic. That's where I parked my pickup."

"You're worried about your truck?"

"No, Dr. Porter. I'm worried about the spread of this virus. You see, my keys are missing too."

Chapter 34

The two of them looked a mess.

The back and right sides of April's head were heavily bandaged; bruises, abrasions and deep scratches on her face, arms and hands were scabbing souvenirs of her crawl through the brush and rocks. Beck's head was bandaged too: an X of adhesive tape held the gauze pad over the shaved patch where the doctors had taken six stitches. He sat in the visitor's chair, his heel resting on the foot of April's hospital bed. His pant leg at the thigh was tight over its thick cocoon of bandages. Gauze and tape also covered his wrists, where the weight of his body had forced the handcuffs to bite deep into the flesh.

Frank Ellis would have felt even more responsible than he already did—*should have known pairing O'Connor with this damn CIA spook was asking for trouble,* he berated himself—except both of his charges were in such high spirits that at first he wondered if they had been given an excess of painkillers. Then the realization hit the FBI supervisor: April and Beck were simply glad to be alive. Not many hours before, neither had expected to be.

"She snores," Beck bitched happily. "And not a dainty little whistle, either. The damn windows rattle."

"Nobody forced you to sit there," April countered. "You could have hung around the cafeteria, tried hitting on the nurses. Play on their sympathy, maybe."

It had been like this in the room since Ellis entered almost a half hour before. He understood the two were performing—partly for him, but mostly for each other. It was the same kind of postgame bravado that surfaces in any contest where the underdog pulls out a close, come-from-behind victory. There was no mention of the dark man they had both survived, and Ellis understood that too.

The only break had been right after his arrival. April had introduced the two men, and Beck had immediately asked for the status of the search for his daughter. Ellis had looked perplexed—no request for status and location of the missing girl had been relayed by Andi Wheelwright—then covered with professional ease, citing a litany of treatment centers and CDC field facilities where the name of Katie Casey had not shown up on any lists.

"That's *good* news, Dr. Casey," Ellis had insisted, remembering from his training classes at Quantico not to put too much obvious sincerity into his tone. "It improves the chances of her being outside the contagion ring. Your daughter may even have made it out of the state before the quarantine was ordered."

Beck had eyed Ellis without expression, though the FBI man imagined he could see the wheels spinning behind Casey's impassive demeanor. In his peripheral vision, he noted the way April O'Connor captured it all, her eyes flickering between the other two.

Finally Beck spoke. "You'll keep looking?"

"Every agency involved will keep looking," Ellis had replied, and realized that he meant it. Mentally, he made a note to alert every FBI facility to press hard to locate this man's daughter; he made a second note to find out why Andi Wheelwright had not already done so.

At that moment, the telephone on the table between the beds rang, and the shrill sound shattered the somber mood that had descended.

Beck won the almost-adolescent race. He snatched the phone from under April's reaching fingers, and grinned in giddy triumph.

"O'Connor's Seafood Shack," he said into the instrument. "You got the time, we've got the crabs." He ignored April's mock-enraged hiss and listened to the voice at the other end. "Hey, Larry." He winked at April, careful to hold the phone out of her reach. "Nah—we're fine. Be out of here in no time." He listened for a moment. "Yeah, they're both here."

A pause, and then Beck broke into a broad grin. "Sure, I'll tell her. Hold on."

He cupped a hand over the receiver, then turned to April. "Dr. Krewell says some county cop named McGuire's been calling in every half hour, trying to find you," Beck said, and watched as the FBI agent's ears turned pink. "Aha. April's got a boyfriend," he crooned in a mischievous singsong, then raised his hands in mock-terror as she groped for something to throw.

"Sure, I'll tell her," Beck said, sounding stronger than Krewell had expected. "Hold on." As he waited on the line, Krewell half-heard the buzz of conversation in the background. Then there was a loud clatter, almost like a lamp falling to the floor, and the unmistakable sounds of laughter.

"You behave, dammit," Beck's voice came over the line, sounding stern, "or I'll have them tie you to your bed." Then he also laughed. It had been days since Krewell had last heard genuine humor in Beck's voice. He regretted being the one to crush it.

"Yeah, Larry," Beck said. "I'm back."

"When things are bad, they just get worse. We have a report from New York City. They caught a guy in a boat on the Hudson, figured he was trying to hightail it out of town. He tried to make a run for it, and a police sharpshooter in a helicopter had to put a round in him."

"Dead?"

"Yeah," Krewell said. "They searched the boat and found a bunch of pretty vicious pamphlets in a bag on board. Seems the guy was a member of one of those militia outfits — something called the Legionnaires of the Empire State. The guy's name was Dickie Trippett."

"I don't suppose that's a coincidence."

"He's Orin's cousin."

"Uh-huh. So?"

"They found something else too. Three pressurized cans, one of 'em open. Looks like the virus has made it to New York. And I'd bet that Orin is carrying the same package his cousin had. CDC's field lab in New York is testing the contents now."

"Why bother?" Beck asked, and there was bitterness in his voice.

In the silence that followed, he sensed that Krewell wanted to confide in him. He waited for what seemed like a long time.

"We may have a chance — maybe," he said. "One of the voodoo priests out at Fort Detrick has come up with an idea. It sounds dicey, but it's the only one we have left."

After Ellis left, April and Beck returned to something closer to their normal personalities. The banter slowed, and finally ground to a halt as the two retreated into their own thoughts. April surprised herself: she found herself thinking about Beck's antics, and didn't know whether to be touched, amused or alarmed. There was nothing sexual about the way he treated her — nothing overtly so, that is. In her experience, few people — none of them male — could make the jump to

intergender friendship without at least a brief sexual specula-
tion.

Still, it would be good to have a friend.

"You asleep?" Beck's voice startled her.

"Just thinking," she said, and was silent for a minute.
"Leg hurt much?"

Beck grunted, his mind obviously elsewhere. "The guy,
the Russian—obviously, he was waiting for Trippett."

"Yeah. Probably. So?"

"So the guy wanted to know who I was, who sent me—
why I was with an FBI agent. He had a lot of questions, but
he didn't ask the obvious one."

"Which is?"

"He didn't find Trippett at the trailer. So why didn't he ask
if I had an idea where to look next?"

Beck frowned, as if wrestling with a stubborn mathemat-
ical equation.

"He already knew," he finally said aloud. "Or he thinks he
knows where Trippett is now." He rubbed his eyes in frustration. "I'm not getting it. My head's still fogged from these
pills they gave me."

"I'm kind of blurred over, too," April admitted. "You're
trying too hard, Beck. Relax, and it'll come to you. Drift for
a while."

"Uh-huh," Beck said, doubtfully. He did not want to
relax; he did not want his mind to drift. He did not like the
thoughts it drifted toward.

When Beck had been in the hands of the Russian *Mafiya*,
what had sustained him longer than he had thought possible
was a single belief: that within the vast apparatus of the organization for which he worked, wheels were turning. A rescue was—*had* to be—both inevitable and imminent.

What had finally broken him had been neither the psychoactive drug injections nor even the often-hideous pain his
captors had inflicted. It had been the realization that there

could be, would be no rescue. The revelation that, in the end, nobody was out there to come for him.

Before his capture, he had believed that he had two families. One was his wife and child, the other the CIA.

By the second week in the hands of the *Mafiya*, he no longer believed he would ever see Deborah and Katie again. In his guilt and shame, he told himself that was even for the best: he had long been too careless with their love, he knew, drawing on it like a spendthrift draws on a shared account until it is bankrupt.

Finally, when the interrogation had been at its most violent, he had pushed Deborah and Katie outside the torture chamber, locking the door behind them and shattering the key. It was an act of simple self-preservation: their very existence made Beck excruciatingly vulnerable to both hope and despair.

As for the CIA, which had asked for his loyalty and trust, which had demanded so much from him—he had waited, with the inculcated faith of the professional. In the end, the Company had coldly given back . . . nothing. At that moment, under the renewed attentions of the *Mafiya* technician, he realized that he had lost both of his families.

Since then, he had been empty, unwilling or unable to regain either of them.

Yes, and that's why you would have cracked like an eggshell this time—a lot faster, too, Beck told himself acidly. *Admit it—you were ready to tell him anything to keep it from happening. And would have, if she hadn't come stumbling out of the dark with that beautiful gun in her hands.*

Beck glanced at April, and saw her staring fixedly at the ceiling above her head.

He wondered if, in her mind's eye, she too saw a thin Moorish moon in a black sky. And whether she too heard, mingled with the slapping of water against rock, a merciless voice offering the urgent, yearned-for relief of a quick death.

He hoped not; he would not wish that on anyone else.

Then the bedside telephone rang again. This time, April answered. She spoke — at first, with a wary expression. Gradually, her features relaxed, then brightened. And after a few moments more — during which she laughed three times, by Beck's count — April pushed the receiver in Beck's direction.

"It's for you, double-oh-seven," she said. "Remember my 'boyfriend,' Deputy McGuire? Said if we still want to find Trippett, maybe he can help. Wants to know if we're still interested."

As Beck snatched at the receiver, she plucked it back out of reach.

"I said we were," April told Beck. "Please note the pronoun. We're going out of here together, even if I have to commandeer a wheelchair."

Chapter 35

Orin Trippett knew better than to call any of his contacts directly, even from a pay telephone. He, like all members of his militia, was well briefed on the dangers associated with any form of electronic communication.

"NSA's been intercepting every phone call in the continental United States for more than fifteen damn years," he had told his people, reciting the information he and the other platoon officers had culled from various newsletters and militia-oriented Web sites. "Same with fax—and now, e-mail. It all goes through computers looking for key words they've got flagged."

He had cocked his head quizzically at the group.

"You want to have the ATF, the FBI, maybe even the goddamn Boy Scouts show up at your door?" he asked. "Well, then—all you gotta do is use the words 'president' and 'assassinate' in the same phone call. I guarantee y'all have company *real* quick."

The line never failed to bring down the house. Everybody always seemed honestly amused, if in an outraged sort of way. Widespread illegal surveillance, electronic or not, was just more proof that "the G" was capable of any abuse.

Hell, it might even be true, he thought to himself. *But this sure ain't no time to find out.*

Now, still tired from the circuitous drive along backcountry roads that had avoided any police roadblocks, Orin wedged the car between two similarly battered-looking vehicles. The sun was a half hour away from rising, and he walked down a still-darkened street on Denver's gritty southwest side.

It was a neighborhood of dirt driveways and rusted pickup trucks, with the occasional chrome-laden Harley secured by a chain to the porch. These were working-class houses, their windows darkened hours before by residents who were usually awake to greet the dawn from jobs on the early shift. Occasionally, a dog barked at the echoes of Orin's footsteps on concrete chipped and cracked.

Midway down the block, he climbed the steps to an asphalt-shingled bungalow fronted with a weather-grayed porch. He knocked—softly at first, then with a louder impatience. Finally, a light deep inside the structure snapped on and Orin saw movement behind the door's curtained glass.

"Orin? That you, boy?"

"Let me in, Cappie."

The door opened, wide enough for him to slip into the house.

Inside, a heavyset man in a soiled green T-shirt and boxers broke into a wide grin. He shifted the pistol he held, a blue steel Colt Python, to his left hand and extended his right.

"Damn, boy—we've been wondering if you got out." Cappie dropped his unshaken hand, awkward under Trippett's unblinking eyes. "I guess you heard. They kilt Bobby. Gil, too."

"I was there, Cappie."

"Sure. Sure, I know you was. Hey, you want a beer? Some coffee?"

"What I want, Cappie—what I dearly want, more than

anything else in the *fuckin'* world—is to find out how the goddamn feds knew to come lookin' in the warehouse."

"How'm I supposed to—"

"Bitch had a fuckin' warrant, Cappie." Orin's voice was still low, but carried the intensity of a laser. "She and that spic waved it right in my face. Somebody's talking. They knew where to look for the '16s."

"Bullshit," Cappie said, and now his voice was angry too. "If somebody talked, why would the feds come looking now? Damn, boy—we moved them guns outta there three days ago!"

Orin was in no mood for his subordinate's logic. "And then we lose the Jap nerve gas, too," he said. "Fuck did you go off to? Gil and Bobby go down, so you just take the hell off?"

"I was shooting too," Cappie protested. "I had my Russian AK. I burned up two full clips, all I had, out the side window. Damn, same time's I was trying to drive the truck, boy! Then you was gone, and I seen Bobby and Gil take it. All the shooting, you knowed the cops had to be on the way. What'd you want me to do? Wait around and surrender to 'em?"

"Seems that's what you wanted me to do."

Cappie threw up his hands, the gun still gripped in his left. "Jesus Lord! Okay, I'm sorry you got left. I'm sorry I ain't got X-ray eyes so I coulda seen the Spanish guy hadn't shot you dead."

There was a noise from the back of the house, and Trippett's head swiveled so quickly the tendons popped loudly. His eyes, narrowed to mere slits, darted to Cappie's face.

"Fuck you got back there?"

"Jesus, Orin—it's just Lubella. Lubella Tompkins. Bobby Touchette's cousin, okay?" He raised his voice. "Honey? C'mon out here and say hi to Orin."

A woman of perhaps thirty, her features sharp and feral, stepped from the bedroom darkness into the long living room. She wore a man's pocket T-shirt that fell just below the junction of her thin legs; as she moved, the small cones of her breasts bounced against the fabric. She stared at Orin for a long moment, her expression cold; then she moved to the dining table and picked up a pack of cigarettes.

"What you say, Orin? You want Lubella to fix up something to eat? She don't mind—right, baby doll?"

The match flared, and the pool of light it cast around her face caught her in an eyes-tight grimace as she brought her cigarette to the flame. Lubella drew the smoke in deeply, and exhaled it with a sibilance that was sharp and disapproving.

"Cook your own damn food," she said. "Lincoln freed the slaves, or ain't ya heard?"

Cappie colored. "Damn it, Lubella, I said to—"

"Up yours," Lubella overrode him. "I'm going back to bed. You make a mess, I ain't cleaning it up tomorrow." She took several steps, then turned at the door. "Whatever you two got in them pea-brains of yours, leave me the hell out of it," she said evenly.

"You don't know nuthin' 'bout it," Cappie said.

"I know I ain't gonna get killed like poor Bobby," she said. "You take your machine guns and your poison shit somewheres else."

Both men watched the door close behind her, and heard the sharp click of the lock.

Cappie stood for a moment as if poleaxed.

"I'll be damned," he said. He looked at Orin, a helpless expression on his face. "*Fuckin'* women. She don't know shit 'bout it, Orin. Hell—I don't know shit, either. 'Cept that I'm on *your* side, man. You know that."

"Somebody tipped the feds," Orin repeated. "You got any thoughts about that, Cappie?"

"Yeah, but you ain't gonna like it. They went to the warehouse because they knew *you* was workin' there. They was *fishin'*, man. Somebody pushed a button on some damn computer, and your rap sheet popped up. Uh-uh, Orin. If they'd been tipped guns was there, they'd of sent a lot more than four people."

After a moment, Orin's own features relaxed.

"The spic guy was ATF," Orin said finally. The hostility with which he had entered had evaporated, and in its place was an attitude of casual calm. "When I got free of that fed bitch, he was inside on his little-bitty walkie-talkie yelling for help. Shit, I almost run right into him in the dark. Knocked the flashlight right out of his damn hand."

"I heard some shooting in there."

Orin shook his head in contempt. "I got out the back 'fore he even drew his gun, man. Heard him stumblin' round in the dark. That musta been when the fucker knocked over the crate with the nerve gas."

Cappie forehead furrowed. "I heard he got shot by one of his own."

"Maybe. But by then, he was a dead man walkin'."

"Damn," Cappie said. "Think I'd rather catch a bullet."

Orin shrugged. "Probably never knew what hit him."

"Too bad about the sarin, though. Coulda come in handy with the Denver thing."

"Yeah, well. Can't cry over spilt nerve gas, huh?" Orin chuckled at his own joke. "'Sides, gotta figure it took down one fed. And, hell—we still got that other shit the Jap brought. Gets down to brass tacks, a little bit of anthrax goes a long way."

"You still good to go?" Cappie asked. "When you want to do it?"

Orin pulled up a chair and settled into it. "Well, boy— what you say we have some of that beer, first. Maybe get a little shut-eye too. You still workin' at that movie theater?"

Cappie nodded. "Damn flu thing's got it shut down, though. Don't know how long."

"Good. Nobody'll be around." Orin thought for a moment. "Okay. We'll use the movie place as a . . . a rallying point. Need to, that's where we'll tell our people to meet. I'm staying here till we do it, and I don't want nobody to know where I am." He nodded in the direction of the bedroom. "You keep her shut up about me, hear?"

Orin put his feet on the kitchen table, and one hand curled into the pocket of his jacket. It came out holding what to Cappie looked like a small red-and-white labeled can. Orin set it on the table carefully.

"Then—if you think Lubella'll *let* you, that is—we'll saddle up about noon, and go wipe out Denver."

Chapter 36

At first, Katie had found it rather exhilarating, racing along graveled roads and two-lane blacktops in a stolen pickup truck. She had driven throughout the night, trusting both to luck and the surprisingly detailed road maps J. L. had found in Carol Mayer's vehicle. It seemed almost heroic—the two of them on the run, armed with a learner's permit and dodging whatever authority might still be hunting them. She envisioned herself and J. L. as a latter-day Thelma and Louise, though far younger and more attractive.

But the closer she got to her objective, the harder it had become to see the situation as anything but what it was. They were alone, possibly infected with some kind of germ that had already killed one of their friends and traveling through what had become a frightening, virtually lawless land. It got worse the closer they got to Tallahassee, when they traded the largely rural Florida landscape for the city's outskirts. Soon they were motoring through what was an unmistakably urban area, its atmosphere one of tired neglect.

For Katie, it was unfamiliar territory—progressively tougher-looking neighborhoods populated by progressively harder-looking residents. While few other vehicles were moving on the streets Katie drove, people were. The closer she got to the city center, the more crowds she encountered—first in knots along the sidewalks, gradually in larger numbers that spilled into the street. Some were profoundly drunk, others plainly predatory. One of the latter, a man with dirty blond hair and a Seminole tattoo on his bare shoulder, cupped his hands and shouted an obscene invitation as Katie motored past. Other men had similar notions, also appearing to find a pickup truck occupied by two teenage girls a focus of increasing interest. Katie found herself frequently cutting down side streets and alleys to avoid the growing throngs in the street.

After a while, Katie no longer knew in which direction she was driving.

The crowds were getting thicker where she now drove, and angrier. Debris littered the street, and once she had to steer around a brace of tires that had been set afire; sullen orange flames vomited an evil black plume. A bottle arched through the air to shatter on the pavement a few feet in front of her vehicle. A block or so farther down, the crowd had spilled from the sidewalks and completely blocked the street.

There were no police to be seen.

"Let's get away from here," Katie heard J. L. say in a tight voice.

She turned left onto a cracked and pitted roadway, and a smile spread on her face.

There, the distance foreshortened by the low perspective, was the skyline of downtown Tallahassee.

Katie slowed, her attention momentarily fixed on the target finally before her.

Distracted, she did not notice anything amiss—not until the chunk of concrete starred her windshield, a shattering supernova that peppered both of them with small rounded fragments and turned the safety glass opaque.

"J. L.!" she screamed, her heart in sudden tachycardia.

At the same time, the truck rocked to the side and something, a short length of pipe, smashed through the driver's window next to her head. More fragments exploded against her, these sharper ones that stung into her face and neck.

A muscular arm reached through the hole, fingers extended toward the key ring that hung from the ignition switch. Katie struck at it with a closed fist, seeing for the first time the other figures converging toward the slowly moving vehicle. A hailstorm of hard objects noisily dented the hood and sidewalls. She heard shouting from immediately outside her window, angry and demanding words that in her terror did not register as language.

"Go, go, go!" J. L. screamed from beside her, and Katie jammed her foot hard against the firewall.

The pickup lurched forward, tires squealing and raising a thick curlicue of smoke. She felt a muffled bang as something substantial hit hard against the passenger door and spun away; she barely heard the curses shrieked in her wake. Through J. L.'s window, Katie saw other figures sprinting toward their vehicle, and she wrenched the wheel back and forth to scatter them.

The disembodied hand was now clutching frantically at the steering wheel, and Katie fought it for possession. It would not release its desperate grip, not even when the vehicle swerved sharply, bouncing over the curb and speeding toward the lamppost.

There was a loud screeching noise—possibly the scream of metal scraping against metal, or possibly something more human—and the arm disappeared back out the window with a horrifying abruptness. Katie, too terrified now even to scream, cut hard back toward the street, leaning forward to peer around the spiderweb of the ruined windshield.

And suddenly she was clear.

Katie sped on for a few seconds before the realization rose sufficiently to smother the fear. She felt a rush of exhilaration, of triumph even.

Oh, that dirty bastard, she told herself, her thoughts a disjointed ramble, *he thought he could get to the key and he won't try that anymore—*

Oh, God. I think I killed somebody.

Without knowing why, she stood on the brake pedal, locking the wheels and again raising smoke from the tires. Then she ripped the door open and stood, breathing in rapid gasps and with one foot still in the truck.

Thirty yards behind her, the milling crowd she had driven through still roiled like an angry storm cloud. People, some burdened by double armloads of clothing or expensive-looking consumer electronics, stumbled along the sidewalks. A tendril of smoke wafted from a shattered display window, and a flickering light fitfully dappled the otherwise darkened interior of the store. In the distance, Katie could hear sirens and the vicious, flat cracks of what might have been gunfire.

Closer to them, a man lay facedown and spread-eagled on the sidewalk, a few yards past the crumpled half comma of the streetlight stanchion. Aside from a dark pool slowly spreading from under the figure, there was no other movement there.

Katie stared in horrid fascination, unable to tear her eyes from the scene.

J. L. was near hysterics.

"Katie, get back in!" She reached over and pulled hard at her friend's wrist, tugging until Katie finally climbed back inside the cab.

"Keep going," J. L. said. "We've got to get away from all this." Her head swiveled back to her friend, and she saw the streaks of tears on Katie's face.

"Are you all right? Did he hurt you?"

Katie shook her head. She wiped angrily at her cheeks, both sides, with the heel of her hand. To J. L., it appeared that she shook herself physically.

"Damn."

"What?"

Katie pointed to the dashboard.

Near the fuel gauge, an indicator had flickered to life. LOW FUEL, it said in unequivocal crimson letters.

"I'm going to try to get as close to downtown as I can," Katie said. "Maybe there's no rioting there; it might be safer. We'll be out of gas soon."

"Great," said J. L., trying to pretend that she had recovered from their experience. "Then what?"

"Then," Katie said, frowning in concentration as she peered through the starred windshield, "I guess we walk."

Chapter 37

Columbia Falls, Montana
July 23

Carl McGuire was dying for a cigarette.

At least, that's what his doctor told him three weeks, five days, two hours and—he checked his watch—eleven minutes ago, following the annual physical examination required of all department heads in the White Bison County Sheriff's Police.

"Look at the goddamn numbers, Carl," Doc Bartfield had told him. "Your lung capacity looks like hell. Another year, and you'll be at the official disability level. And that is a half step away from having to pull an oxygen bottle behind you." The physician snorted in disgust. " 'Taper off,' my ass. Listen to me, and listen good. As far as you are concerned, smoke another cigarette and you will die."

So he didn't smoke. For a man who barely remembered his childhood catechism classes, it was as close to a religion as he had had in almost four decades. It had as its central article of faith a simple dictum voiced by a high priest who carried a stethoscope. It had as its primary sacrament the foil-wrapped wafers flavored by Wrigley's, with which McGuire celebrated communion frequently. It even had a demon bitch-goddess, sold twenty to a pack and omnipresent as a temptress—a profane seductress who was patiently waiting for him to commit the sin that would be, literally, mortal.

And of course, it had a hell. Every waking minute of every infernally endless day.

He told himself he could take it, would take it—even if it meant facing the devil of nicotine withdrawal every day for the rest of his life. He had taken it all his life.

McGuire had grown up a tough kid—not so unusual in backcountry Montana, where the dream of every other teenage boy is to escape to the rodeo circuit as a bullrider. But McGuire had been exceptionally tough, even in that environment.

A hitch as a Marine, where he had picked up three ounces of shrapnel as well as a three-pack-a-day habit, had only seasoned the already case-hardened leather of his character. He had come back to a job where carrying the badge often required him to exercise a judicious, if unofficial, violence. He could have been elected sheriff, or so it was said, if he had wanted to ride a desk instead of a cruiser.

By the time that seemed a reasonable compromise, McGuire found himself too settled in his ways for the politics such a move would have required. He settled for an appointment as senior deputy, in charge of investigations, and told people he was waiting to see which would get him first, forced retirement or the cigarettes to which he remained wedded.

It was a cocky performance, full of the bravura on which he had built a reputation for being a hard-ass. And it had all changed when, after Doc Bartfield's pronouncement, he found out that he indeed did want to live—even if it meant living with the claws of his devil-monkey sunk deeply into his back.

But McGuire had not spent a lifetime hiding from any of the devils he had encountered.

And so it was that every morning of every day, before he

settled behind the desk he now rode, McGuire followed a set ritual. Almost solemnly, he would remove an unopened pack of Winston cigarettes from his shirt pocket and place it within easy reach. Then, at the frequent moments of stress throughout the day, he would pick up the pack, think about what was inside, and replace it firmly back on the desktop— a devout act of faith not unlike that of a zealot handling live vipers.

But his new faith had not brought him peace, a fact he had taken no pains to conceal. Since his Conversion, anyone who had the misfortune to cross his path had been fair game for energetic, sometimes blistering, abuse.

Hell could not be avoided, but it could be shared.

"Well, thanks for sharing that with me, Deputy McGuire," Beck Casey said, looking across the desk at the county officer and wondering what he had done to piss him off so quickly and so thoroughly. "I just thought you may have known this Trippett fellow pretty well at one time or another."

"I'm really sorry if I've offended you," McGuire said, not looking sorry at all. "And I apologize for the 'son of a bitch' comment, Agent O'Connor. Don't usually talk like that, 'specially around a lady. Guess I'm a little edgy these days. Anyway, Orin Trippett ain't from around White Bison County—hell, he ain't even from Montana. The sorry bastard blew in from out east six, maybe seven years ago. Can't say I'd be brokenhearted to see him go away on a federal rap."

He looked up from under impressive silver eyebrows, thick and untamed. "Agent O'Connor—you gonna be okay?"

April touched the dressing that wrapped around her forehead. "Mild concussion, the doctors say. I've had worse headaches, Deputy."

"Glad I could finally get through to you on the phone." McGuire nodded approvingly. "You sound like a tough lady.

Had a helluva week so far, as I understand." He turned and eyed Casey. "You too, by the look of it. Don't guess you get much of this kind of thing—'specially since, like you say, you're just a college teacher." McGuire's tone was bland, but his eyes studied Beck carefully as he spoke.

Beck nodded. He shifted in the chair, his leg throbbing with a dull ache. The hospital had provided him with a cane, an aluminum model that made him feel foolishly conspicuous. He had left it in the Crown Victoria, preferring to limp along under his own power.

"All of it related to Orin Trippett," Beck said. "You told her you had a lead on him?"

"Maybe. Like I said, he's pretty much a newcomer around here. Fish out of water, so the son of a bitch worked overtime to pretend like he belonged." McGuire shook his head disgustedly. "For a while, the silly bastard took to wearing an oversized Stetson and a pair of them cow boots with the extra-high heel. 'Bout couldn't walk without falling."

Beck glanced at April, wondering where the conversation was going.

"Anyway, he got himself tied in with some good ol' boys who liked to drink beer and cuss out the IRS. Called themselves a militia. Ever' so often, they'd go off upcountry to drink and shoot off their damn guns. Pretty harmless bunch of peckerless yahoos, mostly. But not all of 'em."

McGuire pushed a file folder, dog-eared and covered with penciled notations, across his desk to his visitors. He opened the folder, revealing a stack of official-looking pages. Stapled to the top sheet were the full-face and profile poses of an arrest photo. McGuire fanned the stack like a deck of oversized cards, revealing other photos and rap sheets underneath.

"These boys here, they're the ones I kept an eye on." He fished two from the pile. "Gil Sweeney. Bobby Touchette. Them two—well, I always figured I'd have to shoot one or the other someday. Bad apples, the both of 'em. They're the pair that Agent O'Connor kilt two nights ago outside the warehouse. Did everybody a favor, my opinion."

McGuire leaned back in his chair. Beck watched him pick up an unopened pack of Winston cigarettes, toy with it for a moment with a thoughtful expression, then place it firmly back on the desktop.

"So late last night, Agent O'Connor here called me wantin' to know where maybe Orin Trippett might want to hide out. It's vacation time, so I was fillin' in on the late watch. It was comin' on midnight, and I guess I'm turning into a fat, lazy bachelor. I remembered the damn old trailer Trippett used to own, and I told her how to get out there."

Carl McGuire shook his head, and looked as if he wanted to spit. "And then I went home, and had me my TV dinner. Went to bed right afterward," McGuire said, looking Beck full in the eye. "I got a bad case of the guilts, sending the two of you up to that goddamn trailer alone. Hell, I knowed I should have gone along. And maybe what happened to the two of you wouldn't have happened. I'm sincerely sorry, the both of you."

Before either Beck or April could respond, McGuire pushed a card from the stack. The attached photo showed a heavyset man with what appeared to be a permanent five o'clock shadow blue against his jowls.

"That's Cappie Arnold—Henry Capshaw Arnold's his legal name. Used to run with Trippett and his bunch. 'Bout six months ago, I stopped seeing him around the county. Turns out he picked up and moved—good riddance to bad rubbish, but he and Orin Trippett were always thick as thieves."

He pushed the card to April, who studied it before tucking it into her inside pocket.

"Any idea where Arnold went, Deputy McGuire?"

"After I heard what happened to Mr. Casey and you, I . . . kinda asked some people." McGuire had a look on his face that Beck would not have wanted aimed in his direction.

"Called in some favors, you might say. Seems Cappie went on down to Denver, got him a place down there."

"Thanks," April said. "We'll check with the Denver PD, see if they have an address on him."

"They don't; I already called. But I convinced a guy here to come up with one. Wrote it on the back of the picture. Don't think he's got the stones to lie to me—but if it ain't the right one, I'd appreciate you lettin' me know."

Once again, McGuire picked up the cigarette pack. His fingers caressed it almost teasingly, Beck noticed, before returning it to its place.

"Ask me, that's where I'd start looking for Trippett. Who knows? Maybe run across the guy who done that to your friend's leg too."

McGuire looked at Beck, a pointed look on his features.

"And, my advice? This time, college teacher or not, take along a gun. You get the chance, sir, you use it."

Chapter 38

They parked several houses away from the address McGuire
had provided in a tough-looking neighborhood on the southwest side of the city. It was almost one p.m. by now. There
were few locals in evidence, and those who were looked
knowingly at the Crown Victoria before walking on.

"Maybe we should just hang out a sign," April muttered
to Beck. "This damn thing screams out 'unmarked car.' At
least to these people."

She looked at her companion.

"We can wait here and give everybody a chance to figure
out which house we're watching," April said. "Or we can go
up and kick the door right now."

"You decide." He gestured at his leg. "You'll have to do
the kicking."

April frowned at the house, pensive.

"Rental agent says a woman signed the papers," April reminded Beck finally. "And those flowers on the porch don't
look like something a man would do."

"Okay. So?"

"So let's try the direct approach. You wait here and I'll go
knock. If a woman answers the door—or even some bozo

who works the late shift—I'll play it by ear. If it's Trippett or this Cappie Arnold, I take him down, hard."

"It doesn't sound too gallant of me, sitting in the car while a lady with a concussion does the hard work." Beck grinned at the look April shot him. "Great plan. Go ahead."

She exited the car quietly and walked the distance to the porch, making it look casual. Beck watched April climb the stairs, lift her hand to knock—and then stop, bending close to the wooden door as if to study its grain.

She looked toward the car and beckoned him.

When Beck reached the porch, gamely trying to keep his limp to a minimum, April spoke in a low voice.

"Somebody else had the same idea about kicking doors," she said. "Looks like they got here first."

Beck bent low. The wood around the lockset was splintered, and a piece of the broken hardwood trim had been carelessly attached on the jamb. "*That'll* sure keep out the lowlifes," April murmured. She took a deep breath. "Okay— let's do this."

She raised a closed fist and knocked hard, once.

The impact opened the door a half inch before something solid stopped it.

Beck sniffed the air, suddenly tense. There was a faint bathroom smell, and something else—a metallic odor that was tantalizingly familiar to him, almost like the scent of fresh copper pennies.

April looked at Beck and reached to the small of her back, her hand out of sight under her jacket.

"Ms. Tompkins!" she said, in a voice meant to sound firm and authoritative. "Lubella Tompkins—are you there?" Nobody answered; the apartment was silent in a way that raised the hairs along the back of Beck's neck.

"We've got trouble here," April said in a low voice. "You smell it?"

He nodded.

She drew her hand from under her jacket, producing a surprisingly large automatic pistol.

It's like a replay of yesterday, she told herself, recalling the trailer's ruined door. *Beck's probably wondering if women go through doors the* normal *way anymore.* Irrationally, the thought almost made her giggle.

Instead, she raised her voice and said loudly, "This is the FBI, Ms. Tompkins. We're coming in now," and with her shoulder pushed hard against the door. Something broke with a loud snap, and the door lurched open another half foot.

"Hell with this," April muttered, and slammed her body hard against the wood. The impact forced the door open enough for her to squeeze through. *If somebody's waiting with a gun,* she thought bitterly, *I'm dead meat.*

She pushed hard with her legs, and heard more sounds like wood breaking. With her shoulders and upper body through the opening, the added leverage allowed her to push through completely. The copper-penny smell was much stronger here, as was the stench of feces. As she cleared the stubborn doorway, her arms came up extended, and she swept the room in an arc through the sights of her Glock.

Sunlight streamed through the large side window, dappling the bare wooden floor through curtains that had seen better days. April's peripheral vision noted the chair that had been jammed against the inside doorknob, broken from the force of her entry. Her eyes swept past the low pile of matted, stained rags heaped on a kitchen table in the center of the room, and she felt a wave of relief that the house was empty.

Then her mind registered what her eyes had seen, and it recoiled in horror and disgust.

"Jesus," a voice breathed from behind her. Beck was staring at the pile of rags that were not rags, his mouth slightly open and his eyes almost expressionless in disbelief.

Don't lose it now, April's mind ordered her, and she spoke roughly as much to herself as to Beck.

"If you're going to be sick, do it outside in the yard," she growled, and Beck looked at her as if she were a stranger. But she didn't notice, because the floor and the walls and the ceiling had now caught her full and undivided attention.

"Oh, my God," she said.

The wooden floor under the table had drawn much of the fluid into itself; the walls bore red-brown stripes of varying length and weight where gravity had tugged at the flying drops. She noted all this, almost academically.

But it was the ceiling that held her gaze.

From a fixture that hung over the torn remains of Lubella Tompkins, partially congealed drops of blood dangled like miniature, brown-red stalactites. Until now, April had never realized how much blood a human body held.

"I don't want to do much guessing," April O'Connor said into the telephone she held to her face. "But, unofficially, it appears she died sometime this morning."

"She was tortured?" Frank Ellis's voice, as it came over the receiver, was pitched unnaturally high. *Shock, maybe,* April thought, and felt a flash of anger. *I'm the one who had to look at her, dammit. . . .*

"Yes," she said instead. "Whoever it was had rigged up a kind of gag he could push deep down her mouth, or pull out a little. She could talk when he let her, but not scream. It looks like the son of a bitch took his time with her. And when he was done, he took a little more so he could really enjoy it as she died. Probably took a last look at his work before he went out the door."

The professional demeanor of her voice faltered, for just a moment. "Frank, this was one sick bastard. I've never seen anything so sadistic."

There was silence on the line.

"Is your Dr. Casey there? Rather, is he still functioning?"

April looked over her shoulder. "He's doing fine," she lied.

"Yeah." Her SAC's voice was unconvinced. "Okay. Stick

with him until you hear different from me. I'll give you a few minutes, then alert Denver PD. It sure isn't protocol, but unless you two want to hang out with the Denver homicide squad for the foreseeable future, you better secure the place and be gone. Trippett is still out there. I need you looking, not filling out reports for the local cops. And O'Connor—watch your back, and his. Stick to Casey like glue."

April closed her cellular phone with a snap that was brisk and authoritative, wishing that she felt like either. She turned to Beck, who stood nearby. His eyes were studiously avoiding the table and the burden it bore.

"Let's go, Beck. My boss is calling the locals, and we'll just confuse them if we're still here."

He acted as if he had not heard her. When he spoke, his voice was intense with emotion.

"April, this guy enjoys what he does—I could tell when he had me hanging by my wrists," Beck said. "But he isn't totally out of control. He tortures when he wants information. He knew to come here looking for Trippett; he needed to know where to look next."

Beck looked at the torn figure on the table, and April could see the effort it took.

"Beck, we have to—"

"If this woman knew anything, trust me—she told him." Beck looked around the room and stiffened.

"Or *showed* him," he told April. Beck crossed the wooden floor, careful to avoid the blood smears that traversed it in parallel tracks. Then he bent, and when he came up there was the weighty thickness of a telephone directory in his hands. Beck held the directory up to April.

"Look at this."

On the cover was the red-brown imprint of three fingers.

There were smudges inside, randomly spaced as if by fingers desperate to find the proper listing. The last stain was on a page diagonally bisected by a jagged rip; the bottom of the page had been torn from the book. Only a corner of the display ad that had been the focus of such frantic interest was still visible.

"Something called the Mile-Hi," April said. "It's a theater."

It was 1:11 P.M. when April and Beck arrived at the Mile-Hi Theater; it was also already too late.

On a normal midsummer afternoon, even the Mile-Hi would have been thronged with teenagers, seniors looking for the matinee rate, bored housewives. Not today; today, there were virtually no witnesses at all. Because of the flu, movie theaters had been shut down along with every other form of group entertainment. All they had, as they pushed through double doors and into the theater lobby adjacent to the men's room was a fourteen-year-old freshman at Denver Central High School. His name was Danny Carroll.

Thus far in his young life, Danny had identified two overwhelming passions. One was film: Danny loved movies. His room was festooned with marquee posters and books filled with cinematic lore. He had seen most of the films made by Spielberg—at least once; had worn out a pirated director's cut of *Apocalypse Now;* and had memorized every cut and arcane camera angle in *Psycho*—the Hitchcock original, of course. His single other passion was a slightly less complicated attraction to the Big Gulp soft drinks he habitually bought at a 7-Eleven convenience store near his home.

The former passion had driven him to the Mile-Hi this afternoon for the same reason it did every afternoon: in exchange for old posters and a permanent pass for free admission, Danny handled janitorial tasks at no charge.

But it was the latter passion—indulged freely, possibly excessively, prior to his arrival at the movie house—that compelled him directly to the men's lavatory immediately after he had unlocked the lobby doors.

According to the statement he later made to police, Danny Carroll had noticed a smoky, slightly sweet odor when he en-

tered the men's room—"kind of like after you set off a Black
Cat, you know, or a bottle rocket. I figured somebody had
been screwing around, like maybe lighting a match for a cigarette or something."

Whatever his theories, the inherent internal pressures of
sixty-four ounces of Pepsi Cola outweighed his immediate
curiosity. It was only when he finished dealing with this first
priority and was turning from the urinals that Danny noticed
the pool of bright red on the white-tiled floor. It was slowly
spreading from under the half-closed door of one of the
stalls.

Danny Carroll bent slightly, low enough to see the pair of
shoes flanking the toilet's base, long enough to note the drips
that fell, regular as a leaking faucet, on one shoe's instep.

"Hey," Danny called tentatively. "You okay in there?"
There was no answer. Carefully, the boy pushed against the
stall's door.

Inside was Orin Trippett, sitting half-slumped on the toilet. His eyes were open wide, and a trail of blood was still
oozing from a neat, perfectly round hole precisely in the middle of his forehead. On the wall behind his head, a much less
precise splatter of congealing blood, bone and brain formed
a madly abstract pattern.

Remotely, in a deepening state of shock, Danny noticed
something else.

The side pocket of the jacket the dead man wore had been
ripped away violently. It was as if someone had been impatient to take possession of whatever had been carried there.

Chapter 39

Ilya threaded his way through the traffic as carefully as possible. He was uncertain about who he was following, though he was very clear about what had just taken place.

The theater had been quiet when he arrived a few minutes before one o'clock. He had expected to buy a ticket, intending to pay for it with a twenty-dollar bill because the price of things American still occasionally surprised him. Ilya made a practice of paying with larger bills, on the theory that a man who received change was less memorable than a person whose underpayment was called to attention.

But there had been no one at the ticket window.

He wondered if the woman called Lubella had lied to him. He thought not: she had seemed, ultimately, quite cooperative. At one point, on her hands and knees, she had even scrambled across the bare wood floor of the living room to where the telephone directory was kept: eager—in fact, by then desperate—to find for Ilya the movie theater's address. In her wake, she had left red-brown streaks of her own blood to mark her path.

No, he was sure: she had told him what she had believed true. By now, Ilya had an instinct for such matters.

So he had finished with her—not hurriedly, but in a manner befitting the relationship they had developed. And then he had left, taking nothing but the scrap of paper she had provided. That, and his memories.

All he had to do was to come here and find a way to persuade the man to leave with him—quietly and willingly, if possible, though the latter was a secondary consideration. He did not anticipate significant difficulty in this.

But outside the theater, he had immediately sensed something was amiss. And so he waited and watched from his parked automobile, trusting the unerring instincts that longevity in his particular profession had fostered.

Finally, there had been movement from inside the theater. He had zeroed in on a gut-heavy man wearing a faded camouflage jacket at the far side of the lobby. The man had just pushed through a set of double doors—leading, Ilya presumed, to one of the viewing rooms. Even at the distance, Ilya noted that the jacket was bulky and loose fitting. That, and definitely too heavy for the midsummer weather.

But clearly, Ilya thought, *it is the kind of apparel a man might wear if he had something he wished to conceal beneath. And the man is being cautious as he crosses the lobby—trying, a bit too obviously, to look casual about it.*

He watched as the thickset man walked across the expanse of empty marble flooring, his left elbow pressed against his side. To Ilya's not inexpert eye, the jacket seemed to hang awkwardly there; the warning bells sounded even louder in the Russian's mind.

He is hunting, Ilya decided.

And so he waited. From the corner of his eye, he saw the man enter the lavatory. No more than a minute later, he heard it. Few "silenced" weapons are worthy of the name: even from his car, the muffled pop was unmistakable to one familiar with the technology.

And that was more than enough. Ilya did not believe in coincidences.

The Russian already had his engine started by the time the unknown assassin exited the Mile-Hi and climbed into his own vehicle, parked well down the street. Ilya carefully pulled into position behind it.

And now, more than a half hour later, Ilya had made his decision.

This man I am following has secrets I need to share, he thought. *He is a man I must meet. And now it is time.*

He began to look for a suitable place.

Twenty yards ahead, the vehicle—*a light truck,* the Russian thought, *what they call here a "pickup"*—slowed as it turned a corner onto a tree-lined residential street.

Ilya followed, whistling a tuneless melody of anticipation.

He was certain now. The trailing vehicle had swung in an arc, settling again in his rearview mirror as the car behind him straightened. It was the same car, a dark green Chevy Malibu, and it had been behind him for the past twenty minutes—*hell,* Cappie thought, *maybe even since I left the damn theater.*

He was puzzled, but not worried. Cappie Arnold had been playing a double game for almost a year now, working closely with Orin at the same time he kept the militia's Jap patron appraised of what was happening behind the scenes. It was a situation that would have turned a more stress-prone man into a basket case; ironically, Cappie's lack of imagination had only served to sustain him.

I mean, hell—even a damn Jap got a right to watch his back, dealing with the likes of—Cappie chuckled, dimly aware of the irony involved—*well, of guys like Orin and me. Just shows he's a careful kinda guy.*

Most recently, Cappie had tipped his Asian benefactor to the theft of the M-16s—not the feds, *never* them, though what the Jap subsequently did with the information was certainly none of Cappie's business. Cappie was a pragmatist: it was not so much spying on his old friend as it was helping his new one stay on top of things. Why not? The Jap had been grateful for the heads-up—*guy knowed right away that the feds would be lookin' into that kinda shit,* Orin noted, suitably impressed—and had been suitably generous in return.

Cappie was genuinely sorry about Orin, too. Sort of.

'Course, once he started thinkin' about it, sooner or later he'd of knowed it was me talked, Cappie mused. He shrugged off any regret. *Fuck it; it was him or me.* He touched his pocket, felt the weight of the can he had torn from Orin's jacket. *There's people who'd pay boo-coo bucks for something like this. 'Sides, I got nuthin' against Denver. And when you get right down to it, Orin was an asshole anyway.*

So much for memory lane; Cappie returned his attention to his rearview mirror.

Whoever was behind him had only limited practice in car tails. That ruled out the feds, Cappie figured; certainly they had to know their business better than the solitary silhouette in the Malibu. It also eliminated most of the other persons, law enforcement or not, whose attentions might alarm him. That left an amateur of some sort, and while that made him curious, it barely constituted a concern. Whoever was behind him was either new at this, or his experience was limited to places where it didn't matter if the prey knew he was being stalked.

Okay, my smart-assed li'l buddy. Just keep coming. I know a place where we can go be alone together. I got a few questions for you.

He glanced at the object on the seat beside him. Like every silenced pistol Cappie had ever seen, the thing was a piece of crap. It was a battered .38-caliber revolver, and looked better suited as a throw-down piece than as an actual weapon. The front sight had been hacksawed off and the barrel end rough-threaded like a pipe. He had bought it, along with the bulky extension that gave the gun any utility at all, several months before in a biker bar outside Helena.

Before he had gone to the theater, Cappie had donned

latex gloves and carefully wiped the weapon clean. It had taken only a fraction of the precious minutes he had. He had used a few more to wrap white athletic tape around the grip, the face of the trigger, and the bulky silencer itself. Fingerprints were not a problem on the rough cloth texture, unless you happened to be looking for any.

The silencer was homemade, a cylinder the size of a large soup can. Fiberglass insulation and steel wool had been packed around a perforated steel tube, a half inch in diameter, that was welded inside. The end of the tube had been threaded with a hand tap, and the whole apparatus could be screwed into the matching threads cut into the tip of the revolver's barrel. It was as awkward as it was inelegant. Under the best of conditions, Cappie had estimated, it would hold up for two shots, maybe three.

As it turned out, of course, he had needed only one.

There would not be a second shot—at least, not from this gun. It had already done the only work he trusted it to do. He had intended to throw the pistol and its silencer—separately, of course—into a blackwater borrow pit just off I-70. He still would. But now there was an unscheduled stop he had to make first.

Who knows—depending on how things work out, I might just even leave it with the body, pistol and silencer both. The image made him smile. *Boy, that might mess with somebody's mind,* he thought.

Outside, the neighborhood had turned industrial. He continued west until he came to a gravel road rutted from weather and neglect. He turned onto it. Ahead, he could see the dark outline of what looked like a large, abandoned factory.

Cappie reached under his camo jacket and touched the Colt Python he carried in a shoulder rig. Then he checked his rearview mirror a final time.

There was no sign of his pursuer, but Cappie knew for a certainty he was still there. He began to whistle, tunelessly, as the dark building drew closer. Almost idly, Cappie wondered what Lubella would have on the table when he returned home.

It was much later, almost four p.m. This had turned into an interesting meeting indeed—one with more than a few surprises for both of the participants.

Now it was time to leave. All that was left was the tidying up that was always an inevitable final part of these things.

The strip of cloth he had lighted was almost fully ablaze now, almost at the juncture where it was stuffed into the opened gasoline filler neck. Even from where he stood, under the open sky twenty yards away, he could see the flames licking up the rag's remaining few inches.

And then, with no further preliminaries, the fumes ignited. There was an intense white flash, followed an instant later by a curiously flat boom—no, he corrected himself, it was more like a deep-throated whoosh. The shock wave was little more than a puff of warmed air he barely felt in its passing.

The vehicle was burning furiously now, the flames an angry orange-black. Where various fluids escaped along the length of the chassis, liquid drops of fire dripped to the ground. The interior, which he had soaked with gasoline, was alive with the dancing flames, though with nothing else. The mad dance of firelight reflected against the walls of this ruined place, now competing with the late-afternoon sun in intensity. Black smoke rose in a thick, rolling plume.

It was time to leave.

As he drove away, he could see the smoke and flickering of light in his rearview mirror. He did not know if the fire would attract attention from the curious or the concerned; he did not know who would see it, or who might care. Regardless, even if the flames drew anyone here, it would be too late. Whatever there had been of value, he had already taken.

Chapter 40

The death of Orin Trippett—and the inability of Beck and April to find the canister of the virus they believed he had possessed—had left the pair completely without direction or intent. All they had was the knowledge that the unknown man who spoke soft threats in a Russian accent had been a step ahead of them again.

Aside from that, they had . . . nothing.

"I'm coming back," Beck repeated, this time with more force.

"To do what, exactly?" Andi Wheelwright's voice came over the sat phone, clear in its exasperation. "Beck, you're better off where you are. We have chaos up and down the Eastern Seaboard now. It's even worse in Florida. There's rioting—hell, it's more like armed insurrection down in the quarantine zone. We've had reports of attacks on military units down there. Some of the crazies have begun raiding bases, arming themselves with anything they can steal. Not just small arms, either. Mortars, heavy machine guns, even antiaircraft weapons. It's a free-fire zone, man."

"What's happening in New York?"

"What do you think? Ten million people are caught between an incurable plague and a curfew enforced by a shoot-to-kill edict."

"You're getting reports on new flu cases there."

"Some. Okay, yes—it appears to be spreading faster than we hoped. There are confirmed cases in Manhattan and in Queens. The Coast Guard has had to sink a number of small craft that refused to heave to. They were heading toward the mainland."

"Andi, you can't stop all of them. It will get worse; all it takes is one person to get through, or one infected body to wash ashore along the coastline."

"I know. Nationwide flu in a week. Ten days at the most."

"Then it doesn't matter where I am," Beck said. "Look, Andi—if you won't help me, at least don't stand in my way. I've done what you wanted; I've done all I can. Now I need to find Katie."

There was a long moment of silence.

"Beck—if you have to do something, go to Montgomery and wait. We'll authorize a flight plan to fly you there. Go to the Capitol Holiday Inn; I'll make sure they're expecting you." She drew a deep breath. "I'll do what I can, but we're not getting a lot of information out of Florida anymore."

"I appreciate anything you can do. You have CDC teams still going into Florida. Put me in with one."

"I'll have to clear that with Billy Carson," Andi said.

"Tell Carson I'll talk to him when I land," Beck said. "If he has any problems, he can tell me then. But Andi—one way or another, I'm going in to find my daughter." He broke the connection.

April nodded, grimly.

"Then I'm coming along." She sounded stubbornly determined. "Officially, I'm still assigned to you. Last thing Frank Ellis said was to stick to you like glue. Until I check in with him, that's the directive I'm following." She held up a hand before Beck could reply. "And I'd like to help."

Beck looked at April, then at the waiting CDC jet.

"Plenty of room," he said. "And . . . thank you."

Chapter 41

While April inspected the accommodations — Wheelwright's office had handled the arrangements directly, and in the current emergency the hotel manager had immediately upgraded "Dr. Beck Casey of the CDC" to the only available suite — Beck limped into the motel's dining room. He entered an expanse of empty booths and tables that had, nonetheless, each been set with fresh china and linen. Holiday Inn brooked no surprises for its guests, at least none that could be prevented by the attentions of the staff.

A smiling woman flitted to greet Beck, her pale green blouse starched and her carefully coiffed hair a shade of blond not generally found in nature.

Before the hostess could whisk him to one of the many unoccupied tables, Beck surveyed the room. His double take might have been comical, had there been an audience in the room to see it.

There at a booth, situated so that no one could approach unobserved, sat Alexi Malenkov.

The general's uniform was gone, replaced by a tan polo shirt and khaki shorts. He wore matching socks under the Nike-swooshed sandals on his feet, and a pair of retro-designed

Foster Grant sunglasses peeked from a breast pocket. On the table before him, a copy of the Montgomery *Advertiser* was folded to the sports section, and on his fork was something white flecked with yellow. Alexi was studying the latter with a perplexed look on his face. He looked up as Beck slipped onto the bench across from him.

"Nice outfit, Alexi. How are you enjoying the food?"

"I have not before experienced the culinary pleasure of grits," Alexi Malenkov said wryly. "They are surprisingly good, if only one can obtain a sufficient supply of —" He paused, lost. "To be sure, of *anything* that might give them some measure of flavor."

Beck laughed. "Try the honey, Alexi. Or the Tabasco, if you want a real Southern treat."

The Russian tucked another forkful of hash browns into his mouth.

"Thank you. I will pass, for now. I have news, my friend. Your president has announced he will use Agent VIX around the Florida Quarantine Region, and in New York City."

"When?"

"They estimate perhaps this time tomorrow."

"I'll get ready to be pretty sick in the next couple of days." *Or,* Beck left unsaid, *one of the dead five percent.*

"Yes." Alexi handed across an envelope, the size in which mail-order catalogues are sent. "That is a gift from the Russian people to you personally. You will appreciate it, I believe."

Beck tore across the sealed flap and pulled out a quarter-inch-thick sheaf of paper tacked together in the Russian fashion with a straight pin pushed through the corner. He tensed when he saw the photograph that was affixed to the top sheet.

"Ah, you recognize this man," Alexi noted with satisfaction. "Good. That will make our task easier."

"I remember him pretty well. The last time I saw him, he was sticking a knife into my thigh. Who is he?"

"Like so many of the people we meet in this interesting

profession of ours, he seems to have a number of names,"
Alexi said. He sipped cautiously at his coffee.

His face brightened, and he tipped the cup back for a
deeper draught. "We have listed those of which we are
aware. At present, he appears to operate under the name of
'Ilya,' last name unknown. His vitae is on the second page.
You will please note that Ilya is both an interrogator and an
assassin. You did well to escape with only the chicken
scratch you received, my friend."

Beck did not answer, his face furrowed in concentration
as he scanned through the Cyrillic-lettered text of Ilya's file.

"I am sorry we did not have time to transcribe this information into English," Alexi said wickedly. "Do you wish me
to translate for you?"

"What you can do," Beck said, still reading, "is tell me
what this Ilya is doing in the States."

"A good question. You see that he was seconded from the
Army to the SVR," Alexi said, using the current incarnation
of what was once the KGB's foreign intelligence section.
"Our friend was Spetznaz, and like all soldiers from elite
units he brought his own unique skills into his new employ-
ment."

"Meaning?"

"Meaning that you may recall that I told you we had
placed SVR agents close to your own paramilitary factions,"
Alexi said, chewing a piece of wheat toast. "Ilya was one
such agent. His English is as good as mine, perhaps a little
better. His Czech is excellent, and for that reason he is covered as a former Czechoslovakian Army corporal who defected to this country—seeking, of course, the freedom it
has so unquestioningly offered to all."

Beck looked skeptical. "A man with an Eastern European
accent doesn't usually get very far trying to join that kind of
club, Alexi. Not even a defector is 'right' enough."

"His story is that he became disillusioned—I believe the
legend we provided is that he had some altercation with your

taxation authorities—and became close to several of your more extreme militia groups. Plus, our friend Ilya was able to provide his new comrades—pardon me, 'fellow patriotic warriors'—with a few obsolete automatic weapons he bought from street gangs in your larger cities." His face was impassive, though his eyes were mocking.

Beck grunted. "I'll have to introduce you to my traveling companion. She'll find your information very interesting."

Alexi grinned hugely. "A woman? I am pleased for you, my friend. When may I meet your girl?"

"Her name is April, and I'd recommend against calling her a girl, Alexi. You should probably call her Special Agent O'Connor."

"Ah, she is FBI. And she has already made the acquaintance of our friend Ilya."

Beck glanced up at the Russian. "You are surprisingly well informed, Alexi."

"Ms. Andi Wheelwright has been quite cooperative," Alexi said. "But she did not mention your companion. You have reason not to tell her, perhaps?"

Beck laughed, though his eyes did not leave the Russian's face. "Alexi, have you ever heard the phrase 'sex maniac'? Get a dictionary and look it up—right next to it, you'll see a photo of your face."

"Yes, you are pleased to joke. But our friend Ilya is no product of paranoia. He is quite a serious man, my friend."

"And what does he intend to do now? Come to think of it, what do *you* intend to do, Alexi?"

Alexi motioned for the waitress—a slim girl whose smile seemed permanently set on high—and waited until she had refilled his cup.

"The answer to both questions are remarkably similar, my friend. Our mysterious Ilya is in your country—perhaps illegally, perhaps under some legitimate cover. Either way, he will not be easy to find. It would appear he is looking for one of the murderous lunatics who wish to carry poison to your cities. For what specific reason, we do not know. And I—an official guest whose presence was arranged by my president talking to yours—well, I am here looking for *him*."

He again tasted the coffee, savoring it before speaking again.

"You see, Beck—we believe Ilya is no longer acting as a Russian, much less as an SVR agent. Did I mention Ilya had a previous posting in Japan? It is in his record, there before you."

Beck waited, feeling the chill that rippled the back of his neck.

"We believe," Alexi said, "that he is Aum—in fact, that he is one of the teachers, these sensei who now lead them. His task, I am convinced, is to ensure this virus continues to spread. He wishes, I think, to kill millions of your countrymen."

Alexi Malenkov again sipped at his coffee, and studied Beck over the rim of the cup.

"I am here," he said, "to help you stop him."

Chapter 42

An hour later, Beck lowered himself into a lounge chair on the concrete apron around the hotel swimming pool; as he did, he could feel every minute of the past two days in his joints. His leg throbbed; only the possibility that someone might hear gave him the strength to bite back the groan.

Beck had expected the hotel to be deserted, or close to it. He had not factored in the effect that a near-complete shut-down of transportation would have. Across the country, a tremendous number of people were stranded far from their own homes. Here, in the Heart of Dixie, the Holiday Inn had assumed the role of sanctuary for a significant number of these refugees.

One might not have known that, fewer than two hundred miles away, a plague raged unabated.

Around the pool, a cornucopia of browning female flesh competed for his attention. From behind the protection of his sunglasses, Beck still found himself compelled to look, though without the component of casually omnivorous lust he remembered from other places, other years.

For one thing, his mind was still tumultuous with concern for Katie, despite April's frequent, reassuring analyses of why she had still not been located. Then there was the simple requirement of staying alive; between the dark man and the virus, Beck sensed that the odds had dipped depressingly low. For another, Beck had begun to realize that the most voluptuous figures — those that climbed from the water with a lithe womanly grace that was achingly lovely, those whose lowered eyes noted his glance with a studied, seductive indifference — were, upon closer examination of the males who attended them, no older than fifteen.

It was a realization that might have depressed him, simply as a mature man; as a father of a teenage daughter, it left him feeling more than a bit like the worst kind of dirty old man. He was certain that he did not desire the romantic attentions of a girl-child, and not simply because he recognized both the complications and the inevitable embarrassment it would entail.

His relationships with real women had been difficult enough, he knew; he had not lied when he told Alexi Malenkov that he did not believe himself a divorced man. After the decree, Beck had been surprised to discover that casual sex held no appeal to him; on the rare occasions he had engaged in it, the experience had left him empty and morose. In alarm, he had realized that celibacy was possible — perhaps even preferable.

He needed no further complications to an issue that was, to Beck, already nothing less than perplexing. Having been unable to share his life, his secrets, his fears with Deborah, he found little hope that he could craft a bridge to any other woman.

All this he knew. And still he looked, a bittersweet affirmation of something in himself that he had half believed was dead, or dying.

A part of him envied the boys who attended these young goddesses — envied them the freshness and wonder and even the pain that each young Venus represented. But most of him simply wished them all well, hoped for them a fortunate journey to what a lethal virus suddenly had turned into an uncertain future.

"They're too young for you," April O'Connor said, materializing as a dark silhouette standing next to his chair.

"No kidding," Beck replied. "*You're* too young for me, and some of those kids could be your—"

"Sister," April warned. "Kid sister, of course."

"Of course," Beck agreed. "But they're all the age of my daughter. Maybe a little younger."

April nodded, suddenly serious. "Have you heard anything?"

"Have *you*?"

April colored. "I called Frank Ellis, Beck. He was not happy I'm in Alabama, but I guess we'll deal with that later."

"Can he use FBI resources and pass the information to us?"

"He's agreed to do what he can. Katie is not on any of the quarantine zone lists, Beck. It's pretty chaotic in there; she may have gotten out before the quarantine was declared. Or—I'm sorry. You've already thought about all the possibilities."

"Yes," Beck said. "I have."

"By the way, you might have told me you were tight with the Russian government," she said. "Ellis says that earlier today the State Department routed one General Alexi Ivanovich Malenkov—he is director of Russian state security, as if you didn't already know—through Washington to Montgomery, Alabama."

"He's still in the restaurant," Beck said, "trying to decide between sweet and regular iced tea. He thinks we're an item. I think he's just eager to meet a G-*woman*."

As if on cue, an electronic buzz rose from the bag April carried loosely over her shoulder. She reached inside and snapped open a cellular phone.

"O'Connor," she said brusquely. She listened for a moment. "Thank you. No—I'll come there, if you don't mind.

There's a General Malenkov in your restaurant. Would you ask him to join Dr. Casey and me in your office?"

She folded the phone and looked at Beck.

"No rest for the wicked," she said. "Looks like CDC's tracked you down, and they know I'm here too. There's a package of stuff waiting for us in the hotel office, so I guess we better look at it. You want to see what they sent, or stay here and leer at the young girls?"

Before he could answer, he saw April's eyes flicker upward and look past his shoulder.

"I think you have company," she muttered. "Somebody's coming straight your way, and seems upset—the look you're getting, you might want to borrow my pistol."

Beck twisted in the lounge chair, and looked up into the face of his former spouse.

"Hello, Deborah," he said evenly. He was determined she not see his surprise—nor the rush of pleasure that, to his astonishment, he felt at her presence.

"You son of a bitch," she replied. "Where is my daughter?"

Her face was flushed and animated, belying the long hours of driving that had brought her to this place. She glared daggers at Beck, and for a moment it appeared she was about to strike him.

"I don't know—not yet," Beck said. "You shouldn't be here, do you understand that? You're not going to do Katie any good by catching this virus."

"Go to hell."

Beck flared. "And that's helpful too. Look—you can't go into the Quarantine Region, Deborah. Even if they let you pass through the cordon, you don't know where to look. There are people already there, trying to locate Katie. Let them do their job."

"I am going to find Katie," Deborah said. "You can either help, or stay out of my way. Make up your mind, Beck. I don't care either way."

Deborah walked away, her normally loose-limbed stride now stiff and angry.

"I probably should keep my mouth shut," April said, watching Deborah disappear into the hotel. "But nobody gets that angry if they *really* don't care."

"I don't know," Beck said. "She looks pretty uninterested to me."

April shrugged. "It's an act."

"Uh-huh. Well, she's *really* good at it."

April went ahead alone into the hotel manager's office—a glass-fronted cubicle, really, though it had a door for the privacy she needed; Beck lingered in the outer office to await a tardy Alexi. The manager, unaccustomed to the ways of federal agencies, was eager to please: before leaving, he pointed April to a shipping box the size of a ream of paper, addressed to her and Beck and prominently hand-marked CDC: CONFIDENTIAL MATERIALS.

The box was sealed, reinforced with strips of cellophane tape along the seams of the flap. April looked at it curiously. As Beck watched idly, April produced a small penknife, working the blade under the flap and neatly slicing the tape along the top seam. Then, seizing the loosened flap, she pulled upward.

Through the glass of the window, Beck saw it happen.

April stiffened, her eyes suddenly wide and staring. The box fell from hands suddenly clenched into claws. And then the convulsions began, even as April O'Connor's legs collapsed beneath her and her body fell to the carpet as if poleaxed. A mad St. Vitus's dance flung her limbs akimbo, and her head violently twisted from side to side.

Beck rushed forward, had his hand on the doorknob when he was seized from behind.

"Stop!" Alexi held him in a tight embrace, both hands locked against Beck's chest. "Listen to me! We must get outside!" Alexi's voice sounded peculiar, almost strangled. "Quickly!"

"Let me go, Alexi. We have to—"

He lifted Beck bodily and staggered backward until the far wall was against his back. Only then did he loosen his grip, and only long enough to push the door behind him open. Then he half pulled, half carried Beck through.

In the hallway, Alexi slammed the door shut. "Your jacket," he demanded, in the same tight voice. He ripped the light coat from Beck, tugging it violently off his arms. Then Alexi bent and stuffed it, hard, against the bottom of the closed door.

"You cannot help her, my friend. And if you try to do so, you too will die in there."

The Russian gestured at the closed door with his head; to Beck, the movement appeared callous and impersonal.

"Do not act the fool, Beck. You recognize the signs as well as I. It is sarin gas."

Chapter 43

Beck sat in the dark of the suite, trying not to think. His right hand held a plastic tumbler filled with vodka and crushed ice in roughly equal proportions. The minibar in his room, at least, was performing its task competently; it stood at the ready, waiting to fulfill any need he might encounter in himself.

Hours before, after the FBI hazardous-materials team had finally decided the sarin had dissipated sufficiently to allow April's body to be removed, he had stood in silent impotence as the double-sealed body bag was wheeled to the waiting ambulance. He had talked with Billy Carson three times, and Larry Krewell double that number. Neither man had anything to add or ask, nor orders to guide Beck. Both had now refocused their concentration on the larger decisions and actions yet to be taken.

For the moment at least, Beck was on his own.

The package, of course, was a fake. Beck had not been allowed to examine it—the concentration of sarin absorbed by the cardboard was much too high for him to handle it safely, they had told him—but the photographs provided by the FBI technicians had been sufficient. The pressurized tank, remarkably similar to a CO_2 cartridge for an air pistol and no larger than a Bic lighter, had been rigged with a simple linkage to the box lid. Both his name and April's were block-lettered in heavy black marker on the otherwise unlabeled carton; the hotel's address was accurate, even to the ZIP code. But there had been no postage affixed, nor any of the various labels that would have indicated a delivery by messenger.

Alexi, peering over his shoulder at the photos, had said it first.

"He was here, Beck—this man Ilya. He has tracked you to this place."

But for what reason, neither he nor Beck himself could envision.

Unbidden, an image of April came to his mind's eye: the gas hitting her, the sudden, horrible realization in her expression, if only for the split second before the convulsions began.

He shook the picture from his mind, and drank deeply.

Deborah had not answered his call to her room; like the majority of the other terrified guests, she might have checked out, left his life as abruptly as she had reentered it. He was surprised, then dismayed, at his automatic reaction to that possibility; he had not realized how much he still cared.

Maybe, he thought, *I ought to have another drink.*

As if to answer him, there was a quiet tapping at the door. Beck frowned. It was too late for a call by Jehovah's Witnesses, and none of his neighbors had the appearance of people who socialized easily or well. He had half decided to ignore it when a voice, low and tentative, spoke his name.

He opened the door. Even in the dim light, Beck recognized the figure who stood there.

"All the lights were off," said a voice that had once been familiar to him. "I wasn't sure you were here. I'm glad you're still awake. Or have you started sleeping in your clothes?"

"Hello, Deborah, " he said. "Come in."

Deborah was dressed in a blue oxford shirt that was too

large for her slight form. He wondered if it was one of his,
though a darker corner of his mind suspected it was not. She
had rolled the sleeves to just below her elbows. The shirttail
was tucked into a pair of white shorts that emphasized her
trim thighs. Many women might have pulled their hair into a
ponytail to match the gamine look of the outfit. Not Deborah;
hers fell in a fine ashen cascade that emphasized the compact
beauty of her face. It made Beck remember how soft her hair
had felt beneath his hands.

She walked directly to the sofa and sat in a way that in-
vited Beck to sit beside her. Instead, he drew a chair from the
suite's dinette set. He settled across from her at what he
hoped was a safe distance for both of them.

They sat in silence for a long moment as Deborah surveyed his lodgings. Before she could speak, he did.

"Motel decor," Beck said, trying to make a joke of it.
"I've always wondered where they found decorators psychotic enough to take on the job."

She nodded. Beck wondered if she had noticed the vodka
on his breath.

"I'm sorry," she said. "About your . . . friend."

"I met her two days ago," he said. "But yes. She was my
friend."

There was a silence between the two of them that was not
unfamiliar, but neither was it uncomfortable. Then Beck said
the words both of them had been thinking.

"We'll find Katie," he said. "I promise you."

"You've heard about this VIX thing." It was not a question.

Beck nodded.

He had listened to the President's speech from the hallway
outside the motel manager's office, while the technicians
were still preparing to move April's body. The chief executive had not tried to moderate the facts of the Hobson's
choice, nor attempted to sugarcoat the probable results: one
in every twenty Americans would likely die if VIX was used,

compared to at least eight in ten if it was not. He was, the President said, in consultation with other world leaders to discuss the international repercussions involved. But, he insisted, the decision would be his and his alone—and he would make it soon. Possibly, it had been rumored, within the next six hours.

The message chilled Beck. There was nothing to say: it would either work or it would not. Either way, it sounded like less a plan than a desperate gamble—one that was guaranteed to cost millions of human lives. It redefined "acceptable losses" in a horrifying manner. VIX would intentionally create a lethal pandemic in its own right, "acceptable" only relative to the horror it was meant to combat. By any other definition, in any other circumstances, it would constitute mass murder on an unprecedented scale.

"And those are the people you've chosen to return to," Deborah said, and her voice was bitter.

Beck felt his anger rise.

"It's not that simple," he began.

Her voice was mocking. "It never is, Beck. It never was."

He felt trapped, cornered—and furious, struck back.

"Let's talk about you, shall we? You look well—or is it 'you look good'?" Beck leaned back, and pretended to ponder. "Doesn't matter. You've always looked great, as I remember. Of course, I haven't seen you in more than twelve months. Not since the divorce hearing." Beck drew in a breath. "For a year, we've only communicated through lawyers. Suddenly, here you are, in my room. I have to wonder why."

She was flushed, and silent for a moment.

"I want to apologize," Deborah said suddenly.

"For what?"

"When I discovered that Katie was missing, my first reaction was to blame you. I had convinced myself that you were somehow at fault—that the whole damn escapade was something the two of you had planned."

Beck frowned, puzzled. "Why would we do that?"

"To spite me," she answered. "To keep me outside, both of you."

"I would never—"

"I know, Beck. I know. But I don't understand why she did this. Katie and I . . ." Her voice trailed off.

"What?" Beck pressed.

"We're all either of us have. And I think she hates that fact."

"She has me, Deborah. She has both of us."

"You think so, Beck. But both your daughter and I know it is not true. Especially . . . afterward. When they brought you back."

He felt it: the choking feeling he had whenever the horrific memories rose inside him.

She looked up at him, and a sudden defiance was in her voice. "But it was only a matter of degree, Beck. Nothing was really new about it. For years, I watched you pull everything inside. Everything but me. Me, you pushed away.

"Before Katie was born, I thought it was another woman. I wish it had been. Even that I could have understood. But do you understand what it was like for me to play second chair to . . . to a *damn job*? I raised Katie alone, Beck.

"When you disappeared over there, I was frantic. But I had a daughter whose father was suddenly missing. I had to be strong, even when no one would tell me anything. We didn't know if you were still alive. Then, when you came back more dead than alive, I tried to stand by you—I did. But you still wouldn't bring me inside."

"Deborah, there had to be areas I couldn't discuss, secrets that—"

"It was always *your* secret, Beck. They were all your secrets. Well, congratulations. Your secrets destroyed everything. They destroyed us."

"When I came home, I—"

"You never came home, Beck."

Deborah's voice broke. She bent her head and dissolved in a paroxysm of wrenching sobs.

It's true, Beck thought, and the shame and horror again washed through him. *Whatever love we had for each other had not, could not have, survived that collapse.*

He had no excuses, and understood that she needed none of her own.

When she looked up, she had stopped crying. But the marks of her tears still glistened on her face.

"I wanted to come here tonight," Deborah said, "to tell you that. And to be with you."

She rose from the sofa, and stood over Beck.

"This virus—don't lie, Beck. There's not much hope, is there? For Katie, or for any of us."

His silence was her answer.

"We were in love once," she whispered. "We were a family. Remember?"

His voice was hoarse. "Deborah," he said.

"I need to know," she said. "If there's anything left for us. *Of* us."

Her hands dropped to her waist. In a moment, the shorts fell to the floor. Her body was as he remembered: fine and delicate as a girl, but unmistakably a woman.

With her thumbs, she eased the remaining scrap of fabric past her hips, down her legs. When they reached her ankles, she stepped lightly out of them. The movement revealed her inner thigh, and more. The shadows and textures of her directed Beck's gaze to her secret places, full and moist. He could feel the heat rise within him, and he swallowed with a throat suddenly dry.

The cloth of Deborah's shirt had pulled tight against her chest, vividly outlining her excitement. Her hands worked at the tiny buttons, impatient in her own need. Before Beck could speak, the blouse came away. Her breasts were small, rising and falling with each breath, and tipped with nipples that were hard and erect.

Now she was nude. Deborah looked at Beck as if it was his turn to act.

"For what we had," she said, "for what we lost."

And he reached for her.

Deborah stepped close to his chair. They kissed deeply, and Beck felt her hand move to the hardness that strained against his pants. Soon she drew his right hand to her left breast, holding him hard against her. His other hand stroked and explored, pleasuring her in slow circles timed to their shared, rising excitement. Finally she rose and worked at his belt buckle. Soon she had pushed aside all that stood between their two bodies.

Her scent, her feel, her taste overwhelmed Beck's every sense. Deborah pressed him back and moved over him, her feet planted on either side of the chair. She reached between their bodies, grasping, guiding his hardness into a place of heat and tightness. Beck's body trembled as he slipped deep inside.

She rocked her hips, stroking, teasing. He leaned back in the chair, his thighs straining to match her rhythm.

She rose and fell, the fine muscles of her body rippling with the force of her effort as Beck moved in and out of her. His hands moved along her spine—stroking lightly here, grasping hard there. When they kissed, their tongues fenced in quick, darting thrusts and parries.

Near the end, he pulled back to look at Deborah's face. Her eyes were closed tightly, her head twisting convulsively from side to side. The sounds she made were soft and wordless and increasingly urgent. It was a prayer of need and wonder, chanted just under her breath. Her hips churned against him in a dance as old as human longing.

"Oh. Oh . . ." Suddenly she tensed, her face twisted in a rictus that could have been pain or pleasure. She gripped Beck inside her like a hot, silky fist, and he could feel the intensity build throughout her body. For a long moment, she was lost in the sensations, her body almost vibrating. Then her orgasm rippled and swelled and burst upon them both.

She stared sightlessly into Beck's eyes as she came, a strained keening rising from deep in her throat. Her entire body shuddered as if possessed, and that drew him too over the precipice. Beck groaned loudly as he felt his own climax flood into her. He pulled her close, pulsing in wave after white-hot wave.

"Yes." Deborah's voice was breathy and wild, and another massive explosion convulsed her. Then, as if sliding down a long, dark incline, she fell against Beck's chest, spent. The mad hammering of her heart matched the pounding of his own. They clung to each other like that for several minutes, as their breathing slowly eased. Soon, she shifted slightly on Beck's lap and he felt himself slip out of her.

Only then did he feel the chill of the air on his flesh. Deborah's weight, slight as it was, grew oppressive against his thighs. Beck became aware of a sweaty itch wherever her flesh touched his; for the first time since Deborah had entered his room, he felt the dull ache of his wound pulsing in his leg. Outside, a distant siren faded into the anonymous sounds of the night. He fought a sudden desire to look at his wristwatch.

In the postcoital coldness, Beck held the woman he had once loved, and who had once loved him. He felt a clarity of mind that had eluded him since all this began. During that time, he had been waiting, though for what he did not know.

With a sense of profound loss, he realized what he had understood all along. Something was missing in him, in his character—perhaps it had been torn from him in Russia, by the torturer's art. Perhaps, he thought with something akin to horror, it had never been in him at all.

He could not bear to be alone, but he could not bear to be with anyone else. He wondered, not for the first time, if he had gone mad.

Deborah felt the difference in him. She rose and moved away, but not before kissing Beck's ear softly. Or perhaps sadly.

"Sex was never the problem we had, was it?" she asked,

and there was regret in her voice. "We were always good together that way."

They dressed with their backs to each other.

She was halfway out the door when Beck spoke.

"Deborah, " he said, "thank you for coming here tonight."

She stopped and looked at him as if seeing him for the last time.

"If I hadn't, it never would have happened," Deborah said. "You realize that, don't you? No matter how much you may have wanted it. You've diminished yourself, Beck; you've become almost completely passive."

"That's not true—" he began.

"You've turned into a spectator to your own life," she said with a flat finality. "Why are you so compelled to . . . to *accept* whatever happens, Beck? I can understand that you killed off your intellect—perhaps it deserved to die, after the way you had used it for all those years. But when did you lose your soul?"

His face roiled and clouded; as Deborah had always been able to do, she read Beck's thoughts as if he had voiced them.

"It's not what they did to you in Russia, Beck. It's what you allowed to happen afterward. You've given up, on yourself and everything else. I don't think you even know who you are anymore. For God's sake, Beck—come back to life, or it will kill you."

Abruptly, she turned away and opened the door.

"I want you to know"—he swallowed, recognizing the inadequacy of the words—"that I'm very, very sorry."

"For what, Beck?" Deborah said, not unkindly. "Do you even know?"

When the door closed, he stared at it for a long time.

Chapter 44

Montgomery, Alabama
July 23

He sat in the darkened suite, in the chair where he and Deborah had spent their lonesome passion. Only when the knock came, for the second time that night, did Beck Casey realize that he had been expecting it.

"It's not locked, Alexi."

The door swung open, and filled with a dark, bearlike figure.

"Do I interrupt anything, my friend?" In the doorway, Alexi Malenkov's face was split by a wide grin; he managed to look both lewd and gregarious at the same time. "I certainly hope so."

He lifted his hand, and Beck heard the tinkle of glass against metal.

"I heard movement in the hallway, Beck. Being paranoid, both by nature and by profession, of course I looked. You have reconciled with Deborah? I have come to celebrate with the two of you!"

"She left. Keep your voice down, Alexi."

Alexi nodded, suddenly crestfallen.

"Of course. I perhaps misinterpreted. This business with

Katie must be a terrible strain on her—on you both. Have you any word?"

"No. Deborah intends to go inside the Quarantine Region and look for her." He looked steadily and calmly at the Russian. "Frankly, I haven't been able to figure out what I should do. Not even when my daughter's life is an issue. Isn't that odd, Alexi?"

Alexi entered, closing the door behind him. Beck watched him cross the small room and set a bottle on the dining table. The Russian reached into the pocket of the linen jacket he wore and produced stemmed champagne flutes. There were only two of them, Beck noticed.

"We can, perhaps, ask Deborah to join us later," Alexi said. "Her room, I believe, is only down the hall a little way. Perhaps we can formulate a plan together." He shook his head. "What a day we have had, my friend."

"Why are you here, Alexi?"

"I could not sleep, so I thought to join you. Such sadness, this filthy thing to have been done to your Ms. O'Connor."

"No. I mean, why are you *here*. In Alabama."

Alexi raised his eyebrows. "As I told you. To assist you, to stop this assassin Ilya."

Beck nodded thoughtfully.

"You want to open that champagne, Alexi? I think you're right—we should have a drink together."

Alexi grinned, and turned to the task. There was the metallic rustle of foil being peeled back, and a soft grunt of exertion. Then the pop of a cork, followed by the hiss of carbonation pouring into crystal.

He handed one of the flutes to Beck, and raised his own in salute.

"To luck, Beck. Your Katie will be found, and she will be well."

"Not to luck, Alexi. I don't think luck has been involved with any of this."

"I am the Russian here, Beck. It is I who should make such enigmatic statements."

Beck laughed softly in turn.

"Forgive me, Alexi. I guess I'm not being a good host. This is the first chance I've had to think clearly since all this began. Maybe longer."

"It is understandable. And what have you been thinking, my friend?"

"For one thing, how easy it was to assign the guilt," Beck said. "I'm supposed to be the expert on terrorism, and all of us 'experts' have been warning that extremist groups were the biggest threat we faced these days. Particularly when it comes to biological terrorism. It was inevitable, we said. One day, some cult would use a bioweapon to attack a major power."

"It is a logical assessment." Alexi shrugged. "I do not think one need be a prophet to predict this."

"My point exactly." Beck nodded. "And the Aum—well, you couldn't invent a better villain. Of *course* they were responsible; of *course* they did it because they were religious fanatics. How easy it was to accept: the Aum had an end-of-the-world mind-set, as well as the charismatic leader who believed he was a god."

"Do not forget, my friend—they also had the demonstrated ability to wage biological warfare. These zealots have previously acted on their murderous fantasies."

Incongruously, Alexi chuckled. "To act as a god—for some, perhaps this is the same as to *be* God." He peered closely at Beck's expression. "Ah. You do not think so."

"The majority of the Aum are followers," Beck said. "Follow the leader: that's the nature of such groups. That's why it was so simple to get them to commit mass murder. And, later, mass suicide. Asahara is in prison, awaiting execution. So what 'god' were the rank and file taking orders from?"

"They had their sensei," Alexi said. "Their so-called teachers, who led them to these acts."

"Teachers, or teacher?" Beck asked. "In Japanese, the word means both singular and plural."

"Yes." Alexi's voice had become impatient. "And if any Aum still lived, we could ask them. Perhaps this man Ilya is a sensei, or the Sensei. Or perhaps he too is a follower, and these teachers died by their own hands. What is the point, Beck? They are all dead."

"Nicely put, Alexi. You see, that's part of my problem. The Aum are dead. The man they used in your country— Davidovich, I mean; the same person our CIA had employed as a Russian agent—he's dead, too. All these people, the ones who might be able to provide answers of their own— they all seem to be dead, Alexi."

"Less than three hundred kilometers from us, many more people are dead, or soon will be." Alexi flushed. "My apologies—I do not mean that your daughter—"

"It's all right, Alexi. But I can't think about Katie right now. Not if I want to think clearly. You understand that, I believe."

Alexi nodded. His eyes watched the other man closely, though whether in concern or something else, Beck could not tell.

"Today, April O'Connor died. Just as I would have, if you hadn't entered at that very moment. And pulled me away."

"You were quite fortunate, but I am no hero," Alexi said, his tone trying to lighten the mood. "It was too late for me to go back outside. Had you opened the inner door to your friend, the gas would have killed me too."

"I certainly understand enlightened self-interest, Alexi," Beck said. "Bottom line, then. The Aum created a doomsday virus. They passed some of it along to militias in America, possibly in Russia. Then they killed themselves."

"It is quite a simple story, my friend."

"You've told me that before," Beck said agreeably. "Just as you recently reminded me not to look for logic in an illogical act. I forgot that. I let myself be carried along by the events, the story as it unfolded. I didn't look for anything else."

"You saw what existed. There was nothing else to see."

Beck rubbed his eyes. "So you say. Just as you said that Davidovich was Aum. Just as you said that this Ilya is also Aum. You told me that the virus was brought into Russia by a mysterious Japanese man. And earlier today, after April died, you were certainly quick to conclude that Ilya was responsible. You see, it never even occurred to me to wonder how he knew we were here — let alone how Ilya knew April O'Connor's name. It was printed on the package, you know."

Beck looked up, and saw Alexi Malenkov watching him with eyes that were carefully hooded.

"Yes," the Russian agreed. "That is a mystery, is it not?"

"I just . . . went along with what you were saying. I've been doing a lot of that lately, haven't I?"

Beck smiled at Alexi politely. "You have certainly become a central person in this story, Alexi. As I sat here, tonight, it occurred to me: most of what I know about any of this has come from *you*. Were I a less trusting person, I might start to worry about that."

Alexi reached forward, patting Beck on his knee as an adult might placate a child. Then he stood and stretched. "You are tired, my friend. And worried about your daughter. In such a state, it is too easy to see conspiracies everywhere. It is a very human reaction."

"Right on all counts, Alexi. You see, once again you have framed everything for me, quite logically. Accept the premise, and the conclusion is inescapable. You have convinced me that only one conclusion is possible."

Alexi looked genuinely puzzled. "And what is that, Beck?"

"That you are the one the Aum called Sensei," Beck said.

Chapter 45

There was a moment when neither man moved, nor made a sound. Then a slow smile spread over the Russian's features, finally culminating in what to Beck looked like a guileless grin.

"What am I to do now, my friend?" Alexi asked genially. "Am I to gasp in shock and fear—or to produce a pistol and demand from you how you learned this? I will do one or the other, of course, if you insist. I have always had a weakness for bad theater."

"No need," Beck said. "Just tell me why."

Alexi nodded sagely.

"Ah—you wish the denouement, the melodramatic confession of the guilty party. You make an irrational accusation, Beck; perhaps you do not even recognize how absurd it sounds. Why should I humor you in this foolishness?"

"It's just the two of us here, Alexi. Who else is there to tell? Besides, didn't you come in here to kill me anyway?"

Alexi studied him for a moment, as if considering what expression to paint on his own face. Then he threw back his head and laughed, delighted.

"Ah—*this* is the Beck Casey I knew from before. So

quiet, but such brilliant leaps of insight! I wish I had your gift. Tell me truly: had you really left the CIA?"

"I had, before this—before *you*—brought me back."

Alexi chuckled, a rueful sound. "Beck, Beck. It seems I have worked very hard to accomplish the exact opposite of what I intended. Perhaps you have earned the right to know *my* truth."

He reached into his side pocket and withdrew a knife, its naked blade serrated and similar in length to the one that another Russian had plunged into Beck's thigh. He casually placed it on the table near the champagne bottle, within easy reach.

"I have worried about you, my friend. Forgive me, but you had become quite a boring companion. You were so . . . *compliant*. Malleable."

"Yes," Beck said. "Deborah said the same thing. She said I had become passive—a spectator." He spread his hands amiably. "So tell me a story, Alexi. Tell me *this* story."

"Very well. Where shall I start?"

"The virus. You lied to me. It was Russian-made."

Alexi shook his head. "No. In that, I was quite forthright. This doomsday virus was the product of a man named Anji Suzuki. He was a biogeneticist and a member of the Aum, though his recruitment into the group was somewhat . . . brutish. May I smoke?"

Beck nodded, and watched as Alexi produced the flat package of Russian cigarettes and lit one with a battered Ronson lighter. He blew the plume of bluish smoke skyward in obvious satisfaction.

"Ah. Anji Suzuki. The psychoactive drugs you received when you were a guest of our *Mafiya*—do you remember them? I doubt Dr. Suzuki did; his treatment was weighted much more heavily toward electrotherapy, which I understand creates a significant detriment to short-term memory."

Beck frowned. "He was kidnapped? Brainwashed?"

"In a manner of speaking," Alexi said. "He had needed

skills and no close family. It is not difficult, as you know. The Aum are—*were*—quite adept at eliciting what they called an Enlightenment. The trick, as I understand the matter, is to alter the personality—the part of the mind that contains all the small quirks that makes one an individual—without destroying the mind itself."

Alexi pursed his lips mock sadly. "A pity, Beck. Suzuki was quite a talented geneticist. Afterward, I arranged for him to receive an intensive—let us call it a tutorial—at my country's bioweapon development center in Omutninsk. This instruction allowed him to stand on the shoulders of giants in the field of biological weaponry, and greatly simplified his own work on the influenza virus."

"He's dead, I assume."

Alexi shrugged, a casual gesture.

"How did you get the virus to America, Alexi? Did your Aum create another zombie for that, too?"

Alexi smiled, pleased.

"Such a colorful term. No, Anji volunteered for that task. A quite dedicated person, Beck—a zealot. He disappeared shortly after he arrived in your country on his last visit. It seems likely that he was killed by our mutual acquaintance, Ilya. He succeeded only in spreading the infection to Florida."

"Katie is in Florida," Beck said. "My daughter, Alexi."

"In truth, Beck, the outbreak in Florida was a surprise to me. The plan called for poor Anji to fly across your country—disembarking, of course, in selected cities along the way. The hub cities of your major airlines."

Alexi waved his hand, a dismissive gesture.

"It is of no matter, really. Except to Anji, of course. He was a true believer, and would have been very disappointed to know that he performed so poorly on his last glorious mission."

"At your orders, he was to release mass murder," Beck said. His voice was not quite right—hoarse and distant, the voice of a man who was trying to understand the incomprehensible. "You knew it was a virus with the ability to kill . . . *billions*."

"Of course," the man who had been called Sensei replied. "I would not have thought it could turn out otherwise. Surely you understand that. My friend, perhaps you recall the birth of a female child in the Balkans a few years ago? It was touted as a major symbolic event: the population of our little planet reaching six billion people. There was already a plague under way—a plague of people, voracious as any microbe. We can certainly spare a few billion of them, Beck."

"That's a rather coldblooded philosophy, Alexi."

"I do not agree. Consider every problem facing the world today; the root cause behind it is the same. Famine? Too many people. Poverty? Too many people. War?" The Russian laughed, and shook his head ruefully. "Well, people will always fight with one another, is it not so? But when people seek the resources owned by their neighbors, it is almost always because the very scarcity of those resources has made them valuable—perhaps even essential to survival. What creates this scarcity? Again, it is overpopulation. I do the world a service, you see."

"Alexi," Beck said, "I find it hard to believe you've done all this because you have become a humanitarian."

Alexi Malenkov threw back his head and laughed explosively.

"You are right to be skeptical, Beck," he said, the mirth still in his tones. "Forgive me. I love too much the rhetorical discussion, the debate. In truth, I do not care how many people live on this world, as long as I am one of them. Living, of course, substantially more comfortably than most."

"You are not an Aum, Alexi."

Malenkov looked surprised, then offended.

"Certainly not. To worship the words of a half-witted madman—no, this is not for me, thank you. But this is not to say that I do not recognize a useful tool when it is handed to me. They have much energy, these fanatics. And they are not without resources, of course.

"After their Tokyo farce with the poison gas, I was ordered to eradicate the cult's Russian membership. Beck, I was appalled at the waste! Thirty thousand Russian Aum— all of them already proven quite as gullible as they were energetic. Several thousand more in Japan, even more industrious and vastly more prosperous."

Alexi, still smiling, spread his hands in a what-could-I-do? gesture. "Well. Clearly, this was a valuable resource— one that had been shorn of its previous leadership and was, metaphorically, wandering aimlessly in the desert. I found it unconscionable to cast away such an asset."

"So you spent the past few years assimilating the Aum," Beck said. "I can understand how you could do it in Russia, Alexi. But I'm very impressed you were able to take in the Japanese Aum too."

"Really, it was not difficult to position myself advantageously with the Japanese cultists," Alexi said. "I was their cohort from Russia, a fellow Truthseeker as devastated as any of them at the plight of the divine God Asahara." He snorted, though in derision or amusement Beck could not tell. "And I confess, I rather liked the title of Sensei. I am a teacher, of a sort."

"Is that where you found Davidovich? Among the Aum?"

"Davidovich? I doubt if he even knew what an Aum was," Alexi said with scorn. "He was merely a scribbler who sought to supplement his income by selling unimportant information to foreigners. A convenient—what is the word? Dupe? Stooge? One might almost feel sorry for such a creature."

"Why go to the trouble of pretending an interrogation?" Beck pressed. "Why was it necessary to torture him, Alexi?"

Alexi stitched a mock apologetic expression on his face.

"Ah, my friend—that was for your benefit. Do not look

so shocked; accept it as a compliment. I have a great respect for your intellect, you see."

Alexi shook his head again, smiling as if sharing a joke on himself. "I thought to distract you, playing on your unfortunate experience in my country. He was CIA, abandoned. You also. It was most effective, was it not?"

"Why involve me at all, Alexi?"

"A mistake. You are perhaps my private obsession, Beck Casey. This conspiracy of the virus—it has occupied my mind for almost two years. Each detail, so carefully planned. But all the while—I am serious, my friend—all the while I thought of you. Of *course* you were still of the CIA; of *course,* given your specialties, you would be targeted on any biological threat by terrorists. As I say, I felt a need to . . . distract you."

"That's not a mistake, Alexi; that's crazy. I can't read minds."

Alexi made a dismissive gesture. "You are not psychic, this we both know; you are a trained analyst. Your logic, I did not fear. But, Beck—that gift you possess, that ability to transcend logic and make the intuitive leap—no, this I have seen. This, I feared." He smiled genially. "Well, to err is human, no? To then erase the mistake for all time—that, my friend, is divine."

Beck swallowed in a throat achingly dry.

"I don't believe you are insane, Alexi. I really don't. But the VIX infection has changed everything now. The game's over; you've lost."

"Your VIX deployment was unexpected, but I do not see it as an insurmountable problem," the Russian retorted. "As I said, except as a point of debate, I do not really care how many this virus infects. Even supplying it to your militia crazies was merely an afterthought, you see—insurance, as well as another distraction. If you can stop this virus, please feel free to do so."

Beck started to speak, stopped. His mind churned. *Alexi*

no longer cares about the flu, one way or another, he realized. *This was all about something else entirely. Okay—if he hasn't given up on his plan, that means—*

"You already have what you wanted," Beck said aloud. "You wanted Putin, on a platter."

Once again, Alexi grinned broadly at him.

"That is what I mean—you are gifted, Beck. Can anyone really think that even Vadoly Putin can survive the mass execution of several hundred thousand Russians? Yes, yes—in the past, it would perhaps have been possible. After all, Stalin killed tens of millions. But not today; not in a Russia that watched it happen on CNN."

"Yes," Beck admitted. "It might make it tough to find an impartial jury for the trial."

"There will be no need for a trial, of course," Alexi said. "Putin will be shot while resisting arrest." Alexi pursed his lips, pretending to ponder for a moment. "I have not yet decided if he was also attempting to escape."

"I think I'm starting to understand," Beck said.

"Indeed?" Alexi raised an eyebrow. "Then you know that there will be need of a new President in Russia, very soon. A strong leader, but one whose actions in this terrible crisis were above reproach."

"I imagine you have a candidate in mind, Alexi," Beck said.

"If nominated, I will not decline." Alexi smiled. "If I am elected, I will not refuse to serve." He winked. "And I *will* be nominated and elected. It is, as you say, already a lock."

"Your Russian billionaires," Beck said, nodding. "They've decided to trade one ex-KGB man for another. My compliments, Alexi. You've *really* come up in the world. But how do your new friends feel about having a lethal virus set loose on them? Didn't you think they'd want a vaccine?"

"Beck, Beck—there is a vaccine, of course," Alexi said. "I have taken it myself, as have the others of whom you speak. It is quite effective, I assure you. Our dedicated bio-

genecist Anji engineered his virus with an exceptional sensitivity to the vaccine — it provides immunity within hours of
its use."

"Does your vaccine cure those already infected?" Beck
asked.

"Sadly, no," Alexi replied. "But it is available, in sufficient quantities — at least, to immunize everyone in Russia.
We have stockpiled more than three hundred million units.
The plans for mass immunization already exist; you know of
our very excellent civil defense organization. Updating its
procedures was one of the earliest tasks assigned to me, you
see — by Putin, if you can appreciate the irony."

"And you'll be seen as the savior of your country," Beck
said. "That should help you — a presidential candidate
known as a great humanitarian. Even if he unleashed a virus
that would have decimated the planet."

"Your own president's plan is to save the world by setting
off a second plague that will kill millions in its own right."
Alexi shrugged. "Well, I applaud *his* brand of humanitarianism. After he has set loose this VIX, we will announce that
Russian research has developed a vaccine that is effective
against the original killer influenza — too late to stop the VIX
release, sadly. Still, as a humanitarian gesture, we will make
our vaccine formulation available to the world. Meanwhile,
your VIX will spread and kill — what? Five percent, three
hundred million people? Fourteen million Americans? Very
poor public relations, Beck. I fear it will be seen in a less
kindly light than it perhaps might have been."

He grinned suddenly, a flash of the old Alexi.

"Perhaps you too should consider making an arrest, Beck.
Imagine: our two presidents, both arrested for crimes against
humanity. How ironic, do you not agree?"

Before Beck could answer, another voice spoke in Russian.

"It is an interesting proposition, General Malenkov. Trea-
son, of course — but interesting nonetheless."

Both heads swiveled to the figure standing under the arched entryway that led to the suite's balcony.

"I fear I must interrupt," Ilya said, smiling politely. "Stand, please. There."

He gestured with the gun steady in his hand and pointing unmistakably at the pair. When they had moved away from the table, Ilya sidled to it. He picked up the knife, examining it and nodding in appreciation.

"Quite clever," he said, and looked up to address Alexi. "So I was to return tonight? To—how do you say?—finish my business with this man?"

Alexi watched Ilya with an interest that, to Beck, seemed remote, even academic; he could have been at a zoo, looking at an unfamiliar but mildly interesting specimen. But Alexi did not respond, not even when the other Russian shrugged and carefully dropped the unsheathed knife into his own pocket.

"General Malenkov," Ilya said, as if he were presenting himself in a formal reception line. "It is a pleasure. I bring you the greetings of President Putin, who is as concerned about the state of your health as you are of his." His left index finger pointed to Alexi's belt. "Please. If you continue to move your hand, I will, of course, shoot you in the stomach."

Ilya stepped forward and deftly plucked a small-caliber automatic from Alexi Malenkov's belt. His lip twisted in derision—*Romanian-made,* his mind sneered. *Such a useless toy!*—as his thumb pressed a button above the pistol's checkered grip. Ilya shook the weapon, and the magazine clattered on the hardwood floor. Cupping the pistol, he pressed back the slide with a single finger; his eyes flickered downward for an instant, checking the action.

"Yes," he said, nodding. "I compliment your good sense, General. It is much safer to carry even such a weapon as this without a cartridge in the chamber." He threw the empty pistol into the bedroom.

Throughout, Beck noted, the intruder's own weapon had

not wavered from a point midway between the two men. Ilya had climbed to the balcony, had entered unheard, had waited patiently while Alexi had detailed the entire plot before announcing himself and disarming his captives. It had all been done with practiced ease, providing no opportunity for resistance. That fact alone marked him as a professional, and Beck calculated his own chances for survival sharply downward.

"So—you suffer no ill effects?" the man said, and Beck realized the comment was addressed to him. "From our earlier meeting, I mean."

"I'll limp for a few weeks," Beck said, his eyes steady on the Russian. "I hope."

Ilya grinned at the jest.

"In truth, I have no orders to kill you," he said. "Unless you are inclined to make it necessary, of course." The pistol he held moved infinestimally to the left. "General Malenkov is another matter. For him, my orders are quite clear. I was quite interested to hear of his plans to expedite my country's political process. Sadly, I cannot allow such ambitions to be fulfilled.

"It is good to find you here, General," Ilya said. "I did not wish to miss the final act of this play. You have written it so well. Even President Putin is impressed—no, I speak the truth. He wondered only why the director of state security saw fit to promise American dissident elements an illegal chemical weapon—but chose not to report this activity to his president. I was already in this country and close to these groups; therefore, the assignment was given to me."

"You knew about the sarin," Beck said, "and the Japanese who reached out to the militia groups."

"For some weeks. These militia rabble cannot resist the sweet music of their own voices. They spoke, far too often, of the gift this Japanese visitor promised." Ilya shrugged carelessly. "An amateur, to be sure. He traveled always using the same passport; I knew his arrival time almost before he did. I killed him as he placed his luggage in the car he had rented. A Japanese car—is that not ironic? He barely fit inside the trunk where he fell."

He spoke directly to Alexi Malenkov.

"When I killed him, I did not know he carried your plague," Ilya said, and grinned. "It is my good fortune I used a pistol and not a knife. Had I stood as close to him as I do to you now, I doubt that I would have survived the encounter."

Ilya looked at Beck. "You are perhaps curious why I speak so freely in front of you? It is the expressed order of President Putin. He wishes to leave no doubt where the responsibility for this disaster lies."

Ilya again addressed his countryman. "Alexi Ivanovich Malenkov, had I more time to waste on a traitor such as you, I would enjoy . . . *persuading* you to talk in greater detail about your wealthy patrons. But I am willing to—I do not wish to warn you again. Please keep your hand—"

He was too late.

In his left hand, Alexi held a small red-and-white can; his thumb pressed upward on the pull-top tab, which already flexed slightly under the pressure.

"I leave it to you," Alexi said genially. "Please guess: Does this can contain the influenza virus? Or is it perhaps filled with sarin? In truth, I do not know myself. Not for certain."

He looked squarely at Ilya. "If it is the virus, please remember that I have received the vaccine. Regardless of what else happens here, I am immune to it. You are not. Are you willing to chance that you will not die within the next day or two? It *is* a gamble, my young friend: you can perhaps be saved by this VIX of the Americans. Perhaps not, if you are one of those who succumb quickly."

"But you will be dead," Ilya said, and Beck heard no fear in his tone.

"This is so," Alexi admitted, and he too sounded unafraid. "But please consider this: What if this apparatus contains sarin? In that case, there would be no gamble. We will be dead within a few seconds. All of us."

"Ah. So what do you propose, General?"

"At the very least, that you allow me to leave here unharmed." He cocked an eyebrow. "Unless I can also persuade you that your own interests are best served by not chaining yourself to Putin's future. I could find many rewards for someone of your talents." He nodded toward Beck. "If you find this agreeable, you would also be asked to remove any other impediments. In whatever manner you wish to do so."

Ilya nodded judiciously. "It is a difficult decision. As you say, I must consider my own best interests."

And then he shot Malenkov once, in the forehead.

A mist of blood and pulverized bone jetted from the back of the Russian's head, iridescent in the harsh backlighting. His hand jerked an instant before the fingers spasmed and opened; there was a metallic clatter, and a red-and-white labeled object spun across the carpet.

Alexi stood erect and motionless for a heartbeat, and then collapsed into himself. The body that in life had been Alexi Malenkov twitched furiously for a moment, its heels bouncing on the floor, and then was still.

"I am many things, General," Ilya said, addressing ears that could no longer hear. "But I am not a traitor."

Before the corpse had stopped moving, Beck was on his hands and knees, scrambling after the container. He snatched it up, holding his breath and knowing that, if Alexi's dying act had been to wrench up the tab, it was a useless exercise.

Beck lifted the container with hands whose shaking he could not control.

The tab was bent upward at an angle—but not quite enough, Beck realized, to have pulled the metal disk away from its seal. Relief flooded him; he felt his heart pounding, and reveled in the sensation.

"Good shooting," Beck said, and heard the tight nervous energy in his voice. He looked at the can he held in still-shaking hands. "I'll be interested in the lab report. It will be nice to know what almost killed me, sarin gas or a weaponized virus."

"It is the virus," the Russian said.

He reached into his pocket and removed an identical can, the one he had taken from Cappie Arnold before incinerating the militiaman's body. "You see, I have one just like it." He tossed it, with a light underhand, to the American. "With my compliments. I have no need for such vile things."

Beck looked hard at the Russian. "Is what Alexi said true? Is there a vaccine?"

Ilya shook his head.

"I do not know." He made a gesture toward the body on the floor. "He was a skilled liar. But he did not appear to fear his own virus."

Beck thought furiously. "If there is a vaccine, and if there is enough of it—"

He looked up at Ilya. "We've got to contact Putin. He'll know who among the oligarchs own pharmaceutical companies, drug manufacturers. He'll do what is necessary. And we have to keep my people from releasing Agent VIX."

"Why? It is good a vaccine exists—*if* the pig Malenkov did not again lie, and if this vaccine has, in truth, been manufactured. But your VIX will stop this killer virus, will it not?"

"Yes," Beck said. "But VIX will also kill millions itself. Look—Alexi said there were three hundred million doses of vaccine stockpiled somewhere. We can use it to selectively vaccinate around any contagion zones. At the very least, we can set up a herd immunity that will contain the outbreak, while more vaccine is manufactured. We can stop this thing, without killing people with VIX."

Ilya frowned at the American in genuine puzzlement.

"And why should I assist you? Release your VIX; we understand 'acceptable losses.' Russia will be safe, whether this vaccine exists or not."

"But will Putin?" Beck pressed. "You heard Alexi. The game is stacked against your man, by people who have billions to spend. As it stands now, Putin cannot escape being labeled a mass murderer; do you imagine he can survive this conspiracy?"

"I see the point you make," Ilya said. "But he can become a hero, untouchable—*if* he makes available a vaccine that can save the world."

"We have to move quickly," Beck said. "Once the VIX is released, it's too late. And if we find that the vaccine doesn't exist, releasing VIX is our only hope."

Ilya looked at Beck thoughtfully for a moment. Then he reached into his pocket and withdrew the stiletto Alexi Malenkov had brought.

Beck stiffened, his eyes on the scalloped blade. It was only with difficulty that he looked back at the Russian's face.

Ilya smiled, and tossed the knife onto the table. It clattered loudly in the tense silence.

"When we last met, I had placed a blade very much like that one into your flesh. You are aware of what would have happened next, had we not been interrupted?"

Beck nodded, aware that his throat was suddenly too parched to speak.

"You will forgive me this question, please: Why should I believe you hold no . . . ill will toward me?"

"You're a killer, and probably a psychopath," Beck said, and was surprised to hear that his voice sounded almost normal. "Worry about that later, because I *will* come after you. But right now, there are millions of people who will die unless we work together. One of them may be my daughter. I want to save her, and the rest who will otherwise die from this madness."

"So. And what can you give me? What do *I* want?"

"You want to save Putin. And yourself."

"Indeed," Ilya said, and smiled thinly. "It would seem that, for now, we are on the same side."

Chapter 46

Fort Walton Beach, Florida
July 23

The stench of the unburied dead was now almost unbearable, its assault on the senses magnified by the mingled tang of diesel fuel and burning meat. Carol Mayer had organized the detail, finding recruits among the relative handful of persons still strong enough to drag corpses to the far end zone. There, a makeshift pyre vomited an evil black cloud into the Florida sky.

But there was no way to keep up with the mortality. By her own rough estimate, Carol had calculated that more than two thousand souls had been brought to the football stadium. Of these, no more than three hundred now remained alive — if one could define as "life" the state in which these existed.

Sometime overnight while Carol slept, the CDC field team had left, slipping away without notice or fanfare. Carol had been infuriated, though a pragmatic part of her realized that anything else would have been a futile gesture. There was nothing anybody could do for the dead, and the same was true for the camp's other inhabitants.

Carol had dozed for less than two hours, poorly. She was too much the physician not to recognize the symptoms that she too was finally displaying.

Every joint in her body ached, a dull throbbing pain that was mirrored in the excruciating headache with which she had awakened. Without checking, she knew she had a raging fever. Her head also had filled, a thick red-tinged mucus that stained the tissues she now used almost constantly. Breathing was starting to become painful, punctuated by coughs that ripped things deep in her chest.

Two or three others in the work crew she had gathered still appeared without obvious symptoms, as had Carol only the evening before. By the expressions on their faces as they looked at her now, Carol knew that any hope they might have held was now gone.

She pulled hard at the blanket-wrapped form she was dragging, and tiny white-hot pinpoints of light arched and wheeled across her vision. She straightened, feeling for an instant the caress of a cool breeze against her cheek. But when she touched her fingers to her face, the skin felt hot and brittle.

From deep inside, she tried to conjure up a serene image, the way Choctawatchee Bay appeared from her balcony: an expanse of blues and slate gray, punctuated by the foamy comma of wavelets that textured the surface of the ancient waters. But though she tried hard, she could not hold the image for more than a few seconds before it paled and faded from her imagination.

Briefly, she thought about the two teenage girls who had fled this place of death. In her mind's eye, she saw them speeding along in her pickup truck. Their two faces looked fresh and impossibly happy, and whipping with wild abandon in the slipstream of the wind was the long dark hair of . . .

. . . of . . . of the younger one.

Damnedest thing, she told herself, *I can't seem to remember her name.*

She swayed on her feet, then toppled to the dusty ground.

Chapter 47

From somewhere close, much too close, the flat, jackhammer-like bark of what Katie now recognized as an automatic weapon punctuated the bedlam of lesser noise outside. She could hear faint screaming, drowned by a second long burst; when those faded, the screams had ended too.

She peered upward though the casement window that looked out at ground level. Now and then she caught a glimpse of running feet, some of them in heavy boots and others bare or wearing light beach sandals. Once, the owner of a pair of feet in white-and-red Air Jordans tripped right outside, sliding and bouncing headlong past her vantage in a manner almost comical. Before Katie could even smile, another pair of feet — these, in spit-shined Oxfords below gray uniform pants — skidded to a stop. There had been shouting, unintelligible to her but unmistakably filled with both fear and rage. Two shots, carefully spaced, echoed around the basement where Katie had taken refuge. Then the Oxfords wheeled and sprinted back in the direction from which they had come.

"Katie." It was said softly, though more from lack of strength than any awareness of the need for caution.

J. L. lay on a worn afghan Katie had found discarded in a corner, musty with mildew and dust. The younger girl knelt beside her friend.

"I'm sorry, Katie. Oh, God. I feel so—" J. L. vomited explosively. As the spasm racked her friend, Katie Casey held her as gently as possible, one hand stroking J. L.'s blunt-cut hair in a soft rhythm. When her hand touched J. L.'s forehead, the heat of the fever was like touching a kettle.

"It's okay, J. L. We'll be okay in here." Her voice was reassuring and calm, and unaffected by the tears that were once more tracking through the grime on her face.

Katie fought down the raw tickle that again rose in her throat, telling herself to ignore it, just as she was trying to ignore the headache that was no longer merely a nagging shadow inside her temples.

"It's going to be okay," she repeated. Not for the first time today, she wondered what it would be like to die.

Endgame:
July 24

Chapter 48

"You can't be serious. The President has already authorized the mission."

The voice belonged to Billy Carson, and it was starkly disbelieving.

"Listen to me." Beck gripped the sat phone so tightly his fingers ached. "There is a vaccine. You don't need to release the VIX, Carson."

"You think we want to? Beck, listen—the first confirmed flu cases were reported in New York just over an hour ago. And now we're getting reports that a mob of several thousand people tried to overrun the military cordon at the Lincoln Tunnel. They almost made it. Next time they probably will."

"Oh, God."

"'Oh, God' is right. If the virus spreads into New Jersey or Connecticut, we simply don't have the troops to establish a perimeter. We don't have time to wait for the Russians to search for any vaccine. Not one that may exist only in a murderer's lie."

"Alexi wasn't lying, Carson. He was ready to expose himself to a canister of virus. Doesn't that prove the vaccine exists?"

"It may only prove that Malenkov was a madman," Carson retorted. "And we already know that, don't we?"

The transmission erupted in a brief flurry of clicks and crackles, and a new voice came on the line.

"Dr. Casey, I am talking with Mr. Putin," the President said. "He wishes to speak to the man who shot General Malenkov."

Ilya took the phone from Beck's hand, and spoke into it in a clipped, precise volley of Russian so low that Beck was only barely able to follow. He heard his own name once, and recognized those of several Russian industrialists in what appeared to be a much longer list.

Finally, Ilya extended the sat phone to Beck, a grim expression on his face.

"You are a historian. You are given the opportunity to listen as history is made—or, perhaps, ended for all time."

As he held the receiver to his ear, Beck could hear the conversation already in progress between the presidents of Russia and America.

"There is but one way to get this information quickly enough," Putin was saying. "Could you use such methods on your country's richest men?"

"They threaten you directly," the President said. "Those who are involved in this plot threaten billions more."

Putin laughed, a single harsh bark. "You do not answer my question, Mr. President. No matter. I will do what I can do. If this vaccine of Malenkov's does in fact exist, I will . . . persuade one of these men to give it to me."

"Will you provide us with the supply we require? My advisors inform me that we can still initiate what they call herd immunity, and that will—"

"I too have experts," Putin interrupted, "and they too speak of this immunity. Yes. If vaccine exists, we will share. If it does not—"

"I will have no choice but to release Agent VIX," the President said.

There was a hesitation on the line.

"I do not wish to influence your decision," Putin said. "But were this my decision to make, I do not think I could choose to wait. As I could not, when I was forced to use chemical weapons here." His voice again became brusque. "I will leave you to your advisors. As for the vaccine and this conspiracy Malenkov revealed—we will talk when I . . . know more."

There was again the sound of encryption software reprogramming itself, and when it ended Beck heard only the end of the President's dialogue with his national security advisor.

"Mr. President, it's your responsibility," Carson said, his voice both urgent and intense. "The planes are probably already in the air. I can only advise you—and my advice is to release the VIX. Only you can decide. But you must decide now."

Chapter 49

The last shipment of VIX had arrived just after dawn, in the cavernous belly of a C-5 Galaxy with British markings, joining dozens of other blue-gray canisters that had already arrived from Maryland. All of the VIX containers came off the aircraft shrink-wrapped and stacked on plastic pallets that were attended to by forklifts, quickly but with care. Each canister was ridiculously undersized for the havoc its contents were designed to wreak: their dimensions were those of the propane tanks usually mounted on a recreational vehicle or outside a fishing cabin.

Freed from their polyethylene cocoons, the pressurized units themselves were surprisingly light. Installing them into the flight line of assorted sprayer-equipped fighters and transport aircraft scraped together for the mission, a single airman could easily carry a canister in either hand—even in the cumbersome protective suit that regulations required for the exercise.

Good thing, too, thought Colonel Peter Sivigny, watching exactly that exercise through the polycarbonate windows of his own protective mask. *Since nobody is going to take 'em off. Nobody sane, anyway.*

Sivigny was sweating profusely under the impermeable membrane of his coveralls, and grateful for the opportunity to do so. Many of those infected in the first day of the outbreak no longer perspired; the dead seldom do.

Despite the heat and inconvenience the antiexposure suits caused, for the past thirty-six hours the rubberized outfits had served as the mandatory uniform of the day for all personnel—as a safety measure for the uninfected, even those airmen who had already been displaying symptoms when the order was posted. In theory, any viruses being shed were sealed inside with their hosts. Thus far, the theory appeared sound. Several men had already died inside their rubberized minienvironment, but all of them had been diagnosed before the alarm klaxons had sounded.

Due to its proximity to ground zero for the outbreak, it was inevitable that Eglin had been hit hard by the virus. Casualties had been particularly high in the heavily populated central administration and headquarters sections of the main base. There, the virus had rippled outward from the base hospital; within a day, it had infected much of Eglin's brass and the upper-echelon support staff that thought it actually ran the rest of the huge installation. Some of the infected had died within hours, others within the day. A few still staggered on—literally, dead on their feet—inside the ring of armed and gas-masked Air Police that they, or their late predecessors, had ordered posted around the contagion zones. The action had been too late, of course; the virus had continued to spread itself relentlessly.

The disease might have kept right on spreading too, had not an E-9 made a rapid, accurate assessment of the deteriorating situation.

Eleven hours after the first case was reported at the base, the sergeant, acting on her own initiative, triggered the base-wide biochemical alarm that sent all personnel scrambling for their antiexposure gear. It was potentially a court-martial offense, though the odds were better that the sergeant would be nominated for a Medal of Honor. Certainly, she had the votes of Sivigny and the other Air Force personnel who had heard the story through the base grapevine—and who were still, on this third day of the bioalert, without symptoms of the killer flu. As long as they stayed inside the minienvironment of their exposure suits, they would be safe.

At least for another day, Sivigny thought, feeling his stomach rumble once more.

Four days was about the limit for living inside the rubberized cocoons. Even under the Florida sun, one could stay hydrated well enough, using canteens of chemically sterilized water sipped through the gas mask's built-in straw. But there was no way to eat without removing the gear. And as for waste evacuation—

Well, don't stand upwind when people finally get the word to strip these damn things off, he thought.

Still, though many parts of the base were paralyzed, the sergeant's gutsy move had kept much of Eglin operational—including Duke Field, where the fighter jocks went to work, and here at Hurlburt Field, where Special Ops spookies like Sivigny did their usually covert thing.

Well, we're pretty much out in the open this time, Sivigny told himself. He, like all the other pilots the flight surgeons had certified as still healthy enough to fly, had listened closely to the mission briefing of an hour before, and not just because their cumbersome exposure gear made it harder to hear. Aside from the specifics of altitude and distribution headings, there was little that the President had not already announced to the nation, as well as the world at large.

Except, he reminded himself, *for that one little detail.*

It had come, of course, at the shank end of the briefing. The briefing officer, a major general, had paused to emphasize his gas mask–muffled words.

"You will release weapons"—it had sounded incongruous to Sivigny, hearing the term used in what was officially being touted as a mission of mercy—"at an altitude no higher than one hundred feet. At that altitude, your aircraft will be well within range of small-arms fire," he said. "After the fiasco in Russia, people are understandably sensitive about aerial spraying of any sort. You can expect ground fire. It will at times be intense, particularly over population centers."

One of the pilots in his section, a captain who flew the big Hercules transports and looked to Sivigny too young for the rank, had raised his hand.

"If people are going to be *shooting* at us, sir, do we have clearance to evade?"

"Evade, hell," said one of the fighter jocks from Duke, loud enough even through the rubber of his mask for the room to hear. "How about shooting *back*?"

When the laughter had subsided, the two-star had shaken his head, a hard negative.

"No evasionary tactics—not on the target runs," the General said. "You'll all be flying a tick above stall speed on your approaches. Go evasive, and you'll likely spin in." He had tried a cheery tone that, to Sivigny and the other fliers, sounded extremely pallid. "Suck it up, people. Fly the mission, take the ground fire. Any other questions? Thank you. Be prepared for takeoff as soon as the VIX is loaded in your aircraft. And good luck."

As one, the room rose to its feet and saluted.

As Sivigny gathered his notes and charts, an officer appeared at his side. It took Sivigny a moment to recognize the mission intelligence officer, his visage made insectlike by the goggle eyes of the mask. Like Sivigny, Chuck Mason was normally tasked to the Special Operations squadron.

"You've got the Tallahassee segment of the ring, Pete," Mason said, his voice pitched low. "Be advised that the situation on the ground is highly volatile, understand? Rioting, buildings burning. It's like an armed insurrection down there—probably everything from the Aryan Brotherhood to Greenpeace is packing heavy iron. It's out of control, is that clear?"

Taken aback, Sivigny tried to treat it lightly. "That about covers the whole damn state, doesn't it?"

"It's worse where you're going," the intelligence officer said. "I don't know if you've heard. Civilian electricity's out in a number of areas inside the Quarantine Region, including the state capital. The militants and the crazies are blowing up transmission towers, for God's sake." He looked around, as if he was speaking out of school.

"Thanks," Sivigny said. "I'll watch myself up there. I got the message about the small-arms fire."

His informant shook his head ominously.

"Small-arms fire, hell. That's what I'm trying to tell you. A Florida Highway Patrol aircraft tried to drop leaflets over Tallahassee this morning. The aircraft went down, Pete— right after the pilot reported that somebody was shooting the hell out of his plane. An A-10 flew over on a low-altitude scouting mission about a hour ago. It got holed pretty badly, barely made it back. Fifty-caliber rounds, at least; maybe even forty millimeter—they're not sure. It must be mobile, 'cause we can't pin down a location. But anything that flies over the city is taking fire from it. Pete, somebody down there found themselves a damn big machine gun, and figured out how to use it."

Sivigny pushed the big plane down the runway, watching the ground-speed indicator ease well past V-one before he rotated off the runway. Compared to some loads he had carried, the VIX and its accompanying apparatus were a negligible addition to the takeoff weight; still, there was no need to hot-dog—not with twenty-two canisters of virus affixed to tubing the length of the fuselage.

He passed over Highway 90, which separated Hurlburt from the military housing south of the field; today, no children looked up to wave from backyard swing sets or wading pools. Still climbing in the bright sunlight, he passed over the thin strip of sugar white beach and above the impossible green of the gulf before banking left on a northeast heading.

Pete Sivigny had always displayed a light touch on the yoke, taking a secret pride in the delicacy with which he had trained himself to handle the huge bird even under difficult situations. It was a skill that had come in handy during covert operations in which he had been involved. He had been shot at from Iraqi antiaircraft emplacements, successfully dodged a SAM in a little-publicized incident near Afghanistan, and had his Hercules holed by a dozen heavy-caliber rounds over the high jungle of Peru.

In none of the instances could Sivigny remember being frightened, or even experiencing an increased pulse rate; he did not anticipate a flight over Tallahassee would be an exception. Even wearing the bioprotection equipment — a requirement that he had heard the F-15 jocks loudly bemoaning — did not constitute a significant problem for the Hercules pilot. Maybe the coveralls were heavier and stiffer than the usual Nomex flight suits; so what? But gloves were gloves, and Sivigny found the mask that covered his face less bothersome than the night-vision apparatus he was often required to don while on a mission.

Besides, he thought, *when was a pilot ever supposed to feel comfortable? For damn sure, not at a time like this.*

Not on a combat mission.

Chapter 50

**Three Miles NNW of Tallahassee, Florida
Altitude: 4,700 Feet
July 24**

"Holding pattern? The hell do they mean, 'holding pattern'?"

The voice of the crew chief was outraged. They had reached their rally-point coordinates in less than fifteen minutes of flight time—on schedule, maybe even a little ahead of it. The sergeant knew well the potential of what the aircraft carried in the nylon harnesses he had helped affix to the cargo bay bulkheads; the sooner they jettisoned the damn stuff, the sergeant felt, the better it would be for all concerned. Particularly himself, and the aircraft he considered his personal property.

Sivigny was not happy with the delay, either. But it is a time-honored tradition in the military that important bitching goes upward, following the chain of command all the way up to the gold-plated imbecile who issued the order initially. For that reason, the pilot's tone was mild and conciliatory when he keyed the intercom to reply.

"Relax, Chief. Don't you enlisted personnel get paid by the hour anyway?"

His copilot for the mission, a lieutenant, grinned behind his rubber mask.

Patrick Mayo had not previously flown with Sivigny, but like the rest of the squadron he had heard all of the stories. Distilled, they said this: Pete Sivigny ate fire for breakfast, crapped smoke and sparks, and flew the big Hercules like it was an extension of his body. He had also flown more black ops than anybody else in the service, and it was rumored that had he shown any inclination toward retirement, the resulting security concerns would have forced the CIA to shoot him. If they could.

When Sivigny's usual backup pilot had been dropped by the virus's initial onslaught, Mayo had jumped at the chance to fly left-hand seat with him. Now Mayo's biggest concern was to avoid doing something that might forever mark him as a hopeless rube in the eyes of his idol.

"Give me a fuel status, Mayo."

The copilot jumped, Sivigny's voice snapping him to attention. He scanned the control console, and did a quick cross-check against the notes he had scribbled on his thigh pad.

"Twenty-seven hundred pounds, WATO," Mayo said, "current fuel at two-six-oh-oh-niner." *What did the guy expect?* he thought but did not say. *Weight at takeoff had included a full load of Jet Fuel-1; a ninety-mile flight couldn't cut much into it, not yet.*

"Thank you." Sivigny looked out at the vivid blue of the Florida sky, accented only by the occasional puff of cloud. The delay was no problem; with his current fuel load, he could stay up here all day, if need be. That was, after all, why you flew with topped-off tanks.

But Sivigny could not push Chuck Mason's warning from his mind. He had no fear of ground fire, but no one who has ever taken heavy-caliber rounds at low altitude failed to acquire a healthy respect for it. His bird was not designed to be agile; at the slow approach speed mandated by the mission orders, the controls would be mushy as last week's cantaloupe.

*And if some mutt on the ground gets in a lucky shot, a full
load of kerosene makes for a pretty impressive fireball on impact.*

Sivigny shook the thought from his mind and focused on
his flying. Whatever the reason for the hold, at least it would
let him burn off a few extra gallons of fuel.

Montgomery, Alabama

Ilya lounged in the deep cushions of his chair, idly thumbing
through a magazine he had found somewhere. Occasionally
he would stop, holding the opened page up to the light. Once,
he whistled appreciatively, and Beck looked up from the
chair where he too waited, though with far less patience.

"Playboy?"

Ilya held up the magazine; it was a copy of *Motor Week*.

"You have discovered my secret," he said. "I have a particular weakness for Saab automobiles—the turbocharged
models, of course. Tell me, do you own a vehicle?"

Washington, D.C.

The telephone at Carson's elbow buzzed discreetly. He
picked up the receiver, then listened for a few moments before turning to the man slumped behind the large desk.

"Still nothing to report from Russia, Mr. President," Carson said.

"Putin must know who the conspirators are, for God's
sake. What the hell are they doing over there?"

"It's better if we don't discuss it. That way, we both maintain plausible denial, if we're ever questioned about it in an
impeachment hearing."

The President glared at the ceiling of the Oval Office.
When he spoke, his voice was low and furious.

"I don't have to ask, do I? Hell, I did everything but tell
him to do it." He slammed a fist onto the desk, hard. "Jesus.

The president of the United States encouraging the president of Russia to torture information out of his countrymen. What the hell have I become?"

He did not expect an answer, but Carson provided one anyway.

"With all due respect, you've become what you've been since all of this began," Carson said evenly. "A man who is running out of time."

Montgomery, Alabama

"You are a *teacher*, then?" Ilya's voice was dubious. "This is truth?"

Beck nodded. "Is that so difficult to believe?"

Ilya shrugged. "It is just that I do not encounter many teachers in my line of work. At least, not in some years."

Beck raised his eyebrows in polite inquiry, not fully believing that the conversation was taking place.

"In Chechnya," Ilya said. "With the guerrilla bandits there. Teachers were often officers in their ranks. Occasionally, we would capture one alive."

He shrugged, a gesture that to Beck seemed almost apologetic.

"And I would be summoned."

Washington, D.C.

Once again, Carson hung up the telephone. He looked up at the President and shook his head wordlessly.

For a few seconds, the President sat unmoving, his eyes focused somewhere beyond the far wall of his office. Then his jaw hardened.

"Order the planes in," he said, still not looking at anything in particular. "They are authorized—by direct order of the commander in chief—to release the VIX. Now."

Approach Path,
Above Tallahassee, Florida

"Roger that," Sivigny said. He keyed the intercom that connected him to the crew.

"Okay, folks," he said. "We're back in business and good to go. Chief, final check the dispersal system and let me know when you're green light. I will arm the aerosolizing system when we're thirty seconds from weapons away."

He paused, then keyed the switch again.

"Let's do this right, gentlemen. Once everything is armed and ready, I want every crew member to stand away. That is a direct order. I—and only I—will initiate the final release. Please remember that, all of you."

He released the intercom switch, turned to see Mayo's eyes looking steadily at him through the acrylic lenses of his exposure mask.

"That goes for you too, Lieutenant. Unless I say differently, the only hands on the controls will be mine."

Without another word, Sivigny pulled the Hercules into a wide sweeping curve. When the aircraft finally leveled, it was on a heading of due east.

Through the cockpit windshield, the cityscape of Tallahassee was a glittering jewel. Only the tall columns of smoke that rose randomly from the ground marred the otherwise perfect picture.

Chapter 51

The curious aspect of all this, the interrogator thought to himself in mild bemusement, *is that none of these men expected that this treatment would ever be accorded to them. Odd—in particular since without exception the group was the product of the former Soviet system.*

He shook his head, either in sympathy or at the folly he perceived.

They have forgotten the rules of survival that have always been uniquely Russian. They allowed themselves to become careless, in the belief that they were invulnerable.

He bent forward, made a minor adjustment to the intravenous drip that originated at the now limply hanging bag of clear fluid and terminated in the large-bore needle taped to secure it in his subject's forearm. Carefully, as if he were indeed the physician that his lab coat and stethoscope suggested, he checked the man's vital signs once more.

His forehead furrowed as he listened to the tachycardiac pounding of his subject's heart. It was, of course, dangerously high; the pink flush on the man's bare chest had spread upward, dappling the neck in darker reddish blotches. Still, the face was not yet congested and the whites of the eyes remained relatively clear. That was good; as interrogator, his assignment was not to murder, though at some point the difference became academic.

This was his second subject of the morning; the first had, unfortunately, been unable to withstand the intensity of the session. Regrettable, but it could not be helped—he had been told that there were a number of subjects available, and that speedy results were preferable to the survival of any particular suspect. What was needed were answers—in particular, one specific answer—and without any avoidable delay.

Briefly, he wondered who else had been summoned for this assignment. Kadelov, probably; the Tartar they called Ghengis, almost surely. Perhaps Ilya, though rumor had it that he spent most of his time on foreign assignments these days, specializing in wet work.

Just as well, the interrogator thought. *In truth, Ilya had begun to enjoy this work a little too much. When an interrogator allows his professionalism to erode in that manner, it is inevitable the product obtained begins to slip—and we do not do this for personal enjoyment. At least, not often.*

He touched the forehead of this subject almost tenderly, gauging how much of the man's resistance was simple intransigence rather than the unavoidable semistupor that the drugs and the pain always engendered. He did not consider that the man simply had no information to share; such thoughts tended to be self-defeating, allowing pity to enter the equation and skew the results.

He pondered the man, naked and strapped spread-eagle on the now fouled and stained examining table. This was a healthy man, he noted—a touch too self-indulgent, judging by the slight paunch. Such is the penalty of prosperity, or its reward. But there was an underlying muscle tone, too, and the hair was black and thick, though it was plastered wetly above eyes that—

Ahha!

The interrogator had caught the movement, the glint of

eyes wary behind slitted lids in a way impossible for one truly unconscious.

This one is capable, and an adept playactor. I was almost fooled, and that is a compliment indeed.

He moved to a position where he knew the immobilized man could see him clearly. Then he pursed his lips and smiled in a way that was both chiding and conspiratorial.

"Speak to me of vaccine and viruses," he said. "And this will all cease."

He waited a brief moment, then resumed his tasks. This time, the screams were even louder than before.

Above Tallahassee, Florida

Over the intercom, there was a sound not unlike that of a fire-cracker exploding inside a steel barrel—muffled, but resonating beyond the initial detonation.

"Another hit, dammit." The voice of the crew chief rang in Sivigny's earphones, and sounded peeved rather than anxious. "Colonel, I'm counting a half dozen new holes back here, case you were curious."

"Roger that, Chief. Got a couple up here too. Stand by, and keep a tight one. Two minutes to weapons release."

It was still sporadic, the ground fire that was increasingly peppering the skin of his Hercules. It was also unavoidable, given the near-stalling speed and a flight path that now had the aircraft less than a thousand feet above the rolling hills of Tallahassee's outskirts. Rifle fire, he judged by the size of the hole above his head, where a bright shaft of Florida sunlight now streamed through: nothing heavy, and nothing automatic. Yet.

There were houses now, cars parked on the streets below. A few of them appeared to be burning, as were several of the buildings toward which he was flying. He saw the dome of the state capitol, and beyond it what appeared as a twin-towered castle surrounded by neatly mowed grassy expanses that were themselves flanked by neatly aligned ivy-covered buildings.

Florida State University, Sivigny thought. *Go, 'Noles.*

He banked slightly, a minute adjustment to the target point, then glanced at the GPS time/distance readout.

"Ninety seconds," he said. His gloved hand moved to the console and flipped up a safety shield over the weapons release switch.

Moscow

"Confirm it? Of course you must confirm it." *Idiot,* Vladimir Putin thought but did not say. He listened to the voice at the other end of the line, impatience shadowing his features. "Then *dispatch* the troops and confirm that he spoke the truth. Be quick, but be accurate."

He was quite aware that, on the other side of the world, the American president was close to soiling himself in his anxiety. He—*or rather,* Putin thought with a frown, *his surly lapdog Carson*—had called at least a dozen times in the past half hour.

So be it, Putin thought. *One confession does not an answer make, particularly when that confession is the result of scientific persuasion—and I am not inclined to present myself as a fool.*

Arrangements were already being made to transport vaccine, if it existed, across the expanse between the two continents. Standard military transports would be far too slow, and like the United States, Russia had never developed its own supersonic transport aircraft. The Americans had immediately contacted the British and French governments, which had offered the services of its Concorde passenger SSTs. But only three of the dozen aging aircraft still in service were currently flight worthy; and two of those were now at Dulles Airport outside Washington, where they had been when the flu outbreak grounded most flights.

In the end, it had been Russian ingenuity that provided a solution—based, of course, on the concept that had earlier transported the American historian Casey to Moscow. The Russian Federation could field more than two hundred MiG-27 and Su-35 fighters, each capable of speeds approaching Mach 3. A fleet of refueling aircraft—again, Russian; NATO air tankers lacked the requisite fuel-docking cones for the Russian fighters—were already in the air, heading toward Western bases from Germany to Spain. There they would be loaded with jet fuel, and prepared to be vectored to locations where they would link up and refuel the fighters.

It was an impressive display of aerial logistics, a proud moment for Russian military aviation—*if* there was a need to utilize it, of course. If no vaccine existed, or its location could not be provided by the shifts of interrogators working on the conspirators, it was all wasted effort. Initially, the oligarchs had proven either surprisingly resistant, or completely ignorant of Malenkov's claims.

Then one had broken down—Shenpeliski, himself a petrochemical tycoon, but one who sat on the board of at least two pharmaceutical conglomerates. He had provided several names, plausible all, and a cold-storage warehouse outside St. Petersburg where—he had insisted, loudly and with no small amount of desperation—proof of his statement waited in millions of refrigerated doses.

Troops were now rushing toward the warehouse, and the interrogators tasked to question those whose names had been provided by Shenpeliski had been ordered to redouble their efforts. Something would happen very soon, one way or another, and not even a dozen more telephone calls from the White House could change the situation in the interim.

For the moment, Putin told himself, *restraint is the wise man's policy. When I know for certain, I will inform the Americans. Not before.*

The telephone at his elbow rang again, loudly and insistently.

Tallahassee, Florida

The loud noises from outside the basement window shook Katie from the troubled stupor into which she had fallen. For a moment, she wondered if the voices had been part of the frightening dream, where she had found herself being pursued by demonic figures who grasped and tore at her as she ran. She could not escape them, and the terrible stench of their ruined bodies gagged her again.

No, she decided. *That was the dream, because this is the nightmare.*

She swallowed, wincing as she felt the burning of her vomit deep inside the rawness of her throat.

Katie was sitting on the concrete floor, her back against the wall. J. L. lay quietly in her lap, her breathing ragged but for the moment regular.

"Dammit, boy! Get that belt fed and locked. Do it *now!*"

It was the same voice that had torn through her dream. Gently, she disentangled herself from J. L., pushing the dirty afghan tight around her friend's shoulders. Then, swaying dizzily from the fever, she pulled herself up to look out the casement.

The red Air Jordan sneakers were still there, partially blocking her view of the heavy Dodge stakebed truck parked fifteen yards away. Several men moved in a shuffling gait around the vehicle, straining at the rope-handled wooden boxes they bore. In the bed of the truck, two other figures serviced what appeared to be a length of black pipe that pointed at a sharp angle into the air above their heads.

Then they moved, and Katie saw the bulk of the heavy machine gun, a linked belt of ridiculously large cartridges dangling from it to a metal box affixed to its side. As she watched, one of the men moved to the back and seized two vertical handles. Almost at the same instant, three loud explosions pressured her ears; in the echoes, she heard the empty casings bounce against asphalt, bell-like in their pitch.

"If they'd have had one a these big bastards at Waco"—the man slapped with hard affection at the weapon's cocking handle—"well, damn. They'd of *cornholed* them ATF fuckers, pure and simple!"

Then the one manning the machine gun let loose a scream, or perhaps it was some kind of war cry—Katie did not know, nor did she care to. She covered her ears with her hands and slid down the cool stone of the basement wall. But even as she did, she heard the gunner shout to the others.

"Here one comes, boys—Jesus. It's a big 'un, too."

Then the firing began again, claps of spaced thunder that hammered and hammered and hammered against and into Katie's head. It would not stop, not even when she began to scream, in protest and in terror.

Tallahassee, Florida
Altitude: 300 Feet

"Thirty seconds." The controls were sluggish now, and Sivigny debated for an instant whether to nudge the airspeed a fraction higher. He depressed the yoke almost imperceptibly, and felt the firmness return to the stick, ever so slightly.

"Mayo, when I give the word, bring the throttles up to fifty percent," he said, then twisted his head to emphasize his next words. "*When* I give the word, not before."

He noted Mayo's nod, then turned back just in time to see the first of the tracers arching up to meet him. He barely had time to register that fact when the sound of the serial impacts—much louder than the previous ground fire hits, clamorous in a way that signaled their destructive power—rang through the fuselage.

"That's double-A," he heard the crew chief in the intercom. "Antiaircraft fire, multiple hits aft—"

And then another string rose to meet him, chewing through the aluminum skin before dancing sparks from the starboard engine cowling. The intercom went dead, sudden as a switch being flipped. At the same time, the yoke in his hand sagged as if lifeless. The aircraft shuddered, then dropped hard.

"Secure for impact!" he had time to say, just before the ground mushroomed up to fill the cockpit windshield. There was a flash, vivid even in the daylight, and a roaring sound in Sivigny's ears that was suddenly cut short.

Washington, D.C.

The President's hand gripped the telephone receiver so hard that, even from across the room, Carson could see the knuckles turn suddenly white.

"You're sure?" The President's voice was loud and unrestrained. "It's confirmed?"

He pointed to Carson almost imperiously, his index finger aiming like a pistol. Without removing the telephone from his ear, he shouted to his national security advisor.

"They've got it. Good God, they have the vaccine. Abort the mission—*now!*"

Tallahassee, Florida

The wall shook as if in an earthquake, and dust flew from the rafters above. A scream that pendulumed madly up and down the scale drowned out everything but its own feral cry, and a sudden dancing glare turned the casement glass into a blossom of molten colors.

For a long moment, Katie had no comprehension of where she was or what was happening to her. The noise was deafening and the light blinding, and she wondered if she was already dead.

Then the smell filled the room: an oily, smothering smokiness, followed by an intense wave of heat. It galvanized the young woman, making her scramble across the floor to a still-comatose J. L. Katie stood, locking her arms under J.

L.'s, forcing her muscles to strain against the inert weight. She dragged her friend backward, away from the window that now pooled with dancing flames like mica on a furnace.

Somehow, Katie wrestled J. L. up the stairway and outside. Here, the structure of the house shielded the pair from the inferno on the other side, a shadow from the radiant heat that crisped and smoked the grass and palmetto shrubs ten feet to the side. Then the wood framing of the house burst into flames, sending a rolling wave of thermal energy that reddened Katie's face.

We can't stay here, Katie's mind screamed at her sluggish body.

But her body, racked by fever and ravaged by the viral assault, no longer listened. Katie sat hard, her bottom striking the ground with an impact that made her teeth click together audibly. It did not register; she was unable to move.

The fire had now curled around the burning building and was crackling toward the two girls. Katie resigned herself to it, to dying in the inferno.

Then two hands, clumsy in the gloves that encased them, grasped her upper arms. She looked up dully, seeing first the firefighter's helmet and then the full-face plastic visor of his breathing apparatus. His helmet crest read: TALLAHASSEE F. D.

Vaguely, she felt herself lifted up, a split second before the world went dark.

Chapter 52

"The first wave of Russian Sukhoi-35s are in the air," Krewell said, trying hard not to sound as drained as he felt. It had been three hours since Putin's troops had burst into the warehouse and confirmed the vaccine existed; since then, there had been a frenzy of activity on both sides of the Atlantic, with Krewell at its center.

He sat in a White House conference room that was far too large for the number of occupants: Krewell and two other men. One of them was a White House communications technician manning the camera for this video teleconference. The other was Billy Carson, his attitude of outward calm belied by the ashtray at his elbow already half-filled with crumpled butts.

The voice of the secretary of Health and Human Services came from the speaker phone at the center of the conference table; on the split-screen monitor mounted on the wall, HHS looked wan and frazzled.

"Thank God they're cooperating," he said. "How much time do we have?"

"ETA at Newark is two hours, twenty minutes," Krewell

answered. "Twenty-four fighters—a total of six million doses of vaccine, give or take. Another six Sukhoi fighters are on a direct route to Maxwell Air Force Base in Alabama with a million and a half doses on board."

"Eight million doses? Less?" It was the voice of the junior senator from Pennsylvania, his outrage—and, Krewell observed, his fear—clear and evident despite the distortion of the speaker. "There's two hundred and eighty million Americans at risk, for God's sake!"

"We don't have to vaccinate them all," Krewell snapped. "Not immediately."

"Take it easy," Krewell heard Carson mutter. Krewell took a deep breath; when he spoke, he was surprised to hear his voice sound almost reasonable.

"We'll use the Russian vaccine in a two-phase program— first, to inoculate people in a ring immediately outside the contagion zones. We'll use them as containment, to wall off the virus from the rest of the country. If it can't find any susceptible hosts, it can't spread past the barrier rings. The second phase is more traditional: we send medical teams into northwest Florida and New York City to vaccinate everybody possible."

On the video screen, HHS looked doubtful.

"You're talking between eight and ten million persons inside New York alone," he said.

"We don't need to inoculate them all," Krewell repeated. "Just a high enough percentage of coverage to break the chain of contagion."

He scribbled for a moment on his notepad, then held it up for the video camera; obligingly, the technician zoomed close on it. Drawn large on the top sheet, perhaps a dozen circles were bunched together. One circle in their midst was bisected by a bold "X."

"The circles represent individuals," Krewell said. "X indicates a person infected with the virus. If the other circles are unprotected, the virus is easily passed in sequence from one to the next. There's no magic involved; it's a chain, a classic disease-transmission model."

He filled in half of the circles, creating a random pattern of black spots on the page.

"The filled-in circles are persons that are now immune, due to the vaccine," he said. He drew a line from the infected "X" to one of black-filled circles. "A carrier comes into contact with this person, nothing happens. Same here, or here, or here."

He tapped one of the unfilled circles. "The virus has to find one of *these* before it can spread—and then it faces the same problem all over again. That's herd immunity; ranchers have used it for decades. You take a percentage of the potential hosts out of the contagion chain, and that protects the rest."

"So now you're down to maybe five million in the city, and what—another million or so in the Florida Quarantine Region?" HHS shook his head. "It's still a hell of a big job, Dr. Krewell."

"There is precedent," Krewell said. "Back in '76, with the swine flu emergency. In the fifties, when the polio vaccine first became available. In the sixties, with the oral polio vaccine. In each case, you had millions of Americans standing in line to get the treatment."

"There weren't riots going on at those times." The senator's voice was pitched higher, tighter than Krewell remembered; he stifled the automatic retort. Instead of responding to the politician, he spoke directly to HHS.

"Operationally, it's a matter of organization and logistics. Fortunately, New York has an existing emergency response plan that divides the city into manageable areas—based, they tell me, on voting precincts. We'll use soldiers to set up security and deal with crowd control—Swede Brandt has been authorized to use whatever degree of force is necessary. The actual vaccination is a fast, simple process. Hell, you don't need a physician to handle a pneumatic needle or a hypodermic."

Carson spoke for the first time. "Where possible, we will use doctors and nurses from the city hospitals to supervise. General Brandt has informed the President that he can field almost two hundred Army medics. That's in addition to the several thousand paramedics and EMTs that can be mobilized from inside the city itself. We can set up more than a thousand inoculation stations, spread among the boroughs. In Florida, we'll do the same at armories and high schools. Whenever possible, we're using the existing local emergency reaction plans; there's a mass vaccination component in all of them."

"How long?" HHS's voice was blunt.

Krewell shrugged. "Six hours to mobilize and get the word to the populace. After that, it's a matter of cycling people through." He was silent for a moment, once again doing the math. "Within twelve hours, we should have enough patients processed to establish the herd immunity scenario—in Florida, maybe sooner."

"This will work, Dr. Krewell?" asked HHS.

Before Krewell could respond, Carson answered.

"It will," the national security advisor said. "It has to."

Maxwell AFB

The Sukhoi fighters touched down one by one, ninety seconds apart. The flight leader was Gregori Stipilanov, a colonel who had earned his wings long enough before to find landing at an American Air Force base incredible, if also wryly amusing.

Stipilanov would have preferred something more showy —perhaps a simultaneous landing in twin echelons of three planes each, a tricky maneuver designed to demonstrate the verve and proficiency of Russian pilots. But that would have been irresponsible, he admitted to himself, particularly given the critical importance of the cargo they were delivering.

The Air Force ground crew that met his flight rode in closed Humvees, and so it was not until he had powered down on the concrete apron that he noticed anything unusual about his hosts' appearance. The Americans who swarmed out to place chocks around the Su-35's landing gear moved awkwardly, clumsy in the bulk of olive-drab exposure suits.

A moment later, Stipilanov raised his canopy at the gesture of a spacesuited crew chief, who helped him disentangle himself from the straps and hoses of the cockpit.

"You take no chances, yes?" Stipilanov said pleasantly, in an accent that made the American airman smile behind his acrylic faceplate.

"It ain't nuthin' personal, Colonel." The voice, which carried undertones of kudzu and red clay, was muffled by the full-face protection.

Stipilanov saw the American's eyes look at the rear of the cockpit, a space usually occupied by a weapons officer. Instead, a bubble-wrapped bulk was wedged tight, similar to the cardboard boxes now being removed from the cargo compartment in the fuselage. The exercise was being repeated at each of the six Sukhoi fighters parked on the apron. Already, the first pallets of vaccine were being rushed by Humvee toward what Stipilanov assumed was a medical center.

"Welcome to Maxwell AFB, sir," Stipilanov heard, the Southern accent humorous to his ears. "You don't mind me sayin'—we're surely glad as hell to see you guys."

Chapter 53

The digital feed into the HHS's Crisis Management Office made the audio sound lifelike — almost, Andi Wheelwright thought, as if Frank Ellis were standing next to her desk here in Washington. She even nodded, before realizing that he was somewhere in Montana and unable to see her assent.

"Yes," she said calmly. "I have the report on the screen now. It's confirmed, Mr. Ellis. It was Dr. Casey's daughter." On the monitor before her, under a large-font heading that read TALLAHASSEE CONTAGION/SITE ECHO, several columns of names had scrolled past before stopping. Now, highlighted, was the name she had called for in her file search.

Ellis's voice came over the line again, and Andi could hear the effort it took him to keep it calm and even.

"Are you going to tell him, or should I?"

Andi Wheelwright stiffened, but her voice was equally professional in reply.

"I suggest that you deal with your own responsibilities, Agent Ellis," she said. "We will determine when Dr. Casey should be informed of . . . this development."

"The man deserves to know that—"

Andi flared. "This crisis isn't over, Agent Ellis. Dr. Casey is an asset we may need. Could you function effectively, given the same situation?"

There was silence on the audio feed. Then Andi spoke.

"I'll bump this up the line for a decision," she said. "That's all I can promise."

"That's pretty cold-blooded, in my opinion," Ellis said.

"Yes," she said. "Given the circumstances, I'll take that as a compliment."

Chapter 54

"Mr. President, there is news," Krewell said. Across the expansive desk, the President's eyes snapped open and he straightened in his chair. At the same time, Billy Carson stirred in the leather chair where he too had been unable to fend off the exhaustion that had become a palpable presence in the Oval Office.

"Talk to me, Dr. Krewell. What is the present situation?"

Krewell rubbed his eyes; for the past fourteen hours he had been monitoring hourly reports from the CDC field teams in New York and Florida.

"Sir, the first consignments of Russian vaccine have reached the Florida Quarantine Region. Immunization is under way now, focusing on a wide band outside the contagion zone. By tomorrow we project we will have vaccinated a sufficient percentage of the population to have created the herd-immunity situation we need."

"And New York?"

"Essentially the same, sir. It's a bigger program, but we have a lot of resources working there. CDC reports indicate that the immunization will be complete in the states that border New York by midnight. We've already begun a mass program to vaccinate uninfected persons inside the contagion zones of Florida and New York."

"We're sure the vaccine is working?" Carson's tone was carefully neutral.

"I have field labs analyzing the antibody counts of the earliest vaccination subjects," Krewell said. "In each case, we're getting strong positives. There's no reason to believe the vaccine is not effective."

The President took a deep breath, and Krewell heard the relief in his voice. "Then this nightmare is almost over."

Krewell nodded. "The spread of the virus appears to be contained. And with the availability of a vaccine, even if an isolated case appears we should be able to deal with it." He paused, choosing his words with care. "The general population should be secure, sir."

The President looked at Krewell closely. "But?"

"But the vaccine cannot help those already infected with the flu virus. That's a core group of perhaps thirty thousand persons, maybe more. Their only hope is the accelerated immune reaction from Agent VIX."

Carson, who had listened without comment until then, shook his head vigorously.

"Mr. President, I see where this is going. It is only by the narrowest of margins that we were able to avoid disaster once. Twice, if you include the crash of the transport in Florida."

The President's face was impassive, but Carson had made a telling point. Had the Hercules not carried a full fuel load, there would not have been the intense fireball on impact. Instead of being incinerated, the VIX that had been on board would have been released, triggering its own plague. As it was, the other aircraft had been recalled only by the narrowest of margins. It was a near miss to a catastrophe.

Carson's voice was insistent.

"We cannot risk a free release of a substance that could spread and kill millions here and abroad."

The President eyed his national security advisor narrowly.

"Billy," he said, "I'm becoming concerned by your lack of consistency."

Carson reddened. "Sir, if the Russian vaccine had not existed—or if it had not been acquired in time—VIX would have been the lesser of two evils. Now it is the greater. My advice remains consistent: as president, you must make decisions based on saving the greatest number of people. However difficult they are."

"Yes," said the President. "And now I must decide if I will kill thirty million, instead of three hundred million. I do not consider that an easier choice."

Krewell interrupted.

"Sir, Ray Porter has been working with the CDC field coordinators on-site in Florida studying the situation during the outbreak," he said. "He's come up with an idea based on the containment strategy—"

"Which was only a contingency plan," Carson interjected, though with less heat than previously.

"But now we're dealing with a far less widespread contagion," Krewell said. He turned again to the President. "There are risks involved, but I think Dr. Porter has come up with a way to use VIX effectively. *Without* a free release that could spread. If so, we can save a significant number of the flu victims, sir."

Krewell waited silently for several long minutes. Finally, he glanced pointedly at the clock on the wall.

"What is your decision, Mr. President?"

Chapter 55

The satellite phone buzzed insistently as Beck pawed through the bags piled on the backseat of Deborah's Mercedes. They had left in the late-night darkness, Deborah unable to wait any longer. The pair had successfully bluffed their way past the first checkpoint, though Beck realized that the Army sergeant who had finally waved them through did so only because of the direction of their travel. Had they been going north instead, he had no doubt their expedition would have ended at that point, suddenly and without further debate: Beck had seen the two M-60 machine guns that flanked the intersection.

Deborah was at the wheel, concentrating on her driving. She had said scarcely a word to Beck since he had appeared alongside her car, his own luggage slung over his shoulders and two military-issue exposure masks dangling from one hand. Since then, he had initiated most of the limited conversation, sketching in the details of the past few hours. Only when he told her the VIX release had been aborted did she react visibly.

Now they were on a two-lane highway twenty miles south of Florala, passing Spanish-moss-covered oaks that competed with rough-looking pine and fir along each side of the road. Fort Walton was still more than a hundred miles distant when the buried sat phone sounded.

From the corner of her eye, Deborah could see Beck—his features largely concealed by the full mask—awkwardly hold the portable telephone to his head. There was a moment while he listened.

Then his entire body tensed, and though the words were too muffled to discern, Deborah heard the sudden tight intensity in her ex-husband's voice. Before she could speak, he clicked the phone closed and began pawing through the road atlas with which they had been navigating.

"There—take this crossroads east. *Now!*" Beck said, and the tires of the Mercedes squealed as she automatically cut hard into the turn. "Tallahassee, Deborah. Larry Krewell says he'll meet us there. He's in the air now."

She flared into an anger that was white-hot in its intensity. "I'm not going to—"

"It's Katie, Deborah. Larry got word: a CDC team located her in Tallahassee. She's alive, Deborah. Katie's very sick, but she's alive."

Chapter 56

They had commandeered the Tallahassee-Leon County Civic Center, one of the few buildings both large enough to handle the number of active flu victims, yet sufficiently self-contained to facilitate the modifications and additions needed for the VIX treatment process.

Beck looked around the vastness of the fieldhouse. He was frantic, preoccupied with concern for his daughter. Still, he marveled at the sheer scope of the work under way here, knowing the same activities were being duplicated elsewhere in northwest Florida and in New York City.

All involved knew the risks: should the Agent VIX virus escape the containment they were constructing, its virulence would infect anyone it chanced to reach—and thus very likely begin its leapfrog through the outside population with amazing speed. Almost inevitably, they would trigger the very pandemic the vaccine had allowed them to avoid. But without treatment with VIX, anyone infected with the flu virus was doomed to die; current totals—mainly in Florida, but with a significant number now reported in New York—exceeded twenty-six thousand persons.

A tight hermetic seal was impossible, of course. Instead,

technicians had hastily rigged fans and ventilation pumps to create a negative-air-pressure system, ensuring a flow would come only from the outside into the large building. Large-diameter ductwork would move the airflow to an industrial kiln that had been pressed into service; in it, any organic particles the vented air might carry would be incinerated in a twenty-two-hundred-degree inferno.

As an added safety measure, what was in effect a huge rubberized tent was being erected inside the building, encompassing everything up to the third tier of seats. Overhead, the cube of a scoreboard hung suspended, securing the steel cables that uniformed men were even now using to affix the last of the top tenting. At midcourt on the hardwood floor, the Seminole warrior's impassive visage surveyed the beehive of activity that was now nearing its culmination.

The olive green rubberized fabric blocked the civic center's high windows and the majority of the overhead lighting. Instead, a large number of stand-mounted banks of lighting panels had already been wheeled along the perimeter of the tenting. Many were standard halogen lamps—but a substantial number of the panels held banks of longer lighting tubes that, as they were tested by the military electricians, glowed with an odd blue-white intensity.

"We're trying to cover every base," Krewell told Beck, as both men watched from the second row of seats in the cavernous fieldhouse. "Ultraviolet lights will be in alternating banks around the treatment enclosure. The CBW people swear that it will neutralize the VIX even faster than natural sunlight—two hours, three at the most."

The physician nodded to a line of soldiers topping off plastic canisters from a green-painted tank trailer that had been pulled in by a Humvee.

"We've also cornered the market on liquid bleach and hand-pump sprayers, Beck. It's not Level Four containment, but it's as close to it as we can get in a field situation."

He looked at Beck though the full-face exposure masks both of them wore concealed any expressions.

"How is Katie doing?" Krewell asked.

"Not good. She's in and out of consciousness, and her fever is spiking. Deborah won't leave her side."

"It won't be long now, Beck. Ten minutes. I promise."

Krewell had taken pains to ensure Katie and J. L. were in the first bank of flu patients awaiting treatment with the VIX. Their symptoms were advancing ruthlessly; whether their weakened systems could deal with the demands that were about to be placed on them was, the doctors had made clear, an open question.

As if on cue, a parade of stretchers had begun to wind through the entrance. They were placed in rows on the hardwood floor, and from Beck's vantage point it looked as if a line of ants, two to a litter, were depositing some hard-won bounty for inspection by the queen. He scanned the lines until his eyes locked on one stretcher, this one accompanied by a third exposure-suited figure that walked at the side, holding the hand of its occupant.

He turned to see Krewell watching him.

"Go on," Beck heard his friend say. "Get the hell down there with her, man."

By the time he reached courtside, the treatment had already begun. The infective process was simplicity itself: while an assistant held the face of a patient steady, a green-garbed medic placed the tip of an inhaler tube against a nostril. A squeeze of the bulb, and the team moved on to the next stretcher.

Beck reached Katie's stretcher simultaneously with the treatment team. Deborah, sitting on the hardwood floor and white-faced behind the rubber mask, looked up at him once. Then, still holding Katie's hand in her own gloved one, she waited as the medics performed their ritual. On the stretcher, Katie was only semiconscious, but she had pulled away as the inhalator tip touched her and grimaced at the puff of moist air that followed.

Beck was staring at his daughter, hot tears on his own cheeks under his mask, when he felt Deborah's touch. Her hand took his, forming a chain that linked child and parents. Wordlessly, he knelt beside her.

Together, they waited.

Aftermath

Chapter 57

"You did *what*?" Beck's voice was dumbfounded. "He's a sociopath who killed at least four people in this country alone. Probably more."

Carson was unmoved. "Calm down, Beck. It was a direct request from Putin. A demand, actually. What were we supposed to do? Put your friend Ilya on trial for murder?"

"So instead you put him on a plane for Moscow."

"We haven't forgotten what he tried to do to you. But perhaps *you* should. It's history, man. Move past it." He smiled, but not as if his heart was in it. "Concentrate on the bright side. The President wants to make you a national hero."

"Thank him for me. I'd rather he didn't."

"You may not have a choice. He feels strongly that you were the reason he is not facing an impeachment hearing — or worse — this very minute."

"I still don't want it. There would too many bodies draped over any medal he could give me. I know how we got the vaccine in time — what the President asked Putin to do over there to get the information."

"There was no choice, Beck. Not with what was at stake."

"I understand that too. That's what bothers me: I *do* understand it. I'm a historian, remember? I know that the same choice has been made before, countless times. And will be made again, the next time."

Beck's eyes looked steadily at Carson. "We're the good guys. But we still act on our sense of expediency. We make our decisions, compromise what we are—*who* we are. All in the name of the greater good. I've been on both sides of that line now, and I don't know if I can straddle it ever again."

Carson nodded, and shrugged.

"I'll pass that along," he said, and something in his voice made Beck look up.

"The President and I have come to a mutual decision," Carson said. "I will tender my resignation within the next few weeks. He will accept, with regrets." He looked at Beck from under an arched eyebrow. "That's still confidential, by the way."

"What are your plans?"

"I have not yet decided," Carson said. Then he smiled thinly, at an unspoken but shared jest. "Perhaps something in the defense industry. Selling shoes to the Army, maybe."

He stood, his hand outstretched awkwardly enough so that even if Beck had not known him, it would have been obvious the friendly gesture was an unfamiliar exercise.

"You could write your own ticket at the Company, you know," Carson said, making it sound like an afterthought. "Or even here, in my old office. The President would be open to the suggestion. National security advisor isn't a *bad* job, you know."

"Thanks," said Beck. "I already have a job, in Arlington. I just have to start doing it again. If they'll take me back, that is."

Chapter 58

The balcony looked out over Choctawatchee Bay and beyond, a vista that stretched so wide and so open that it could leave those unaccustomed to it delightfully dizzy.

Far to the east was the arch of the Destin Bridge, its simple lines carved sharp against the slate blue sky. Southward, just over the low swell of Okaloosa Island's sugar white dunes, was the Gulf of Mexico, an unimpeded expanse of emerald greens and white-flecked cobalt. In the distance, its single sharp horizon bisected the world into two distinct realms.

But it was the bay to which her eyes always returned, whether to watch the timeless grace of sails filling like the wings of a gull, or simply to gaze upon a surface in ceaseless, soothing movement. The bay was a living thing, an underappreciated artist who worked in wind and wave and current — crafting an unending series of intricate patterns, never duplicating the same one twice.

Carol Mayer sat unmoving, the salt breeze stirring her hair. It felt cool and fresh against her scalp, and she savored the way it fenced with the morning sun's warmth.

To her, it felt like life restored.

For a moment, she tilted her head back to take the full measure of the elements in conflict. Had there been anyone to see, the hollows under her eyes and the residual sallowness of her skin would have signaled a woman whose convalescence was not yet complete. The hand that held the china mug still shook, though less than in previous days, whenever she lifted it to her lips.

But she was alive. It was a still-surprising knowledge that now made her smile, but which had rocked her only a few days before. Then, she had just swum to the surface of her consciousness; through fever-blurred eyes, she had stared in confusion at the olive canopy far overhead. Panic began to flood her when a figure in fatigues and gas mask bent close.

"It's all right, ma'am," a soft Southern voice had said. "This here's a hangar at Eglin we fixed up special. You're pretty sick right now, but it's gonna be okay soon."

It was the voice of an angel, and she had believed it without question. She had drifted away again, this time with a sense of peace.

Carol opened her eyes again, drinking in the panorama and feeling the same peace flood into her now. The angel had spoken the truth, though as a physician Carol knew it would be some time before her recovery would be complete. Someday, even the memories that regularly plagued her dreams might begin to fade.

So many had died—the figures were still uncertain, she had read, but in Florida they were sure to exceed twenty thousand persons. New York had escaped the worst of it; but before the vaccine and the VIX treatment facilities had stemmed the virus, more than eleven thousand deaths had occurred on the densely packed island of Manhattan.

As for Russia—well, nobody knew the mortality figures. The Russian government simply would not release the numbers, though that had not stopped the commentators in the Western press from speculating in the mid-six-figure range.

That, not including those who had been killed in the nerve-gas cauterization of the outbreak.

It was a ghastly tally, the most devastating terrorist attack in history. What made it all the more horrifying was a knowledge all the world now shared: it could happen again at any time.

The thought made Carol shiver, and she fought it down to the deepest recesses of her mind.

What was it Scarlett O'Hara said? she mused. *Oh yes—"I'll think about that tomorrow. Tomorrow is another day."*

She waited, willing herself calm again. After a moment, she looked once more at the vastness of the Choctawatchee.

A fresh swirl of breeze skipped across the waters of her bay, and the reflected disk of the morning sun exploded into a kaleidoscope of glittering jewels.

Carol Mayer leaned back again, and let the warmth of life wash over her.

Epilogue

Beck sat in his car, watching for the figure that occasionally moved behind the sheer draperies that covered the picture window.

He had been there when Deborah pulled her car into the driveway. She had taken the turn too quickly, the way she always did, and the wheels bottomed out on the steep incline with a scraping thud. When they were married, living in this house, the sound had been an ongoing source of irritation to Beck. He hadn't known how much he would miss it, would miss knowing each time Deborah came home.

Beck did not know how long he sat in his car. He did know that he almost drove away several times, once even touching the key that hung from the ignition. Finally, he found himself standing on the porch, his finger pressed against the bell.

The door opened, and she stood there as if she had expected him. Beck hesitated on the doorstep, for a moment unable to find words for what he wanted to say.

Then he spoke.

"I made the first move, this time."

She must have read something in his face, because she smiled briefly before she responded.

"You better come in," she said. "Katie's still down at the mall, with J. L." She looked at him closely, as if looking for something deep inside him that she alone could see. Her eyes were serious, almost solemn; but they were not without welcome. "We don't have much time before dinner."

Beck Casey stepped through the door she held wide, home at last.